SHEARS, S.
RETURN TO
RUSSETS

CW00376183

This item should be returned on or before the last date
stamped above. If not in demand it may be renewed for a
further period by personal application, by telephone, or in
writing. The author, title, above number and date due back
should be quoted.   LS/3

Return to Russets

Sarah Shears

PIATKUS

Copyright © 1990 by Sarah Shears

First published in Great Britain in 1990 by
Judy Piatkus (Publishers) Ltd of
5 Windmill Street, London W1

British Library Cataloguing in Publication Data
Shears, Sarah
  Return to Russets.
  I. Title
  823'.914

  ISBN 0−7499−0000−8

Phototypeset in 11/12pt Compugraphic Times by
Action Typesetting Limited, Gloucester
Printed and bound in Great Britain by
Butler & Tanner Ltd, Frome and London

PART 1

Chapter One

He was eight years old, and really too big to be sitting on Aunt Lucy's lap, but it was such a nice comfortable place to be sitting on a Sunday afternoon. Everything about Aunt Lucy was nice – her soft bosom, her warm smile, and her hair that was white as snow but had once been the colour of ripe corn. That was before he was born, according to Uncle Julian, who was also his step-father. It had taken some time to get the family sorted out, and even now, when he should know better, he sometimes addressed his step-father as Julian, and that, according to his mother, was most disrespectful. Why should it be respectful at the age of three, when Julian came home from the War in a wheel-chair, and disrespectful after he had married Mum? Even Aunt Lucy, who could usually be relied upon to answer all his questions, had been a little vague on this particular matter.

"I expect you will be calling him Julian again when you are grown up, love," she told him, and he had to be content with that.

"How old are you, Aunt Lucy?" he asked, as they rocked to and fro in the old rocking chair.

"That is not a very polite question," she reminded him.

"I was just wondering when you would be a hundred, because then you will get a telegram from the Queen."

She chuckled, and her soft bosom trembled under his head.

"I've some way to go yet before I get that telegram."

"How far?"

"Another twenty years."

He began to count backwards on his fingers. "That makes

you eighty," he mused. "You eighty and me eight."

"Yes, love."

"When I am eighty, shall I have white hair and a white beard like Father Christmas?"

"That will be the day!"

"Only there isn't a Father Christmas, is there?"

"No, love."

He sighed, remembering the shock of that discovery on his first day at the village school. It was a long time ago, but that first day in Infants was still fresh in his memory. He had been so proud of his new pencil box. It held a pen-holder, a box of nibs, two pencils, a ruler and a rubber. Teacher had admired it, and promised he should use one of the pencils, but the pen would have to wait till he moved up into Standard One, where they had inkwells in the desks.

"I had a lot of presents. Father Christmas filled my pillow case when I was asleep," he told her.

"There ain't no Father Christmas, silly!" jeered the boy at the next desk.

To this day he remembered the awful feeling of being cheated, but he still wouldn't believe it, and he was fierce in defence of that beloved old gentleman.

"There is a Father Christmas! I've heard his sleigh bells ringing. He comes all the way from Greenland with sacks and sacks of toys."

All the children in the class were staring at him and shaking their heads, while Teacher explained gently that it was a sort of fairy story for little children, and now he was a big boy.

"A fairy story? Like Jack and the Beanstalk and Peter Pan?" he had asked.

"Yes, Peter."

"But who fills my pillow case?"

"Your mother or your granny or perhaps a big sister."

"I haven't got a sister, and my granny lives at Tunbridge Wells."

"An aunt, perhaps?"

"Yes, Aunt Lucy." He couldn't believe it. Aunt Lucy, who never cheated at Ludo and Snakes and Ladders, had cheated over Father Christmas. It was the end of the world. He had burst into tears, and run out of the room. But he got no

4

further than the playground that was covered in snow, and a pretty little girl in a red pinafore was sent to bring him back.

"Do *you* believe in Father Christmas?" he asked her, like Tinker Bell had asked all the children at the pantomime, "Do you believe in fairies?" and they all had shouted "YES!"

But this little girl shook her head. "No I don't, because I've always known it was Mum what fills our stockings. We don't have pillow cases, not with four of us, and Dad out of work. But we all get something from Woolworth's, and an orange and a sugar mouse. It's like Teacher said, it's just a fairy story, and our Mum is too busy to bother with fairies." She kissed his wet cheek and gave him an aniseed ball to suck. "You can be my sweetheart if you like," she offered.

"I don't mind," he said. It was his first proposal, but there would be others who fancied him, not only because of his golden hair and blue eyes, but because of the gingerbread and the apple he brought for his elevenses!

When the rocking chair stopped rocking on that peaceful Sunday afternoon, he knew that Aunt Lucy was having her forty winks, and he sat very still, watching Rusty's tail twitching on the hearth-rug. He would be chasing rabbits in his dreams, Aunt Lucy would say – and Aunt Lucy knew everything about everybody. After she had finished her forty winks, she would tell him a story about the family, and about Russets, the old farmhouse that was so old it had been built in the reign of the first Queen Elizabeth, when the first Sir Neville Franklin had been the squire of Marston Park and owned the whole estate. Russets was one of the farms on the estate, and the Blunts had been tenant farmers of Russets for generations until the last Sir Neville Franklin had died and left a Will in which all the tenant farmers became the legal owners of their own acres and houses.

"It was the proudest day of our lives when we received that letter from the solicitor," said Aunt Lucy, "and we had a party to celebrate the occasion here, at Russets. I was baking all day and half the night. It was like a Harvest Supper, only more so. More of everything, and all home-made. The men drank cider, the women drank elderberry wine, and the children drank lemonade; the cider and the elderberry wine

5

are still home-brewed to this day, and the lemonade made with lemons and brown sugar. The same with the baking, for it's still my proud boast that I feed my big family on home-baked bread, pies and cakes, and pure dairy produce. Fresh butter and cheese, eggs from our own hens, vegetables from the garden and fruit from the orchard."

Aunt Lucy's voice was strong, and her eyes as blue as a summer sky when she related all these stories of bygone days, because the past was more real to her now than the present, as she had explained to him.

"When you are as old as me, love, you live in the past, and today is just an extension of yesterday. Does that make sense to you, or nonsense?"

He had answered truthfully, "Nonsense."

Her chuckling laugh was a measure of her good humour, for she seldom lost her temper. "That's why I am so fat. We are what we are, Peter, love. Mother Nature endowed your Aunt Lucy with a happy nature and a contented mind. It's a great blessing when your little world collapses, and you have to pick up the pieces and carry on."

"What pieces?" he had asked, for he was often puzzled by her train of thought these days.

"Pieces of strength and faith and courage, that get lost when the bottom drops out of your world. It can happen when you least expect it, on a bright Summer day, like the day when my dear old Bert fell off the hay wagon and broke his neck. One minute he was there, on top of the wagon, waving his pitchfork, and the next minute he was lying on the ground dead. And all because a baby rabbit got tangled up in Prince's big hairy hooves. That's something you never forget, love."

"What happened to the baby rabbit?" he had asked, anxiously, for he was much more concerned about the rabbit than uncle Bert, who was not his real uncle anyway.

"It was only frightened. It was not hurt."

"That's good." He couldn't bear to think of that baby rabbit squashed under one of those big hairy hooves. They still had a Shire horse called Prince that pulled the wagon, and an old mare called Betsy that pulled the milk float Auntie Carrie drove to the village.

"I remember the day Julian came home from the War. He

6

gave me the Spitfire," Peter mused, thoughtfully.

"You chose it, love, from all the other models, and Julian was pleased as Punch because he had been flying a Spitfire in the Battle of Britain."

"I know. Dick told me."

"You were only three when Julian came home from the War. What else do you remember?"

"Hay-making, and my small little rake, and Mum crying because she was happy, and John was jealous because Julian gave me the Spitfire, so Julian said he could choose, and he chose the Gladiator. Why does John have to be jealous of me?"

"Because you are the youngest of the family, and he thinks we spoil you. But John would be jealous of his own grandmother. It's his nature, he can't help it."

"Midge is not jealous of me, and they are twins."

"Not identical twins. They are different as chalk from cheese."

"I like Midge."

"Everyone likes Midge."

"Why didn't she come home this weekend?"

"Because she has a new boy-friend with a car, so they have gone to Brighton. She will be home for her birthday next Sunday. John's birthday, too, of course. I must bake a chocolate cake. It's his favourite, and Midge won't mind what it is. She is so taken up with this new boy-friend, she won't even notice!"

"Aunt Lucy."

"Yes, love?"

"I don't want to be a farmer when I grow up."

"That doesn't surprise me, not with Franklin blood in your veins on your mother's side of the family. Only the Blunts get their hands dirty!"

"I want to be an actor."

"An actor? That won't please your mother, Peter, love. Whatever gave you that idea?"

"Nobody gave it to me. It was there all the time."

"Well, now, supposing we keep it a secret just between you and me? After all, you may change your mind."

"I shan't. I'm POSITIVE." It was one of the big words he had recently added to his vocabulary since he became a pupil

7

at The Firs Preparatory School at Tunbridge Wells, where the Headmaster, an ex-Wing Commander, was very positive indeed! Not that he used the cane – he didn't believe in corporal punishment. "The punishment fitted the crime" – whatever that might mean. This was his first term at The Firs. He was a weekly boarder. He liked the village school best because you came home every day, and he had his own little room with all his belongings. Sharing a dormitory with five other boys was hateful, and the food was rotten. It was Uncle Julian who persuaded Mum the time had come to make a change, and she didn't need much persuading.

"The sun rises and sets on her Julian," Aunt Lucy would say. "But then it was a miracle he survived the War. We all thought he was dead."

"Where are they now, Mum and Uncle Julian?"

"Now you know where they always spend Sunday afternoon."

"In bed?"

"Yes, love."

"And Uncle Tom and Auntie Carrie?"

"Yes, love."

"Why do they?"

"Because they are tired. They have a very busy week. Are you going to help me get the tea?"

"All right." He slid off her lap. Sunday tea was rather special. It was the only day when they all sat down together. Sunday was a rest day, apart from milking and feeding the animals. Sunday was the best day of the week for Peter. It was a high tea on Sunday, with home-cured ham, tomato chutney, pickled onions and salad. While Aunt Lucy prepared the salad, Peter laid the kitchen table with a clean white cloth, and counted the willow pattern plates he took down from the old Welsh dresser – "Uncle Tom, Auntie Carrie, Dick, Maggie, John, Uncle Julian, Mum, Aunt Lucy, ME." Only Midge was missing, and Katie, the servant, who spent her free day with her friend at the Home Farm.

"Why doesn't Midge bring her new boy-friend home? She always does bring her boy-friends home to tea on Sunday, doesn't she?" he asked, as he counted out the cutlery.

"Perhaps he didn't want to come, or perhaps he is too new.

8

They can't have known each other very long. This is Midge's first term at the College of Art. She told me on the telephone that he was the art master, and he was absolutely smashing. You know what Midge is like. She's over the moon with her enthusiasms, but it doesn't last long. There are no half measures with our Midge. It's all or nothing. She is either on top of the world or down in the depths of despair. I sometimes wonder where my grand-daughter gets her zest for life. Not from either of her parents. They enjoy their way of life, but in moderation. Midge doesn't know the meaning of the word, bless her. I suppose you could say she takes after me. Once-upon-a-time I felt the same way. It was a long time ago. I'm an old woman now, and slowing down, like old Betsy!" she chuckled. "When I was Midge's age, I was already married to Bert, and expecting Harry. Would you believe that, Peter, love?"

He shook his head. He knew what "expecting" meant. Buttercup was expecting a calf, and Flossie was expecting kittens. But his eight-years-old imagination could not stretch as far as Uncle Harry being "expected". He was just another figure in a frame on the mantelpiece in the front parlour, like Uncle Bert, who had fallen off the hay wagon and broken his neck, and Uncle Albert, who got killed by a falling beam when young Julian set fire to the barn, one Christmas Eve. He couldn't really feel too much about people who were dead before he was born.

Aunt Lucy went on talking as she arranged the red radishes among the green lettuce leaves. There was colour everywhere in this farm kitchen, he noticed, for the first time — blue plates on the dresser, red geraniums on the window ledge, pale green walls and shining copper pans. It was his favourite room in the house, because he knew he would always find Aunt Lucy in the kitchen.

"I think I love you best, Aunt Lucy," he told her, gravely.

"Do you, love?" She smiled affectionately at the child, remembering the other small boys who had sat on her lap in the old rocking chair and counted out the plates for Sunday tea. Peter was the last of her boys, she would not live to see a great-grandchild. The thought saddened her, because she was still young at heart, and only her body was wearing out. She

9

had to sit down when her racing heart reminded her the pots and pans she had been lifting so easily for years were too heavy. Her legs were ugly with varicose veins, under her long skirts, and her back never stopped aching. Only in bed, that big, lonely marriage bed she had shared with Bert in those early years, and with His Lordship in later years, only there could she relax her tired old body and shed a few tears of self-pity. Never, never in front of the family. She had to keep her image of glowing health and cheerfulness. The Matriarch of Russets had an important role to play, and she was a good actress. In that lonely marriage bed she could still have enjoyed a "cuddle" from one or the other, her husband or her lover, and that was shocking, wasn't it? Her thoughts wandered as she sliced the crusty, home-baked bread. Who would look after them when she was no longer here? A cold shiver ran down her spine. "Not yet, please God," she prayed, silently. She often spoke to God now, as though he were an old acquaintance. It was a nice feeling.

A rich fruit cake, gingerbread, and her own strawberry jam, completed the Sunday tea. Tom would slice the ham. The big silver cruet she had inherited from Bert's parents graced the centre of the table. She had mixed fresh mustard, and filled the decanters with vinegar and salad cream. Such small items she had to attend to personally, for Katie was too clumsy. Katie was an orphan, one of hundreds of orphaned girls sent out to service at the age of thirteen with a tin trunk containing three of everything. Three sets of underwear, and three flannelette nightgowns, laboriously stitched with her own clumsy fingers, three print dresses, three aprons and three caps. She had never worn the caps.

A simple-minded, sullen girl, she had grown into a big, strong woman, who still had to be reminded every day of her duties, and who took orders only from her mistress. She worshipped the ground her mistress walked on, and revelled in scrubbing, washing day and black-leading the kitchen range. Every Christmas she received a jumper, a cardigan or a blouse from Aunt Lucy, and small gifts from every member of the family, that she hoarded, like a magpie, in her "bottom drawer". At hay-making and harvest, she was out in the fields, chasing the youngest boy with her rake. First it was

Charles, then it was Julian, now it was Peter.

There was a time when Katie would be tumbled in the hay by any Tom, Dick or Harry, but of recent years, she had settled down with Fred, the cowman at Brook Farm, and she found her sexual pleasure in Fred's heavy breath and clumsy fondling on market days. "Poor old Katie," they would say, but Katie was happy enough in her own small world.

"I can hear Julian and Wendy on the way," said Aunt Lucy, pushing the kettle over the fire. The big brown teapot stood warming on the hob. Everything was ready.

Peter ran into the hall to watch his step-father sliding down the stairs on his backside, while his mother stood waiting with his two sticks.

"Hello, darling," she greeted him absentmindedly, not taking her eyes off that slim, boyish figure with the eloquent dark eyes. He was smiling and confident, while the young woman who watched his descent was frowning anxiously. There was no other way for Julian to get up and down stairs except on his backside, and he was so proud of the achievement. For more than two years after he came home from the hospital in the Channel Isles he had been confined to the wheel-chair and the bed, with a pulley, in the front parlour. Wendy and Peter had shared a bedroom upstairs. Julian had never given up hope. The German doctor had insisted with gruff kindliness that the age of miracles was not past, and that it would depend on Mother Nature and his own determination. It was Aunt Lucy who had seen the suffering in those dark eyes, and shared his desperate efforts to be mobile when they were alone together. And when, at last, he had taken those first faltering steps, leaning heavily on two sticks, they both had wept with emotion. Then the bed and the pulley had been dismantled, and all his belongings taken upstairs. The front parlour was quickly converted into a comfortable sitting-room, where the rest of the family could settle down after supper, on Winter evenings, and Wendy could play her piano. But the front parlour had never been used as a sitting-room before the War. It had always been reserved for special occasions, and special visitors. It still held a kind of reservation that only Julian and Wendy seemed to overcome, quite naturally. Aunt Lucy still preferred her rocking chair in the kitchen with Carrie and Tom for company. That left Dick, John and Peter prowling restlessly between the two rooms, disturbing both parties with their constant demands for television. It was already an established feature of most homes, and Aunt Lucy had reluctantly to agree to a set being installed in the back parlour, thereafter known as the "telly room". Katie was absolutely enthralled by this new toy that provided a variety of non-stop entertainment every evening. As for Dick and John, they would have stayed up half the night, but the deadline was ten o'clock, when Julian switched off the set. Katie was packed off to bed at nine. Aunt Lucy retired at nine, and Peter was sent to bed promptly at seven on Winter evenings. He soon tired of the new toy, and was back to sharing the rocking chair with Aunt Lucy, or persuading Julian to play a game of Ludo or Snakes and Ladders.

Summer evenings, after supper, were pleasantly different. Tom and Carrie would lean on a gate, watching the placid cows in the water meadow. In companionable silence, these two were still sweethearts, with a family of four grown children. Julian and Wendy would take a quiet stroll at a pace that suited Julian, but they always had a lot to talk about because they lived in a wider world, met more people, and had more interests. Since Julian had been provided with a small car, specially built for the disabled, he travelled to Cranbrook five days a week to work as secretary to a retired Colonel who was writing his memoirs. Wendy travelled by train to Tonbridge. She taught music at the Grammar School. Peter and Wendy travelled home together at weekends, and Tom or Carrie would collect them at the station in the utility van, which smelled strongly of the farm, for nobody had the time or the inclination to clean it out.

Grinning happily from the bottom stair, Julian reached for the sticks, and heaved himself to his feet. A lesser man could have spent the rest of his life in a wheel-chair, reconciled to the role of a crippled war hero, but not Julian. He was a fighter, one of the undefeated, his courage and determination a shining example to young Peter. There was a mutual affinity between them, and the boy had a closer relationship with his step-father than with his mother. She was too impatient, too

12

critical, too absorbed in Julian to get to know her growing son, and to recognise the inevitable change that took place when a boy is flung into the battlefield of boarding school, if only as a weekly boarder. Julian could recognise himself at the same age, when he had run away from home to escape the same fate. It's true he was back the following day with an infection he had caught from a sick gypsy boy that proved to be scarlet fever. It had so frightened Aunt Lucy that nothing more had been said about boarding school when he recovered. It had pleased them both, however, when he won the scholarship to Grammar School at the age of ten. But if he had his time over again, he would have accepted that boarding school would provide the right approach to manhood. It taught a youngster the self-reliance and independence he had still to learn at the age of seventeen, when he was plunged into the world of men and the rigours of the Royal Air Force. So he had voted in favour of his young step-son and The Firs Preparatory School, and Aunt Lucy had reluctantly to part with her youngest boy.

Bad habits and bad language had to be corrected. Already, in his first term, they all had seen a marked improvement in both, for children are quick to adopt the behaviour of the majority. To be odd man out was unthinkable.

So, on this pleasant Sunday afternoon, Julian smiled at the boy as he took the sticks from Wendy, and asked, "Well, Peter, what's it to be after tea — fishing for tiddlers or batting a century?"

And Peter, determined to get into the Junior Eleven, answered promptly, "Batting a century!"

"OK."

Wendy was still frowning. Her love for Julian was so possessive, she could not bear to share him, even with the child. If she had her way, they would be living in splendid isolation, and in perfect harmony, in a woodman's cottage. But that would soon spell boredom for Julian, who thoroughly enjoyed the lively company of the family at Russets, and his independent excursions in the motorised vehicle, five days a week, to his place of work. His dearest girl would have wrapped him in cotton wool, bless her!

He waited till Peter had run on ahead to report the exciting news of the cricket match, then he bent his long, lean body to kiss that pouting mouth. "I love you," was all he needed to say to restore her confidence. She was so sensitive, so vulnerable, he had to protect her from her own smothering devotion. Tom and Carrie followed them down, yawning, only half awake, for they had made love and slept heavily till they were awakened by the heavy thudding on the stairs. Dick and John were called from the telly room, strongly protesting they would miss the end of an exciting cowboy film, but they knew better than to suggest they had their tea later, for the animals had to be fed, the hens fed and watered, and the eggs collected. That was John's sole responsibility and nobody was allowed to encroach on his domain in the orchard, except to gather fruit in season.

Aunt Lucy had been clever in providing an outlet for her younger grandson's backward mentality. With a chip on his shoulder because of his twin's bright intelligence, John suffered the pangs of jealousy that would never allow him to be completely happy or content. The nearest he came to happiness was in the pleasant sight of a mother hen with a brood of newly hatched chicks; even then he would be worrying about their future safety with the constant danger of a prowling fox or ferret. He still kept a few nesting boxes for the broody hens, though the majority of chicks were bought in the market and reared in the incubators. The shed containing the bins of corn and meal, the egg racks and boxes, and bundles of clean straw, all this provided his haven. Here he enjoyed a sense of ownership and authority, and here he would spend an hour or so every afternoon, keeping the ledger up to date and grading eggs for the market. Broken eggs were used for cooking, and the eggs for Sunday morning breakfast were counted out precisely in a bowl on Saturday. Brown eggs were popular on the market stall and fetched an extra twopence for the half dozen. A few unnaturally large eggs, with double yolks, provided a good breakfast for Tom and Dick, with several rashers of bacon. It was Tom who wrung the necks of the chickens for market, and Carrie who plucked them and prepared them for the table, for if John had his way, they would roam free in the orchard until they died of old age. When the hens were past laying, they were sold cheaply as boiling fowls, providing a good meal with vegetables for a working-class family.

The drum of paraffin for heating the incubators was replaced by the oilman on his regular visits to the farm. The routine of feeding and watering, cleaning and collecting eggs, seven days a week, suited John, whose mind could only cope with such an established order. Any emergency would see him rushing in a panic for Tom or Dick. On one such occasion, when fire destroyed one of the incubators, and a hundred pathetic little corpses littered the floor, John went berserk, screaming and sobbing, and only Aunt Lucy had known how to soothe him. He had no explanation for the accident, and insisted he was not to blame, but everyone knew he smoked a packet of ten cigarettes every day, and a carelessly dropped match could have started such a fire. Aunt Lucy's comforting arms, together with a mug of strong sweet tea, softened the blow. In the meantime, Tom, Dick and Carrie cleared away the blackened ruins and the tiny corpses. When a new incubator was installed, John was so anxious to avoid another accident, he gave up smoking, so he must have known he was responsible for the accident, but would never admit it. One way and another, John was a problem, but he had an endearing way of spending his small allowance on flowers and chocolates for Aunt Lucy, and never forgot a birthday. Like Katie, John would take orders only from one person, and only Aunt Lucy had foreseen the day when she would no longer be there to manage these two immature members of her family.

Her grand-daughter, Maggie, slipping quietly into her place that Sunday afternoon, had brought one of the orphans from the convent school at Marston Park. This was a normal practice on Sunday afternoon, so there was no embarrassment, and Peter would be reminded to fetch another plate and another knife and fork.

"But I am not going to play with her," he told himself, yet again. Girls were soppy. Besides, she was a Roman Catholic, and he was Chapel!

Without Midge's lively company, Sunday tea at Russets was a much quieter family gathering, and only Wendy and Julian had refreshed their minds as well as their bodies, with the afternoon rest. They talked of events beyond the small world of the farm, and Peter listened, absorbed by the nature of things in the adult world of which he had seen enough to whet his natural curiosity. As for Dick and John, still riding the range with the cowboys, they were wondering if the villain would get his deserts and the hero rescue the girl from almost certain death. They ate their tea in silent protest at having to return so abruptly to reality.

Maggie and her orphan seldom contributed anything to the conversation, but were avid listeners, and would tackle all the washing up.

Tom and Carrie, still feeling the effects of their weekly indulgence in sex, exchanged meaningful glances, and listened to Wendy's pleasant, cultured voice relating the usual bulletin of her pupils' progress on the pianoforte and the violin. The breeding was there in her voice and in her manner, from her mother's side of the family. Upper class had married working class, and Wendy was the only child of this particular union. It had been a nine days' wonder in the village when a daughter of Sir Neville Franklin married the young clerk in the solicitor's office, whose father was a ganger on the railway, and his mother a charwoman at the Three Nuns public house. It took courage in that day and age, before the Great War, to defy the traditions of the upper class and the principles of the working class.

"It ain't right. Class is class!" Ruby had protested, meeting her daughter-in-law for the first time. It had taken all that young woman's tact and diplomacy to convince Freddy's Mum that the barriers between the classes were not insurmountable. She proved her sincerity most emphatically, however, by working as a nurse in a London hospital, and by sharing the misfortunes of war in the return of a severely handicapped husband. With an artificial leg and a tenuous hold on life, it had taken all of two years for Freddy to pick up the threads of his former life. The day he opened his small office in their terrace house for working-class clients, was a milestone in the life of the young solicitor. By that time Cynthia was a nursing Sister, with a reputation as a strict disciplinarian. Her young daughter, Wendy, was reared in a home where the mother's personality was so much stronger

16

than the father's gentle influence. She in turn had rebelled. The consequence of that rebellion was sitting at the table on that Sunday afternoon — eight-year-old Peter, her bastard son.

"Why do you have a step-father?"

"What happened to your real father?"

Such questions had to be answered at prep school, and Wendy was ready with the answer.

"Your own father was an Army Lieutenant. We met at a dance in the Pump Rooms in Tunbridge Wells, and we fell in love. We were married before his regiment was posted overseas. But he never came back. He lost his life when he gave up his place on the boat at Dunkirk to stay behind with his blinded corporal."

It all sounded very romantic, and highly commendable. Peter was impressed. He could now boast a real father *and* a step-father, and both were heroes!

Leaning heavily on the sticks clutched in his left hand, Julian swung his arm, aiming for the wicket — an empty petrol can. Wendy and Aunt Lucy watched his unsteady stance anxiously. Peter demanded over-arm bowling these days, and defended his wicket from the old tennis ball with aggressive determination. His future was at stake. He could see himself as Captain of the Junior Eleven next season, an honour as coveted as the champion roller skater. Team spirit was encouraged at prep school, but Peter concentrated on his own individual achievements, probably because he still remembered the tough battles in the playground of the village school, and also as the only child in the family these days, he had no competition. It was Wendy's job as wicket-keeper to retrieve the ball and hand it back to Julian, for neither Dick nor John could be persuaded to join in the game. Animals and hens had to be fed and watered, then they would be back in the telly room. Tom and Carrie were bringing in the cows for milking.

At the end of half-an-hour Wendy called a halt. She could see Julian was tiring.

"Oh, *Mum!*" Peter protested, swinging the bat at an imaginary ball, while Julian collapsed thankfully on the bench beside Aunt Lucy, wiping the sweat from his face.

"Ungrateful child! Say thank you," Wendy reminded her son, tartly, as she joined them on the bench.

Aunt Lucy smiled at the child, and wished she could put back the clock. In her younger days, she had bowled for Julian, but had never mastered the over-arm. She chuckled at the memory. "Do you remember that time I hit one of the farmyard cats sun-bathing on the roof?" she asked Julian.

He nodded, his eyes twinkling with the memory. "You have never seen anything so funny as Aunt Lucy trying the over-arm," he told them. "I thought she would dislocate her shoulder. Talk about energy and enthusiasm!"

"That was twenty years ago, love," she said, with a heavy sigh.

"What happened to the cat?" Peter liked to hear all the details.

"It scooted out of the way, none the worse. Cats have nine lives, anyway," Julian teased.

"I hope Flossie has nine lives, then she will have nine lots of kittens," he mused.

"Heaven forbid!" Aunt Lucy exclaimed.

"I know when she's expecting. It shows. It shows with all the mother animals, doesn't it? And it shows with human mothers. Their stomachs get fat."

Julian exploded with laughter, but Wendy was not amused.

"Now you are being vulgar," she said. "Give me the bat. Run along and help Dick."

He handed over the bat, his mind still baffled by that vexed question nobody seemed willing to answer. How did the babies get inside? He walked away slowly, his hands stuffed into his pockets. He found a sticky aniseed ball wrapped in a grubby handkerchief. A nice surprise. He rolled his tongue around it. It was no secret how babies were born — but how did they get there in the beginning?

Rusty was squatting on the step, wagging his tail. An intelligent Welsh Collie, he seemed to sense Peter's disappointment. Rusty was the same age as Peter, and that may have explained the affinity between them. Peter loved to watch him rounding up the sheep for dipping, or for market, and when snow covered the Weald of Kent in the months of January and February, he would help to dig out the ewes that

18

had sunk in the deep drifts. Sheep were stupid creatures, and could not help themselves, especially when they were heavy with their lambs.

So they went off together, the boy and the dog, on this warm Summer evening, and climbed the steep slope to the wood. It was their favourite haunt. While Rusty chased rabbits, Peter swung from the branch of one tree to another, in the manner of the legendary Tarzan, still to be seen very occasionally on television. It had taken a lot of practice and several broken branches had landed him on the ground, bruised and shaken. But he hadn't complained of his bruises, for it would have worried Aunt Lucy to know he was playing such a dangerous game. The danger was all part of the fun of flying through the air. Nobody came to the wood to interfere with his games. They were all too busy about their own affairs. Dick had promised to build him a tree house, but he hadn't got around to it yet. It had been promised as a sort of bribe when he had to leave the village school and the friends he had made for the strange new world of prep school. Making new friends and learning about the importance of the team spirit had marked his first term, but he hadn't wanted to bring a boy home. That would come later. He was in no hurry to share the privileges he enjoyed at Russets.

It was different with Maggie. There were so many orphans at the Convent School they had to take turns to accompany her for tea at Russets on Sunday afternoon. Maggie loved them all, as though they were her own children, and she had been no more than a child herself when the Sisters brought them away from the war-scarred streets of the East End. Even as a little girl, Maggie had been different from the rest of the family, reading her Bible, saying her prayers, and determined to be a missionary in Darkest Africa. Then she forgot her zeal for the mission field in the demands of the children just across the park. They were all God's children as she had explained to Aunt Lucy, especially the orphans, and Maggie had a special flair for teaching the difficult and backward children who seemed to respond to her gentle patience and understanding. The only Catholic in the family, inspired by the dedication of the Sisters, Maggie would soon be accepted into the established Order. It takes courage to be different in a family, but they had long since accepted another "cuckoo in the nest".

Charles was the last "cuckoo", but there was a very good explanation, and it was no secret. Charles was the bastard son of Aunt Lucy and Sir Neville Franklin, with no sense of belonging either to the working class or the upper class. He had made his home in America, in a classless society.

Three boys born out of wedlock in one family was quite a record, Aunt Lucy supposed, when she considered it − a rather shameful blot on the family's otherwise splendid record. In her old age, mellowed with time, the anguish and anxiety of the world wars, and the sad loss of two of her sons, Aunt Lucy had come to terms with life, and felt no shame or regret. What had happened had not been deliberately shameful. It was the natural and instinctive urge of a normal man to mate − as natural and instinctive as the animals with which she had been surrounded all her married life. She herself had been quite willing to bed with His Lordship, after the initial shock and surprise. To be seduced by such a handsome, virile gentleman was a most enjoyable experience. And Charles was a chip off the old block. She adored him. Her spoiling of the boy in his early years had upset her other three boys − Harry, Tom and Albert, fathered by Bert, her former husband. Such was the penalty of her "fall from grace" as her twin sister, Ruby, had described it. Dear Ruby. She had never been tempted so had not fallen. Faithful to one man to this very day, and that man long years in his grave.

Both married at sixteen, and both expecting a child, but clever enough to get the wedding ring on their finger before the pregnancy became too obvious! Many a girl had realised her mistake too late, and a romp in the hay had to be paid for in a lifetime of disgrace. The working class had their own method of dealing with daughters "in trouble". As for the innocent young maids seduced by a careless son of the house and dismissed by an unsympathetic mistress, they found themselves in the workhouse or in the river.

Looking back on those early years of marriage, Lucy would wonder how she managed to cope with the never-ending work on the farm, the smells and the mud, all so foreign to a girl

20

brought up in the village, to bear three sons in quick succession, all with only one pair of hands for the kitchen and the dairy, the milk round and the market stall. Lucy soon discovered a farmer's wife was busy from morn till night at all seasons of the year, seven days a week, and no holidays to break the monotony and the drudgery. But she and her family were strong and healthy. They lived off the land, and never went hungry.

As for Ruby, married to a ganger on the railway, surrounded by squalor and poverty, she was fighting a losing battle with her neighbours, their swarms of children and their stinking privies. Scrubbing the floors of The Three Nuns public house, Ruby would be wondering on the nature of the useful "bits and pieces" she would be taking home. Would it be the remains of a joint from the meals served to passing travellers, a jug of nourishing soup or beef or rabbit pie?

The sisters had one thing in common, a happy nature that defied the hardships and counted the blessings. From the landing window of The Three Nuns, Ruby could look down on the tall Elizabethan chimneys of Russets in the valley, but there was no envy in her heart for her more fortunate sister. With three boys and a girl to feed and clothe, and rent to pay on the pittance her man was earning on the railway, Ruby counted herself fortunate to have a husband who handed over his wages intact every Saturday. She handed him back a shilling for his beer and baccy. Her Irish neighbour was not so lucky. Her man never came straight home on Saturday, but indulged his taste for the strong brew they served in his favourite pub till closing time. Regularly and methodically he then beat his wife, followed her upstairs, dropped his trousers and climbed on top of her.

"With all them kids sleeping in the same room, it isn't decent," Ruby declared emphatically.

"But it ain't our business, love," her man would reply, sober as a judge after a single mug of ale.

Ruby was blessed with a daughter, a lively, intelligent child, who had played quite happily with her rag doll while her Mum scrubbed the floors, emptied the spittoons and polished the brass. Carrie had watched the children running past on their way to school, and when she reached her fourth birthday, she

21

was no longer satisfied with the rag doll and her perch on the window sill. So "Teacher" had included her in the crowded classroom, and the Infants class had opened up a fascinating new world of delight and discovery. The relationship between teacher and pupil had a close and lasting affinity, and they were still sharing all the joys and sorrows of life. Teacher had married the Schoolmaster, but was long since widowed. She and her grandson would be joining the family at Russets to celebrate the twins' birthday.

Russets had seen many changes and would see many more, for each generation left its mark. They had electricity now, but Aunt Lucy still lit the lamp in the kitchen on Winter evenings. The Ford van had replaced the wagon and the tractor had replaced the plough. Machines cut the grass and the corn, but human hands still gathered it into stooks, milked the cows, and delivered difficult calves. Aunt Lucy still clung to the old-fashioned kitchen range, though several of her farming neighbours had modern stoves installed at the end of the war. There was no substitute for her home-baked bread and pies, or her jam. Carrie preferred the old methods in the dairy. It was the men who delighted in the new methods. Tom, Dick and John would attend the annual Agricultural Show, fascinated by the variety of gadgets and machinery on display.

"What you never have you never miss," was Aunt Lucy's sensible observation, but it did not alter the views of her son and grandson. They were biding their time, and progress was slow but inevitable. The combine harvester would soon be lumbering round the country lanes and hay-making and harvest would lose their charm, but also their hard labour for those who could afford to pay for its services; spilling neat little parcels of hay and corn from its gaping mouth would be a nine days' wonder in the Weald. Neither Tom nor Dick would persuade Aunt Lucy to sample the monster's unique performance. She still had the last word.

Tom welcomed his daughter with a slow smile as Midge jumped off the train and ran into his arms.

"Darling Dad!" she breathed, her glowing face under the halo of curls expressing all her happiness.

"Hello, Midge. Many happy returns of the day." She was

his favourite child, though he did his best to hide it. Midge was so like her mother and her grandmother in looks, but had her own individual personality, her own special place in his heart.

The train went on its way along the quiet branch line linking the villages, so familiar now to Wendy and Peter. Only a half dozen passengers had alighted and were making their way to the exit. Midge stepped gaily along, clinging to her father's arm.

"How's Gran and Mum?" she asked.

"Fine," he answered.

She did not bother to enquire after her brothers. They were not very close, and she would see them later. "Julian OK?"

"Yes, fine."

She loved Julian. "What's Peter been up to lately?"

"That new school has made quite a difference. He's stopped saying bugger, and he's stopped kissing."

Midge giggled. "Why didn't you bring him to meet me?"

"Because this is the only chance I get to have you on my own."

"Oh, *Dad*!" She reached up to kiss his weathered cheek. "You smell nice," she said.

"How's the new boy-friend?"

"Smashing."

"Thought you might have brought him home today."

She sighed. "Not today. It's family. Next time perhaps. I do love him, terribly."

"Serious, eh?"

"Deadly serious."

"Not thinking of getting married?"

"No."

"Too young, anyway."

"Mum was married at seventeen and Gran was only sixteen. Anyway, he is already married."

"Midge!" Tom pulled up short and looked down at her. The glowing face had clouded, and there were tears in her eyes.

"Don't tell them. It would spoil the day."

"I don't like it, dear. It can only lead to heartache."

"I know, darling, but I can't help myself."

"What age is this man?"

"I haven't asked. About fortyish."

"Forty, and you are seventeen today!" He shook his head. "Any family?"

"Yes, three."

"Then he should be ashamed of himself."

She smiled, tremulously. "He's so funny, Dad. He makes me laugh, and he has the most heavenly smile, and brown eyes that crinkle at the corners. He thinks my animal studies are good, especially the Shire horses."

"So this art master's praise means a lot to you?"

"But of course, darling. He's a professional."

"Do you meet him out of college?"

"Only at the café where most of the students meet for coffee. The other girls are green with envy."

"I don't like it, Midge. It's dangerous, and I don't want you to get hurt."

"I can take care of myself. I'm not a child."

"I was afraid something like this would happen when you left home to live in lodgings in London."

"I love it, Dad."

"Promise me you will be careful."

"I promise. Don't worry about me, darling. I'm a big girl now!" she teased.

That word "darling", it came so readily to her tongue these days. His little Midge had changed.

"Let's go," he said.

Peter was hanging over the gate when they got back to the farm. "Happy birthday, Midge!" he shouted.

"Hello, Peter, you rascal. Got a kiss for me?"

"I've stopped kissing. It's soppy. But I don't mind kissing you this once 'cause it's your birthday."

She giggled and gave him a hug. His mouth was sticky, and his cheek bulged.

"Aniseed ball?" she asked.

He nodded, took it out, examined it carefully to see if it had changed colour, and put it back. "I've got a present for you. Have you got one for me?" he asked.

"Pete, you're incorrigible!"

He grinned disarmingly. There was a gap in his mouth.

"You've lost two teeth since I was last here," she said.

"I shall grow some more. Aunt Lucy says they were only milk teeth."

"When you two have finished nattering, you might open the gate," Tom reminded them, amiably.

"Sorry, darling." Midge swung open the gate, and he drove into the yard.

"It smells like home." Midge wrinkled her nose and wondered what Brandon would think of it. Perhaps it would be a mistake to invite him here now that Dad knew he was married. Dad could be rude. Anyway Brad liked to spend Sunday with his kids. They were going to the Zoo today.

Gran was standing at the kitchen door. Gran mustn't know about Brad. She had very strong principles, yet she had loved another woman's husband *and* had his child. That was really naughty. She dropped Peter's hand and flung herself into those welcoming arms, wishing she hadn't to pretend. It was not her nature to have secrets, especially from Gran. She wanted to cry. Already she knew there must be lies, and that one lie would lead to another.

"Many happy returns, love," Gran was saying. And she lifted her head to kiss the warm responsive mouth − a mouth made for kissing. She didn't care to be pecked on the cheek. "You haven't brought the new boy-friend?" she asked.

"No, it's difficult for him to get away on Sunday. He usually has an engagement of some kind." (That was true, wasn't it?)

"Not working on Sunday?"

"He wouldn't call it work. He is probably completing a river scene. He has his favourite haunts." (That was a lie, well, partly.) "I shall be seeing him this evening. He is meeting me at Victoria," she added, for good measure.

"The usual train?"

"Yes."

"Midge has brought me a present," Peter interrupted.

"You shouldn't be expecting presents when it's not your birthday. Not now you're a big boy," Aunt Lucy reminded him.

"I don't actually expect it. I just sort of wonder," said he, with a disarming grin. They laughed at him and Midge opened

25

her handbag and took out a small package. "Thanks!" He tore off the wrapping and exclaimed, excitedly, "A pocket-knife! Coo, thanks Midge. I've always wanted a pocket knife. Now I can carve my initials on that tree in the wood where Uncle Tom and Auntie Carrie have carved theirs."

"I didn't know. Which tree?" Midge was surprised to discover her practical parents could be so sentimental.

"I'll show you after dinner," Peter promised.

"Are we expecting any visitors today, Gran?" she asked.

"Yes. Aunt Martha and Mark."

Midge sighed. Mark had been in love with her for years, since they were kids at the village school. Now he was a junior bank clerk. He lived with his grandmother in a cottage some two miles from the station, and had to cycle to catch the train to Tonbridge. She liked Mark, but not as a boy-friend. He was more like a brother. You didn't have fun with Mark. He was too serious. But he loved Russets. It was like a second home. Everyone loved Russets.

There was no time to think of Brad. The family claimed her. She looked up to see her mother hurrying across the yard from the dairy, and her brother, Dick, waving in the distance.

"Where's John?" she asked. He was always last to greet her, but when they both were celebrating their seventeenth birthday, he should be here. They had never been close. She wondered if other twins had a closer bond, and whether they could boast identical thoughts and feelings. She felt only impatience for his slowness and his sullen moods. But the warmth of her mother's greeting and the rough hug from Dick more than compensated for her twin's lack of affection. Then she saw Julian following Dick on his sticks, and she ran to meet him with the same eagerness of the little girl who had greeted him on his return from the war.

He was grinning cheerfully as he hobbled along, followed by Wendy, who had always been a little jealous of Midge. Now the girl was cupping her husband's face in her hands and kissing him on the mouth, and Julian was enjoying the kiss.

"Sweet seventeen and never been kissed?" he teased. She blushed. "The new boy-friend?" he asked, gently.

She nodded tremulously, and answered, "He's smashing."

"Bring him home. Let's have a look at him."

"All right," she said.

Now Wendy had her arm on Julian's shoulder in a proprietary gesture. Her smile was too sweet, her manner too gushing. "How does it feel to be seventeen, darling?" she asked, and pecked Midge's cheek.

"Marvellous!"

The constraint between them could be cut with a knife, but Julian was there, and he loved them both. There was no need for jealousy. There was room in his heart for both.

"Just in time for elevenses," he said, and led the way into the house.

"There's John." Wendy was waving to the boy climbing over the orchard gate. She was sorry for John, who always seemed to be hovering in the background while his twin stole all the attention. Now that Midge was living in London all the week, it was not so noticeable, and he seemed more manly. Now today, he was going to be sulky, lagging behind as they flocked into the kitchen in a noisy group. Everyone had to admire Peter's new pocket-knife before Midge and John received their presents.

The family had bought them identical radio sets, and Peter had bought Midge a small box of liquorice allsorts that he knew she would share and a tin of toffees for John who would take it into the hut in the orchard. Wendy was not at all pleased about the pen-knife. "Too much spoiling and too many presents are bad for a child," she insisted.

"Nonsense!" Midge retorted.

"I *am* his mother."

The implication was not lost on Aunt Lucy who was pouring tea into mugs.

"Would you say I was a ruined character, my love? Heaven knows, I had plenty of spoiling and masses of presents at Peter's age," Julian teased. And they all laughed.

"Sorry, darling," Wendy kissed his cheek and peace was restored.

Leaving Midge and Mark with a stack of washing up, Dick and John slipped away to the telly room. Tom and Carrie, Julian and Wendy retired to bed for a couple of hours, while Lucy and Martha settled down comfortably in the front parlour for a good gossip, but their white heads were soon

27

nodding. Peter rocked to and fro in the old rocking chair, nursing Flossie, heavy with kittens.

"Shall I wash and you wipe?" Mark was asking.

"If you like," Midge answered, absentmindedly. She was wondering if Brad was enjoying the day at the Zoo with his kids. They would be feeding the monkeys with nuts and the bears with buns. They would ride on the elephant and sit on a bench in the sun, licking ice-cream cornets. It would be fun. She sighed.

Mark was sorting the pile of dishes on the draining board. He was very methodical. He was never quite natural with Midge. She was so casual in her manner, she seemed to be warding him off, and so alive he felt inadequate.

"Do you like living in London?" he asked.

"It's super!"

"It must be exciting. I mean, all those students and everything."

"It is. I adore every second. Two of my paintings have been picked out for the Summer Exhibition in the Embankment Gardens. People walk through the gardens in their lunch hour. It's fun to listen to their remarks. Not always complementary. Wonder if anyone will buy my Shire horses?"

"They should do. They are good. It's very clever. They are so life-like."

"Not bad, but I am still learning. It's all I care about really, and it's my only talent so I may as well cultivate it."

"It's a wonderful talent, so creative."

"Everyone has a talent of some kind. It need not be especially creative. It's just a question of using it and not wasting it."

"That sounds like Gran."

"It's true."

Mark shook his head. "I think I was missing when the talents were handed out."

"Don't be silly. If you hadn't a talent for maths, you wouldn't be in the bank. I was an absolute duffer. Still am, for that matter. Decimals and percentages have me biting my nails. As for algebra, it could be Chinese for all the sense it makes."

"You don't need to bother your brains with such mundane

28

things. A creative talent must be so very satisfying, and so absorbing. Look at Wendy with her music, and Julian with his wood carving."

"Yes, both creative, but don't forget Gran's talent for hospitality and Maggie's talent for teaching backward children. There are so many kinds of talents."

"There is no talent in adding up figures. It's just a boring job. Now if I could change places with Dick . . ." He sighed, his hands busy with the dishes.

"I thought you liked your job at the bank with such good prospects?"

"You must be joking. Ten years from now I could be a senior clerk, but only if old Hawkins moves up a peg, which is very unlikely. He's stuck in a groove, poor blighter. The whole system of promotion is so slow in our particular branch, it's almost stagnation."

It was not often that Mark mentioned his job, so she had naturally assumed he liked it.

"Did you have no option? Who decided on banking?" she asked.

"Mother."

"But your mother lives in the Congo. You only see your parents once every five years. What difference can it possibly make whether you're a banker or a dustman?"

"You don't know Mother. She still has the last word on what she considers really important issues. She's a bit of a snob, bless her. A parson's daughter, upper class. I hate this class business, Midge. It still crops up, even after two world wars."

"That's one issue I don't have to bother with. The Blunts are working class, pure and simple. We have no pretensions to upper class."

"Am I upper class? Aunt Lucy says I'm a Franklin on my mother's side of the family," Peter interrupted.

"But not on your father's side, so that makes you fifty-fifty, doesn't it, darling?" Midge rumpled his hair affectionately.

"But my name is Franklin, so why can't I be altogether upper class?"

Mark and Midge exchanged a meaningful glance. "This is

where you get into deep water, Midge, if you are not careful," he warned.

"When you were very young, before your mother married Uncle Julian, you took her name, Simmons. Then she had it changed to Franklin by deed pool."

"What's deed poll?"

"You tell him, Mark."

And Mark explained in simple terms. He was good with children. It seemed to satisfy Peter for he dropped the subject and told them importantly, that Flossie was expecting her kittens any day, and he wished she would wait till next weekend, when he would be here to see them born. "I still don't know how the kittens get inside her. That really puzzles me. I suppose you wouldn't like to tell me, would you, Midge?"

"No, darling. There are still some things that can't be told till you are older."

"How much older?"

"A couple of years or so. It depends on whether you are still interested enough to ask the question again at a later date."

Peter sighed. "That's what I thought you would say. I've already asked Aunt Lucy, and she said I had to wait. There's a boy in my class who says he knows, but he won't tell me unless I give him a shilling."

"It's not worth a shilling, Peter. I have a hunch you will find the answer to your question long before you are ten." It was Mark talking in the quiet way that seemed so very knowledgeable. "Living on a farm, you are bound to discover the facts of life earlier than most children. Just keep your eyes and ears wide open. Isn't that so, Midge?"

She nodded, trying to remember what age she had been when she first noticed the Welsh collie climbing on the back of Maisie, while her brother Dick stood laughing at their antics. "Make him get off, he's hurting her," she had demanded.

"Don't be silly. He is making her puppies," he answered, and walked away, whistling. When the puppies arrived, some months later, she remembered what she had seen, but was still too young to see the implication. It was magic, like the conjuror who pulled rabbits out of a hat at the children's Christmas party in the village hall. Mark was right, however, and the facts of life were disclosed on the farm, in her early years, surrounded by breeding animals, and a father who believed in answering his children's questions truthfully. Her own avid curiosity had been satisfied. It was natural. There was no mystery about the cows being "serviced" by the bull at the Home Farm. Male and female, and the seed that was planted by the male grew into a living creature in the body of the female. It was a fascinating subject for Midge, with her enquiring mind, as she followed Tom around the farm in those early years. Even so, he hadn't been quite so forthcoming over the conception of human babies. "Ask your Mum," said he, doggedly. And Mum had answered, "Ask your Gran."

"Plenty of time for that, love." Gran had also evaded the issue, making it a mystery of profound importance to Midge, at the age of ten, and ready for Grammar School, bursting with knowledge on the facts of life in the animal kingdom, but sadly ignorant on human behaviour.

It was Brenda Smith, her best friend, born and bred in a crowded tenement, who knew all the answers, and Midge was duly impressed.

She was sorry for Peter, for whom the facts of life were still a mystery. Being so much younger than the rest of the family, he was cossetted and protected, yet he had faced up to prep school in his first term without tears or tantrums.

"I think I'll go down to the pond and catch a few more tadpoles," he told them as he placed Flossie gently on the hearthrug. There was no mystery about tadpoles. They turned into frogs.

Chapter Two

Brad was waiting at Victoria. He was so tall she could pick him out over the heads of the crowd waiting at the barrier. Her heart missed a beat. All day her thoughts had wandered involuntarily. His personality was so strong, his influence her guiding star. She could not imagine how she was going to get through the long Summer vacation. This could be their last meeting apart from class for six long weeks, unless she could persuade Brad to spare an hour or two from his family if she came to London. She could always pretend to be meeting Leonie, the girl who shared her lodgings. If only he were free, she knew he would want to see her more often. To have picked her out from all the girls in class, in her first term, must be proof that he liked her, and she had made no secret of her own feelings. If only she could stop blushing every time he spoke to her.

"I can read you like a book, kitten. Your face is a mirror to your thoughts," he had told her. Kitten was his pet name for her.

Now she could see his hand raised in salute, and she ran the last few yards, dodging the passengers streaming towards the barrier.

"Brad!" she breathed ecstatically, hugging him round the waist with such impetuous enthusiasm he was quite startled, and more than a little embarrassed. You never knew who you would run into at Victoria on a Sunday evening. So many Londoners escaped to the coast for the weekend, or even for the day. He must remind her to be a little more discreet in future.

"Well, well, somebody seems pleased to see me!" he teased, unfolding her clinging arms. "Happy birthday, kitten. Had a good day?" he asked, as he took her hand and they walked away.

"Super!"

"Is that your present?"

"Yes." She was carrying the transistor set.

"I've got a surprise for you. I give you three guesses."

She shook her head. "I haven't a clue. Tell me."

"We are having dinner at the Strand Palace Hotel."

"The Strand Palace?" she gasped. "I have passed it a number of times, but it looked so imposing I wouldn't have dared to step inside. Brad, are you sure you can afford it? I mean, it must be frightfully expensive."

"I've been saving my pennies," he teased, and hailed a taxi with that laconic air of a man of the world she so admired. It was going to be fun.

"Do you normally travel by taxi?" she asked, when they had settled down.

"Only when I am in a hurry. I normally travel by Underground."

"I travel by bus or I walk. I am still petrified of the Underground."

"You would soon get used to it. Close your eyes on the escalator, but don't forget to open them when you get to the top, or the bottom, or you might find yourself falling flat on your face!"

"Oh, *Brad!*" she giggled, happily, squeezing his hand. Being with Brad was so stimulating, she felt she was being swept along on a voyage of discovery. His world was so terribly interesting, and exciting, compared to her own small world of Russets. She was a country girl by birth and breeding. Brad knew all about Russets, and she would be thrilled to show him off, but she had already realised the two worlds must be kept apart or there would be trouble with Dad. It wouldn't be easy to keep making excuses. She had always taken her boy-friends home. Gran encouraged it. If only Brad were free — if only.

When the taxi pulled up at the hotel, a burly, uniformed figure stepped forward to open the door and handed her out.

He wore a row of medals on his chest from two world wars.

"Good evening, Madam," said he. "Good evening, sir."

Brad paid the driver, including a generous tip, and slipped half-a-crown into the doorman's hand.

"Thank you, sir." The smart salute was automatic from an ex-sergeant-major.

Midge was blinking in the brilliance of the foyer. It was a cosmopolitan scene, lively and fascinating to her country bred senses. Music drifted out from the lounge. Brad had seen it all before, and hurried her along to the restaurant, where the head waiter, recognising Brad, escorted them to a small side table, saw them seated, and handed them both a menu.

"You choose," Midge whispered, nervously.

Brad smiled reassuringly at his young companion, and handed back the menus. "No need to peruse all that rigmarole, Alphonse," said he. "What do you recommend?"

"The steaks are particularly good, sir, but perhaps Madam would prefer a grilled sole?"

"Madam would indeed prefer the sole. I know her taste pretty well. And the steak for me. Three minutes as usual. Don't forget the mushrooms."

"Very good, sir."

A young waiter stood by his superior. He would serve the meal, under strict supervision. When they had walked away, Midge whispered, "How did you know what I liked, Brad? This is the first time we have had a meal together."

"It's a safe bet," he chuckled, and ordered a bottle of wine from Pierre, the jovial wine waiter who was hovering expectantly.

The large steak, served on an oval dish, was garnished with mushrooms, tomatoes and fried onions. It smelled delicious. The sole was garnished with lemon. There were dishes of sauté potatoes, french beans and endive.

"Brad, this is super," Midge smiled her appreciation. They ate well at Russets, but nothing to compare with this. She was still a little worried that Brad was spending too much money. A cup of coffee and a hamburger in the station buffet would have pleased her just as well, for her tastes were simple, but Brad was obviously enjoying it. When he had tasted the wine,

34

the waiter filled the glasses. Midge had never tasted anything more potent than a glass of elderberry wine at Christmas and Harvest Supper.

"Don't talk. Eat!" said Brad, slicing a portion of steak. It was almost raw, and Midge concentrated on her grilled sole, feeling a little sick.

The loaded trolley of varied desserts was tempting, but Midge chose an ice-cream, and Brad asked for his favourite French cheese, and a liqueur brandy with his coffee. He had finished the bottle of wine when Midge had refused a second glass. She was amazed at his capacity for food and drink.

"I enjoyed that," said he, dabbing his lips with the starched napkin. "How about you, kitten?"

"The best meal I've ever tasted," she lied, but it pleased him. Now it was time to go, but Brad seemed in no hurry.

"What time does the last bus leave the Strand for Bayswater?" she asked, tentatively.

"No need to worry about buses. I have booked a room," he told her, with deliberate intention to shock and surprise.

"B-ooked a room?" she stammered. "Brad, I can't — I mean ..."

"Of course you can. You owe it to me. I want to make love to you, darling."

He got up and took her hand. She walked out of the restaurant, dazed. What had she expected? Not this. It was too soon, too sudden. She was not ready. The lift door slid silently into place. There was no escape.

"Fourth floor," said Brad, pressing a button.

The long, carpeted corridor seemed to stretch for miles, till Brad stopped, took a key from his pocket, unlocked a door, and pushed her gently inside. She stood there, feeling trapped and helpless. She wanted to cry, but it was too late for tears. Brad was so calm. She watched him remove his jacket and drape it carefully over a chair. Then he sat on the edge of the bed and opened his arms. "Come here, you adorable child. I'm waiting." he said, coaxingly.

And she went to him, mesmerised into obedience, to stand between his knees while he took off her clothes.

"You won't give me a baby, will you, Brad?" she asked, anxiously, as he lifted her on to the bed.

35

"No babies with Brad, my sweet innocent," he chuckled. "Close your eyes and relax. I am not going to hurt you."

Relax! Was he joking? She was tense, and the tears still threatened. Then he was kissing her breasts. She could feel the nipples hardening. His hands were cool and caressing on her hot body as they moved over her stomach and lingered on the pubic hair.

"Open your legs. There is a little button here," he said, and her whole body trembled as he massaged it gently with a wetted finger till her thighs were damp, and her back arched. Her eyes were closed, so she did not see the protruding penis in the gaping buttons. Then he was on top of her, and when she cried out with the sharp, sudden pain, he thrust deeper, splitting her thighs. She heard herself moaning with pain and pleasure, for the pain was only momentary, and a prelude to such ecstatic sensuality she could never have envisaged in her wildest dreams.

When he slid away, she heard herself protesting, "Don't stop! Don't stop!"

Brad was laughing triumphantly. He hadn't been mistaken. She was a peach of a girl, and he had captured her first, an unspoiled virgin, on her seventeenth birthday.

Midge was reluctant to open her eyes, and when she did so, she was surprised to see Brad sitting on the edge of the bed, still immaculate in the silk shirt and the white flannels — he had been playing cricket all afternoon. There was no sign of the penis.

"Brad, did you like me? Was it good?" she asked, anxiously.

"It was very good, and I like you very much." He kissed the tip of her nose.

"I love you, Brad."

"That's fine. It calls for a repeat performance. Yes?"

"Yes, please."

"Yes, please," he mimicked. His ego was satisfied. He stood up, stretching his long, lean body. A giant refreshed. When he pulled on his jacket and smoothed his hair, Midge demanded, "Where are you going?"

"Home," he answered, laconically.

"What about me? I can't stay here on my own," she wailed.

"Of course you can. Snuggle down and have a nice sleep. Don't fuss, there's a good girl. When you wake up, just lift that telephone, ask for room service, and order breakfast. OK?"

"OK," she echoed, miserably.

"Be seeing you." He lifted a hand in salute, then he was gone.

It was all over so quickly, she could hardly believe it had happened. But her thighs were still damp, and there was blood on the sheet. What would the chambermaid think? But she was no longer a virgin, and she had a lover. It was a consoling thought. She was a woman, and her sex life was important. Brad said she was good, and that was the highest praise. Then why was she crying? And why was she still waiting to hear those three magic words – "I love you"? Was it sex, or love?

The following morning, Brad greeted her with his customary brusque "Good morning, Midge," and not a trace of embarrassment. Her own face was flushed, and her heart melting with love for him. Those slim fingers, painting out an error of judgement on Toby Barnes' lake scene, had been exploring her young, virgin body only a few hours ago.

It was Toby who had taken her to the pictures one evening, and fumbled clumsily under her skirt. She had slapped his hand, and reminded him she was not that sort of girl. He was still sulking from the rebuff. Poor Toby!

Now she had surrendered to Brad, and he had taken her in a way that could never be forgotten. She belonged to Brad. Their two bodies had been joined as one in the intimacy of intercourse. Life could never be the same again. She sighed ecstatically as she took up her brush to put the finishing touches to her latest animal study, "Portrait of Bessie". Brad had been amused at her choice of subject. They were all allowed a certain time each day for their own individual preference, and for Midge it was always the farm animals. Bessie was enormous, and she wallowed in a bed of clean straw while her ten piglets fought for a place at the milk bar. Midge had captured them on the sketching pad she always carried as she wandered about the farm. It was a perfect setting for her own particular talent, for all her

37

subjects could be found in their natural habitat.

Gran thought she was clever, but it was not cleverness. It was as much a part of her as her curls and her blue eyes. She had been drawing cats and dogs before she started school. It had not been an easy victory. Mum and Dad had wanted her to enrol at the Secretarial College at Tonbridge. Why couldn't she keep her painting as a hobby? Dad had suggested.

"But it's *not* a hobby, Dad!" she had protested in a vain attempt to make them understand.

"But how will you earn a living, dear?" Mum could foresee a bleak future for their beloved daughter in a Pimlico garret.

"And what about the white slave traffic? The streets of Soho are teeming with potential seducers of innocent young girls."

"Oh, *Mum*. Don't be so ridiculous. You read too many cheap novels," Midge retorted.

Finally, it was Julian who turned the scales in her favour. In his opinion, Midge was old enough to know her own mind, and should be allowed to live her life the way she wanted. But what if he knew of her true relationship with Brad? She must be careful. She would act the part of a flighty teenager, trailing a retinue of boy-friends. It shouldn't be too difficult. The future was in the lap of the gods, and now she could not visualise a time when Brad would not be the centre of the universe. Several of the students, including Midge, sold their pictures at the Summer Exhibition in the Embankment Gardens. It boosted their morale, and proved to their reluctant parents that they were taking their careers seriously.

Gran giggled when Midge explained how necessary it was to have a nude model for the students to draw the structure of the human body.

"I call it downright disgusting!" Carrie exploded, still hankering after that Secretarial College.

"Student doctors and nurses have to get accustomed to seeing the naked body, so why not student artists?" Julian had argued. "At least the models are healthy and shapely, and that is more than can be said for some of the pitiful creatures to be seen in hospital."

When Julian mentioned hospital, they all were silent and ceased to disagree among themselves, for they knew he was remembering the war years in that hospital under German occupation, after his Spitfire had been shot down. He seldom mentioned it now, but the disability he had suffered was a serious handicap to a young man. Never again would he dance with Wendy at Harvest Supper or chase Midge round the haystacks. Never again ride the bicycle that had been given to young Dick, or gallop a frisky horse across the fields. Never again skate on the frozen pond, or sledge down a steep hill in the snowy mid-Winter, or climb the ladder into the loft over the stables. His small world could be measured in the limited terms of a cripple, as he staggered around on his two sticks, watching the activities of the family. Even Aunt Lucy, in her eightieth year, could move more freely. And the antics of the new-born lambs in early Spring, brought a lump to his throat and tears to his eyes. How he envied those little creatures their healthy leaping limbs.

Only Wendy really knew what he suffered in those bleak moments of frustration and despair. He had long since conquered the self-pity that had made life a misery for his Uncle Albert — a victim of Turkish atrocities — and his long-suffering wife and mother. Russets had seen so much suffering, and also its share of family joys in the happiness of marriage and the birth of children, the prosperity of the farm and the sweet contentment of their small world.

It had been the German doctor who had refused to allow the germs of self-pity to establish themselves in any of his patients. His outlook was healthy and optimistic. Mother Nature was the best healer, he contended. All his patients were treated alike, German and British.

"I am a doctor, not a policeman," he told Julian.

This traumatic experience in early manhood had left its mark, not only on Julian's crippled legs, but on his mentality. They all relied on him to settle their problems and disputes, though he never asserted his authority over that of Aunt Lucy. It was Julian who had taken over the farm accounts and supported Tom in his desire to invest in new machinery. It was Julian who had recommended The Firs Preparatory School for Peter.

If only she could confide in Julian, Midge was thinking, on her first Sunday at home after the bitter-sweet encounter with

Brad. To keep such a dark secret to herself was almost impossible to a nature so candid and trusting. Life had always been an open book for Midge until that night, and in her anxiety to be careful of betraying her thoughts, she was unusually quiet and subdued.

"You feeling all right, love?" asked Gran, as she poured a cup of tea from the big brown teapot.

"Yes, Gran. I'm OK," she lied. Her secret love demanded so many lies.

"What's the matter with Dick? He's mooning around like a sick calf," Tom complained, when his eldest son refused a second helping of his favourite plum duff, and left the table before his Gran had poured the cups of strong tea that always followed the main meal of the day.

"Dick's in love!" John jeered, spitefully. John had never outgrown the childish habit of telling tales. It made him feel important.

"Dick has never looked twice at a girl to my knowledge," his mother reminded him.

"Well, he's looking now, and she's a smasher!"

"Anyone we know, John?" his father asked, with only mild curiosity, for John's tales had to be taken with a pinch of salt.

"Not likely, Dad. This girl's a gypsy."

"A *gypsy?*" his mother echoed in shocked dismay. "Are you sure? I mean, where would he meet a gypsy girl?"

"Probably at The Three Nuns. He likes his pint of beer, and the village pub is a lively place in the hop-picking season," Tom suggested. "We have never grown hops at Russets, so we don't need to employ gypsies to help pick them. So Dick fancies a foreigner for his first tumble in the hay. Can't say I admire his choice, but there's no harm done. The gypsies will be moving on to their Winter quarters when the hop-picking is finished, and the girl will go with them."

"I don't like it, Tom. Why can't Dick pick on one of his own kind? There's Hetty, at the Home Farm. She's been keen on our Dick since they were school kids. Born and bred on a farm, she would make a good farmer's wife," said Carrie.

"Hetty Smith's a soppy thing. This gypsy girl is a real smasher," John insisted.

40

Carrie sighed. "He wouldn't be serious, would he?"

"We can't choose partners for our children, love," her mother-in-law reminded her, kindly. "Let him alone. If it's just a passing fancy, it will die a natural death. Talk about history repeating itself. Tom, do you remember when Harry fell in love with that young servant girl from the Orphanage? She had gypsy blood in her veins, and was always running away. She had to be outdoors. It was like trying to tame a wild bird."

"I remember, Mum, and when Harry got killed in the War, she disappeared, and we never saw her again," Tom reflected. He would tell Carrie not to worry, but Carrie was a born worrier. When her children were little, she loved them dearly for they needed her. She was like a mother hen with a small brood of chicks. Now they were grown up, and even John liked to be left alone in that hut in the orchard. She worried about Midge in London, and she worried about Maggie turning Roman Catholic when all the Blunts had been Chapel. Now she would worry about Dick. You couldn't trust a gypsy. Dick was no match for one of those sloe-eyed beauties, with her sly ways. If only Hetty Smith had a bit more gumption, she would have married their Dick years ago. Some men were ready for marriage and only waiting to be persuaded. The occasion of the Harvest Supper had seen a number of lukewarm courtships suddenly aflame with the madness attributed to the potency of the cider. Be that as it may, more than one child had been conceived at every Harvest Supper in the Weald of Kent since the days of Good Queen Bess.

Carrie wanted to spare her children the suffering she had endured with her cousin, Albert, in her first marriage, but Fate had a way of surprising even the wary. Who would have supposed that healthy, good-looking farmer's son, who had volunteered so eagerly in 1914, would return to Russets so physically and mentally maimed? Yet she had married him, out of pity. There was no alternative.

"Saw them again tonight. Sneaking into the barn!" John announced, gleefully, as he hung the key of the hut on the hook in the kitchen.

"I told you to leave them alone," Tom reminded his younger son.

41

"Just telling you what I see, that's all. I got eyes in me head," John retorted.

"No need for rudeness, John." Carrie spoke sharply. Her tongue was not normally sharp, except when she thought one or other of her children was in danger. She could foresee trouble for their Dick in the near future if he was serious over this girl. Supposing he got her in the family way? There would be the devil to pay in the shape of an angry father and brothers demanding money. Dick would be threatened. The gypsies had a kind of vendetta to avenge their own kind. But Dick was a man who knew his own mind, and he could be as stubborn as a mule. If he was enjoying sex for the first time as a man of twenty, and not a young boy, it would have the effect of a drug. Too much sex, especially with a hot-blooded gypsy girl. Carrie remembered watching the fights on the forecourt of The Three Nuns from the house across the street in her own young days. She had been engaged as nursemaid to the doctor's grandson. They were a wild crowd, and had to be left alone to settle their own affairs. The men could be brutal and dangerous by closing time, rough with their women and cuffing their children. The gypsies were a law unto themselves, and the village constable was reluctant to assert his authority.

Nobody knew how Dick had managed to get acquainted with the girl, or dared to bed a young female so closely guarded by her father and brothers. She must be sneaking away under cover of their drunken state, as they made their way down the country lanes to their camping site. Dick would be waiting at a chosen spot. He knew every inch of the countryside for miles around, and had the eyes of a cat in the darkness of night. No, the danger was in his recklessness in taking a sweetheart from such an alien people.

Carrie was too tired to keep awake at night till her first-born crept upstairs to bed, but she knew it must be well past midnight by the time he had taken the girl back to the gypsy camp several miles away. His reluctance to get himself out of bed in the morning, and his lack of energy during the day, was sufficient proof that a nightly tumble in the hay was sapping his strength. It was difficult to ignore, but his Gran was right. "Let him alone." Even a sensible, steady-going chap like her eldest grandson had to sow his wild oats. It was natural.

Market day, the following week, saw the exodus of the gypsies to their Winter quarters at Maidstone, and Carrie watched the caravans pass with a sigh of relief. When she returned home, however, in the late evening, she found Dick and the girl seated at the kitchen table, and her mother-in-law calmly dishing up sausages and fried onions, while the rest of the family stood around staring in blank astonishment at such audacity.

"Mum, this is Anna. She has run away from her people, and Gran says she can stay here," said Dick, defiantly.

"We will see about that!" Tom glowered at the girl. Not more than sixteen, she was beautiful with her black eyes and black hair, her olive skin and high cheek bones.

"If she goes, I go, Dad," Dick threatened.

"Another cuckoo in the nest," Julian whispered to Aunt Lucy, under cover of Peter's scrambling in Flossie's basket for one of her kittens.

Leaning heavily on his two sticks, Julian's face was pale and strained. He was tired, after a trying day with the Colonel and his memoirs, those interminable memoirs.

"Sit down in the rocking chair, love. Dick and Anna will soon be finished. I served them first because they had walked from Cranbrook, and had nothing to eat since breakfast."

John was staring at the girl in ardent fascination. He wondered if the dangling gilt ear-rings were gold, and whether the stones were real in the rings on her fingers.

When she spoke for the first time, they all were surprised to hear plain English, for she looked so foreign in that farm house kitchen.

"We are engaged. See, Dick has given me a ring." She lifted her hand, pointed to a ring and went on eating her supper with the healthy appetite of a hungry child.

Dick was blushing, and not quite as confident as he would have them believe. For one thing, he hadn't really expected Anna to leave the tribe. He thought she would funk it at the last moment, once the caravans were on their way. As for the ring, he had bought it for her from the stall in the market, and hadn't intended it to be an engagement ring. But if Anna wanted it, then he was willing — as Barkis would say. Charles Dickens had been a firm favourite with the whole family on Winter evenings till television proved a rival attraction.

Julian was right about Anna being a cuckoo in the nest, and she would disturb the peace and harmony of this family as the last "cuckoo" — the bastard son of Sir Neville Franklin — had divided their allegiance all those years ago. They had not seen him since the war. He had married the daughter of the wealthy industrialist who had bought Marston Park, the ancestral home of the Franklins, and they were living in the States. It was better so, for now there was no reason for Julian to be told that Charles was his father. It was just another skeleton in the cupboard, and Aunt Lucy had locked the door on it. Now she was trying to reconcile her mind to this unexpected invasion in her close-knit family. "If she goes, I go." She had no reason to doubt that Dick would carry out his threat, and they could not manage without him. He was indispensable, and he knew it. Born and bred at Russets, he could turn his hand to any job on the farm. Dick had been ploughing with a team of Shire horses while other youngsters of his age were still kicking a football around. He drove the tractor, and his capable hands kept all the machinery in good working order. They never had to pay for any outside mechanic. Nothing had seemed to disturb his contentment, or the even pattern of his days, until this alien creature from another world had ensnared him with her melting black eyes and her sly glances.

When they had eaten more than half of the treacle tart, and washed it down with cups of strong tea, Dick muttered "Thanks, Gran", and took the girl's hand. They went out together.

"Is she going to marry Dick?" asked Peter, perched on the window sill, nursing his favourite kitten.

"It seems more than likely, Pete." Julian answered quietly.

"But she doesn't *belong,*" Peter objected.

"Don't you let Dick hear you say that, or you're asking for a good hiding." Julian warned. But the child was right. You get the truth from children, Aunt Lucy was thinking.

They all started talking at once, but were quickly silenced by Aunt Lucy's raised hands. "Quiet, all of you. Dick has

44

every right to please himself. He has chosen this girl, and she must be made welcome. She must be very fond of Dick to leave her people, for she's naught but a child. Give her time to settle down. Everything will seem strange to her, and we ourselves are strangers. It won't be the first time our family circle has been stretched to include an outsider. We shall manage. We *have* to manage." She dropped her hands and smiled, that all-embracing smile. As always, she had the last word. Anna would stay.

But the shock and excitement had taken its toll on her tired heart, and she swayed as she bent to open the oven door.

"You all right, Mum?" Tom steadied his mother with an arm about her buxom figure.

"Thanks, Tom. It's nothing." She pushed him aside, and reached for the piled dishes of sausages and fried onions. But the giddiness persisted, and she handed him the oven cloth.

"Here, you do it. I do feel a bit shaky," she admitted.

"Sit down, Aunt Lucy." Julian was struggling out of the rocking chair.

"Thanks, love." She was glad to sink into its familiar shape. It was like an old friend. But she still held the reins in her capable hands.

"Now sit down and eat your supper. Carrie will serve. Peter, love, put the kitten back in the basket and wash your hands. Yes, Wendy, I should like a cup of tea." Breathlessly she marshalled them, and when they were seated at the table, her fond gaze travelled round the room and she tried to find a place for the gypsy girl in their midst, but for all her brave words, the girl would remain the cuckoo in the nest.

Midge took her place at the table. She was home for the weekend. All the heated controversy over Dick's girl had passed over her head, for her mind was filled with thoughts of Brad. It had been a long, disappointing week after their emotional meeting at Victoria Station last Sunday evening. She blamed herself for making a scene. Brad had been embarrassed and impatient with her tears. He was not a man of warm sympathy. Perhaps he had seen too many tears in the classroom. That sarcastic tongue could be very scathing, and Midge was not the only young student to shed a few weak tears behind his uncompromising back. The family seemed to have taken sides, Dad and Mum, Julian and Wendy, with opposing views on whether or not the girl would settle down. What did it matter? Her brother Dick would know how to handle it. Dick was no fool. Her own fluctuating love affair was demanding all her senses. Every moment of that disturbing interlude had been dissected over and over again. Had Brad forgiven her? She would die if he replaced her with that snooty Forrester girl, with her upper-class accent and her green eyes. The thought was intolerable, and the smell of fried onions quite nauseating.

"Excuse me." Her muttered apology was lost in the babble of voices, and only Aunt Lucy saw her disappear through the back door.

The Summer vacation had seemed interminable to Midge. She had spent a week with Wendy's parents at Tunbridge Wells, but since they were both working, she found herself sitting idly on the Pantiles, dreaming of Brad, who was on holiday with his wife's family in Portugal for the whole month of August. Surely he could have found an opportunity to send a postcard? He said not, because the children were with him wherever he went.

The following week had been spent with Mark, who was on holiday from the bank, and Aunt Martha. It was rather boring. Long walks with Mark to see whether the hops were ready for picking, and visiting Aunt Martha's ex-pupils from the Infants and *their* grandchildren.

When they had helped with the harvest, Julian, Wendy, Midge and Peter spent a week at Hastings. The weather was perfect, and Julian spent hours in the sea, watched over by an anxious Wendy. With his strong arms, he made good progress with the over-arm stroke. Midge and Peter had both learned to swim in the river, supervised by Dick. After helping with the harvest, a swim was refreshing in the cool of the evening. But for the thought of Brad, these holidays would have been as enjoyable as all the other holidays for Midge, but his image intruded. Her body yearned for the touch of his hands, her breasts awaited his kisses.

When the holiday was over, she had hurried back to London on the Sunday evening, expecting to find him waiting at Victoria, but he was not there. Her disappointment was so acute, she had wept all the way back to her lodgings on the top deck of the bus.

"Had I promised?" he asked, casually over their mid-morning coffee the following day.

"No, you didn't promise."

"You just thought I would be there?"

"Yes."

"Why?"

"Because I hadn't seen you for six weeks."

"And you missed me?"

"Terribly. I ticked off the days in my diary."

He seemed pleased to be the recipient of so much devotion, but the week had passed without any further mention of a rendezvous at Victoria on the Sunday evening. The suspense was awful as the train slowed down. She was the first out of the carriage with her fingers crossed for luck, and her heart racing. Yes, he was there at the barrier. Her feet had wings as she flew down the platform.

"Hello, Brad!" she gasped, and he laughed as she hugged him exuberantly.

"Hello, kitten. Sorry I can't stop. I just stopped by to say 'hello'," he told her.

"Oh, Brad. NO!" she wailed, and burst into tears.

"Now don't make a scene. People are staring. Here, mop up your face." He pushed a handkerchief into her hand, took her elbow, and walked her away from the group of interested spectators.

"I – I'm sorry," Midge gulped, as he pushed the damp handkerchief back in his pocket.

"Come along to the buffet. I can spare half-an-hour for a cup of coffee, and I'll explain what's happened."

By the time he had queued at the counter and brought the coffee to their table, Midge managed a warm smile, and another apology.

"You mustn't get yourself in such a state, sweetheart," he scolded. "You know I am married. I have been perfectly honest with you. I love my wife and my children, and they must come first. Do you understand? If you can't accept my terms, we must call it a day."

47

"Your terms?"

"Yes, that I can only meet you here when I can think up a very good excuse. It's dashed awkward, I can tell you, and I'm not a very convincing liar."

"Neither am I, for I can't stop myself from blushing."

"So I've noticed!" He patted her hand and smiled disarmingly.

She loved him so terribly, she would do anything he asked.

"It's my daughter's birthday, and now she is ten she settled for the cinema and supper at Lyons Corner House instead of a party. My wife was rather relieved, for a party makes a lot of work, and the children have to be amused for a couple of hours or so. Penny has naturally outgrown Punch and Judy and the conjuror, though the boys are quite happy with either. I am meeting Joan and Penny at the Strand Corner House," Brad explained.

"Penny?" Midge questioned.

"Short for Penelope. The boys are Philip and Peter. We call them the three P's."

"I do understand, Brad, and I hope Penny enjoys the rest of the day."

"That's my girl!" He reached for her hand. His long fingers curled about her small hand with a sensuous clasp. "I am very fond of you, sweetheart. You know that, don't you?" He really meant it.

She nodded, tremulously.

"Very soon I mean to repeat that date at the Strand Palace. Did you think I had forgotten? My dear child, do you take me for a villain? At the very earliest of opportunities it shall be arranged. That's a promise. Happy now?"

"Yes, thank you, Brad."

"Now I must be off. You will be all right? You know the number of the bus?"

"Yes, thank you."

"I can just make it if I take a taxi. Do you want that coffee?"

"No, it's horrid."

"Filthy stuff." He pulled a face and took her hand. They hurried across the forecourt, and he hailed a taxi. "Au revoir, sweetheart." His lips brushed her cheek, the door slammed, and he was gone.

48

She stood there, watching the cab till it turned the corner. It was all so rushed, so very disappointing. She wanted to cry again. Then she reminded herself of the promised date in the near future — and he had called her sweetheart. Hugging those small crumbs of his affection, Midge boarded the bus some time later.

"He *does* care. He *does* love me," she told herself, as she hunted in her purse for the fare.

"Guess what, Mum?" Peter panted breathlessly, after racing the full length of the station platform at Tunbridge Wells one Saturday morning.

"MOTHER," Wendy corrected, for the umpteenth time since her son became a pupil at The Firs Preparatory School.

"Mother," he echoed impatiently. Why did she have to spoil everything when he was bursting with such important news? Automatically straightening his cap and tie, she supposed he had been selected to captain the junior football team or the Head had praised his efforts to learn the rudiments of percentages.

Anything in the nature of maths appeared like so much Greek to her, but Julian was coaching him for half-an-hour after supper. Something had put a sparkle in his lively blue eyes. She could see herself at the same age, and should have been more understanding of his enthusiasms, but her mind, as always, was wandering from her small son to her crippled husband. The weekends were all too short. If only she could find a post nearer home, and they hadn't to be separated all the week. She had applied for the post of music teacher at both the girls' colleges soon after the War, but both had been filled by ex-pilots of the RAF, and Julian had approved, whole-heartedly, of such a decision. Of course the chaps should be given top priority. Hadn't they fought in the Battle of Britain? You couldn't argue with Julian about the RAF. It was still his world, and his crippled body had a heaviness irrelevant to his soaring spirit.

Peter was prattling on excitedly as the train pulled into the station, and she bustled him into an empty carriage. "You were not listening," he complained, as he flung his satchel on the seat and stood, facing her, hands in pockets, exasperated by her lack of interest.

"I'm sorry, darling. Start again, and don't gabble." She gave him her whole attention now.

"I am playing the lead in the Christmas pantomime!" he announced, importantly. "It's 'Dick Whittington', and I'm Dick," he added for good measure.

"That's splendid, darling. Congratulations." She leaned over to kiss his cheek, her mind racing back through the years. She saw herself escaping from her mother's domineering influence to join a small travelling concert party in the early days of the War. Ignorant of the facts of life, she had been seduced, in their lodgings, by the leading man, and the tour had finished abruptly when their disgusted comedian had knocked him down and walked out, taking her back to London, and handing her over to her father. *Nigel Bannister.* Peter was the son of Nigel Bannister — a handsome, debonair, middle-aged actor, who could still charm a bird off a bough on stage. Show business was his life.

"You all right, Mum?" Peter was scared. Was she going to faint? Pale as a ghost, she was staring at him as though he had suddenly sprouted horns.

"I – I'm OK," she insisted, and he smiled, reassured.

Why hadn't she realised when Peter was chosen to play Joseph in the Nativity Play at the village school that he was his father's son? Now here was further proof. He was a new boy, yet out of two hundred youngsters, he had been chosen to play the lead in the Christmas pantomime. She clenched her hands and shivered. He was such a handsome little boy. Was he destined to follow in his father's footsteps? "Over my dead body!" she told herself, decidedly, and snatched at the sliver of chewing gum on its way to his mouth.

"Nasty horrid habit!" she scolded. "The GIs have a lot to answer for."

"Don't throw it away, *please,* Mum," he pleaded.

"Then put it away."

"OK. Thanks, Mum."

That disarming smile was Nigel Bannister's. Why had she never noticed?

Tom was waiting with the Ford at the end of the short journey, and they scrambled in. Peter was wedged tightly between his mother and uncle.

"Guess what, Uncle Tom," he began as soon as they were settled.

"You've been caned for being cheeky."

"The Head doesn't believe in caning."

"A pity. It didn't do me any harm."

"Were you cheeky?"

"I was often late. Had no use for learning. Stopped on the way to hunt for birds' nests, climb trees, catch tadpoles, all that sort of thing."

Peter looked at his uncle with new respect. "Did it hurt?"

"You bet it did. The Head of the village school in my young days had no fancy ideas about corporal punishment. 'Hold out your hand, Blunt.' Whack! Whack! Whack!"

Peter winced. Sensitive to pain, he could feel the cruel cut of the cane across his open palm, and he tucked both hands under his buttocks.

"What were you going to tell me then?" Tom asked, kindly, as he narrowly avoided a hare in the lane.

"They've given me the lead in the Christmas pantomime. I didn't ask. They just told me I had to play Dick."

"Dick who?"

"Dick Whittington."

"Never heard of the fellow."

"Oh, *Uncle!* You must have. He was famous. He walked all the way to London with his cat, and he became Lord Mayor of London."

"Sounds like a fairy tale to me."

Peter looked at his mother for confirmation, and she nodded. Peter sighed. Fantasy and reality had a way of getting mixed up, but Dick was already as real as Joseph in the Nativity Play at the village school, last Christmas. He *was* Dick, from the moment he strutted on stage with a hunk of bread and a slice of cheese tied up in a large red handkerchief slung over his shoulder.

"What happened to the cat?" Tom was doing his best to show interest, but he was not brought up on fairy tales. Even at the age of eight life was real and life was earnest for a farmer's son.

"The cat fed on cream and got fat as fat."

"I'm not surprised."

51

"The littlest boy in the school plays the cat."

"*Smallest,*" Wendy corrected automatically.

"What about all the other boys? Don't they get into it?" asked Tom.

"Yes, every single one. Nobody is left out. They dress up in all sorts of costumes. The Head's wife keeps them in big trunks in one of the attics. Matron plays the piano, and Mr Featherston, the sports master, writes the songs. They have a lot of fun singing and dancing. It's a pantomime, you see."

Tom stole a glance at the small boy who was showing such a lively interest in play acting. Ask him to help muck out the stables on a Saturday afternoon, and Peter would wrinkle his nose in disgust. Environment was supposed to influence a child, but Peter had lived all his short life at Russets, and still disliked the stink of dung and silage. Another "cuckoo in the nest"?

Julian was waiting at the farm gate with Rusty. Peter scrambled out to push the gate wide, then knelt on the cobbles to hug the dog. A rough tongue licked his face, and a tail wagged in frantic welcome.

"Good old Rust," said the boy, offering his last sliver of chewing gum. But the dog rejected it. Once was enough. He remembered all too well that sticky substance that clung to his jaws as he rolled in the yard, trying to dislodge it with a paw. Peter had removed it. He was not a cruel boy.

"OK, Rust. I forgot you didn't like it," he was saying.

Mum was too busy hugging and kissing Uncle Julian to notice the gum had disappeared. Chewing gum was a favourite pastime. It lasted even longer than the aniseed balls, and could be stuck under the desk in class and chewed again later.

Aunt Lucy was standing at the kitchen door in her long, white apron. Her white hair still curled. Her cheeks were pink, and her eyes were blue.

"Aunt Lucy!" he shouted, as he raced across the yard.

"So there you are, love." Her plump arms closed about his small body, and he buried his face in her warm, motherly bosom. She smelled nice.

"Guess what, Aunt Lucy?" he began, when he had had his fill of her clean, sweet smell.

"You tell me, love. I'm not much good at guessing games," said she. "Put the gum in my clean hanky. You can have it back later," she added.

"OK. Thanks." They understood one another perfectly, and she was pleased as Punch about Dick Whittington.

"You can come and see me. All the family can come. It's on Christmas Eve, and it won't cost nothing," he told her.

She thanked him, but she knew her aching back and her tired heart would prevent such an excursion in mid-Winter, so she changed the subject quickly, and took a batch of hot scones from the oven. "Just in time for elevenses. Hang up your cap. The kettle is on the boil."

"The best part of school is coming home," he said.

She chuckled as she brewed the tea.

"Can I blow the whistle now?" Peter asked eagerly, when he had finished munching the hot scone, dripping with butter.

Aunt Lucy handed him the whistle that hung on a nail at the side of the mantelpiece. Her husband, Bert, had driven in the nail when they were first married, and told her to blow the whistle when a meal was ready. Working with the sheep or the cattle, or ploughing the boundary fields, he would forget the time. At hay-making and harvest, when they hired Irish labourers, Lucy would take bread and cheese and cider for their refreshment at midday, jugs of tea and cake for elevenses and tea-break, then cook a substantial meal in the evening. The hired labourers slept in the loft over the stables. Lucy was only sixteen when she married Bert, and was plunged into an unfamiliar world of hard work, but she was strong and healthy.

Harry, her first-born, arrived seven months after her marriage, and only Bert was surprised! As soon as he could muster enough breath, he was blowing the whistle to summon his dad to meals, and when he started school, his brother, Tom, took over, followed by Albert two years later. At weekends, and during the school holidays, the boys would fight for the whistle, and Lucy had specified one week for each boy in turn and no nonsense. It was Lucy who had kept the boys' behaviour within reasonable limits, for Bert was too easy-going to bother. It was Lucy who insisted on clean hands before sitting down to the table, and Lucy who corrected their manners and their speech. They got their ears boxed when they answered back.

"*Somebody* had to keep them in order, or they would rule the roost," she told Bert.

The years had slipped away, and Albert was twelve when Bert had been killed on that bright Summer day. Harry, at sixteen, had stepped manfully into his father's shoes, and Tom left school to take over the milking, with his mother, and the milk round in the village. He was ploughing with one of the Shire horses the following year, and when Albert left school to join his brothers on the farm they made a good team, and Lucy was proud of her strong, healthy sons.

The dairy was her place, and her butter and cheese sold well on her market stall. Now, as she listened to the shrill blast of the whistle, she could see all her boys in turn, standing in the doorway, blowing out their cheeks, and she smiled at the memory.

Charles, the first "cuckoo in the nest", had grown into manhood in upper-class society, but her strong influence had lasted much longer than the environment into which he was plunged at the age of seven. He loved his mother, but had to follow in the tradition of the Franklins. Sir Neville doted on the handsome son that had arrived after a family of daughters. He had shocked his lady wife, and all the tenants on the estate, when he bedded the farmer's widow only twelve months after the tragedy. When Charles, in turn, had seduced his half-sister, who died in childbirth, he had fled the country, leaving the baby, Julian, to grow up at Russets. Lucy had gathered the tiny scrap of humanity to her warm bosom, and he was so happy and content with his foster-mother, he asked no questions about his parents until the children at the village school wanted to know why he called Sir Neville Franklin "Grandpa".

Now it was Peter, and in her old age, he seemed to be the dearest of all her boys. Yes, *her* boys, for her strong maternity had claimed them all, and fathers stood aside for the Matriarch of Russets.

As the shrill blast of the whistle summoned the scattered family to elevenses, Julian and Wendy still lingered by the gate. He had been trying to calm her fears, but she was adamant in her refusal. Never would she allow her son into show business, never!

"But my darling, there must be something of his father in the child. It's natural," he had argued, quietly. And she had burst into tears. Julian looked at her with the dark eyes that had seen so much suffering, and wished he could put back the clock to those happy, carefree days before the War. Why had he not realised the age of chivalry was dead on that last day, before he left home for the RAF station? Why had he hesitated to take his little sweetheart when she had practically offered herself with such trusting devotion? Why leave her to lose her virginity to that swine, Nigel Bannister? Why? Why? Why? What good did it do to harbour such thoughts. It was too late. Peter could have been *his* son, and Aunt Lucy the very same foster-mother he himself had known and loved. That innocent girl he had left behind was an embittered young woman when he returned. Now her bitterness and her reproaches had fastened on the child.

"The sins of the fathers," he told himself, as he leaned heavily on his sticks and waited for Wendy to recover her composure. He could see Tom in the distance and Carrie hurrying from the dairy, drying her hands on her apron. John climbed over the orchard gate, and Dick brought Anna with his arm draped protectively over her thin shoulders. The only time they were separated, and then for a mere half-hour or so, was when the grandfather clock chimed the hour of ten, and Anna retired to Dick's bedroom, while Dick climbed the attic stairs to the room next to Katie's.

Aunt Lucy had no illusions about the gypsy girl. She moved with the stealth of a young animal, and would not sleep in her lonely bed. Never in her short life had she slept alone. Packed into a tight cocoon of warm bodies, she had listened to her parents copulating with noisy pleasure. All her senses had been awakened to sex at an early age, and Dick was not the first to bed her.

Tom watched the girl covertly as she clung like a limpet to his eldest son. What had happened to Dick? He was neglecting his work and playing the fool, like any young village lad, but Dick was a man. He came of age this year.

55

"What's the attraction?" he had asked Julian. "What does Dick see in her?"

"It's something called sex-appeal," Julian had answered, with that boyish grin that no amount of suffering had extinguished.

"Is that what they call it? Like a bitch on heat?"

"Exactly, only the heat is there all the time."

"I'm glad my Carrie don't feel that way or I should be proper worn out. Once a week is enough for me. It weren't sex-appeal what got her in the family way before we was wed, but sheer bloody frustration, knowing Albert were incapable, and knowing she loved me."

"So Dick was born on the wrong side of the blanket, as Aunt Lucy would say?"

"Yes, he were!"

"Well I'll be damned! A family of little bastards!" Julian chuckled. "Between you and me, Tom, have you ever wondered why my aristocratic grandfather bedded your mother?"

"I reckon she were real pretty when she were young."

"It was more than just prettiness. His Lordship could pick and choose. I'd say it was sex-appeal."

Tom looked quite shocked, as though his mother had been accused of rifling the petty cash in the tea-caddy on the mantelpiece.

"Not like Anna, but certainly attractive to a man like Grandpapa Franklin, God rest his soul, as Maggie would say."

"I do recollect His Lordship was the first on the scene that time our Dad fell off the hay-wagon and broke his neck," Tom mused, thoughtfully. "And Mum turned to him for comfort. We three boys was dumb with shock. That must have been the start of that love affair, I reckon, for they was in love, and made no secret of the fact. A bloody scandal!"

Julian nodded. "As a family, we seem to have a knack of scandalising our neighbours. Now it's Dick, and I would bet The Three Nuns pub is already buzzing with speculation on Dick's intentions. Poor fellow. I shouldn't care to be in his shoes. If he doesn't make an honest woman of Anna, his life won't be worth living. Everyone knows how gypsies take

56

revenge on anyone who insults their womenfolk. And it would be a kind of insult to court the girl and then discard her."

"Dick has no intention of discarding her. 'If she goes, I go'. That's what he threatened, and that's what he intends. Dick knows his own mind. We can only wait and see." Tom sighed heavily. He was a man of peace, and the only time in his life he had resorted to force was one evening, long ago, when he raped his brother's wife on the hillside late in the day of the Michaelmas Fair. He had lived with a guilty conscience for months while Carrie, still sharing her husband's bed, wept her silent tears in the anguish of the spark of sexuality that Tom had set alight.

"What's the matter with Mum? Has she got a bad headache?" Peter enquired, anxiously, for they were the last to sit down for their elevenses. Julian answered for his wife.

"Yes, she has. A nice cup of tea and a couple of aspirins and it will soon be better." He was quoting Aunt Lucy, and Wendy smiled wanly, but could not speak, for her throat was still choked with tears of regret and remorse. The skeleton in the cupboard had been let out to taunt her, and the past had caught up with her. Unwittingly, for he seemed quite unaware of her reaction, Peter had proved, without a shadow of doubt, that he had inherited his father's talent for acting. Show business was in his blood. Even Julian had let her down. It was natural, he said, and sooner or later the child must be told the truth. A legendary hero was no substitute for a real-life father, whatever crime he had committed.

Aunt Lucy poured tea, and the family helped themselves to the hot scones and the dairy butter. The gypsy girl was silent, but she watched and waited, one hand clasping Dick's under the table, one leg entwined around Dick's. They had made love twice in the night on the attic floor, but still their strong healthy bodies were not satisfied. Dick was conscious now of his aching loins as she held him prisoner. The days were too long, the nights too short. If only she would help Gran in the kitchen, or his mother in the dairy, but she had no desire to make herself useful. Desire was in her small, intense body, and in her senses. She had dropped one of Aunt Lucy's treasured willow pattern dinner plates the first time she was handed a tea towel. Carrie had shown her how to make the cream cheese that was so popular on the market stall, but she soon lost interest and slipped away to find Dick, as soon as Carrie's back was turned.

"It's being indoors she can't abide. You can't blame her. It's the way she's been brought up." Dick would not have her blamed.

"What's a DOXOLOGY?" Peter demanded, as Aunt Lucy served her family with apple pie at midday. She never ceased to be surprised at the nature of the questions the boy asked. His enquiring mind was a source of interest and amusement in her old age. She was just about to answer "Never heard of it, love", when a rich baritone voice interrupted, and they all stared at Mark as he sang, with feeling —

Praise God from whom all blessings flow,
Praise Him all creatures here below,
Praise Him above the Heavenly Host,
Praise Father, Son and Holy Ghost.

"I didn't know you could sing?" said Midge.

"You've never asked," he said, blushing with embarrassment, for Julian and Wendy were both applauding.

"My son Philip had a good voice. He was leading choirboy till his voice broke." Aunt Martha had tears in her eyes as she continued, "He sang solo at all the festivals, Easter, Harvest Festival and Christmas. When my son sang the opening verse of 'Once in Royal David's City', in the processional hymn on Christmas morning, it was like an angel singing, it was so pure. Now it's my grandson, bless him. We never miss a Sunday morning service, but he doesn't sit in the choir-stalls. Says he's too shy."

"Shy, with that voice?" Midge shook her head, but she knew Mark's shyness was so much a part of his gentle nature, he would never face the congregation from the choir-stalls.

Peter had already forgotten why he had asked the question, and was asking another. "Can I get down?"

"*May* I get down," Wendy corrected, automatically. "No, sit still. We are not finished. There is plenty of time. The Show opens at 2 o'clock, after the judges have finished judging all the exhibits and have had their lunch."

"But I want to be there to see whether I have won a prize for my painting and my pressed flowers."

"Don't worry, Pete. We will get you there in good time," Tom promised. He thought Wendy was inclined to be too strict with the boy. "How many of you want a lift in the van?" His eyes travelled round the table, counting the show of hands – Carrie, John, Peter, Midge, Mark, Wendy.

"I have my own transport," Julian teased.

"And you and Anna?"

"We shall walk. It's no more than a couple of miles," Dick decided.

"A tight squeeze in the van even so. Couldn't you walk, John?" his father suggested.

"No, I'm too tired. Been mucking out all morning, and traipsing around the place after those bloody hens what won't lay in the egg boxes."

"No swearing, please, John, in front of the child," Carrie reminded him.

"Sorry, Mum," he muttered, sulkily, for he couldn't bear to be scolded in front of Anna. She was watching him with sly glances, and his young, virginal body trembled with new, conflicting emotions. It was not fair. He was better looking than Dick. He was seventeen and he wanted her.

They piled into the van, leaving Aunt Lucy and Aunt Martha with the washing up, but it was no hardship to these two old women. When they had finished, they settled down comfortably in the warm kitchen, had a little doze, brewed a cup of tea, and repeated the tales of their younger days they had told so many times, but were not aware of repetition. Living in the past, brewing more tea and making toast in the late afternoon, the hours would pass pleasantly till the family returned for supper. Very little time was spent on the present-day problems of the family, for they did not weigh heavily on their old shoulders.

"The young ones will sort things out for themselves as we had to, Lucy, and we both had a hard time, heaven knows," Martha reflected. "Looking back on those early days when Father turned me out to have my baby in that wretched hovel in Richmond Row with a nagging mother-in-law, I sometimes wonder how I survived. Yet the only alternative was the workhouse." She shivered at the memory, and drew her shawl more closely about her shoulders. Then her grave face shone with the kindly smile that three generations of Infants remembered. "But it all turned out well in the end, didn't it, my dear old friend. God in his mercy gave me a second chance of happiness, and Father forgave me. Who can resist the tiny, clinging hands of a baby? 'Bring my grandson home, Martha. That dirty hovel is no place for him,' he ordered. So I went back and carried on teaching, with my baby lying in his pram in the classroom."

"You had courage, Martha. We all admired you."

"Andrew had more courage when he defied the school governors in permitting a fallen woman to teach in his school. He was such a splendid headmaster, they had to capitulate, for it would have been difficult to replace him."

"Did you know Andrew was in love with you?"

"Yes, a woman always knows, but it took him two years to make up his mind to propose, even after I was free to marry again. Such a confirmed bachelor, bless him. Mind you, Lucy, Andrew was not an easy man to live with. He was so set in his ways. Yet compared to my first marriage and the misery of that short period as the wife of a bullying Army sergeant at Tidworth, it was very pleasant. Andrew was a kind man, and a good influence on a growing boy. He coached him for the entrance examination to the Grammar School, and when he passed, he could not have been more pleased than if Philip had been his own son. My biggest problem, I suppose, was the jealousy between them, for both wanted all my love and attention. I couldn't help spoiling Philip a little. It was a protective, maternal love, so different from the love of a woman for a man, but Andrew would not accept that, and I had to be so careful. In a sense, I lost my own identity keeping the peace between my husband and my son. I hadn't your strong personality. Nobody would dare to suggest *you* had lost your identity! Why, I have heard you called the Matriarch of Russets."

"Have you, love?" Lucy asked. But she was pleased.

As soon as the gates were opened in the Vicarage field, a crowd of children swarmed towards the big marquee. Peter was one of the first to dive into its warm, scented interior. Midge and Mark followed the children, and were just in time to see the boy's hand reach out to touch a card lying on the open page of a book of pressed wild flowers. A blue ticket had been stuck on the card. "SECOND PRIZE" Peter announced, flushed with pride.

"Congratulations, Pete." Midge hugged his small shoulders.

"I would have given a first for that collection," said Mark, turning over the pages.

"I didn't know all the names, that's why Sandy Taylor has beaten me."

"Couldn't someone have helped you?"

"No! That's not allowed. We are on our honour. It must be all our own work."

Mark and Midge exchanged a meaningful glance. Such honesty!

But Peter was already on his way to the artists' section, where his *Portrait of a Clown* had won third prize.

"Why a clown?" asked Midge.

Peter shrugged. "I dunno. I just thought it was funny."

The rest of the family had gathered round admiringly, and Peter was the centre of attention, as usual, being the youngest. Then they wandered away to check on their own exhibits. Carrie had won third prize for a bunch of wild flowers. Tom had a second for a huge marrow, and John had won a first for half-a-dozen brown eggs. He was telling everyone he met.

"Anyone would think he had laid the bloody eggs!" Dick muttered, as he led Anna away to the coconut shies. He knocked one down with the third ball, and Anna carried it around. There was little to choose between the pride and pleasure of the boy and the two young men.

Anna coveted a bracelet on the hoop-la stall, but Dick spent three shillings and only succeeded in winning two pieces of Goss china, that he would take home for Aunt Lucy and Aunt Martha. Peter spent all his pocket money on the roundabout and swings. The village band played marches and waltzes till tea-time, then disappeared into the beer tent till after the prize giving, timed for six o'clock.

There were so many classes, and so many prizes, it took the Honourable Charlotte Fitzgerald nearly an hour to distribute them. The children came first, accepting the envelope with a muttered "Thank you", and lost no time in tearing it open. Five shillings for a first, three shillings for a second and two shillings for a third.

"It ain't the money, it's the honour," Sandy Taylor's mother was heard to remark, but Sandy had other ideas as he raced for the sweet stall, with two young sisters in tow, clamouring for sherbet bags.

The entire village seemed to have spilled into the Vicarage field that day. The elderly Vicar wandered around, patting those choirboys on the head who were not quick enough to escape. It was a bright day of late September, with hop-picking over for another year and the harvest gathered in. Apples would be picked in October, and blackberries were ripening on the hedges.

The next exciting event in the country calendar was the Michaelmas Fair, followed by Bonfire Night. Then came Church Parade on Armistice Sunday, with the Scouts' bugles competing with the drums of the village band, and the Guides out of step. Christmas Day was followed by a family social in the village hall on Boxing Day. "Never a dull moment, love," as Aunt Lucy would say. *She* had always been too busy at Russets to attend any of these events, but had taken a keen interest in village affairs, and encouraged the grandchildren to take an active part. Dick had won prizes for the Shire horses. Maggie and Midge had been Guides. Now it was Peter, who had joined the Cubs because he liked the uniform. Her own three sons had followed the Boxing Day Hunt on their Welsh ponies, and Charles had jumped all the hurdles at the Children's Gymkhana on his spirited mare.

The two old women were still looking back when Peter burst in, waving his prize tickets. They had left Dick swinging Anna in the swing-boats, watched by a sulky young brother. Dick was standing up, pulling on the ropes with strong, muscular arms, and Anna was screaming with pretended fright as they hovered precariously in mid-air. All the village lads had claimed a swing-boat, and were showing off to their sweethearts. It was a dangerous game; the boats were rocking

62

and all the girls were screaming. Naphtha flares had been lit by the fair people, and the scene had a kind of bizarre beauty. The band played on, fortified by mugs of ale and cider, and couples were waltzing on a patch of shorn grass to the strains of "The Blue Danube" when Peter was dragged away by an impatient Wendy, who had been showing signs of boredom for some time. Tom and Carrie had left earlier for milking, and Tom brought the van back to collect the rest of the family, leaving Dick and Anna still enjoying the swing-boats. They followed Julian's little car at a slow pace round the winding country lanes.

"Next year I shall know all the names of all the flowers, then I shall get first prize," Peter decided as he cuddled close to Midge, his eyes drooping with sleep. Mark looked at them and wished he could put back the clock. Midge was in love with that art master at the College, and he hardly seemed to exist for her now. They had lost that precious something on which he had built his dreams. His safe little world no longer attracted Midge. She was reaching out to a wider, more exciting world, and he had already lost her.

Mark was not the only one in the van to wish the clock could be put back. Wendy had envied Dick and Anna in the swing-boat. There had been a time, before the War had spoilt their lives, when Julian had swung her high and she had screamed because she really was frightened. When she closed her eyes, she could see his lean young body balanced dangerously on the well of the boat, his laughing boy's face. "Youth and glowing health and his favourite little sister", for they were not yet sweethearts. All of life was before them. They thought that youth and glowing health would last for ever. Hot tears stung her closed eyelids. Such a cruel fate had crippled that eager young body, and sent him back to stagger around on two sticks for the rest of his days.

When Mark squeezed her hand, her eyes flew open, surprised by the gesture. "I understand," he whispered.

"Do you?"

He nodded. "It was the swing-boats. Remembering how he used to be."

"Yes. He was so − so beautiful, Mark."

"I know."

"But Julian is not bitter. I'm the embittered one. It makes me irritable, especially with Peter. I'm a poor sort of mother." Her voice was scarcely audible, and the deep sigh seemed to be drawn from the depths of her being. Then she squared her shoulders and blinked away the tears. "We must be nearly home. A cup of tea will be nice," she said.

Chapter Three

"I have to take Prince to the forge today. Can you amuse yourself, Anna, for a couple of hours or so?" Dick asked, as they drank the cups of strong tea that followed the midday meal.

Anna shrugged. She was not very clever at amusing herself. She had always had company. Her young life had been spent in close proximity to her parents, her aunts and uncles, brothers and sisters and cousins.

"Would you like to gather blackberries, Anna? I shall need them now the apples are picked for jam," Aunt Lucy suggested.

"I don't mind." She shrugged again.

"Plenty in the orchard," John muttered.

"You help me pick?" Anna asked, innocently. Her dark, lustrous eyes held a promise of something he could only guess at. He was both eager and scared at the prospect of being alone with Anna, so his manner was casual and his voice was brusque as he followed her to the orchard after she had waved Dick on his way, leading the big Shire horse.

"You hold the basin, I'll do the picking. The best are out of reach for you. I am so much taller," he told her.

She smiled, showing her perfect teeth. She was really beautiful when she smiled, he thought. Only a few of the blackberries went into the basin, the rest went into Anna's mouth. Her white teeth and her pink tongue were soon stained with the juice.

They were giggling together like two naughty children, caught out in mischief, but there was nothing childlike in the gypsy girl's intentions as the boy continued to feed her with the biggest and best of the berries. She was teasing him, with her head thrown back and her dangling ear-rings catching the sun's rays, on this bright Autumn day. There was no obvious urgency in her desire for him, for she knew how to prolong the agony of waiting. She had practised it since she had the curse, at the tender age of eleven, teasing and tantalising her young uncles and her cousins. They would chase her into the wood, and she would hide, smothering her giggles. It was fun, the only fun she was allowed, for the women and girls worked hard, and the men were lazy, harsh in their treatment and quick to punish.

For young John Blunt, reared on the farm, sheltered and cosseted since his earliest recollections, the gypsy girl had an irresistible attraction. When she caught his hand and thrust it into her loose blouse, he stood there blinking and blushing, in nervous agitation. He was ready for sex, had been ready for sometime. Masturbation was only partly satisfying his latent senses. His roughened hand, stained with juice, touched the soft hollow between her breasts, and a violent tremor shook his whole body.

"You want me, John?" she asked.

He nodded.

"Come, we go to hut. I show you."

Withdrawing his hand from her breast, she led him across the grass and up to the hut, and closed the door. Few preparations were necessary for Anna had never worn knickers. The earth floor was more to her taste than a feather bed. The lesson was prolonged, for John was an apt pupil, and once was not enough. It did not surprise her. She knew he was ready for sex. But they both were surprised when the door burst open and Dick's furious voice shouted, "Filthy young swine!"

In a matter of seconds, John was hauled to his feet, punched on the jaw, and sent sprawling. Then they were gone, and he was left lying there, whimpering, surveying the havoc of the dozen smashed eggs!

Anna was crying her crocodile tears as she was dragged away. Dick's anger would soon be appeased, for he could not bear to see her cry. "The first time I leave you alone I come

66

back to find you on the floor with that young brother of mine!" he scolded.

"It was not my fault. He forced me," she sniffed. "John is very strong, too strong for me to fight." She looked at Dick with wide, tear-wet eyes, her stained lips trembling.

"Poor little girl. Don't cry. Bloody young swine! I bet he thinks I've broken his jaw. He can't bear pain. Never could. That will teach him to keep his hands off my girl. We won't mention it to the others. Let them think what they like, and John will be too ashamed of himself to tell them the truth. Where's the basin? How many blackberries did you pick?"

"Not many."

"Then we had better find the basin and get it filled, or Gran will be suspicious."

They found the basin under a hedge, and Dick set to work to fill it. Anna was holding it carefully, feeling a little sulky, for she had been enjoying that lesson. Her thighs were still damp, and her nipples were hard. But she must be more careful. Jealousy between brothers could be dangerous. She had once seen a fight where the elder brother nearly killed the younger. Jimmy had spent many weeks in hospital. That was two years ago. Jimmy was seventeen now, and grown into a man. Next time he would win. She liked Jimmy. They were two of a kind. She wondered if he was searching for her.

"Little bitch! You wait. I'll pay you out for this!" he had threatened. Those were his last words as they carried him away on a stretcher. She had been afraid of him ever since, but he had avoided her. Gypsies could wait years for revenge. They never forgot an insult or an injury.

Her thoughts wandered to their Winter quarters at Maidstone. She liked the other seasons best, when they were on the move. Making pegs and selling them in the town was no fun. She had to carry one of the babies, slung in a shawl, and pretend it was hers. The baby was heavy and her arms ached, but it helped to sell the pegs. When a housewife shut the door in her face, Anna would mutter a curse. The old Matriarch of the tribe had taught her to curse effectively, and she firmly believed that disaster would strike the house where she had been rejected. In a sense she was homesick for her own people. Dick was spoiling her, and she had never had such an easy life. He bought her trinkets on market day, and had promised her a new dress for Christmas. She could twist him round her little finger. Marriage to Dick would mean living here always, bearing his children. No more wandering, no more caravans, no more beatings, no more pegs. Yet the prospect was not entirely pleasing.

Rough speech and threats. "If you don't work, you don't eat!" She had often gone hungry. Here they fed like fighting cocks. She was growing fat and lazy. She sighed.

"There, that should be enough for Gran to be going on with," said Dick, when the basin was filled. He bent to kiss her stained mouth, and asked, "Still love me?"

She nodded.

They could hear John cleaning up the mess as they passed the hut. "Serve him right! Young swine!" said Dick.

And Anna giggled.

"Anna is going to be my wife." The announcement was entirely unexpected. Three months had passed since Dick brought the gypsy girl home. Aunt Lucy was the first to wish them happiness, and the rest of the family quickly followed her example.

High tea on Sunday was a good time for anything of importance to be discussed, with all the family present, including Aunt Martha and Mark, who had been collected by Tom after dinner and would be taken back later in the evening. Tom was doing his best to hide his dismay and disappointment. To have his eldest son married to a gypsy was the last thing in the world he had expected of Dick. Besotted, there was no other word for it.

He looked at the girl soon to be his son's wife, and saw her for what she was — sly as a little fox, a trouble-maker in the family, another cuckoo in the nest. It hadn't escaped his notice that, on the very day when Dick had taken Prince to the forge, young John had sat down to tea with a bruised jaw and two missing teeth.

"Slipped on the wet floor and hit my face on the cornbin," he had explained, sulkily.

Gran had fussed over him, cooling his tea with more milk, and his mother had cut the crusts off his bread. After tea,

Gran had tucked him up on the sofa in the back parlour, and he had watched a film on TV. Dick and Anna had ignored him completely, but Katie was kind, and brought him more tea when the film was finished. Nobody was really deceived, for it was all too obvious.

"What are you thinking, Mum?" Tom asked, as they gathered round the kitchen fire.

"I'm thinking the same as you, love," she answered, and they all laughed.

"Christmas Eve is as good a day as any," Dick suggested, when they rejoined the family for hot cocoa and biscuits at 10 o'clock.

"Christmas Eve? Not a lot of time for all the preparations," his grandmother was looking a little worried.

"Nothing much to prepare. I don't want a big fuss. Just a quiet wedding at the Chapel."

"But I don't want a quiet wedding, Dick. I want a *proper* wedding," Anna wailed. "A white wedding, with a satin gown and orange blossom. *Please,* Dick," she pleaded, coaxingly.

"All right. You win, provided you don't expect me to dress up in tails and a topper."

"Silly man! Your best suit will do." She clung to his arm, purring like a kitten. But a kitten also has claws, and it would not be long before Dick felt them, Carrie was thinking.

Her heart ached for her firstborn. Dick had never questioned her about the date of his birth, only seven months after her marriage to Tom. She still could blush at the memory. Young Julian had caught scarlet fever from a gypsy boy and had to be isolated. Albert had volunteered to amuse the child in the afternoons. She met Tom in the wood, and they made love under a tree – a sturdy oak that had seen several generations of Blunts grow old and die. Since the night of the Michaelmas Fair, when Tom had seduced her, she had yearned for him, and he knew it. Their mating was a natural outcome of that night, and a promise of their abiding love.

How could Carrie refuse her son when he asked if she would take Anna to Tunbridge Wells to buy the wedding dress? Pressing a roll of notes into her hand, he was like a little boy asking a favour, not certain if it would be granted.

"Buy anything you think she needs, Mum. Shoes, size four,

silk stockings, pretty underwear. I leave it to you. This money should cover it. I drew it out of my Post Office Savings Account yesterday. Been saving a bit each week since the War. It pleased Gran. 'Everyone should have a bit put by for a rainy day, love,' she told me. Well, you could hardly call it a rainy day, could you?" He grinned. Then he was serious again. "Thanks, Mum. You've been very decent about it. I expect you were hoping I should marry Hetty at the Home Farm, for she's been around the place since we were kids. Hetty's a nice girl, and I'm fond of her, but it's Anna I love, and Anna I want to be my wife."

"I understand, son. Your dad is a bit upset, but he will soon come round to accepting it when he sees you are happy. It's just that Anna is rather young, and she has been brought up so differently. Will she settle down, do you think, after she is married, or will she always be so restless?"

"That's a risk I have to take. Providing I take her with me on market days, and to the pub for a drink most evenings, she should be happy enough."

"What do they think of it at The Three Nuns?"

"Teasing me, of course, but I can take it. Can you persuade Dad to give her away?"

"Leave it to me."

"Don't fancy John for best man. Do you think Mark would oblige?"

"I'm sure he would. He is so good-natured. He is so fond of Midge, but she seems to have set her heart on that art master at the College. She hasn't brought him home yet, but she's obviously in love, and can hardly wait to get back to London after the weekend. We only know that he's smashing, and all the girls are crazy about him. Well, we shall see this paragon in due course, I suppose."

"Plenty of time, Mum. Midge is only seventeen." Dick was too involved in his own affair to spare much thought for his young sister. He supposed she was quite pretty, but she couldn't hold a candle to his lovely Anna.

So Carrie went off to Tunbridge Wells with her future daughter-in-law, and they spent every penny of Dick's savings in the big drapery store. Anna was not in the least intimidated by the rather haughty saleswoman in the fitting room, and tried on half-a-dozen wedding gowns before deciding on the most expensive.

"Dick will like me, won't he?" she asked, as she smoothed the ivory satin over her small hips.

"Dick will love you, dear." Carrie was choked with emotion. Such a vision of loveliness would take Dick's breath away on their wedding day.

All the accessories were brought to the fitting room. Such a good customer could not be expected to exert herself. Two satin nightgowns completed the trousseau – an unnecessary expense, since they slept naked!

The "grape-vine" at The Three Nuns had spread the astonishing tale of Dick Blunt's engagement to a gypsy girl, and the actual wedding date, and not all the women were regular Chapel worshippers. A great number only attended a place of worship three times in their entire lives – at their own christening, marriage and burial.

Curiosity was the main factor that filled the Chapel that Christmas Eve. Some of the women had brought their children, even babies in arms. Their menfolk were working, and some would be enjoying the free beer that would be served so generously at The Three Nuns later in the day. The upper class were not invited. The War had changed a lot of conventions, but the barrier between the classes in the Weald of Kent still existed. Local gentry had lost their big estates to the New Rich, and to property developers, and were living in quiet retirement in Worthing, Bournemouth and Cheltenham.

The Chapel had been decorated with a Christmas tree, sparkling with coloured bulbs and tinsel. Holly and ivy draped the pillars, and choir-stalls, and a small vase of Christmas roses from the Minister's garden graced the table with a touch of delicacy.

Two cars had been hired from the local garage to convey the Russets family, and a third car lent by a neighbouring farmer to convey the bride and her prospective father-in-law. White ribbons fluttered from the bonnet. This car was greeted by a group of excited children from the Convent.

When the strains of the Wedding March thundered to the rafters, the congregation rose, and heads turned to stare at the girl who had left her own people to marry the young farmer. It took courage, some were thinking, while others were wondering how long it would last. But few of the working-class women gathered in the Chapel that Christmas Eve would deny that Dick Blunt had found a little beauty. Their own daughters seemed pale in comparison. It was noticed that only Hetty was missing from the Home Farm contingent, and the reason was plain. Hetty had loved Dick since they shared a desk in the Infants, and Teacher had taught them the three Rs. They had collected conkers under the spreading boughs of the chestnut trees on the Marston Park estate, played "mothers and fathers" in the hay loft at Russets, kissed under the mistletoe at Christmas, and pledged themselves afresh at every Harvest Supper. They were two of a kind.

The unchanging seasons followed the same pattern year after year. It was inconceivable that Dick should lose his head over a gypsy girl. He was so sensible, so reliable. Yet he was actually marrying the girl this very day, while Hetty sat alone in the farm kitchen, her grey eyes wet with tears as the grandfather clock ticked away the precious moments.

Only Dick and Mark remained standing, stiffly erect in their best suits and did not turn their heads till Anna's small hand reached out for Dick's. Only then did he turn to look at her — a breath-taking vision in ivory satin he hardly recognised as the same girl he had last seen sprawled naked on the floor of his attic bedroom. But the Minister was smiling, and Anna's small hand was warm in the clasp of his own big, roughened hand.

In a daze of unreality, he listened to the sombre voice of the Minister and the meaningful words that would set the seal on the weeks of tormenting sensuality they both had enjoyed. The urge to lie together was stronger than anything he had ever known. It ruled his will and dominated his thoughts. The future was vague. He had no thought for the morrow as his bemused senses recognised the moment for which Mark had prepared him, and the vital question that had to be answered, "Will you take this woman to be your wedded wife?"

The Minister got no further, for he was rudely interrupted by a commotion in the doorway, and the pounding of heavy boots on the tiled floor. A fierce-looking black-eyed gypsy lad pushed Dick roughly aside.

"Jimmy!" Anna gasped as she was snatched up, and slung over his shoulder.

Then he was gone, clattering down the aisle and out the open door. There was no time to protest. It was too sudden. So totally unexpected.

Midge and Peter were the first to recover, and they dashed in pursuit. They were just in time to catch a glimpse of a billowing veil and the little bride perched precariously on the back of a shaggy pony, the lovely wedding gown clutched carelessly in the rough hands of her gypsy sweetheart.

"Will he bring her back?" Peter asked, with only mild curiosity. He did not like Anna. She did not belong to Russets.

"I shouldn't think so. He seemed a very determined young man," Midge replied.

The rest of the family had joined them on the forecourt. Dick and Mark walked slowly down the aisle, followed by the Minister, too shocked by the desecration of the marriage ceremony to offer sympathy to the jilted bridegroom. In all his fifty years in the ministry, he had never witnessed such a disgraceful disturbance.

Back at the farm, the lavish wedding breakfast, so lovingly prepared by Aunt Lucy and Carrie, was a further reminder that there had been no wedding, and the family stood around in their best Sunday clothes, feeling slighted by the arrogance of a gypsy of alien blood, for whom they held no respect. Invited guests had melted away, and the congregation dispersed to spread the news of the extraordinary scene they had witnessed.

Katie sighed wistfully. "It were proper romantic. I wish I 'ad a lover what would sling me over his shoulder like that gypsy."

"He would have to be a giant to sling your hefty body over his shoulder," jeered John.

"Put on the kettle, Katie. We could all do with a nice cup of tea," Aunt Lucy reminded her servant automatically.

"Not to worry. A nine days' wonder in the village, and everyone will have forgotten poor Dick Blunt was jilted by his gypsy bride."

John helped himself to a sausage roll, gloating over his brother's misfortune.

"Will you shut up!" Dick had had as much as he could stand, and he was near to tears. In all his young life he had never felt so alone, surrounded by the family who had witnessed his humiliation. For them it would always be remembered as the day a Blunt had been rejected by a gypsy. He turned away from their sympathetic glances and went out. Carrie would have followed him, but Tom laid a restraining hand on her arm.

"Let him alone," he said.

Six months later, on top of the hay wagon, one bright morning in June, with the larks' joyous song cascading from the heavens, and the sweet smell of hay all about him, young Dick Blunt finally emerged from the gloomy depths of despair and disappointment, and recovered his lost pride. His shrill whistle surprised and pleased Tom and Carrie, and sent Peter scampering away to the house to report the fact to Aunt Lucy, who was busy slicing fresh home-baked bread and chunks of cheese for the midday snack.

"Dick's whistling, Aunt Lucy," the child announced importantly, reaching for a sliver of cheese.

"That's all right then, love. I've missed that whistle." The old woman's face was flushed, and the palpitations made her sound breathless, but her smile was warm and her genuine delight in this information could override any discomfort in her ageing body. She really had missed Dick's cheery whistle. It was a shrill, penetrating whistle that hung on the air as he ploughed a stubbled field or trimmed a hedge, or repaired a fence or shifted a bale of straw.

"Aunt Lucy," the child interrupted her wandering thoughts.

"Yes, love?"

"Can I stay home from school on Monday to help with the hay-making?"

"You must ask your Mother."

He sighed. "She won't let me. She never lets me do what I want."

"Your Mother knows best, love. I mustn't interfere."

74

"I wish I had a proper father. All the boys in my form have got a proper father. Having a step-father makes me different."

"That's not such a bad thing, to be different."

"Yes it is, at prep school. It didn't seem to matter at the village school. It's not only that I'm the only one with a step-father, but I'm the only one who wants to be an actor."

"So you haven't changed your mind, love?"

He shook his head and dropped his voice to a whisper. "If I tell you a secret, you won't tell Mum?"

"I won't tell anyone. A secret is a secret."

"Cross your heart."

Aunt Lucy crossed her heart.

"I have been chosen to play Hansel in the 'Babes in the Wood'. It's the Christmas pantomime at the Theatre Royal. Mr Sinclair, the producer, came to see the Head yesterday, and I was sent for. He said they had auditioned nearly a hundred children, most of them girls, and it was easy enough to find a Gretel, but the boys were not suitable for the part of Hansel. Then he remembered me. He was in the audience on Boxing Day, when I played Dick in 'Dick Whittington'. He said I was just right for the part, and I said, 'Thank you, Sir'."

"Well, would you believe it, love? But isn't it a bit early to be talking of next Christmas?"

"It's not too early to choose the characters. We don't start rehearsals till after the Summer holidays. I shall be excused sport on Friday afternoons. The Head says it is an honour for the school."

"So it is."

"Mr Sinclair has given me the story to read. He says I can get acquainted with Hansel during the holidays. So I can, just like I got acquainted with Dick."

"Your mother won't like it. She should have been consulted."

"Mr Sinclair is writing to her. He seems to think she will be pleased and proud, but she is going to be upset again. She cried over Dick, didn't she?"

"Yes, love."

He frowned, puzzled by his mother's disapproval.

75

Shrugging his small shoulders, he asked, "Can I have the crust?"

The normal Sunday routine could not be observed that weekend, for rain was forecast, and the hay must be gathered into the Dutch barn. The Sunday dinner of roast beef, Yorkshire pudding, roast potatoes and cabbage, followed by fruit pie and cream would lie too heavily on the stomach, and Aunt Lucy had baked a batch of Cornish pasties to supplement the bread and cheese for the midday snack in the hay-field. Liberally flavoured with chopped onion, the savoury smell wafted over her as she lifted the flat tins from the oven to stand on top of the stove to keep warm. Allowing herself a few minutes respite in the rocking chair, she fanned her flushed face with the oven cloth, and rocked to and fro, well satisfied with the effort.

When a tall, handsome man appeared in the doorway, she thought she must have dozed off and was seeing the ghost of the lover who had died long years ago. But the teasing, cultured voice was real enough.

"Hello, Mother darling. Had you forgotten your cuckoo in the nest?"

"Charles!" she gasped, choked with bitter-sweet memories of his father.

He stepped inside, followed by an elegant young woman.

"You remember Diane? Diane Maloney, from Marston Park?" he asked, and draped an arm over her shoulders.

"I – I think so." The face was vaguely familiar.

"It's the hair, darling. I was a brunette when we last met," Diane explained, as she kissed the old woman's cheek. The expensive French perfume was as alien to the farm kitchen as Anna's cheap Ashes of Roses from the market stall. There was a time when young Julian was crazily in love with this only daughter of a rich industrialist who had bought Marston Park, but she had married the son of a German industrialist who had made a fortune in the First World War, and added to his industrial empire in the Second. A dedicated Nazi, and a fanatical disciple of Hitler, the marriage was dissolved, and Diane enjoyed the war years entertaining American officers in the house at Little Venice, Maida Vale. Still an American citizen, she was not obliged to register. Charles Franklin had

76

claimed her with his charm and distinctive looks. After the war, they settled in the States. His mother was not even sure they were married, and now it did not seem to matter.

Charles stood there, looking down at her, feeling guilty for neglecting her, and wondering whether it had been a mistake to take her by surprise. She had aged, and she seemed quite stunned. He had never seen her sitting down in her kitchen. Always she had greeted him with hugs and kisses, but not today. Till he bent to kiss her mouth, then something stirred in her, and she trembled like a young girl, and wound her plump arms about his neck, drawing his head down to her warm bosom. He was the only one of her sons who kissed her mouth. It was a sensuous kiss, a lover's kiss, his father's kiss, the kiss that had melted her bones twelve months after losing Bert.

"You are looking very well, Mother darling," Charles told her, and she cupped his face in her hands, seeing His Lordship in every feature, for there was nothing of herself in this illegitimate son.

"How long can you stay?" she asked.

"Only a few hours. We are catching the night flight to Paris."

She sighed. He was her darling, the best loved of all her children, but she had never been able to hold him, not since his father removed him from her care at the age of seven, to be brought up with his half-sisters at Marston Park. From working class to upper class. No wonder the boy had been confused and rebellious.

"Where is everyone?" he asked.

"Hay-making," she answered.

"I rather fancy a tumble in the hay," said Diane, who couldn't bear to be ignored.

"Not your type, my sweet." Charles kissed the tip of her nose, and she touched his lips with a finger. Her painted nails matched her painted lips.

His mother watched them, choked with sadness. Why did he come back to disturb her peace of mind with these bitter-sweet memories? She was an old woman now, content in her small world, surrounded by a loving, devoted family.

"These cookies smell delicious. We don't have them in California," Diane hinted.

"Come along with me to the hayfield. I have made two dozen pasties, so there should be enough for everyone, even with two extra." Aunt Lucy was packing them into a basket lined with a clean tea-cloth. Another basket held the bread and cheese. Jugs of cider and lemonade, together with mugs, had been lying in the long grass under the elm tree all morning, for the men and the boys to help themselves. The women and girls preferred to drink hot tea from the flasks.

So they went out together, Charles carrying the baskets, and when they reached the open field gate, he halted, staring at a scene that had once been familiar to him in early childhood. It was like a tableau, framed by tall green hedges and blue sky. The big Shire horse in the wagon shafts, with a sturdy figure at the halter. His half-brother, Tom, on top of the wagon with a pitchfork. Three women in faded print dresses and sun-bonnets, two girls in short skirts and blouses, and a little boy in a bright yellow jumper, chasing a dog round the hay-cocks. It was putting the clock back and strangely moving to a man from the New World.

"It hasn't changed, Mother," he murmured. Then he saw the young man in a wheel-chair in the shade of the tree. "Who is that?" he asked.

"Julian."

"Crippled?"

"Yes."

"I didn't know."

"We hadn't got your address."

"I'm sorry. I should have kept in touch. Mother, does he know?"

"That he is your son? No. Family skeletons are best left in the cupboard, love."

"Has anyone ever told you that you are a very remarkable woman?"

"Yes." Her smile was wistful. "It would only upset him, and he is so brave and cheerful. He married Wendy."

"And this little boy is theirs?"

"Peter is Wendy's, not Julian's."

"Ah, another little bastard!"

"I don't like that word, love."

"Sorry, Mother."

78

They all were closing in on the newcomers, and Charles smiled disarmingly.

"Damned if it's not young Charlie!" Tom waved the pitchfork. His mother shuddered. On just such a day in June, many years ago, Tom's father had stood on that same wagon, and he fell to his death.

"Tom! Come down off that wagon. It's dinner time," she called, authoritatively.

"OK, Mum." He obeyed with his customary good humour. "Give Prince his nosebag," he told Dick, and walked across to shake hands with Charles. A roughened hand gripped the soft hand of a man who had never known the hardship of manual labour in all kinds of weather, but there were no hard feelings. "Nice to see you again, Charlie boy – and you too, Miss Maloney," said he.

"So you remember me?" Diane asked coyly.

"Once seen, never forgotten, Miss!" He smelled of earth and sweat, but she would have enjoyed a tumble in the hay with this healthy, sun-tanned farmer!

"Who are you?" Peter demanded.

"This is your Uncle Charles," Aunt Lucy explained.

"I didn't know I had an Uncle Charles," he retorted. And they all laughed.

The strangeness was lost, and Charles had a feeling of kinship he had not known for a very long time. When he had shaken hands with everyone, and Diane had presented her be-ringed fingers with amused condescension, they drifted across to the shade where Julian was waiting. The Franklin features and the air of good breeding matched the older man's, and they smiled the same enchanting smile that most women found quite irresistible. It was the first time that Charles had touched his son, and once again the feeling of remorse swept over him as they shook hands. Tongue-tied and embarrassed, he waited for Julian to speak.

"Hello, there! What a nice surprise for Aunt Lucy," he said.

That lean, sensitive face and eloquent dark eyes held memories for Diane. The last time they had met, she had been recovering from a vicious beating by an angry husband, infuriated by her infidelities. She had expected sympathy

79

from Julian, who had regarded her bruised body with contempt and walked out. It had rankled for some time, till she met Charles. They were two of a kind, and still enjoyed sex at any hour of the day or night. Julian had not forgotten, but he met her coy glance with the frankness of a man who had long since found his true love.

"You are looking very beautiful, Diane," he told her.

Then Wendy was beside him. She did not trust this woman with the false smile and the expensive perfume. There had been a time when Julian was infatuated. As her hand rested on his shoulder, Julian could sense her resentment. Her possessive love for him could still be hurt by any reminder of those pre-war days, when he had regarded her with brotherly affection. Julian squeezed the small hand reassuringly. She was hot and tired and grubby.

Diane looked cool and elegant in a Dior dress of exquisite simplicity. She had to diet to keep her figure, but she would spoil herself today with one of Aunt Lucy's delicious cookies.

"Mum, can I have a turn holding Prince after dinner?" Peter interrupted.

"Prince is much too big for you." She answered the child absentmindedly, staring at the immaculate blonde with her blue-tinted eyelids, and sensuous mouth.

"Oh, Mum, he's not too big. He's gentle as a lamb." He was quoting Uncle Tom. His eager little face was streaked with dirt and sweat, his knees were grazed. He had tripped over a rake and gone sprawling into the stubble. His mother's voice was sharp, and she was upset about something. He always knew. He sighed, and turned away.

Charles rifled his pocket for a handful of coins and selected half-a-crown. "Here you are. Forget about the horse. He's a monster," he said, kindly.

"Thank you, Sir!" It was a fortune to a small boy who received only a shilling a week pocket money.

Charles and Diane drifted away to sit in the long grass on either side of Aunt Lucy. Peter was kept busy filling mugs with cider and lemonade, while Midge poured tea from the flasks. She was thinking of Brad. He was taking his family on the river today. How she envied them. Maggie, too, was hot and tired, but her thoughts wandered to the cool, peaceful

80

chapel where she had shared in the early Mass before joining the family at Russets. Her lips moved in silent prayer. "Holy Mary, full of grace, blessed art thou among women. Blessed is the fruit of thy womb, Jesus. Holy Mary, Mother of God, pray for us sinners now, and at the hour of our death. Amen."

In half an hour, the family were back to work and only Charles and Diane remained in the shade, chatting to Aunt Lucy and Julian. It was Diane who did most of the chatting, about their life in California, their holidays in Switzerland and their trips to Paris. Their life-style was so alien, it hardly stirred the surface of that hay-scented little world, where the seasons of the year and Mother Nature dictated the pattern of their lives. These pleasure-loving parasites from the New World had only a superficial interest in the family at Russets on this bright Summer day, and were soon bored with the scene.

Julian was silent, and took no part in the conversation. It peeved Diane that he no longer found her attractive. Glancing at her watch, she pretended surprise at the lateness of the hour, and took out her compact to powder her nose and a lipstick to restore the damage of the picnic meal. "We are meeting friends and dining at the Savoy," she told them, importantly.

"How are your parents?" Aunt Lucy asked, in a desperate effort to detain them. She could not bear to say goodbye to Charles. She would not live to see him again. As she reached for his hand, Diane was explaining they often saw her father, for he still had business associates in the States. "Mother and Sammy visit us once a year. They travel by sea. Mother is too scared to fly. She hasn't changed. Still has a working-class mentality. Sammy would have made a better partner for Daddy, but she happened to be my governess, and she was fond of Mother. Daddy sold the flat and kept on the house at Little Venice. He is away on business most of the time. He has a good manager in the London office. Mother was never happy at Marston Park. It was too grand. She couldn't cope."

Aunt Lucy bridled, and her voice betrayed her feelings. "Your mother liked coming to Russets. It was more homely. She once told me that her happiest years were those in a poky little apartment in New York, when you were a baby, before your father made his money. I can understand that. Money does not make for happiness. Too much money can destroy it."

Diane shrugged. "Perhaps, but you can't blame Daddy if the marriage fell apart. Mother just couldn't adapt to the new life-style."

Aunt Lucy said no more, but she was remembering a time when the new owners of Marston Park were labelled "The New Rich", and not one of the old servants would work for them. They had to import foreign servants, refugees from Europe, who had settled in London and didn't like the country. Diane knew nothing of the servant problem. She was away at a finishing school in Switzerland, or was it France? The old servants had their own hierarchy, and the Maloneys were despised for having no breeding. It was true. It was still true, Aunt Lucy was thinking. This adored daughter of the rich industrialist had been given everything that money could buy, but money could not buy blue blood.

"Mother, darling, we really must be on our way," Charles was saying. "Come and see us off." He pulled her to her feet.

"You going already?" Tom shouted from the top of the wagon.

"Unfortunately, yes. Sorry we have to rush away," Charles called back, and smiled disarmingly on the scattered family.

"Push me to the gate," said Julian, and Charles trundled the wheel chair over the stubble field. Only Peter followed them, for he couldn't bear to miss anything. For the rest of the family it was nothing more than an incident in their busy lives, a flying visit of two comparative strangers from the New World, soon to be forgotten.

Peter climbed on the gate. "That's a smashing car." He was very impressed. The half-crown was burning a hole in his pocket. He submitted to their kisses with a good grace because of the half-crown. A boy of eight was too old to be kissed, but he supposed they would not know about that. Aunt Lucy held him close. He could feel her sadness, and he knew she would cry after they had left. The car roared away in a cloud of dust. Two hands waved from the open windows, then they were gone.

"They've gone, love." Aunt Lucy's voice quavered.

"Don't cry." Peter gave her one of his warmest bear-hugs, and asked, "Can I have a crust? I'm hungry."

Aunt Lucy smiled through her tears. "I never knew a boy to eat so many crusts. Before we had you, the crusts went into the pig swill. You know where to find them, and the butter is in the crock in the larder."

"OK, thanks." He ran off, planning how to spend the half-crown.

Aunt Lucy took the handle of the wheelchair, and Julian spoke gently. "Charles is my father, isn't he?"

"Who told you?"

"I have known since I was a kid. Servants talk, my dear. There was a parlourmaid at Marston Park who had seen Charles and Penelope making love. It seems she had blackmailed him for years, and when he finally stopped paying her to keep her mouth shut, she took her revenge. I believe she eventually married the groom, and they emigrated to Australia."

"Fancy you knowing all this time and not saying a word to anyone!"

"It didn't seem to matter. I had you, Aunt Lucy. I was a very lucky child," he told her, as she wheeled him back across the yard. "Shall we sit here? I think I have had enough of the hayfield for today," he said, and she sat down on the bench. "Tell me about my mother. Was she pretty?" he asked her.

"Not exactly pretty, but attractive. All four Franklin girls were attractive. They had that air of good breeding, and they all had lovely eyes. Penelope, they called her Penny, was very animated and popular. She had enjoyed the war years working as a VAD nurse in the hospital for American officers at Marston Park. Then there came a time when the last of the patients was well enough to be sent home, and Penny was not the only one to feel lost and lonely in that big, empty house. According to Charles, he found her lying on her bed crying, and only wanted to comfort her. They were both very emotional, and it just happened. To make love to his half-sister was understandable under the circumstances, but to leave her to face the consequences was weak and cruel."

"She died in childbirth?"

"Yes."

"Poor little Penny."

"You are like her, love."

"Am I?"

"Did you feel anything for Charles today?"

"Not a thing."

"And Diane?"

He chuckled. "Left me stone cold."

"She was flirting with you. Wendy was furious."

"I know. My poor darling still thinks I'm a catch, bless her," he sighed. Sometimes it was smothering to be loved so passionately and possessively.

They sat there in companionable silence till Peter came to join them with his buttered crust. He was pleased to see that Aunt Lucy had stopped crying.

"You've still got me and Julian – *Uncle* Julian," he corrected, with a mischievous glance at his step-father.

Julian ruffled his hair affectionately. He could not have been more fond of the boy had he been his own son. He had the ability to see himself at the same age. Peter would also have to know the truth about his own father one day. He often entertained them with lively impersonations of the masters and schoolmates at The Firs. It was quite uncanny. His voice, his expression, his gestures, were no longer Peter's, and he obviously enjoyed the applause. Acting was in his blood, and nothing and nobody would prevent it coming out.

When he had finished eating the crust, he gave them a good impersonation of Diane Maloney powdering her nose and applying lipstick. It made them laugh, and that was his intention, for he had sensed the sadness when he joined them. He always knew. "To make people laugh and cry, that is the essence of playing a part," Mr Sinclair had insisted when he was offered the part of Hansel in "Babes in the Wood". "You played Dick in 'Dick Whittington' most convincingly. You can do it again with Hansel."

"Yes, Sir," Peter had answered. He knew he could.

The rumble of the hay-wagon reminded them that the last of the hay had been gathered. Aunt Lucy hurried away to put on kettles; fresh pots of tea and hot water for washing off the sweat and dust.

Peter ran to meet the wagon. "Can I lead Prince, *please*," he begged.

"OK." Dick handed over the halter. Peter walked proudly beside the huge horse, his small figure completely dwarfed. Prince had finished his work for the day, and he knew it. Dick would not drink his tea until he had fed and watered his horse. Cows and horses had top priority. This was one of the golden rules on the farm. Prince would soon be enjoying his retirement, cropping the grass through the long Summer days, and the comfort of his stable in the Winter.

Julian watched the scene from his wheel-chair, his crippled legs twitching. Nobody could really understand the unbearable frustration, or the agony of waking each morning to the realisation that nothing had changed. He often wept for his lost youth and strong, virile body, while Wendy slept soundly beside him. But self-pity was an indulgence he had to avoid at all costs. He remembered Uncle Albert, a physical wreck of the First World War, who made life a hell for his long-suffering wife and mother with his black moods and violent temper.

When Wendy came to sit beside him, he smiled and kissed her. "You're tired, sweetheart," he said, gently.

She nodded, and laid her head on his shoulder. He knew she was still wondering about Diane Maloney. "I love you, my darling, now and for ever," he told her, convincingly.

For Midge it was still a time of uncertainty, of dashed hopes, and unfulfilled longing. Brad still occupied her mind and her heart, and she travelled back to London every Sunday evening in a fever of nervous anticipation. Would he be there to meet her? Would they sit in the station buffet for a brief half-hour, drinking that awful coffee, and making polite conversation that had nothing to do with her thoughts? She knew now that he was never going to suggest another night at the Strand Palace. She had embarrassed him with that scene on Victoria Station.

It seemed she had always known Brad, but it was not yet a year, for this was her third term at the college. But because he had been the first man to touch her body intimately, and to arouse all the latent senses in that virgin body, he had become the symbol of her heart's desire. Once awakened to sex and the trauma of intercourse, she had only to see him in class, to watch those long, sensitive hands pointing out some fault on a student's canvas, to feel those same hands exploring her naked body. Yet she still questioned the normality of his approach to intercourse. Was there something strange and rather abnormal about a man who made love fully clothed? In her dreams, they both were naked, and they would lie together, sated and satisfied. But the reality was altogether different. Brad seemed to be using her body as an instrument, not with affection. She loved him to distraction, and made no secret of her love.

Not once had he told her that he loved her. "I am fond of you, kitten. You are so young, so intense," he had told her.

So she had allowed herself to be seduced, had actually welcomed it, because in her ignorance she had imagined it to be the prelude to an intimacy of lasting duration. The voice of reason told her that she had disappointed him in some way, and failed to prove her complete readiness to be moulded into the woman for whom he was so obviously searching. It was humiliating to be left wondering what had gone wrong. She had re-lived every moment in her mind, time and time again. He had taken her with a kind of desperate urgency, but it was quickly over, and he was pulling on his jacket, smoothing his hair, lifting a hand in farewell.

For a young woman born and bred on a farm, it should not have been such an alarming initiation, but she had always separated animal and human behaviour in her mind.

So, on this Sunday evening, when she had spent all day in the hayfield, she bathed, washed her hair, changed into a clean cotton dress and white sandals, and travelled back to London with a premonition of impending disaster. Brad would not be there to meet the train. He had not been there last week, nor the week before. It could only mean that he was tired of her, and had found someone he liked better.

She scanned the small crowd at the barrier hopefully and foolishly, and stood there, choked with disappointment, while a message shaped itself in her tortured mind. "Take a bus to the Strand. You will find him at the Strand Palace." It was now or never. She had to know the truth.

The foyer was crowded, but it took only a few seconds of her searching glance to discover Brad at Reception, with a tall, elegant young woman in a tailored trouser suit. They were sharing a joke. Midge turned away and walked out. It was over. Perhaps it had never really started.

Back at Victoria Station, she caught the last train home. It was too late to phone Russets. They would all be in bed. She walked the two miles in bright moonlight. The sweet scent of hay still lingered in the stubble fields, an owl hooted forlornly and a vixen screamed. Midge was neither surprised nor disturbed by these night creatures.

She let herself into the silent house and climbed the stairs. It was only when she had undressed and slipped between the cool sheets that the full significance of that evening overwhelmed her.

Her smothered sobs woke Aunt Lucy, who had always been a light sleeper, and she padded into the adjoining room in her long cotton nightgown.

"Come in with me, love," she whispered.

It was putting back the clock. The big marriage bed had often been a haven of comfort in childhood. Unhappiness over some childish quarrel, or a nagging tooth. "Can I come in with you, Gran?" Now, on this night of such bitter disillusion, the old woman enfolded her young grand-daughter in her loving arms while she sobbed, distraught, on the warm, comforting bosom.

Chapter Four

It was customary for Tom to take his mother a cup of tea at five o'clock, when Carrie made a pot of tea before the milking. He was startled to find Midge tucked up in the bed when he had last seen her waving from the train. His mother put her finger to her lips, so he made no comment as he handed over the mug. Midge was sleeping soundly. With her flushed cheeks and curly hair she looked like a little girl, cuddled to that warm, motherly bosom. Midge was his favourite, though he prided himself on absolute fairness and affection for all his children. Carrie was inclined to favour Dick, her first-born. She had been so terribly upset when he brought the gypsy girl home, but because it was Dick, she had accepted the situation and even accompanied the girl to buy her wedding clothes. That particular episode had ended happily for Carrie, if not for Dick. Now she would worry about Midge.

"Did she look poorly?" she asked, anxiously.

"No, she looked no different from when I saw her off on the train."

"Then something happened at Victoria. If that art master has jilted her, Tom, she will break her heart. She's crazy about him."

"No future there, love. He's married."

"*Married?* She told you?"

"Yes, some time ago."

"Why keep it to yourself? We never have secrets between us?"

"Midge thought you would be upset."

"I *am* upset. Silly girl. It's asking for trouble. Now we

know why she hasn't brought him home. Married." She shook her head.

"Middle-aged, with three children," Tom said, rubbing salt into the wounds.

Carrie choked on her tea. She was so angry. "That poor woman. She must be out of her mind. How could our Midge behave so badly, Tom, when she's been brought up decently? She ought to be ashamed."

"Don't be too hard on her."

"You don't think . . . ?"

"If he has got our Midge in the family way, I'll ring his bloody neck!"

"This comes of gallivanting off to London. I was always against it."

"But she won that scholarship."

"What's a scholarship compared to happiness?"

"But she *was* happy. Who could have foreseen she would fall in love with a married man, old enough to be her father?"

"Midge is just the age to be attracted to an older man. Mum will know if she is really in trouble. Mum is always the first to know. This family seems fated. It crops up in every generation, starting with Mum and His Lordship."

"You and me only just managed to get wed before I was showing, don't forget."

Tom grinned, and pulled her into his arms. "And weren't you in a right old panic, love!" he teased her.

"I think I should have died if you hadn't married me."

"As though I hadn't been waiting all those long years you were tied to Albert. Oh, Carrie, love, shall I ever forget the misery and frustration?"

"Poor Albert." She shivered at the memory.

"Suppose we had better get on with the milking." Tom suggested, laconically. And they went out together, hand-in-hand, into the freshness of early morning, still sweethearts, with four grown-up children.

Two hours later, they were sitting down to an appetising breakfast of eggs and bacon and fried potatoes. If the heavens were falling, Aunt Lucy would have their breakfast waiting in the oven.

"What happened to Midge?" Tom asked, anxiously.

89

"It's all over with that art master. She broke her heart, poor lamb. It seems he has found someone he likes better."

"So long as he hasn't got her in the family way?"

"No, nothing like that."

"The man's a swine. He should be reported."

"You can't blame the man if all the girls are like Midge. It must be quite embarrassing."

"You taking his part?"

"No, I'm sorry Midge has to learn the hard way. She will get over it. Leave her alone. A day in bed won't come amiss after all that emotion."

"It must have been pretty bad for Midge to cry."

"She cried plenty last night, son. I thought she would make herself ill. She says she is not going back."

"I don't blame her," said Carrie, buttering a slice of bread, and much relieved that another family crisis had been settled.

But they all had underestimated the depth of feeling and the importance of that first love affair. It would be a long time before they saw the old happy Midge again. Even when the wound had healed, it would leave a scar. For a whole week she lay in bed, refusing food, till Aunt Lucy threatened to call the doctor; then she got up and came downstairs in her dressing-gown, unwashed and heavy-eyed, to rock to and fro in the rocking chair.

"You would feel better outdoors, love," Aunt Lucy suggested, tentatively.

"I shall never feel better. I wish I could die. Nobody cares," Midge muttered, as she pulled herself out of the chair.

"Don't talk that way, love. We *do* care," the old woman insisted, enfolding the girl in her arms. But there was no response. The close contact of that first night had not been repeated. They all had tried. Even Dick had shown his young sister a gruff sympathy.

Julian, with his sensitive understanding of his wife's frequent emotional upsets, left Midge alone to find her own way back to normality.

Only Peter refused to accept the obvious fact that his favourite cousin — if she was a cousin — had changed her image.

He still shared his sweets with her, and the first strawberries,

90

and brought an offering of tadpoles in a jam jar.

In this black mood of depression, Midge had taken on the likeness of her twin brother for the first time. The blank stares, the sulky mouth and the self-pity. Now John was upset because Midge was getting too much attention.

The fact remained, in such a close family, the small world of Russets revolved around the Matriarch, and she was beginning to feel the weight of her responsibilities. Only Aunt Martha noticed the obvious signs of failing strength in her old friend, but she herself was feeling her age, and had only her grandson depending on her, while Lucy had all the family at Russets. Mark had not been seen at Russets since May Day, when he and Midge had leaned on the gate, watching the cows being driven out of their Winter quarters to spend the long Summer days in the green pastures. This was one of the traditional signs of the changing seasons, and tradition was still strong at Russets. The new machinery that made seedtime and harvest less arduous, and the tractor that carried Dick over the furrowed fields, were still regarded with suspicion by Aunt Lucy and Carrie. It was the men who had to keep abreast of their neighbours and not lag behind. In Aunt Lucy's kitchen and Carrie's dairy, the old-fashioned methods were still considered the best.

It was the first year that Mark had not helped out with the hay-making, but he had his own reasons for keeping away from Russets that Summer. He had loved Midge since he first made his home with his grandmother − Aunt Martha to the family at Russets − after the tragedy. It was inconceivable that his little brother Matthew should be killed by a car, crossing the road, after the school had been evacuated to a safe area in the early days of the War. Yet it had happened, and Mark had not returned to the school. In the shocked state of the aftermath, secure in the loving care of a fond grandmother, Mark had found in Midge the cheeky, self-assurance he had always lacked. He spent all his holidays at Russets. One more child, especially a boy, was welcomed. In a sense, the relationship had developed in much the same way as that of Julian and Wendy, from brother and sister, but it was Mark, not Midge, who saw in their relationship something more. His shyness was an embarrassment, and his gentleness regarded as weakness by his contemporaries at the bank. The Grammar School, followed by the banking career his parents had chosen on his behalf, had left him singularly vulnerable and unhappy. What did the parents know of their son when they saw him for only three months every five years? All their energies were deployed in the Mission Station in the Congo.

Generations of children suffered the same compulsory separation, and grandmothers played the role of parents with loving devotion. For the young bank clerk, on his bicycle, pedalling furiously round the country lanes to catch the train to Tonbridge, there was no joy in the day ahead, and he would gladly have changed places with any one of the farm labourers he met on the way. Sunday at Russets had been his only consolation, and Midge the only girl in his small world. Since she went to London, the gap had widened between them. She had moved into a wider world. She was in 'love, and he couldn't bear to listen, so he stayed away.

The bored young woman who sat with idle hands had no place at Russets. The weeks went by, and it seemed a mistake to let her alone to find her own way back to normality, as Julian had suggested. Yet they all were wary of upsetting her still further. A nervous breakdown following such a long bout of depression was not uncommon, even in farming circles. The aftermath of the War had left its mark on town and country alike, and children who had grown up since the War seemed to lack the stamina and resilience of the older generation. "What shall we do with Midge?" became a pressing question when the harvest had been gathered, and the Michaelmas Fair the next date on the calendar to be enjoyed in time-borrowed fashion, in holiday mood. To leave Midge mooning about at home was unthinkable, but Aunt Lucy reminded them she was too old for such gadding about anyway, and they would keep each other company. She would make pancakes for dinner, and a chocolate cake for tea to tempt her grand-daughter's poor appetite.

The family departed in fine style after breakfast. Tom and Carrie, who had been up since dawn for milking and delivery, would have to leave the Fair early for the evening milking, but they did not complain. It was their life. Twice a day, seven days a week, cows had to be milked and animals fed and watered.

Katie was waiting in her Sunday best with a purse full of shillings the Mistress had saved for her. Like a child in her enjoyment of such rare outings, ten single shillings meant more to her than a ten shilling note or five florins. Katie was not the only one to remember the days when they travelled in the wagonette to the Michaelmas Fair, picking up stragglers on the way. Tom and Carrie had good reason to remember this particular date on the calendar. It marked the day when the patient Tom had lost his patience, and could wait no longer to claim his brother's lawful wife. He had carried the protesting Carrie to the top of the hill, and taken her by force, on the homeward journey.

As soon as the crowded van had disappeared down the cart-tracks, Midge was wishing she had joined them. They did not want her. She would spoil their pleasure. Leaning on the gate she thought of Brad. Three months had passed since that awful night, and she had long since given up hope of hearing his voice on the phone. Hope had died a slow, lingering death, but the ache was there all the time. "Nobody cares," she muttered, miserably. Aunt Lucy would be putting on the kettle for another cup of tea in her firm belief that a nice cup of tea could cure anything from a headache to heartache. The long day stretched ahead.

She turned away from the gate, wandered back across the yard, and into the wide open doors of the big Dutch barn. She was tired. She was always tired, in body, mind and spirit, for idleness can be more wearisome than work. Stretched on the sweet-smelling hay, she fell asleep.

Aunt Lucy was beating the batter for the pancakes when the pain gripped her chest with such violence, she gasped for breath and clutched the table. She was not a stranger to pain in latter years, but this was the worst pain ever. Every breath was agony. The kitchen spun. Cold sweat damped her brow.

Staggering to the old rocking chair, she sank into its creaking, familiar comfort, and closed her eyes. This was the end. She knew it. She was glad to be alone in her kitchen. Earlier in the day she had gone in search of Midge, and found her sleeping soundly. She left her undisturbed. Her last coherent thought was of Midge, and the pancakes she had promised. Then she slipped away.

Midge woke refreshed, and lay quietly savouring the sweet-smelling hay. She had not bothered to wind her watch, for time had stood still since she came home to Russets. One day had been so much like another. Her dry throat reminded her of Gran, who was putting the kettle on for a nice cup of tea when they last met. Not a sound penetrated this peaceful haven. She remembered the family had left for the Michaelmas Fair soon after breakfast, but if it was dinner time, Gran would have wakened her. She had promised to make pancakes, and Gran's pancakes, sprinkled with caster sugar and a squeeze of lemon, were the best she had ever tasted. Their London landlady had served up pancakes that would have soled your shoes! She giggled at the memory, surprised to find herself in such a good mood. Yawning and stretching, she sat up and put her feet to the floor.

Sunlight dappled the cobbles as she crossed the yard. The smell of Autumn hung in the air. A hen cackled in the orchard, and Prince neighed in his stable. These were the only sounds to break the silence of the deserted farm. She shivered involuntarily, and hurried towards the kitchen. In all her short life, the kitchen had been the one place in the house to which all the family had fore-gathered at all seasons of the year. A fire would be glowing in the old-fashioned range. The smell of baking lingered long after the ovens were empty. The big brown tea-pot stood warming on the hob. But it was Gran who gave the kitchen that special atmosphere of homely comfort. It was her domain. Gran was Queen in her kitchen.

"Here I am, Gran," she called, cheerfully, from the open door.

There was no response from the huddled figure in the rocking chair, and the chair had stopped rocking. In a matter of seconds, Midge was across the kitchen, falling on her knees, clutching at the prone figure.

"Gran – GRAN! Speak to me!" she screamed – and buried her face in the folds of the white starched apron.

They came home in high spirits, packing into the van, recounting their separate pleasures. They all had brought a "fairing" for Aunt Lucy. Tom had reminded the rest of the family they would be leaving for home at four o'clock. They would find the van in the stable yard at the George and Dragon. Tom and Carrie were rather surprised when they all turned up; for different reasons they had had enough. Dick was remembering last year, in the company of Anna. John had spent all his money, and was not prepared to walk such a distance. Wendy was tired of pushing Julian in the wheelchair, and Peter was tired of being told not to get lost. He wanted to see the Fattest Woman in the World, and the Man with Three Legs, but Mum said it was all a fake and a waste of money.

Last year, he had lots of fun with Midge. They had sampled everything, and he had been sick twice! Once on the Giant Chair-o-Plane, and again after eating candy-floss, a toffee apple and a hot-dog too soon after the swing-boats.

As for Katie, she was sulky and bad-tempered. The fun of the fair for Katie, and other farm servants, was after dark, lying with their sweethearts under the empty wagons. There was a time, in her younger days, when Katie's attraction to the opposite sex was quite an additional worry for her long-suffering mistress. But another little bastard had been avoided, more by luck than judgement, and Katie was a woman of fifty now.

Peter was squeezed between Tom and Carrie in the cab, his pockets bulging. Peanuts for Midge and peppermint humbugs for Aunt Lucy.

Back at the farm, he jumped out of the van to push open the gate, and raced across the yard, waving aloft the bags of peanuts and the peppermint humbugs. "Look what I've brought you!" he shouted, importantly — and froze with shock on the threshold. Aunt Lucy was slumped in the rocking chair. Her eyes were closed, and her face waxen. Midge was sprawled at her feet, her curly head buried in the folds of the clean, starched apron. *The rocking chair had stopped rocking.*

Tom pushed him aside, too stunned to speak, and gathered Midge into his arms. Her eyes were red and swollen with crying. "She's dead, Gran's dead," she told him, in a choked voice.

Carrie moved quickly to cradle the white head to her breast, her own tears falling silently. Katie was crying hysterically.

"The Mistress is dead! The Mistress is dead!"

"Shut up!" John growled.

And Katie turned on him, her face ugly and distorted. "You ain't got no right to talk to me that way!"

"Sorry," he muttered, and plunged out of the door.

"Phone the doctor, will you, Dick?" his father asked.

Dick nodded, mutely, and went to the hall.

Julian wore the stricken look of one who has received a mortal blow, but Wendy was dry-eyed. She would weep later, in Julian's arms, when they were alone together.

"I want to be sick!" Peter wailed; dropping the bags of peanuts and peppermint humbugs on the kitchen floor, he dashed for the scullery sink. Nobody came to hold his head and give him a drink of water. "Nobody cares," he sobbed, and crept back to the kitchen. Julian reached out a hand to draw him close. The child was shivering.

"Can you die just like that? I thought it took a long time to die," he gulped.

"Not always, Pete. It must have been a heart attack. See, she was mixing the batter for the pancakes. Aunt Lucy could not have wished for a better place to die. She loved that old rocking chair." They spoke in whispers, out of respect for the dead. It was all so strange.

"Who will tell us what to do? Who will bake the bread and the pies?" asked the child, his wet eyes wide with a sorrow he was too young to understand. The full significance would come later.

It was the end of a chapter, and Russets would never be the same again without Aunt Lucy.

"The doctor will be here in half an hour," Dick was saying.

"Shall we carry her upstairs?" his father asked. Was it the proper thing to do? Nobody seemed quite sure.

"I will stay with her," said Carrie, following them up the stairs.

"She wouldn't like to be left alone, would she? Aunt Lucy always liked company," Peter reminded them, as he bent to pick up the packages he had dropped.

Midge had slumped in a chair, her face buried in her hands.

"I brought these for you, Midge," a small voice whispered.

She lifted her head, and stared at the child as though he were a stranger, and he dropped the bag of peanuts in her lap.

"You can have the peppermint humbugs if you like, Katie," he told her.

But she shook her head and shuddered. "T'would be like robbing the dead," she sniffed, miserably.

The young doctor seemed a little brusque, but it was only his manner. "Upstairs?" he asked.

"Yes, please, Doctor." It was Julian who answered from his wheel-chair. They exchanged a glance of mutual interest, for Julian was a survivor from the Battle of Britain, and a hero to a young man who had spent the war years in a military hospital only a few miles from his own village.

Carrie was standing at the top of the stairs. "Jimmy," she exclaimed.

"Hello, Carrie." He smiled at the plump little woman he remembered from his earliest years. Carrie had been engaged as nursemaid soon after she had left the village school, and had proved to his sceptical grandmama that a girl raised in Richmond Row could be as capable and intelligent as the fully trained Norland Nanny on whom she had set her heart for young James. Jimmy had loved her. She had travelled out to India with her small charge, helped to nurse him through a nasty bout of typhoid, and brought him back to England.

"It has been a long time, Carrie, but you are such a healthy lot at Russets," he said, as they turned towards the still form on the big marriage bed.

She watched his sensitive hands moving gently over the old woman's body. She looked so peaceful lying there, but already a little remote.

"Her heart was tired. That is the simple explanation. Don't cry, Carrie. It's a good way to die. Only a few brief moments of suffering, then oblivion." He laid a comforting arm about her shaking shoulders.

"I am so afraid, Jimmy," she confessed.

"Afraid?"

"I can never take her place. They will expect too much of me."

"You can only do your best. They must help you."

"We have depended on her for so long. She had the last word on everything."

"A kind of matriarch?"

"Yes."

"Take heart, my dear. You will find the strength, as you did all those years ago in India. You saved my life then. Don't think I have forgotten. Mother was kind, but it was you I wanted. When she sent you away to rest, I cried."

"You did?"

He nodded, gravely.

"You were such a dear little boy," she sighed, nostalgically, and asked, "Are you married, Jimmy?"

"Married, with two children, a boy of three and a baby girl. I married a nurse at St Thomas's after I had qualified. Then I took over my grandfather's practice in the village. I was lucky."

They talked in low voices, and now it seemed that Aunt Lucy's brave spirit was still there. This young doctor, with his pleasant, boyish face, had reminded her that she was no weakling.

"It's so good to see you, Jimmy. I often thought of you," she told him.

"We lost touch, I'm afraid. There was prep school, public school and medical school, then marriage. But that's a poor excuse. We won't lose touch again. I shall bring my son, Jonathan, to see you."

She smiled at the pride in his voice. Then she remembered her new role and asked, "Would you like a cup of tea?"

"Thank you."

"I will put on the kettle," she said, and he followed her downstairs.

They could hear the cows calling plaintively as they drank their tea. "They know it's milking time. If we forget, they remind us," Carrie told the young doctor, as she put down her mug and held out her hand. "Goodbye, Jimmy."

He stood up, took her hand, and kissed her cheek. "For old times' sake," he told her, gravely. Then he shook hands with everyone, including Katie and Peter. And Katie, still in her Sunday best coat and hat, stopped sniffing and poured herself a second cup of tea.

They all knew they were going to have trouble with Katie, for she had always refused to take orders from anyone but Aunt Lucy.

"Can I have a crust, I'm hungry," Peter asked, when the doctor had gone. "Aunt Lucy always let me have a crust when I was hungry," he reminded his mother.

Were they going to have trouble with Peter as well as Katie and John? Wendy sighed. She was starting another migraine, and would have to lie down.

"Can I, Mum?"

She nodded, and he flew to the larder.

Tom put his head round the door to ask, "Can I leave you to do all the phoning, Julian?"

And Julian answered, "Yes, of course." Wendy pushed him into the hall and left him there. All the numbers were there in the book on the hall table. Aunt Lucy's sprawling, childish hand had not changed since she left the village school, and his throat tightened with tears as he leafed through the pages. How to break the news gently to her twin sister, Ruby? – Wendy's beloved Gran. Aunt Martha must be told, and their farming neighbours on the big estate. A cablegram to Charles in California and a telegram to London to their old friends, the Maloneys. For nearly an hour he sat there, and when he had finished, he put down the phone, feeling completely drained.

It was Midge who came to look for him and pushed him back to the warm kitchen. Normally he walked about the house with his two sticks. Today, however, his legs were numb, and his whole body felt bruised and battered, as though somebody had given him a good hiding. This terrible shock was only just beginning to penetrate his dulled senses.

"Thanks, Midge," he said, gratefully.

But when she burst into a fresh flood of tears, and sobbed, "It was all my fault. I left her alone to die. I shall never forgive myself," he forgot his own anguish in the need to comfort her.

"My dear, it was nobody's fault. You heard what the doctor said. Her heart was tired."

"But if she hadn't been beating the batter for my pancakes ..."

99

"Then it would have been something else. The slightest exertion when the heart is worn out can be the end."

She shook her head. To blame herself was a kind of penance. She had needed to be rudely awakened from that self-absorbed state of unrequited love.

Peter was munching a buttered crust. Dick was washing up the tea mugs. Why not Katie? Somebody would have to remind her she was still a servant, but it was too soon.

"Ain't we 'aving no supper tonight, then?" she asked, some time later. She had hung her best coat and hat on the hallstand, patted her lank hair, and smoothed her best dress over her big hips.

They stared at her, and wondered how her simple mind would cope with this drastic change in her life. Dick was glowering, and his voice was gruff.

"You know what you can do if you want your supper — GET IT!"

"The Mistress never spoke so sharp to me." Her lips trembled, her pale eyes flooded with tears.

"Oh, for God's sake, Kate! I'm sorry."

"I'll make her a sandwich," Midge volunteered, helpfully.

Katie watched while ham, bread and butter were collected from the larder, and Dick made a clumsy attempt at slicing the ham.

"The Mistress knowed 'ow to slice that 'am proper like. She never let nobody else touch that 'am," sniffed Katie, miserably.

Nobody answered. The empty rocking chair served to remind them of the wonderful woman who had become a legend in her own lifetime. Lucy Blunt would be sadly missed in the village. Although she rarely left Russets and never took a holiday, she was mindful of those in need of practical help, and Carrie kept her in touch with such customers on the milk round. Harassed mothers with sick children would be grateful for a few free pints of milk and a dozen eggs. Aunt Lucy had not seen herself as Lady Bountiful, but remembered her own childhood, when too many mouths had to be fed on a working man's wage.

It was late evening and most of the family in bed when Aunt Lucy left Russets for the Chapel of Rest. It was a quiet departure, watched only by Tom, Dick and Julian, leaning heavily on his two sticks. All three men were weeping unashamedly as they carried her out, and Rusty howled dismally from his kennel.

"I won't disturb Wendy. I will sleep on the sofa," Julian told them.

So father and son climbed the stairs and left him alone. But when their bedroom doors had closed, he put more coal on the kitchen fire, and eased himself into the old rocking chair. Never had he known such heartache. Even in the darkest days of the War, in the German hospital, there had been hope and a cheerful comradeship. This was the end of a chapter, and he was not yet ready to start another. His earliest memories were rooted here. He had taken his first steps in the farm kitchen, and been rocked to sleep on that warm, motherly bosom. Surrounded by love, familiar faces, and familiar smells, he had accepted his small world as children do, without question. The questions came later.

"Am I upper class or working class?"

"Neither one nor the other, love, like your Uncle Charles," Aunt Lucy had answered.

To have a grandfather who answered to the name of Sir Neville Franklin was very gratifying. And he had a real pony, while other boys had only "shank's pony".

The chair rocked slowly. Aunt Lucy was very close to him now. He could feel her presence, warm and comforting. She had lived too long, spent too many hours in this farm kitchen to be banished for ever. "I'll put on the kettle and make a nice cup of tea," she would say.

"God rest her soul," Maggie would say. Maggie was very concerned with souls.

When Julian slept, the old rocking chair went on rocking. Who else but Aunt Lucy would know his greatest need that night?

"I've been thinking," said Tom, ponderously, as he sliced the top of his boiled egg the following morning. For the first time they found no cooked breakfast waiting in the oven, no table laid, no pot of tea brewing on the hob. They were "making do" with boiled eggs.

"That hearse is too grand for Mum. Why don't we use the wagonette like we did for Dad's funeral?"

Carrie carefully tapped the top of her egg with the spoon and peeled off the fragments of shell. Only the men sliced the top of their eggs.

"You think she would like that?" she asked, in a small voice. Her eyes were swollen with weeping. She had wept on the warm flanks of the cows, and her troubled mind was so beset with anxiety for the future, she had boiled the eggs in the milk saucepan, and the eggs were hard, like picnic eggs.

Tom went on talking. "There hasn't been another funeral like Dad's in all these years. It was so right and proper for a farmer. Even His Lordship's grand funeral, with all those black plumes and carriages, couldn't hold a candle to Dad's in my opinion. There's nothing like a freshly painted wagonette, lined with evergreens, and the coffin piled with the wreaths."

"But Mum has been taken to the Chapel of Rest."

"They can bring her back here in the hearse, and we can have the wagonette waiting all nice and shining. No black ribbons or black crepe."

"People will talk."

"Let them talk. She's our Mum, and we know what she would like." Tom was the head of the family now, and he had the last word on the matter.

The undertakers obligingly followed the cortege in the empty hearse, and that in turn was followed by a long procession of cars. The mourners from the other farms on the big estate had followed Bert's cortege in the farm wagons, but that was before they all owned cars, and had television sets in their front parlours. Wreaths had been delivered at the farm all morning, and were piled in the cobbled yard, freshly scrubbed for this important occasion. Julian sat in his wheelchair, taking the names in a notebook, since all would be thanked in due course by letter. Children brought bunches of drooping late Summer roses from cottage gardens, and the Maloneys had sent an enormous wreath of Madonna lilies from a Tunbridge Wells florist.

As the procession wound its way through the village, all the blinds were drawn, and the shops closed, out of respect — for Lucy Blunt and her family who filed quietly into the reserved pews.

The heavy perfume of the Madonna lilies was too much for

young Peter in his emotional state. "I want to be sick," he gulped, halfway through the solemn service. It was Carrie who took his hand. Tom might be the head of the family now, but it was Tom's wife who would be expected to step into Aunt Lucy's shoes. Even as she held the child's hand, her thoughts wandered. Who would take over the dairy and the milk round if they expected to find her in the kitchen? The kitchen was not her place. She couldn't even boil the eggs as they liked them, and they would soon be complaining once the funeral was over.

"I don't want to go back in there," Peter was saying, plaintively.

"You don't have to, love. You and me will wait here," she told him. And they sat down to wait on a flat gravestone. They could hear the congregation singing the hymn, "The day Thou gavest, Lord, is ended", as they stared at the open grave a few yards away. It was lined with imitation grass.

Peter shivered, and clutched Carrie's hand. How could Aunt Lucy find her way to Heaven if they buried her in that deep hole? All the good people went to Heaven, and Aunt Lucy was the best person in his world. So many questions had to be asked, but who would answer them now?

It was quiet in the church. They must be saying the prayers. The sun came out from behind a cloud and a robin sang sweetly from his perch on the wall. On the other side of the wall, Prince was enjoying a bag of oats.

If he sat on the wall close to Prince, he wouldn't have to watch.

"Where are you going, love?" Carrie asked, anxiously, as he slipped off the gravestone.

"Just to keep Prince company," he answered, and ran from her smothering embrace.

Their farming neighbours had all contributed to the funeral tea at Russets. The older generation remembered the appetising feast of home-cured ham, pork pies, sausage rolls, baked potatoes, rich fruit cake, custard tarts and trifles that Aunt Lucy had prepared, single-handed, for Bert's funeral tea, but Carrie was obviously incapable of providing anything more than a cup of tea and a biscuit. As for Wendy, Maggie and Midge, they were like children, waiting to be shown what

103

to do, and nobody had yet asked Katie to help. The entire household had the muddled confusion and chaos of a ship without a master. Only the animals had not suffered. They were fed and watered, and the cows milked, in a kind of dazed regularity — because it was as natural as breathing to attend to the livestock.

John went about his own domain with baskets of corn and water, and collected eggs in silent protest. Nobody cared. Nobody would understand his weak stomach like Gran, or tuck him up on the parlour sofa when he felt poorly. Tears of self-pity ran down his cheeks as he scattered the corn to the clucking hens.

Aunt Martha had collapsed in church, been taken home and put to bed. Mark had taken a week off from the bank to nurse her.

In the little terraced house in Tunbridge Wells, Lucy's twin sister, Ruby, found herself comforting her son and her daughter-in-law, when her own heart was desolate. Ruby was a tough old woman, who had spent all her married life in Richmond Row. It had been a hard life for the wives of the gangers on the railway in those dilapidated cottages, with their leaking roofs and earth closets. But Ruby was a cheerful soul, and accepted her role as a working-class wife and mother with sturdy independence.

"The rich man in his castle,
  The poor man at his gate,
  God made them high or lowly,
  And ordered their estate",

they sang in the village school. It was true. Ruby had seen no reason to doubt such a sensible arrangement with the Almighty until her son, Freddie, married into the upper class. Ruby was "proper flummoxed" by such a disturbing contradiction to all her deeply rooted principles and prejudices. The son of a charwoman and a ganger had no right to fall in love with a daughter of Sir Neville Franklin. But that was a long time ago, and the upper class daughter-in-law had proved the class barrier could be bridged with tact, tolerance and affection. Wendy was her favourite grandchild, and Ruby had long since "spoke proper" and picked up her dropped "aitches". In her old age, she enjoyed the comfort

104

and security of the little terrace house in Tunbridge Wells. She cooked and cleaned, and loved them dearly, these two, who had defied convention for love.

Now Lucy was dead, but life went on for Ruby and life was good. They made a great fuss of her at the funeral tea because she was Lucy's twin. She sat in the old rocking chair, and drank three cups of strong, sweet tea and ate two slices of the home-baked bread and farm butter. Then she took Peter on her lap, and they rocked together, to and fro, to and fro. The old woman and the little boy felt very close to each other and to Aunt Lucy.

With the funeral over, a sense of anti-climax descended with heavy foreboding on the family. Tempers were short, and Katie's obstinate refusal to take orders only from the Mistress sparked off an angry ultimatum from Tom.

"My wife is Mistress now, my girl. You will do as you are bid, or you can pack your trunk and get out!" said he, with unaccustomed severity.

Katie's ready tears poured down her pallid cheeks. She rushed from the room, and clattered noisily up the back stairs.

Carrie sighed. She had managed to persuade Midge into the dairy, and a reluctant Dick had started on the milk round.

"This is an antiquated system, Mum. Fill up milk churns and have them collected by the Co-op, like all the rest," he grumbled. Dick was right, of course, but she had rather enjoyed the milk round, and having a little gossip on the doorsteps.

Peter had been sick again, but was not allowed to miss any more schooling.

"After all, I *am* his mother," Wendy pointed out, for Carrie was inclined to spoil the child. He was bundled into the van with his satchel, sucking a peppermint, his blue eyes wet with tears. Tom drove them to the station.

John had picked at his breakfast of chippy rashers and over-cooked fried eggs, in gloomy silence. Julian had eaten nothing but a few cornflakes before he left in his little car for Cranbrook, and the endless catalogue of the Colonel's memoirs.

With breakfast over, and the rest of the family going their

105

separate ways, Carrie found herself alone in the cluttered kitchen. Tom had cleared the ashes and lit the fire, but the stove was dull and dusty, and the grim prospect of feeding the family four times a day, seven days a week, for the rest of her days was daunting. She felt completely inadequate. For the past three days, their midday dinner had consisted of the cold ham left over from the funeral tea, with baked potatoes, followed by a stodgy rice pudding that had to be cut with a knife. There had been no complaints from the family. Only Katie had hinted that it was not the kind of dinner that the Mistress had provided. As if they didn't know! The shelves in the store cupboard were stacked with bottled fruit and vegetables, jars of jam, chutney and pickles. But how long would it last? Even in the darkest days after Christmas, they were eating gooseberry pies and plum tarts. Runner beans, salted in mid-Summer in an earthenware crock, and young carrots, were served as regularly as Winter cabbage and sprouts.

Food was important. They all enjoyed their food. Only John was picksome, and that was to get attention. There was no waste. The pig bucket stood beside the scullery sink, and received all the scraps.

If Katie was going to sulk in her room till dinner-time, somebody had to wash the dishes, clean the kitchen, prepare vegetables and cook the dinner. Maggie should have helped, but she had left for the Convent School soon after seven, where she taught the youngest children and supervised their meals, baths and bedtime. Maggie was a dedicated convert to the Catholic faith, and devoted to the Sisters. The Convent was her true habitat, and she had gradually become almost a guest at Russets. She would work in the fields with the rest of the family at hay-making and harvest, but would hurry back across the park at the end of the day, like a bird to its nest. As a young girl, Maggie had announced with great earnestness that she wished to be a missionary in Darkest Africa, and would ask Mark's parents to take her back to the Congo when they came on leave. But the War had changed all their lives, and they had no leave.

In the meantime, Marston Park had seen several changes since the Franklins sold the ancestral home to the rich

American industrialist, and Maggie forgot her missionary zeal in a new outlet for her dedication. Carrie had never been close to her eldest daughter, and now she resented the dutiful kiss and the quiet "God bless you, Mother". Surely her first duty was here, with her family at this time of sorrow and difficulty. For the first time, Carrie saw her daughter as another "cuckoo in the nest" as she watched her hurry away across the cobbled yard.

By the time Tom, Dick, John and Midge were ready for their elevenses, Carrie had managed to wash the dishes, prepare the vegetables, mince the remainder of the pork and ham for a shepherd's pie, and mix the dough for the bread. It was warming in a bowl on the fender. She was feeling quite pleased with herself, but Tom was cross because she hadn't fetched Katie down to help.

"This has gone on long enough," said he, and clattered up the back stairs in his muddy boots. He came back pushing Katie before him, like a naughty child, and sat her down with rough impatience at the kitchen table. Carrie poured a mug of tea and offered bread and cheese.

"The Mistress always give us hot scones for our elevenses," Katie grumbled sulkily.

"Really, Kate, you would try the patience of a saint!" Dick protested. "If you pull your weight, we may still get our hot scones for elevenses. Be sensible. There's a good girl." If anyone could change her attitude it would be Dick, his father was thinking, for there had been a time when Katie worshipped the ground he walked on. She would wait for him in the barn, her big heavy body slumped in the hay, but Dick did no more than slap her bare buttocks and send her back to the house. That was a long time ago, when she lusted after the young farmer and had to make do with the elderly cowman at Home Farm.

"That stove could do with a bit of blacklead," said Katie.

Dick grinned and patted her work-worn hands affectionately. She wasn't such a bad old girl.

In the unaccustomed coldness of the dairy, Midge skimmed milk, and turned the handle of the old-fashioned butter machine with aching arms and a heavy heart. Her mother had explained what had to be done and left her to get on with it.

107

Midge agreed with her brother, Dick, that such out-of-date methods should be scrapped, and they were lagging behind their farming neighbours. The fact remained, however, that they had hardly given it a thought till this week. Their mother had delivered the milk in a float, spent hours in the dairy, helped Dad with milking twice daily, and manned the market stall once a week. Midge felt a little guilty that she had always taken for granted the generous allowance of fresh butter, the cheese and thick cream to pour on their fruit pies.

All thoughts of Brad, the College of Art, her lodgings and the tearful scenes at Victoria Station had no meaning for her now. It seemed to have happened to another person a long time ago. The chapter was closed. She would never go back, yet she could see no farther than this day-to-day drudgery, and herself growing old, like Gran, with white hair. It frightened her, this vision of the future. To work and eat and sleep like her parents. No time to lean on the gate with her sketching pad, tracing the shape of a splended Shire horse, a ewe with her lamb, the patient cows with their heavy udders waiting to be milked, the enormous sow wallowing in the mud with a dozen piglets at the "milk bar". A hen with a brood of yellow chicks, Flossie with her kittens and Rusty begging for a bone. Without Gran's strong personality to bind them together, like sheaves at harvest, they would drift apart, each seeking the missing link, the warmth and affection they had assumed would last for ever. Carrie had Tom, Wendy had Julian, Maggie her religion, John, her twin, would grow ever more isolated in his small domain. Dick would eventually marry the girl from Home Farm. They had grown up together. A farmer's daughter would be so suitable, so sensible, everyone would agree. That left young Peter, an intelligent little boy, but still a child, with a child's limited capacity for understanding the problems of the adults with whom he was surrounded.

Faced with a sense of duty and responsibility for the first time in her life, Midge felt as much a stranger to the dairy as her mother to the kitchen. Resentment made them irritable. The three men, lost and lonely, sought comfort in the farm kitchen and found only conflict. The shepherd's pie had dried in the oven, and Carrie made fresh gravy from an Oxo cube.

Thickened with flour, the gravy was lumpy, and John pulled a face. The dough was slow to rise in the bowl on the fender, and Carrie was impatient to get it in the oven.

"How long do I knead that dough?" she had asked, but nobody had the answer. They had left it to Aunt Lucy. Home-baked bread had been there on the table at every meal. Just one more item they had taken for granted.

Carrie's bread was heavy as lead. She was shamed into tears. "It's so hopeless!" she wailed — and sobbed on Tom's broad shoulder.

Dick reminded her kindly, "It's not at all bad, for the first attempt. Cheer up, Mum. Rome was not built in a day."

"My hands were not made for kneading dough. They were made for milking cows and making butter. I don't belong in the kitchen. I don't want to be stuck here all day," she mumbled, despairingly.

They looked at each other and the heavy loaf on the trencher. Then Julian spoke quietly, but authoritatively. "We will buy our bread from the baker. All you have to do, my dear, is to pick up the phone and ask him to call here. If he can't manage every day, every second day would do. The time has come to have a few changes. We have been spoilt. Why should we expect home-baked bread?"

Carrie lifted her head from Tom's shoulder and blew her nose on the wet handkerchief. "It's not only the bread, Julian, love. It's the pastry. I haven't told you, but I have been experimenting. Yesterday I thought I would surprise you with treacle tarts for tea, but the pastry crumbled all to pieces and wouldn't cover the plates. Perhaps I used too much lard, or not enough. I just don't know, and I feel such a fool." She shook her head, her wet eyes still troubled. "We *must* have pastry. We've always had it, haven't we, almost every day? Meat pies, fruit pies, sausage rolls, Cornish pasties, treacle tarts and jam tarts."

"Perhaps Midge or Wendy could make the pastry, if you did the rest?" Tom asked, hopefully.

"And have it compared to Aunt Lucy's? No, thank you!" said Wendy, decisively.

"Not me, either." Midge was equally firm.

"We can't live on stews and casseroles and stewed fruit. It's deadly dull," Carrie pointed out.

John spoke for the first time. He was surprised at the fuss they were making. Gran had never grumbled, so he, too, had taken for granted they would always eat like fighting cocks at Russets. As for the pastry, he had watched her often enough, in his school-days, when he found so many excuses to play truant. He had hated school, and the three Rs had no meaning. Gran's kitchen was a warm homely place on a bleak day in January, and when she rolled out the pastry, she left the strips for his little men, with currants for buttons.

"I don't mind having a bash," he said.

"You!" they chorused, and he immediately lost confidence, and began to blush and stammer.

"No-b-body thinks I can do anything, only chuck around that b-bloody corn!" he growled. Why was he stammering? He hadn't stammered for years.

Carrie spoke kindly. She was all maternal now. Losing his beloved Gran had been a terrible shock. He was not like the others. "Thank you, love. Of course you can try."

"Our John a pastry cook? Watch out for the grit!" jeered Dick.

"You shut up!" John retorted, pushed back his chair, and stalked out, slamming the door.

"I wish you would let him alone, Dick," his mother chided. "He was only trying to help."

"That in itself is surprising, coming from John," Julian mused, thoughtfully. "Let him try his luck, Carrie. After all, men are supposed to make the best pastry cooks, though Aunt Lucy's pastry would take a lot of beating, bless her."

Peter was manfully struggling through the crust of the new loaf. He had been brought home by one of the young masters on Matron's recommendation. Wendy was furious to have her authority questioned.

"He can sleep with me," Midge suggested, helpfully. Gone were the days when he could curl up comfortably on that warm, motherly bosom.

For the first time in the history of Russets, the village baker called to deliver bread and cakes. The variety was so appealing and appetising, each member of the family would gather round the van in the yard to help Carrie make up her mind, and to choose his or her own particular fancy. The baker stood by, grinning, in pleased anticipation, for it was already a fact that Russets would prove to be one of his best customers. It was such a novelty, Carrie explained. From henceforth, Tuesdays, Thursdays and Saturdays would be called "Baker's Day", and the fragrant smell of freshly baked bread and cakes issued from the van as soon as the doors were open.

In a few short weeks, the hot smell of Aunt Lucy's baking was almost forgotten. Such is the changing nature of our modern world, and the weakness of human nature, that a lifetime of loving labour and loyalty to the standards of a previous generation should be so easily lost in the effortless procedure of escorting the baker from the van to the kitchen. It would prove to be an expensive luxury, as Julian, who kept the accounts, would soon discover, but there was no alternative.

John's pastry was not only eatable, but surprisingly good. It lacked all the finishing touches of pastry leaves, scalloped edges, and a shine from the milk brush. John couldn't be bothered with such fiddling, and he left his mother and Katie to clear up the mess and muddle. They rolled up the coconut matting before he started, and the brick floor had to be scrubbed when he had finished.

"The Mistress never made all this mess with her flour," Katie would grumble, but not in his presence. Nobody wanted to upset John in his new role as family pastrycook. It had boosted his flagging morale at a time when he was lost and lonely without the support of that strong personality who had ruled their lives with such cheerful kindliness. As he dusted the flour from his hands and took off her long, white apron, he seemed to grow in stature. His hunched shoulders straightened, and his sulky mouth twitched with a wry smile. He, who had always been regarded as a weakling, now saw himself as a splendid fellow. To sit at the table, watching them eat and enjoy *his* pastry, pleased him enormously. But he liked to be praised, and Dick's casual "Not bad, kid" as he pushed his plate across the table for a second helping was music to his ears. To have his brother's approval meant more to him than Julian's "This pastry is really excellent, John", or his mother's proud boast, "It's as good as your Gran's".

111

When the meal was finished, he would saunter back across the yard, whistling tunelessly, swing open the orchard gate, and scatter the clucking hens that swarmed about his Wellington boots.

He even invited Peter into his private domain to search for eggs in the secret hideouts that some contrary hens preferred to their warm, hay-scented nesting boxes. Peter was thrilled at such an unexpected honour, for he had never been allowed to do more than peek at the pretty yellow chicks in the incubators, with John standing over him in scowling disapproval. Actually, it was the younger boy's bright intelligence that John had resented. It no longer mattered. They depended on him. They liked his pastry.

That first Christmas without Aunt Lucy would have passed without any of the traditional enjoyment of the festive season but for Peter, who was too young to be denied the pleasures of opening a bulging stocking, eating a sugar mouse before breakfast, and stuffing himself with mince-pies, marzipan dates and marshmallows. (It was expected that he would be sick on Christmas night, and he did not disappoint them!)

Then there was the PANTOMIME on Boxing Day. He was word-perfect in his role of Hansel, and could prompt Gretel if she forgot her lines. "Babes in the Wood" at the Theatre Royal was good family entertainment, with two performances on Boxing Day. Peter would stay overnight with his grandparents in the terrace cottage on the edge of the Common. Grandmama was upper class. She had married into working class in the early days of the War, and defied tradition. The marriage was frowned upon by both classes of society, but Cynthia and Freddie had weathered the storm, and their daughter, Wendy, had passed on to Peter that indefinable air of good breeding. It was there in his shapely head, his features and a certain arrogance in his small person.

Supported by the entire family, they forgot their sadness in the professional performance of the child, still happily unaware of the father in show business, and still puzzled by his mother's strong disapproval.

As one theatre critic reported in the *Kent Messenger*,

"Young Peter Franklin did not play the part of Hansel. He *was* Hansel."

"Babes in the Wood" played to a full house every night till the end of January, and Peter received his modest salary with the innocent remark, "Oh, do I get *paid?*"

PART 2

Chapter Five

Carrie was back in the dairy. With only meals to prepare for her family, the baker calling three days a week, John making the pastry, and Katie reconciled to her new mistress, life at Russets had settled down to its new chapter.

Only Peter had to be reminded of the anniversary when another Michaelmas Fair had dawned, and they were packed into the van, like sardines in a tin.

"A year ago today Mum died." It was Tom who spoke, but he did not take his eyes from the road ahead, so he could not see the shadow on the child's face.

But Carrie understood and squeezed his hand. Peter was too young to be reminded of the tragic events of that day or of the gap in their lives, for school demanded all his energy and attention, five days a week. He had missed her in the long Summer holidays, but he had Midge all the time, and there was so much to do on the farm. Only at weekends, when he came home to Russets and climbed out of the van in the yard and ran to the kitchen door, expecting to see that dear, familiar person with the welcoming smile and the warm hug, only then did his safe little world tremble with the sad realisation she was gone, for ever. Then he would turn away, and walk slowly back across the yard to find Midge. She always knew how he felt on Saturday morning. They were very close, these two. He would find her in the dairy, busy with the butter, for it had to be weighed and patted into shape on the marble slab, and every half pound marked with the cow. It was a kind of trade mark, and the wooden butter pats had been used by three generations of women. Carrie would be churning the butter in the same machine, for nothing had changed in the dairy. For one thing, there was no money to spare for modern appliances; the housekeeping bills were so much higher since Carrie had taken over the reins. It did not worry her that she had to "make do" because Tom had ordered a new hay-binder, or John had demanded another incubator. She preferred the old-fashioned methods, and she liked the feel of her well-worn instruments as she liked the feel of her well-worn clothes.

Mother and daughter worked well together these days, though Midge would never be so completely absorbed that she could forget her sketching. Her sketch book was handy in the apron pocket, and when the work in the dairy became too tedious and her arms ached, she would slip away to lean on a gate. The animals in their natural habitats never failed to present a fresh picture to her observant eyes. Only once in the past year had she remembered that her early attempts at portraying the human form had been quite commendable, and she sat down in the deserted kitchen to sketch a portrait of her beloved Gran in the rocking chair from memory. It was so good that Julian had it framed, and it hung over the kitchen mantelpiece. Gran still seemed to be watching over them as they gathered around the table, or pulled up their chairs to warm their stockinged feet on the fender. They had almost forgotten the smell of yeast in the rising dough and the taste of home-made jam and chutney. The fruit fetched a good price on the market stall. Only Katie would occasionally complain.

"This jam don't taste nothing like what the Mistress used to make, do it?"

"You're right, Kate," Dick would agree, for you seldom disagreed with Katie or you found yourself without a servant while she sulked in her room. But then she had always been unpredictable and sulky, even with Aunt Lucy. The Orphanage had left its mark on her for life, and she had never matured.

On the first anniversary of Aunt Lucy's death, Katie was there, as usual, in her Sunday best, packed into the van with the family, clutching the new handbag Carrie had given her for her September birthday, with no thought in her head but

118

the spending of the shillings her new mistress had saved from her wages each week in the red pillar box on the kitchen mantelpiece. Dick had prised it open with a knife while Katie stood counting, her pallid face flushed with pride and pleasure in her achievement. The shillings were heavy in her purse, and the anticipation of spending was matched by the temptation to keep them, for her miserly nature would eventually regret the spending of such accumulated wealth. "Poor Katie" was as cunning as a fox in scrounging free cups of tea, sandwiches and cakes from warm-hearted farmers' wives in the refreshment marquee. But the highlight of her day was the arrival of Fred, resplendent in Sunday best suit and bowler hat, and the boots that squeaked in the chapel aisle on Sunday evening. They went regularly to Chapel because it filled in a pleasant hour after tea. The long sermon was lost on Fred and Katie, who would be anticipating the cuddle in the barn at the end of the day. They were well matched these two, in mentality and in their strong healthy bodies. In her younger days, when Katie would lift her skirts to any Dick, Tom or Harry with a shilling to spend, Fred had taken his turn on Sunday evenings, and never questioned her light-hearted approach to sex. In their dull, uneventful lives, the Sunday evening cuddle in the sweet-smelling hay was as near as they would ever get to ecstasy. It provided a fitting climax to a week of toil, and their grunts of pleasure could be more articulate than the spoken word.

"Why don't you marry the wench?" Fred had been asked by his cronies at The Three Nuns.

To which he had replied with blunt honesty, "Never give it a thought."

"Want any help?"

The question surprised her, but Hetty had no need to turn her head for the voice was as familiar as the voices of her own brothers. A blush swept over cheeks already glowing with health, and grey eyes brightened. She had been trying to win another vase for her mother on the hoop-la stall to add to the collection on the parlour mantelpiece. Crippled with arthritis, Meg Smith could no longer attend the Michaelmas Fair, and all her devoted family brought her "fairings" to prove she had not been forgotten.

119

Hetty handed Dick the hoop without a word, and he aimed it, straight as the darts for which he had become the local champion at The Three Nuns. It landed within a fraction of an inch, and the lad in charge of the stall was quick to point out this fraction with the long cane, and to smile disarmingly at the customer.

"'ave another go, Mister. Three for a tanner," he invited.

Dick paid over the sixpence, took the hoops, and aimed for the vase. Twice he missed by the smallest margin with the hoops lodged on the base. Dick licked his lips, and his eyes squinted in the last determined effort. Honour was at stake, and he couldn't bear to lose with Hetty watching.

"Got it!" he shouted, in boyish delight, and the lad handed over the garish trophy with obvious reluctance, and replaced it with another.

"Thanks, Dick," Hetty murmured, suddenly shy of this good-looking young farmer who was no stranger. Their eyes met and asked the question that should have been asked before he met the beautiful gypsy girl. Eyes cannot lie, and now there was no doubt and no barrier between them.

"I'm sorry, luv," he said, contritely. "I must have been mad."

"A man has the right to please himself," she answered.

"Then you don't hate me?"

She shook her head. "You should know me better than that, Dick. Haven't I been following you around since you were in short pants, with a gap in your teeth?"

"Honest Hetty!" he teased. "I could always get the truth from Hetty Smith!"

"Somebody has to be honest."

"Could we start again? Could you forget and forgive?"

Her lips were tremulous, her eyes bright with tears. "Yes," she whispered.

Dick draped his arm about her shoulders. She was short and plump, sweet and wholesome, and one day she would be very like Aunt Lucy.

They walked away, Dick carrying the precious vase. Away from the crowd, at the far end of the field, they found a stile, and sat down. Dick sighed. So much time had been wasted.

"You haven't said when you will marry me, luv," he prompted.

"You haven't asked me!" she answered, coyly.

"Well, I'm asking you now!"

They laughed, and hugged each other, then they were serious, for Hetty was asking, shyly "Could we have a quiet wedding, Dick? I mean, just our two families. No fuss and no frills. Something nice and homely."

"Something nice and homely," he echoed. That described her. Why had it taken him so long to recognise his true mate?

"Anything you say, luv." He kissed her gently. "When shall we tell them? Tonight?"

"Tonight. I wish Aunt Lucy could have been here," Hetty sighed.

"Yes, Gran always wanted this to happen, bless her." They sat quietly, wrapped in thought of the woman who became a legend in her own lifetime — a woman who had defied convention and broken the barriers of class and was still respected — a woman who had borne four sons, and one of them on the wrong side of the blanket. There had been Charles, Julian and Peter, all born on the wrong side of the blanket. She had loved them all.

The local brass band was competing with the canned music of the roundabout, the raucous cries of the stallholders and the screams from the swing-boats. But for Dick and Hetty the noise was neither disturbing nor distracting, and the Michaelmas Fair would always be remembered with nostalgia. It was part of their lives, this annual festival, that even two world wars had not prevented.

The Michaelmas Fair had a long history, and being a public holiday for the farming community, was regarded as an occasion for family outings. Only the very old, and the very young, stayed at home. Even the disabled like Meg Smith could have been pushed around in a wheel-chair, but pride and an independent spirit refused to accept it. Animals had to be fed and cows milked. All other work was suspended until the morrow.

For the family at Russets, the day had a special significance of recent years. Tom had seduced his brother's wife on the homeward journey, and Carrie had known she was carrying his child two months later. Aunt Lucy had died, alone, in her rocking chair, and now on the anniversary, Dick had proposed to Hetty. All these events had a significance in the history of the family, for each generation contributed its share to the endless pattern of seedtime and harvest, life and death. To have the two families united in marriage would release Midge from the drudgery of the dairy, for Hetty was an experienced and efficient dairy maid. It would be taken for granted that Dick would bring his wife to Russets, for there were no cottages on their acres. Hetty would fit into her adopted family as though she belonged there, while still in daily touch with the Home Farm. Her dreams had been realised, in spite of his infidelity, when they had seemed to be permanently shattered. To marry Dick, her childhood sweetheart, and to bear his children, was a goodly heritage, since Dick was the eldest son, and would inherit Russets. Her thoughts had wings as she envisaged their children growing up in that big, friendly house, with the Elizabethan chimneys and the mellowed walls.

"What are you thinking, luv?" Dick asked, after a long, companionable silence.

"I was thinking if we got married the same day as the Harvest Supper, we could call it our wedding breakfast."

Dick shouted with laughter, and hugged her exuberantly. "That would be champion," he agreed.

"It would save a lot of trouble and expense," she pointed out. "And your big Dutch barn is bigger than anything we have at the Home Farm." She sighed contentedly, and stroked his face. "I love you, Dick," was all she said, but it was enough. They were two of a kind, not given to elaborate on their feelings with fancy talk.

"And I love you, Het, old girl. Give us a kiss," he answered her.

Blunt in name and blunt in nature. That was Dick, *her* Dick, the *real* Dick she had known all her life. That brief madness was best forgotten. It was the start of a new chapter at Russets.

When the phone rang that Saturday morning, the family were gathered round the kitchen table for elevenses. It was Wendy who answered it. She came back to announce, "It's for you, Midge. It's Mark."

Midge looked surprised. She had not seen or spoken to Mark since Aunt Lucy's funeral, when Aunt Martha had collapsed in church and been taken home. It was understandable that she no longer visited Russets, for it was not the same place without her dear old friend. As for Mark, he had his own reason for staying away. Midge was in love with that art master, and the only way he could forget her was to put her out of his mind. So far he had not succeeded.

"Hullo, Mark. Is anything wrong?" Midge asked.

"Yes, it's Gran. I found her moaning with pain when I got home yesterday, and called the doctor. After he had examined her, he phoned for an ambulance to take her to hospital. I went with her and stayed till she dropped off to sleep. They gave her a sedative. I phoned the hospital this morning. She is having an operation tomorrow. I wondered whether you would care to meet me and we could visit her together this afternoon?"

"Yes, of course I will meet you. What time?"

"There's a train from here at twelve-fifteen and not another for a couple of hours. Visiting hours are from two till four. We could get a cup of coffee and a sandwich at the station buffet at Tunbridge Wells."

"OK. I'll get Dad to run me to the station. Poor Aunt Martha. Has she complained of feeling ill?"

"Gran never complains, but she has been looking poorly for some time, and she seems to have lost a lot of weight. She was always rather plump, more like Aunt Lucy. Now she is pinning up her skirts with a safety pin. I don't think she feeds herself properly. She is supposed to have her dinner midday, and to give me my share in the evening, but I doubt whether she is telling me the truth."

"Poor Aunt Martha. I do hope it is nothing serious."

"So do I." He sighed, and she could sense his anxiety. "It's market day, isn't it?" he asked.

"Yes. Not to worry. Hetty will take over the stall."

"She won't mind?"

"She doesn't mind what she does. She's marvellous, and Dick's on top of the world. I'm looking for a job. They don't need me here!"

"Have you finished that course at College?"

"Ages ago. I've been working here as Mum's dairy-maid, but Hetty is worth two of me."

"What sort of job are you looking for? Could you teach art to children?"

"The basic principles, yes, and my own natural talent would help."

"The Firs Preparatory School have been advertising for someone to teach art in the local paper for several weeks."

"Peter's school?"

"Yes."

"Should I apply? What do you think?"

"I think they would be darn lucky to get you. If I had your talent I wouldn't be slogging away at the bank."

"Is it still boring?"

"Deadly."

"Are there no alternatives?"

"Plenty. Money is the problem, or lack of it. It's having no capital."

"We will talk about it, Mark. I don't have to hurry back."

"That's good. I've missed you, Midge."

"I've missed you, too, Mark."

"See you later then. 'Bye for now."

"'Bye for now."

Midge hung up the receiver and stood there, feeling guilty. Why had they lost touch? Why had she allowed Mark to think she was still in love with Brad?

Mark was fastening the padlock to his bicycle when the van from Russets drew up in the yard. He had already purchased the tickets. He greeted them with his shy smile, his eyes dark-ringed, for he hadn't slept at all last night. When they had shaken hands, and Tom had asked for love to be delivered to Aunt Martha from all the family, Tom drove away and left Mark and Midge waiting for the train. Few people travelled on this branch line on Saturday afternoon. Shoppers had caught an earlier train.

They climbed into an empty carriage and sat facing each other from corner seats.

"Thank you for meeting me, Midge. I'm scared stiff of hospitals," Mark confessed.

"So am I." Midge wondered whether to offer him her fare,

124

but decided against it. She had brought eggs and a bunch of brown and yellow chrysanthemums from her mother's flower garden. Carrie was the only one to grow flowers and to tend Aunt Lucy's grave. Tom grew vegetables, and Peter had his own small patch for lettuces and radishes in season. Out of season, he grew a fine crop of weeds! Mark also had eggs and flowers. Aunt Martha's flower garden was much admired, and she had always kept a few hens since the War, when eggs were worth their weight in gold.

It was a bright Autumn day, and the trees spread their own particular beauty over the wooded landscape at this season of the year. For Midge, with her artistic eye, it was even more beautiful than Spring. For Mark, it passed unnoticed. He was watching the girl. There was a change in her, a subtle change it was hard to define. It was not only her quiet manner, but the sparkle had gone from the periwinkle-blue eyes. Her zest for life was something he had always envied. Life for Mark had been a very serious business. Gran was a tower of strength. If he lost her? He shivered, and his throat tightened with pain.

"Shall you send for your parents?" Midge was asking.

"Not yet. I will wait till after the operation. Gran wouldn't want to bother them. Besides, they were over here on leave two years ago, and it's a big expense."

"I should die if I had to wait five years to see my parents."

"You wouldn't. You would accept it. I was lucky to have Gran. We are very close. My parents are strangers. It's always quite a relief to all of us when their leave is up. I believe they expect to find me in short pants, knee high to a grasshopper, and I am taller than Father."

"If I ever had children, I wouldn't want to leave them. But perhaps I should be too possessive. Sooner or later they would want to spread their wings. That's human nature, isn't it?"

Mark nodded gravely. "For Mother the Congo is a second home. She spent her early childhood there, but I'm not so sure about Father. Gran told me he fell in love with Mother, and it was a case of where thou goest I will go. Mother was, and still is, the stronger character. My little brother, Matthew, was like her. If he hadn't been such a daring little devil, he would be alive today. We had been repeatedly warned not to cross that road without a master. Matt was bored with the cricket match, and who could blame him? He had two pennies burning a hole in his pocket, and the sweetshop was just across the road. He was still clutching them when the car knocked him down."

The memory was still painful, but it helped to talk about that beloved little brother for whom he had felt so responsible when their parents left them behind in England, to start on their formal education at The Firs Preparatory School at Tunbridge Wells. Matthew had been rather spoilt at the Mission, and he was his mother's favourite. He cried a lot that first term, but they had a lot of love and fun in the holidays with Gran and the puppy she bought for them.

"Do you remember that day we all had tea at that tea-shop in the Pantiles, and Matt burst into tears over his ice-cream, and you finished it?" Mark asked Midge.

"I was a greedy little pig," she answered, smiling at the memory.

"And Maggie trying to comfort him. 'Let him alone', I told her rather rudely, I'm afraid, 'He wants Mummy'."

"You were only speaking the truth."

"Yes, and when he was killed, I blamed myself for not taking better care of him. I should have realised he would be bored, just sitting there, watching the cricket, and when he was bored, he got into mischief. But I was fielding, and I didn't see him disappear."

Midge had heard the tragic story from Aunt Lucy, and her sympathy was all for the elder brother who had seemed to take his responsibility so seriously.

"Mother left him in my care," he reminded her.

"But you were only eight."

"Yes."

"And homesick for the Congo."

"We loved it there. We were the only white children at the Mission. That's what I missed more than anything, all those happy black faces. They always seemed to be laughing and singing. And the sun, of course. That first Winter is best forgotten, Midge. We were wretchedly cold and miserable. Matron dosed us with cod liver oil, and rubbed our chests with Vick. Matron was our other grandmother. We called her

126

Grandmama when she was off duty, but the role of Matron suited her better."

"What happened to her?"

"She married the Austrian professor who taught music and French. They went back to Austria at the end of the war. It was Grandmama's third marriage."

"Good heavens! Was she very attractive?"

"I suppose she was, but we didn't care for her. It was Gran we loved."

"Everyone loved Aunt Martha. Mum used to call her Teacher. Wasn't she teaching the Infants at the village school before she married the schoolmaster? And wasn't there a bit of a rumpus with the school governors when she brought her baby in his pram?" That was another story Aunt Lucy had related with such obvious amusement. She had a fund of such stories for her grandchildren. "A good baby, fortunately, and the Infants loved him," she mused.

"Aunt Martha has had quite an eventful life, hasn't she, one way and another. The baby in question was born on the wrong side of the blanket as Gran would say, and when she married the child's father, an army sergeant, they were stationed at Tidworth, and he gave her a hell of a life, according to Mum, who was also at Tidworth as nursemaid to the small son of an army officer, and saw it all happening. Coming from the same village, and already close friends, it was natural they would grow so fond of one another. Mum would have liked to come with me today, but I promised her she could come next time we visit Aunt Martha."

Mark agreed to that. He was glad to be alone with Midge today, with the warmth and companionship of shared memories, the breach between them healed.

Changing trains at Tonbridge, they arrived at Tunbridge Wells a few minutes later, and found they had plenty of time for a snack in the station buffet. It reminded Midge of the several occasions at Victoria, when Brad had met her, and they had spent a brief half-hour together in the station buffet. There was the same grey liquid in the coffee cups at Tunbridge Wells, but the sandwiches were fresh. No two men were so completely different, however, and Brad was forgotten as she gave her whole attention to Mark. He had noticed the wistful

127

expression on her piquant little face as he waited in the queue at the counter, and wondered what she was thinking. He loved her so much, his dearest Midge, but was afraid to show his true feelings, since so often in the past he had been reminded that he was regarded with brotherly affection, nothing more. Their relationship was natural, for they had shared so many happy hours at Russets, while Aunt Lucy was alive. Those Sunday teas with her delicious home-baked bread and cakes, and his favourite blackcurrant jam. The Cornish pasties, eaten in the hayfield in the shade of the trees, and the mugs of home-brewed cider. Those harvest suppers in the Dutch barn, with the trestle tables groaning with food fit for a king, the picnics on the river bank, and the fun in the woods, knocking down conkers for young Peter in the mellow Autumn days.

Since he made his home with Gran, after losing Matthew, Russets had become his second home, and Peter had grown from a baby into a handsome little boy. Nobody could ever replace Matt, but Peter was very lovable.

"Shall we go?" he asked Midge, when they had finished the sandwiches.

They walked out of the station and made their way to the hospital. When Midge slipped her hand in Mark's, he clutched it gratefully. The contact gave him the courage to face the ordeal of the women's ward, and the twenty patients in tidy formation, under their red blankets. Gran was at the far end of the ward, but tomorrow, after the operation, she would be at the top, under observation. She was smiling serenely, and stretched out her hands in greeting, but Midge was shocked at the change in her since their last meeting. She looked — and was — a very sick woman.

When they had kissed her, they sat down on either side of the bed and took her hands.

"The flowers are lovely. A nurse will be along later. All the flowers are put on that table in the centre of the ward, where everyone can share them. Some patients get too many, and some none at all," she explained. "I shall enjoy the eggs later. Thank you, my dears. Now, tell me, what has been happening at Russets? It's so long since I was there." Determined to keep cheerful, for Mark's sake, she kept chatting when Midge had brought her up to date with events.

128

Her poor darling looked so strained and anxious, and Midge was pale. They were so young and vulnerable. If only she could leave them engaged to be married, she would die happy. She knew she was going to die. She had asked the doctor for the truth a year ago — and he had told her. Of recent years, her grandson had become more dear to her than her own son. She felt no acute anxiety for Philip as she did for Mark. He had his wife, Harriet, a very strong-minded woman, and they had the Mission. It was their life's work. They had lost touch during the long years of separation. No, it was Mark who troubled her now. He was so shy and sensitive, and hadn't the stamina to walk alone. He needed someone like Midge. But had she got over that sad affair with that married man? Martha wondered, as she chatted cheerfully about this and that, and squeezed their hands affectionately.

When the nurse rang the bell in the doorwary to warn the visitors it was time to leave, a wave of desolation swept over her. The time had come to say goodbye, the final goodbye, and she swallowed the heart-rending cry of old age — "Don't leave me! Stay with me. I'm afraid."

But they were already kissing her soft, withered cheeks, and she told herself sternly, "Now Martha, no silly nonsense. No clinging and no tears." In her desperate anxiety not to break down and make a scene, she pushed them away quite roughly, and her voice was sharp.

"Off you go now! Time's up. You heard the bell." She shook her white head reprovingly, and pursed her grey lips in mock severity. She was Teacher again! Now they were smiling as they left her bedside, and walked away, hand-in-hand, down the long ward. When they turned in the doorway to wave, she waved back, smiling bravely. Then they were gone.

She closed her eyes and lay back, exhausted, on her pillows, her throat tight with anguished tears.

"Please, God, let them be happy together," she prayed.

"Your tablets, dear."

She opened her tear-wet eyes. The young nurse smiled sympathetically, and patted her shoulder. Old age was so pathetic, she thought, as she gave the tablets into the trembling hand and held out the glass of water. It was difficult

129

not to get involved. The very old and the very young were so vulnerable, and their tears upset her.

"It's always a bad moment when that bell rings, isn't it?" she said. "Was that your grandson?"

"Yes."

"And his fiancée?"

"Yes."

"You can always tell when two people are in love. There is something about them." She spoke with all the wisdom of nineteen years, and her own young observations. She was kind, and her words were comforting.

Waiting for the pain to subside into a dull ache, Martha repeated them under her breath.

"You can always tell when two people are in love. There is something about them."

She was smiling as she drifted off to sleep.

"She will be all right, won't she?" Mark asked hopefully as they walked away.

"Yes, she will be all right," Midge answered, with the confidence she was far from feeling. Her woman's intuition had seen beyond the façade of the cheerful chatter and the brave smile. Aunt Martha would slip away, like Gran, in lonely isolation because she wished to spare her loved ones the trauma of the deathbed. This old generation, who had lived through hard times and two world wars, had a strength and stamina the young generation would never know. One by one they died, and left behind a lasting memorial of courage and steadfastness as an example to their children and grand-children. Midge was shamed by her own moral weakness and the wasted months of self-pity and disillusion.

As she walked away from the hospital, holding Mark's hand, her love for him had a new depth and understanding, and none of the passion and possessiveness she had known for Brad. Mark was going to need her in the future. She felt protective, as a mother with a child, knowing he must suffer the pangs of separation from that beloved old woman who had rescued him from the scene of that early tragedy, and brought him back to the warmth and welcome of her cottage home.

130

Putting aside Mark's immediate problems, Midge knew she must concentrate on the interview with the Headmaster. It was important to find a job. She had telephoned for an appointment, before going to see Martha, and been invited to call after they left the hospital. They could hear the boys shouting and cheering as someone kicked a goal in the football field.

"That brings back memories," said Mark. "Though it wouldn't have been me who kicked the winning goal. I was more likely to kick the ball in the wrong direction on the few occasions I managed to get a hold on it. We were never any good at sport, Matt and I, and for that reason alone were branded as useless members of a community in which the team spirit was the most important factor in a boy's education. We hated it, everything about it, the system and the harshness of its discipline."

"I suppose it depends on the nature of the child. Peter seems to be happy enough, but Julian hated it, and ran away from home when it was first suggested. His bid for freedom ended in bed with a nasty bout of scarlet fever he caught from a gypsy boy, so the story goes. Gran was so relieved to get him back, she nursed him at home, and refused to send him away to the isolation hospital."

"Just the sort of thing Aunt Lucy would do, bless her," Mark reflected, as they walked towards the house. "Shall I wait outside?" he asked.

"No, come in. As an old boy you will know your way around."

The front door was open, so they went in.

"The Head's study is down that passage," Mark pointed out. He kissed her cheek and wished her good luck. "I wish I had half her courage," he thought, as she walked away.

"Come in," a deep voice invited, and Midge went in, to confront a tall, lean man, with greying hair and a kindly smile, standing behind the desk.

"Miss Blunt?" he asked.

"Yes."

They shook hands. His hand was firm and strong. "Sit down, Miss Blunt," said he. "It's a pleasure to meet another member of that big family at Russets. It has been quite a long association.

131

Julian was a bit of a rebel and opted for the village school, but distinguished himself as a fighter pilot in the Battle of Britain. We have heard all about it from young Peter, who has already distinguished himself in the field of acting. A talented youngster, and singularly modest. It would not surprise me to see him on the London stage one of these days."

Midge agreed, for she often acted as prompter at weekends, when Peter was rehearsing his part in the current production.

"You remember the little boy who was killed crossing the road in the early days of the war?" she asked.

"Indeed I do. Poor little Matthew. It was a great shock for all of us, when I had thought that by evacuating the school to the West Country the pupils would be safe. There was an older brother, but he left us after the tragedy, and we lost touch."

"That was Mark. He attended the village school for the following two years, won a scholarship to the Grammar School, and joined the staff of Lloyds Bank at Tonbridge at the age of eighteen."

"Splendid! I have often wondered what became of him."

"He is here with me now. We are engaged to be married."

"Indeed? Congratulations! Shall we call him in? This will concern him, will it not, as your future husband?"

"Thank you." Her heart was racing. What had she done? It was quite spontaneous, absolutely unrehearsed, yet she had no wish to deny it.

The Head picked up the phone and called Matron. In a matter of minutes, Mark was tapping at the door and been invited in.

"How do you do, Sir," said he, shyly, more than a little puzzled to be invited to participate in the interview.

"It's always a pleasure to meet an old boy." The kindly smile and the firm handshake soon put his ex-pupil at ease. "I thought you would like to join us, Mark. Miss Blunt tells me you are engaged to be married."

"I beg your pardon, Sir? Did you say *married*?"

"I did. Why? Am I speaking out of turn? My dear fellow, I do apologise."

Mark was not listening. He was staring at Midge with wide,

incredulous eyes, a slow blush spreading over his face. "Is it true?" he asked, tremulously.

She nodded.

"You have my permission to kiss the young lady!" teased the Head. He was enjoying this unexpected situation.

"Thank you, Sir!" Mark wasted no time, for he could hardly believe his good fortune. He brushed her cheek with his lips and whispered, "Dearest Midge."

She knew him too well to expect an emotional scene in the Headmaster's study. That would come later in the empty railway carriage, en route for home, when she would be surprised by the nature of the kiss. It would not be the brotherly kiss to which she had been accustomed, but a lover's kiss, so gentle and tender, but so utterly convincing. She would respond with an eagerness and joy that swept away the last vestige of that unhappy affair with Brad.

In the meantime, the Head leafed through the portfolio of animal studies that Midge had placed on his desk. "These are excellent. The boys will enjoy copying them. You may even find a kindred spirit amongst that mixed bag of youngsters. Ah, here is the diploma from the College of Art. I see you had only one year at the College. Scholarships are normally for two years, are they not? But perhaps you had a personal reason for leaving at the end of the first year?"

"I was ... homesick." Midge had not been prepared for such a question, and the slight hesitation was not lost on the man behind the desk.

"Understandable when home is Russets," he said, kindly. "Full marks for Art. Now what about the French?"

If she was surprised by the question in that language, she gave no sign of it, but answered with an easy assurance and no trace of an English accent. It had been one of her favourite subjects at the Grammar School, and they had been lucky in their French mistress — a wartime refugee from Lyons. It was Mark who was surprised, listening to their conversation, for his own "schoolboy French" was limited to such phrases as were found in the *Guide to Tourists*. But his dearest Midge was full of surprises today, and he was proud of her. He loved the way the colour flushed and faded on her cheeks, the new liveliness of the vivid blue eyes, the soft curls under the brim

133

of the Sunday-best hat, and the expressive gestures of the small gloved hands.

"Full marks for French," the Head decided, with a twinkle in his eye, as he handed back the portfolio. "Now, if our terms are agreeable to you, how soon could you start?"

"Next week?"

"Splendid!"

When they had discussed the salary, the number of hours to be allocated to both the junior and senior pupils, the accommodation, and the holidays, and Midge was agreeably satisfied on all the issues, they both were invited to join the Head's wife for tea in the big, shabby drawing-room that was her particular domain, and where she dispensed tea and cakes and sympathy every Sunday afternoon to half-a-dozen homesick little boys. Presiding over the teapot with a natural charm, it was easy to see how quickly a small boy could forget his shyness. She remembered Mark and Matthew. Indeed, she never forgot a single child in the hundreds that had passed through the school in the last decade.

While Mark handed round the dainty sandwiches and cakes, she was making the acquaintance of a new member of the staff — very young, and very pretty. The boys would love their new teacher!

If the aftermath of that pleasant afternoon should end in sorrow the following day, when Aunt Martha slipped quietly away under the anaesthetic, the joy in two young hearts that had re-discovered love would have pleased that gentle soul as she was laid to rest, a week later.

It was a moving ceremony, and another of those memorable occasions when the shops were closed, and the blinds drawn as the cortege passed through the village. The school children marched two by two to the church on the hill, and were seated in the front pews reserved for them. They knew all about the teacher who had taught the Infants when parents and grandparents had sat at those tiny desks with sand trays and slates and coloured chalks. The coke stove that had warmed the classroom, and dried the wet boots had been replaced by hot pipes, and the sand trays by exercise books, but mustard and cress were still grown on the window sill and the children's drawings papered the walls. They knew all about that gentle teacher who had brought her baby in his pram, and the girls who had escorted him like a little prince on the homeward journey at the end of the day. Grandmothers remembered her with affection and admiration, for she had weathered the storm of criticism and scandal over that affair and married the school master. Some could not even remember her name. She was always "Teacher". So it was not surprising that a collection had been made and a wreath of lilies carried by a senior girl bore the inscription, "To our beloved Teacher, from pupils past and present".

The church bell tolled solemnly as the long procession of children marched up the hill, and the stately swans on the village pond waited in vain for the crusts of bread that day. Three old men, smoking their pipes, on the seats facing the pond, found the mournful tolling of the bell a sad reminder of their own declining years.

"One for a man, two for a woman, three for a child," muttered Isaac Peabody, in his nintieth year. "That be for old Martha, what died last week in 'orspital. Seems only yesterday she got 'erself in the family way with that young rascal from Richmond Row," he added, musingly.

"There weren't 'arf a rumpus when 'er Dad got to 'ear of it. Turned 'er out of the 'ouse, so 'e did!" The youngest of the trio, a mere seventy-five, chuckled at the memory.

"Ah, but 'e took 'er back, didn't 'e, when 'e see'd it was a boy," Isaac reminded them. "A grandson what would carry on the wheelwright's business, so 'e thought, the silly old bugger, but young Philip went off to foreign parts to be a missionary."

"Young 'uns goes their own way. Stands to reason. 'Tis only natural," Albert Lindridge, a more tolerant observer, commented drily.

"What do it matter?" growled Isaac, who always had the last word. "A man don't never consider the consequences when 'e fancies a gel. Remember the Squire, with that pretty widder at Russels? Why 'e bedded that young woman afore poor old Bert were cold in 'is grave! Mind jew, the Gentry 'as always been allowed to pick and choose. Stands to reason. They got the upper 'and." He sucked on his pipe. The past was past. When that blasted bell stopped tolling, they could

135

toddle up to The Three Nuns for their daily pint.

Mark was surrounded by the family from Russets, and Midge was holding his hand. The church was crowded, and the children sang Gran's favourite hymns — "All things bright and beautiful" and "The day Thou gavest, Lord, is ended", with shrill enthusiasm.

Mark went back to Russets for the funeral tea in the big, warm kitchen. The cottage would be a lonely place without Gran. He had dutifully cabled his parents, but they had not flown over for the funeral. It was too expensive. They had sent their love and God's blessing. It was a poor substitute for the close relationship he enjoyed at Russets. The thousands of miles that divided them were too vast to negotiate. Even before he married Midge, the sense of belonging to the family was real and comforting. Martha had left all her worldly goods to her "beloved grandson". That included the cottage, and £700 in the Post Office Savings Bank. They would live in the cottage after they were married, and cycle to the station five days a week to catch an early train to Tonbridge. Midge would change trains for Tunbridge Wells to finish the journey.

It would be a long day, wet and cold in the Winter months, but they were young, and they wanted to share everything. Until the wedding — after a decent interval of mourning for Aunt Martha — Mark was sleeping in Aunt Lucy's bed, the big marriage bed, in which she had borne her four sons, and lain with Bert and His Lordship. Mark had no illusions about his dearest Midge. He was not marrying a virgin. But Midge was wishing she had kept herself for Mark. She was shamed by her foolish infatuation for a man whose ego had to be constantly bolstered by the pursuit of every pretty girl he fancied.

So she tossed and turned impatiently in her own single bed, and only Peter divided them. It would have been easy to creep along the passage and slip into bed with Mark. Would he be shocked? What if Peter woke with a nightmare, and came in search of her and found her bed empty? Since they lost Gran, he came to her for comfort. Such doubts and fears that troubled Midge in those lonely nights since their engagement did not trouble Mark. He had waited for years, and could wait a bit longer.

136

They would lie together in Gran's marriage bed on their wedding night, not here, at Russets. In that same bed he had been gathered to her warm bosom, night after night, when the little brother had been killed, and he was blaming himself for negligence. In that same bed Gran had nursed him through measles and chicken-pox. Yes, he could wait, for he was blessed with a quiet, contented nature like his dear Gran. They were two of a kind, and had lived in peace together. Now she was gone, and his sheltered little world could never be the same. But he would have Midge, glowing with health and vitality, creature of moods and mischief, and sudden wild extravagance. And the bank would be seen with different eyes, as a means of providing for a wife and family. He would ask for a rise in salary. To be a husband and father was an incentive to better prospects. When his dearest Midge became pregnant, he would insist that she gave up her job at the school and stay at home. Though he couldn't really believe she would comply with his wishes. "Don't be silly, darling. I'm as strong as a horse," she would say!

If thoughts had wings, then they flew on ahead, and Mark was happy in his plans for the future. And if he still had a lingering desire for an outdoor life, he thrust it aside, and listened to the voice of reason and commonsense. He would cultivate the cottage garden at weekends, grow vegetables and plant fruit trees. The swing still hung on the branch of a tree to remind him of those happy, carefree holidays before the War. Now he could visualise another small boy swinging to and fro, or a little girl with short curls and blue eyes. "A boy for you and a girl for me," he whistled cheerfully as they sped, side by side, along the winding country lanes.

"Oh can't you see how happy we shall be!" Midge carolled, teasingly.

There was a steep hill to climb on the outward journey to the station, where they had to dismount and Mark pushed both bicycles. On the homeward journey, they could free-wheel into the valley. It was hilly country for cycling, but they were young, and it was no hardship.

Tom took Wendy and Peter to the station in the van on Monday morning, and met Wendy off the train in the evening. They returned together Friday evening, unless Peter had rehearsals over the weekend, when he stayed with his grandparents in the little house on the other side of the Common. They made a great fuss of him, for he was their only grandchild.

"I'm glad I'm me, Grandpa," Peter told Freddie one morning, on their favourite walk along The Pantiles. Grandpa walked slowly with a stick, because he had lost a leg in the War. The artificial leg was called "James" and when James got tired, they sat down to rest on one of the seats, and Peter would chatter about the part he was playing in the Christmas pantomime at the Theatre Royal. Next to Aunt Lucy, Grandpa was the best listener in the family, and never interrupted with his own personal views, like most grown-ups. Now that Aunt Lucy was no longer there, waiting to welcome him home, he quite enjoyed spending the weekend in Tunbridge Wells. It upset Mother to talk about rehearsals, and Midge had no time for him now she was engaged to Mark. But Grandpa had all the time in the world to listen to a child who had brought such joy into their lives during the darkest days of the War.

The talent for acting that the child had inherited was as natural as breathing, and his mother would never suppress it. Why hadn't she told the boy the truth about his real father, instead of some silly trumped up story about a gallant young officer who died fighting for his country? Silly girl. She couldn't hide the truth for ever. If Nigel Bannister was still in show business, there was a good chance that father and son would eventually meet. Freddie would have liked to tell the boy the true story, of how his young mother had run away from home to join a small troupe of entertainers, and travelled all over the country to entertain the army and airforce at bases and factory workers in canteens, too isolated to be patronised by the official troupe ENSA. Travelling in dimly-lit railway carriages, crowded with weary, hungry passengers, and often arriving too late to get a proper meal in their lodgings, was not what Wendy had expected when she left home. Freddie remembered the phone call from Lennie, their old neighbour in Richmond Row, as though it had happened only yesterday: "I'm bringing Wendy back. She's expecting. Will you meet us in London?"

The blunt statement had infuriated Freddie, but Lennie had cut him short.

"Don't blame me, Fred. I'm not the father. It's Nigel, and I've given the bastard a good hiding and walked out. Without a pianist and a comedian, the show's a bloody flop!"

It was true. Lennie had been the life and soul of that small troupe, with his lively personality, and his bawdy jokes. Born and bred in the village slum, he had cultivated a Cockney wit and accent, and claimed to have been born within the sound of Bow Bells. His cheeky self-assurance and endearing generosity had provided the young pianist with a much-needed morale booster in those early days of stage fright and homesickness. Nigel and Nancy Bannister, in their Edwardian costumes and fixed smiles, provided the romance. Their duets and sketches, composed for an older generation, still appealed to the girls in the audience. Show business was their life, and they lived in a world of make-believe.

Behind the scenes, their relationship was near to breaking, but on stage they appeared in perfect harmony. This was the professionalism that Wendy had envied but could not emulate. With Lennie's support and encouragement, and her own youthful charm, the quartet had been popular. But the middle-aged Nancy was madly jealous of the newcomer, and only Lennie kept the troupe together. It was ironic, however, that on the morning Wendy received the fatal letter from Russets, with the cruel information that her beloved Julian had been shot down in his Spitfire, Lennie was drinking beer in the local pub, and Nancy keeping a dental appointment. Without Lennie's sturdy shoulder to cry on, and without his brotherly protection, she was too emotionally immature to resist the soothing blandishments of an accomplished seducer.

This was the story that Peter must eventually hear, but not yet. He was too young, and Wendy still so sensitive to a situation over which she had no control. Her beloved Julian had returned to Russets at the end of the War, and found the little sweetheart he had left behind the mother of a three-year-old boy. For so many prisoners of war, reported killed or missing, the homecoming had been a bitter experience.

Unfaithful wives and illegitimate children, broken relationships and conflicting loyalties. The young Julian Franklin, with his crippled body, must have wished that the girl he had left behind would have kept her virginity, but he revealed nothing but love and understanding, and in his own particular way had never ceased to convince her that she would always be his adored sweetheart. The battles he had fought with his own disability had strengthened his mind and warmed his heart, so that he returned home a better and a wiser man, eager to prove he could still play a useful role at Russets. The family's joy and thankfulness in his safe return, together with his own courage, helped to smooth the difficult days of readjustment, and the sense of belonging was fully restored. As for Wendy, she forgot his disability in his comforting arms, but could never forget her own foolish abandonment to Nigel Bannister, and Peter was a constant reminder of what Gran would call "her fall from grace".

"I wish children wouldn't grow up so quickly," Tom sighed, as he settled himself more comfortably on Carrie's plump bosom, on the Sunday afternoon before the wedding. Carrie kissed the top of his head and echoed the wish. There were grey hairs in that head, and it frightened her to see the years slipping away so quickly. She knew Tom had not been concentrating on their regular Sunday afternoon cuddle, and his thoughts had followed Midge and Mark, as they climbed the steep slope into the wood that held so many memories of their own secret rendezvous and the guilty courtship of his brother's wife.

But Midge and Mark had no need of secrecy, and no sense of guilt. The whole world could witness their happiness.

"We are going to miss her, luv." Tom sighed again.

"Yes," Carrie agreed.

Midge had always been his favourite, and Russets would not be the same place without her. It had taken a long time to adapt to a home without Tom's Mum. Even a wife cannot compensate for the loss of a mother. There had been disagreement and disharmony in the family that Mum would have settled amicably over a "nice cup of tea". Dick and Midge, with their unsatisfactory love affairs, had found a measure of understanding and tolerance in that warm-hearted woman, and John, a sympathetic ear for all his troubles.

Young Peter had been the first to recover, but then he was away at school all the week, and not involved in the day-to-day activities of Russets. He had been play-acting to take his mind off the emptiness of the old rocking chair.

"It's something we've always wanted for Midge, isn't it, luv?" Carrie reminded Tom, sensibly. "Thank God she got over that affair with that art master. I was really worried. She was so smitten, silly girl. It wasn't like Midge to get herself in such a state over a boy-friend."

"If Midge hadn't been so obsessed with that man, she would have noticed her Gran was feeling poorly that day, and not have taken herself off to sleep in the barn. Stands to reason," said Tom, who always defended Midge.

"She won't ever forget that day as long as she lives. Remember how she blamed herself for that heart attack, because Mum had been beating the batter for the pancakes she had promised when she collapsed? Then that young doctor explained it could happen any time with a tired heart."

They were silent for a while, but it was a companionable silence between these two.

"I still wish children wouldn't grow up so quickly," Tom reflected, sadly.

"We still have Dick and Hetty, and Midge and Mark will only be living a couple of miles away. Cheer up, love," said Carrie comfortably.

The trees were bare in the wood, and the naked branches, etched against a grey sky, had a special kind of beauty for the young lovers as they wandered, hand-in-hand, in perfect harmony on that Sunday afternoon. This was their world, and they loved it. Yet the time had come, almost, to leave it, for another, smaller place with no spreading acres and no animals.

"We must have a cat," Midge had decided. It would be Midge who would decide most things, and Mark would agree, amiably. Her strong personality had always dominated her twin brother, and it was natural for her to take the lead. Never again would she allow herself to become subservient to anybody. The middle-aged charmer had left his mark. Nobody could pass through fire without getting scorched.

In that short year, Midge had climbed to the heights and plunged to the depths. There had been no tenderness in her first love affair, and no hope of a future together. Now she knew the meaning of both. She had been reading the marriage service in the book of Common Prayer she had discovered in the glass-fronted bookcase in the parlour. The true significance of the blessed state of matrimony had moved her to tears. "To have and to hold, from this day forward, in sickness and in health, till death us do part". It was a solemn thought, a thought to be shared with the man who walked beside her in such quiet harmony. It was his quietness and his kindness that she had recognised at last as the very essence of love. Who else but Mark would have remained faithful through the turbulent years of adolescence into manhood? His strength was in his determination to wait till Midge was ready for marriage. His patience had the inexhaustible quality that only his beloved grandmother had really understood. So Jacob had waited for his Rachel.

But his principles and his dogged determination, on these last few days before the wedding, would almost shatter Midge's new found faith in her own opinions. What harm could there be in making love, here and now? Hadn't her own parents lain together under this very tree, where she now stood with Mark? Yes, this was the very spot for here were their initials carved on the bole with Dad's penknife. And Mum had confessed to the guilty secret on one of those rare moments when a mother opens her heart to a growing daughter. Here, on this earth, their firstborn had been conceived. It was a kind of agony to lean against the bole of the tree, with all her senses clamouring for the touch of his hands on her naked breast, and he did no more than cup her face in his hands, and murmur, "Dearest Midge, I love you."

"Take me then!" Had she shouted in the anguish of her throbbing thighs and trembling limbs? How could he be so calm and so cruel? she wondered, and wound her arms about his neck, in a throttling hug, and pressed closer, closer. But his tall, lean body was stiff and tense, and he would not yield.

142

"Come to the barn. *Please*, darling," she whispered. "Nobody will disturb us there."

"No," was all he said, but it was a very definite refusal. He knew the history of the old Dutch barn. He shook his head and kissed her pouting mouth. It was a tender kiss, and she felt humiliated by her own urgent desire. She pushed him away, roughly, and ran back through the wood. There was no beauty in those naked branches against the sky. She had been mistaken. They were UGLY, UGLY, UGLY!

"Midge! Wait!"

She was running as fast as her short legs would allow her to run, but his long, loping stride soon caught up with her. She struggled, but she was no match for him in his righteous indignation that he was misunderstood.

"You don't love me!" she panted, her blue eyes blazing.

"I *do* love you. I want you as badly as you want me. What do you think I am made of? You tempt me almost beyond endurance. I have waited for years, and I can wait a few more days. Don't you see, it has to be perfect. To take you now would soil that perfection. The act of intercourse is not something to be snatched at in any hole or corner, like animals. I could be wrong, sweetheart, but *please* bear with me."

She stopped struggling, and looked at him wide-eyed and puzzled. She had known him for most of her young life as another brother, but this was no brother to appeal to her senses.

"Why didn't you tell me you feel this way? I felt awful, being rejected when I was so certain you would feel the same urgency. Now I feel cheap," she sighed. There was still so much to discover about this man who did not wear his heart on his sleeve and was often inarticulate. This must be the longest speech he had ever made for her sole benefit, and he was so desperately in earnest, he was almost in tears.

"I'm sorry, darling," she told him, and she really meant it, but he hadn't finished what he had to say, and his brow was creased in frowning concentration.

"This is neither the time nor the place. The time is our wedding night, the place is the marriage bed. Do I sound sanctimonious? I don't mean to be, my dearest. I believe so

143

strongly in the sanctity of marriage. Children have a right to be born in wedlock. There have been too many little bastards in this family!"

"Oh *Mark*, who said anything about children?"

"I thought we had decided on a boy for you and a girl for me?" he teased.

She stroked his lean, sensitive face and touched his lips with a finger. The engagement ring on the finger had been bought with his savings. He had not touched the legacy Gran had left. It was already banked and gathering interest. The ring had cost much more than a junior bank clerk could afford, but Midge had liked it, and only the best was good enough for Midge. There were ways and means of cutting down on his expenses – sandwiches for lunch – walking instead of taking a bus from the station – giving up smoking. That was a test of endurance when the smoke drifted over his head during the morning coffee break and afternoon tea break. But he had an incentive! A married man could not afford to smoke, and more than anything else in the world he wanted to marry Midge. So he kissed the top of her pert little nose, but did not kiss her pouting mouth.

"Feeling better?" he asked, huskily.

She nodded. "Bless you." His shy, boyish smile illumined his grave young face.

"Shall we go back now?" he asked.

"Yes," she answered.

"Are you hungry?"

"Starving!"

"Sunday tea at Russets is too good to miss."

"Not as good as the teas we had when Gran was alive. Do you remember her home-baked bread, and the lardy cake?"

"And the blackcurrant jam."

"And that mellow ham that simply melted in the mouth."

"Why is it that nobody can cook a ham like Gran?"

"I suppose because she had been cooking hams and baking bread and all the rest for about sixty years."

"Gosh! – Mark."

"Yes, Midge."

"I'm not sure I can even boil an egg."

"Not to worry. I'm quite a good cook, *and* I make a nice cup of tea."

144

"I'm going to like being married to you, darling."

"That's what I intended," said he. And they both laughed.

As they stepped forward, a bough cracked overhead, and a small figure dropped like a bolt from the blue in their path.

"You were listening, you little sneak!" Midge accused, angrily, grabbing his arm.

He winced. "Careful. It hurts. I think it might be broken."

"Serves you right if it is. What were you doing up there?"

"Climbing the beanstalk."

"Beanstalk?"

"I'm Jack. Had you forgotten? The Christmas pantomime. You *had* forgotten, Midge, hadn't you? You don't care about anybody now, only Mark."

Midge had the grace to blush.

Mark was on his knees rolling up the sleeve of the child's jersey, feeling and flexing the small arm. Being a member of the local Red Cross branch was useful.

"Nothing broken, old chap," he confirmed.

"But it *hurts*. I hurt all over," Peter complained.

"Bruises. You will probably find yourself black and blue all over tomorrow."

"Shall I?" he asked, hopefully. "Then I shan't have to go to school."

"I thought you liked school."

"Only the drama and the gym."

They looked at him with the fond affection of a young couple already anticipating parenthood. Mark was seeing a small boy on the swing in the garden. Midge was seeing a replica of Mark. But the tousled fair head and blue eyes were not Mark's. And Mark, at this age, would never have pretended he was Jack or Hansel or Dick. Life had been real and earnest for a child separated from his parents at an early age, to face the trauma of boarding school, and then to lose his younger brother in such tragic circumstances.

Mark pulled Peter to his feet and brushed him down. "If that is your best jersey, your Mum will scold," he warned. There was a jagged tear in the sleeve and green smudges on the front of the garment where he had clung to the bough.

"What shall we do with you, Peter?" Midge shook her head. She was really very fond of the child, but, as Mark had just reminded her, there was a time and a place for everything, and they really had thought they were alone in the wood.

He was standing there, surveying them with fresh interest.

"You said there had been too many little bastards at Russets," he reminded them. "I know what a bastard is. It's a baby what's born on the wrong side of the blanket, but what I don't understand is why the baby was there in the first place? I mean, why put it on the wrong side? Why couldn't its mother or father have put it on the *right* side?"

But they only laughed. They thought he was being funny. The only time he was really important, as a person, was when he was somebody else, not himself, and that was odd. Here, with Mark and Midge, he was just a little boy asking silly questions and disturbing their privacy.

"Well, anyway, I'm not one of the bastards because I had a father, didn't I? Everyone knows I had a father," he said, importantly. "You can't be a bastard if you had a *proper* father. Aunt Lucy told me that, and she almost always answered my questions," he sighed. "It was Aunt Lucy who said it was not a nice word, and much kinder to say a child was born on the wrong side of the blanket. When I'm grown up, I shall tell my children *everything*, even how babies are made!" He dug his hands in the pockets of his short trousers and stalked away, every inch a Franklin.

"Pete, darling, you're priceless!" Midge called after him. But he didn't stop. He had just remembered he still had to slay the giant and had left his sword up the tree. Sometimes his make-believe world was more real than the real world.

"Will it be a *proper* wedding?" Peter had asked.

"What do you mean?" Midge had been polishing her nails and wondering whether she dare suggest making new curtains for the cottage. All the original colours and patterns had long since faded, and nothing matched. Each small room had been decorated with patterned wallpaper in bold designs. The curtains and carpets were also patterned, and to Midge's artistic taste, it was just an appalling jumble. Diplomacy was the key-word, however, for Mark was loth to change anything. Aunt Martha had simply taken over the heavy mahogany furniture, the Victorian bric-à-brac and faded carpets and curtains from the schoolmaster's mother when she had married the schoolmaster, on the principle that what was good enough for Mother was good enough for a wife. Now Mark had inherited all this ugliness and could be stubborn in his quiet way.

"Midge, will it be a *proper* wedding?" Peter had persisted.

And Midge had dragged her mind back from new curtains to answer the child. "You mean, will it be a white wedding?"

He nodded.

"No."

"Why not?"

"Because the last time this family had a white wedding, it was an absolute fiasco, and one feels a bit superstitious."

"That time Dick nearly married the gypsy girl?"

"Precisely."

"But she didn't belong. You would look pretty, much prettier than a gypsy."

"Thank you, Pete."

"What *are* you going to wear?"

"I shall be wearing a suit, in a pretty shade of blue, with a matching hat."

"Blue is my favourite colour."

"Me, too."

"Why does it have to be a Church wedding when we always go to Chapel?"

"For the simple reason, darling, that everyone remembers the gypsy wedding, and it would be embarrassing for Dick and Hetty. And I want Hetty for my maid-of-honour."

"What's a maid-of-honour?"

"A kind of bridesmaid when it's not a white wedding."

"Where are you going for your honeymoon?"

"To the cottage."

"That's a funny sort of honeymoon."

"We can't afford to go away, and we don't really mind."

"Why can't you stay here when you're married? Russets is your home."

"Russets will be our second home, Pete."

"I don't want you to go away."

"We shall be coming to tea every Sunday."

"Will you bring the baby when it's born?"

147

"Oh, *Pete*!" She gave him a hug.

"How soon?"

"A year, perhaps two."

"I *almost* know how babies are made."

"Do you, darling?"

"Gerry Siddons knows. His sister tells him everything. He was new this term, and we're friends. I wish I had a sister."

"What age is this sister?"

"Twelve."

"You've met her?"

"Yes, she's pretty. I am going to marry her when I grow up."

"Love at first sight, eh?" she teased.

"I just know," he insisted, gravely.

"What does the young lady say?"

"She says she doesn't mind."

"Where did you meet her?"

"In the tea-shop at The Pantiles. We had three cakes each, Gerry and me, and she paid for our tea."

"Clever girl. She evidently knows the quickest way to a man's heart is through his stomach."

Peter looked puzzled. Midge often spoke in riddles, but he was very fond of Midge.

"It won't make any difference will it, not having a white wedding?" he enquired, anxiously. "I mean, the wedding breakfast?"

"Don't worry. Mum has it organised. The baker is doing the catering and making the wedding cake. OK?"

Peter was satisfied. He wandered away to the old barn to rehearse the final scene in the pantomime with the full cast. He could see them all spread across the stage in their fancy costumes. The climax was tremendous fun, but he always felt a little sick and a little sad when it was all over. He had to swallow hard and dry his wet eyes on his sleeve. It was the only time he allowed himself to cry. Boys don't cry, normally, but a boy playing the lead on the stage was permitted the luxury of a few tears – according to the Director. In fact, it was expected. A buffet supper was provided for the cast after the final curtain, but Peter was too choked to eat. The ginger beer was nice.

When the old barn echoed to the clear, resonant voice, Rusty would sneak in the door and squat on the floor, wagging his tail. An audience of one, even a dog, gave the performance an authentic quality, and the excited barking when the young actor made his bow, was a splendid substitute for clapping. The slight disappointment over Midge, that she was too occupied with Mark to listen to these impromptu rehearsals, was forgotten in the company of the faithful Rusty. They had grown up together, and understood one another perfectly.

"A dog is a boy's best friend," Julian had reminded him, and Julian was an authority on most things. They were happy memories, his earliest memories, when his hero came home from the war in a wheel-chair, and he rode on the canvas cover stretched over the crippled legs because he was only a little fellow, aged three, and small for his age. They went everywhere together, the three of them. He remembered that he was lifted down when they climbed the steep slope to the wood, and he would help Dick pull on the rope while Mum pushed from behind. They laughed so much they nearly toppled the wheel-chair, but Julian was laughing too, and not in the least afraid of being shot out. It was his courage and his good humour that Peter remembered to this day. His example had helped to fashion his own character. Without Julian, he could have been a spoilt little brat, for he was everyone's darling.

Among those earliest memories was a picture of Mum bending over Julian in the wheel-chair, to give him a kiss. Her long, fair hair had almost covered his upturned face, but their happiness had been felt so keenly, he was outside the magic circle of their love for that brief moment.

"Come on!" he would insist, impatiently.

Then Mum would lift her head, still starry-eyed, and they both would smile at him, and all would be well again between them. Was it jealousy he had felt so acutely? he wondered.

Aunt Lucy hovered in the background of those early memories, a buxom figure in a white apron, smelling of sweat and yeast, and embrocation. Her lap was the most comfortable place in his small world, a chariot in which they would ride to the Land of Nod. Next to Julian, he loved her best. They shared secrets.

"Do you love me best?" he had asked.

"Bless you, child. What a question. I love you all," she had answered.

It wasn't true, of course. He was kind of special because he was the youngest.

Chapter Six

Midge woke early on her wedding day, and lay still, listening to the familiar sounds of her small world – the cock crowing in the orchard, and the answering bark of Rusty; cows lowing in the byre, the old mare coughing in the stable; Dad and Mum creeping downstairs. It was the last time she would wake in her own bed – the last time – the last time. The sad finality of this sudden realisation brought the tears to her eyes. She mustn't cry on her wedding day. She mustn't! Tomorrow she would waken in Aunt Martha's big marriage bed, and Mark would be lying beside her. "Till death us do part." It was such a solemn thought, and rather frightening. "Permanent" and "Everlasting" were not comfortable words, and she always found herself backing away from them. But she loved Mark dearly, and she would feel safe – safe from her own young foolishness, and Brad's disturbing image.

"My sweet innocent" he had called her, and she *had* been innocent. Brad had taken her with the easy assurance of an accomplished seducer, then left her alone to spend the rest of the night weeping. It was so hurtful, so humiliating, yet she had seen in him the very essence of love, and built her dreams around him. How could she not have seen the weakness of his character, the selfishness behind that charming façade?

"Goodbye, Brad," she whispered.

Mark was sleeping at the Home Farm because Mum was superstitious. It was unlucky, she insisted, for a girl to meet her bridegroom before the wedding. Midge wondered if he was listening to the same familiar sounds of a new day on the farm, or whether he was still sleeping. Her dear, faithful Mark. There would be nothing to disturb their waking hours at that isolated cottage. She would miss all these sounds and smells. They had been part of her small world as far back as she could remember. There was continuity here, and contentment. She was a Blunt, and Russets was her home. Her roots were here.

If only she could put back the clock and live those early years over again. She saw herself at the age of three, sitting on top of a gate in Dad's encircling arms, to watch the new-born lambs skipping about on their spindly legs. She would have fallen off the gate in her excitement, but Dad held her fast, sharing her pleasure. Until she went to school, she had followed him round the farm, always at his heels, in all kinds of weather. He was big and strong.

Dear Dad. She couldn't remember when she first started to draw the animals. The talent was there, inborn. Dad was amused and amazed. He would miss her. She had always known she was Dad's favourite. After today, everything would be changed − her name, her home, herself. She must learn to say "we", to lose her identity in another being. For all the years they had known each other, there was still so much they did not know, might never know. Mark had hidden depths she would try to probe. He was an introvert, she was extrovert. Would that make for harmony or disharmony. She couldn't bear it if they quarrelled on such fundamental issues as bringing up their children, or whether to be Church or Chapel.

She shivered, sat up and hugged her knees. Dad was climbing upstairs, his heavy step unmistakable on the creaking boards. He was bringing her a cup of tea, *for the last time*. She was going to miss him terribly.

"Morning, luv." Tom's voice was husky with emotion. She looked like a little girl with her tumbled curls and flushed cheeks, and her blue eyes bright with unshed tears.

"Oh, *Dad*!" she whispered, and reached out her arms. He put down the tea and held her close. She was trembling like a leaf in the wind, and he couldn't bear to lose her. Russets would not be the same without Midge. The love he felt for this younger daughter was a special kind of love, protective and anxious, altogether different from the love he felt for Carrie. He still saw her as a child, not a grown woman, and that was why he was so shocked and upset over that unhappy affair with that art master. Inarticulate and shy of endearments, Tom was a typical Blunt. There was so much he would like to say, had made up his mind to say, as he climbed the stairs, but his mind was a blank as he cuddled his daughter in his strong arms.

It was the women in the family who had the gift of the gab. Three generations of women, so forthright and outspoken they could be irritating. Quite naturally and unconsciously they "wore the trousers". Midge would take the lead in her marriage, and Mark would let her. Today he was giving her away. It was a father's duty to hand over his daughter to her husband. A queer sort of custom.

He had a new suit for the occasion, and Carrie had trimmed his hair and ordered red carnations. All the men in the family would wear a carnation in their buttonholes. He would feel a proper charlie, but Carrie had insisted.

"Don't cry, luv," he said, chokingly.

"I'm not crying, darling, I'm just so terribly, terribly sad."

"Me, too."

"It's so final, isn't it? I want both. I want you, and I want Mark. I want to stay here, and I want my own home. How can I reconcile one with the other? Gran would understand. I wish she had lived to see me married to Mark. She always wanted it."

"Yes, she did."

"Dad?"

"Yes, luv?"

"Do you think she still knows what is happening at Russets? Do you think she still cares about us, in a different way? I sometimes feel her spirit is still here at Russets. Am I being fanciful?" She had lifted her head from his shoulder, and she was looking at him with the bright-eyed eagerness of the older woman. They were much alike.

"I wouldn't be surprised." It was all he could say, but he thought a lot about the hereafter when he was alone, walking his fields. It wasn't something he could talk about, even with Carrie, but he had felt it too, this comfortable assurance that his mother still cared about her family at Russets, and shared all its joys and sorrows. It was not a ghost. Tom was too earth-bound to believe in ghosts. It was something more tangible, more positive. Midge was waiting for further assurance. If only he had Julian's articulate ability to explain certain fundamental issues to the younger generation.

"Don't you fret, luv. I'm as sure about your Gran watching over us as I am that you're going to be happy with Mark. Now, drink up your tea." He handed her the cup, and she sat back on her heels and held the cup in both hands.

"The cup has a handle, Midge," Carrie would say when she was a little girl, but here she was, on her wedding day, still holding the cup with both hands!

"Next to Mark, I love you best, Dad," she said.

"I know."

They smiled at each other, a warm, comforting smile. Then Carrie called upstairs, "You coming Tom?"

And he bent to kiss his daughter's cheek, and hurried away.

As soon as Tom and Carrie had left for milking, Peter slipped through the door and Midge made room for him in her bed. "For the last time — for the last time," she was thinking, as she cuddled the warm little body.

"Am I too big to come in your bed?" he had asked, when he was eight, and again when he was nine. Now he was ten, he had stopped asking, but the habit was too strong to break. Wendy had been shocked and disturbed to see them cuddled together one Sunday morning quite recently.

"He was feeling poorly, weren't you, Peter?" The ready excuse slipped out naturally, for he was hot and flushed on that particular morning.

"If you were feeling poorly, you should stay in your own bed. You may be sickening for something, and you would pass it on to Midge," his mother had retorted, irritably.

But Midge could see no harm in it. They had been doing it for years, every Sunday morning, and Peter was such a small child, he would have passed for eight, still wearing the same pyjamas that Aunt Lucy had bought for him that last Christmas — all the family gave him something to wear as well as a toy or half-a-crown — the trousers had been let down, but the jacket still fitted perfectly.

154

"You haven't left me any tea," he complained. "And where's the biscuit?"

"Sorry, darling, I forgot. Anyway, Dad didn't bring any biscuits."

"Why?"

"I think he was feeling rather upset."

"Why?"

"Because it's the last time he will be bringing me a cup of tea in bed."

"Why?"

"Because I won't be here. It's my wedding day. Had you forgotten?"

"No, I hadn't forgotten. That's why I'm here today instead of tomorrow," he sighed, gustily. "It's a rotten shame. Sunday morning won't be the same without the tea and the biscuit."

"You could get it downstairs. Auntie Carrie wouldn't mind. But you would have to come back to bed till 7 o'clock."

"What should I do?"

"The same as you always do – sleep!"

"Why do I have to wear my Eton suit to your wedding?"

"Because it's your Sunday best, and everyone will be dressed up."

"I look soppy."

"No you don't. You look rather superior – like Little Lord Fauntleroy."

"Who's Little Lord Fauntleroy?"

"A character in one of your Aunt Lucy's Sunday School prizes. Always perfectly immaculate and the perfect little gentleman."

"He sounds a bit of an ass."

Midge giggled. "Not your type."

"Midge?"

"Yes, Peter?"

"You won't ever tell them at school that I come in your bed?" He sat up, suddenly alerted to the awful possibility. He would die of shame. He would never live it down.

"Of course I won't tell them," she promised.

"Cross your heart and hope to die?"

"OK." Midge dutifully complied.

"What we do at Russets is not their business."

"No, of course not."

"This is our place. We belong here."

"Shall I still belong, even when I am living at the cottage with Mark?"

"Of course."

"Even if I change my name?"

He nodded. "Aunt Lucy said it was for always, belonging to a family. Whatever you do and wherever you go, it makes no difference. You could go to Australia but you would still belong to the family at Russets. Fathers and mothers, sons and daughters, generation after generation. That's how it is. That's how it will always be." He was frowning and hugging his knees. Such a serious little boy with such profound thoughts.

"Thank you, darling. I feel better now," said Midge, gratefully.

Katie came down to breakfast all dressed up in her Sunday best, so Hetty cooked the breakfast.

"Really, Katie, you would try the patience of a saint!" Carrie exploded, as she bustled about the kitchen.

"You never said I 'ad to wear me working clothes first thing," Katie grumbled.

Carrie sighed, she was already feeling emotional, and the tears would flow at the slightest provocation. It was no use. She just hadn't got Aunt Lucy's patience with this stupid creature who still had to be reminded of everything, every single day. But she didn't have to be reminded when a meal was ready, and her hearty appetite equalled that of Tom and Dick.

"There is such a thing as an apron," Wendy pointed out, irritably, snatching it from the hook on the back of the door.

Katie looked away. It was like a red rag to a bull. Wendy always seemed to rub her up the wrong way with her superior manner, and her cultured voice.

"All you need is a little tact, and Kate will eat out of your hand," Dick had told them, in those early days after Aunt Lucy's death. It had taken the combined forces of Julian and Dick, and threats of dismissal from Tom, to get her back on the job, and to recognise her new mistress. Only Aunt Lucy

156

had really understood that simple mentality. She was no more capable of thinking for herself than a child of four.

"Well, you are not getting out of the washing-up," Wendy reminded her tartly. She was starting a migraine, and would finish the day in bed, alone, in a darkened room.

"Put it on, Kate. There's a good girl. You don't want to spoil that pretty frock," Dick was smiling placatingly.

"It suits me, don't it? The Mistress said it suited me," said Katie, turning about for his inspection.

"It suits you fine, Kate. You look swell." He slipped the apron over her head and tied the strings round her thick waist. Dick knew how to handle her − a woman with a child's mentality, but the sexuality of a whore. All her senses were excited now, because Dick was tying on the apron. She liked Dick, and she was envious of Hetty who shared the marriage bed, and was already "expecting". But she had Fred, and he wasn't such a bad old fellow. Sunday was the proper day for their weekly cuddle in the barn, but today was sort of special, and she was all dressed up.

"T'ain't Sunday, gal. 'Tis only Sat'day," Fred would protest, but after a couple of glasses of that potent elderberry wine, it would be easy enough to persuade him to leave the party. Dick had a nice smell, not like Fred, who always smelled of cows, even in his Sunday best. Dick was proud as Punch because his wife was "expecting". Katie remembered how worried the Mistress had been when she discovered her to be sneaking into the barn with every Dick, Tom and Harry who had a shilling to spend on sex. But Katie had told her not to worry, for she knew how to take care of herself, and another little bastard would not be welcomed at Russets. The Orphanage had taught her the facts of life long before she was sent out to service, at the age of thirteen. A big, strong girl, she had matured early, and discovered the pleasure of sex at the tender age of eleven. But it wasn't something you could explain to the Mistress, who expected her new servant girl to be as innocent as a babe in arms, and pure as a virgin!

Giggling happily, Katie smoothed the apron over her ample bosom. "I'm wearing me Sunday best petticoat, but I don't never wear no drawers!" she announced.

Dick hooted with laughter, and slapped her fat buttocks. "Behave yourself, Kate!" said he.

Hetty gave a shriek and nearly dropped the egg she was breaking into the frying pan. Born and bred on a farm, she found Katie's vulgar remarks extremely funny, and since she never attempted to give Katie orders, they rubbed along quite amicably. Carrie smothered a giggle as she sliced the bread, but Wendy's disgusted expression would have turned the milk sour. Tom and Julian were straight-faced, and John blushed with embarrassment, remembering the gypsy girl. As for Peter, he carried on with his cornflakes, for it was no surprise and not at all funny.

Sitting next to Midge, he would share her fried bread and probably half a rasher of bacon. It was a good place to be, for Midge was often served more than she could eat.

"You must take a good breakfast today, dear," said Hetty, as she slid the hot plate across the table.

Midge looked at the two rashers of bacon, and the egg on a square of fried bread, and shook her head. "Sorry, Het, I just don't fancy it."

And before Peter could claim his share, the plate was snatched away, and John had scooped it on to his own piled plate.

"Greedy guts," Peter muttered.

"What did you say?" Wendy's voice was sharp.

"Nothing." The mumbled reply was scarcely audible, but it seemed to infuriate his mother.

"Leave the table immediately! Go to your room!"

"I'm sorry, Mum."

"Do as you are told!"

An outcry from the rest of the family saved the situation for Peter, but only infuriated his long-suffering mother. Everyone was speaking at once, and she frowned at the familiar bombardment of voices. Why must they interfere? It was always the same whenever she attempted to punish the child for rudeness or disobedience or swearing. And no wonder he questioned her authority with everyone spoiling him so ridiculously. Katie was another thorn in the flesh. She should be kept in her place. Although she did not actually sit at the same table but ate her meals at a small table in the

158

window recess, she missed nothing of the conversation on any subject under discussion. There was no privacy, no attempt to lower their voices.

Julian was talking quietly and soothingly. He knew the threatened migraine was the direct cause of her irritation, and that her nerves were so ragged, she could burst into tears at any moment. She knew she was unpopular, and only Julian understood and sympathised with the problem of Peter. Dear Julian. If only they could have a little place of their own, but she knew he would never leave Russets. After today it could be a little easier, for Midge would be gone. And Midge was the biggest offender in spoiling her son. At this very moment she was whispering to Peter to sit down, and her throat tightened with the effort to control her tears and her temper. The smell of the frying was nauseating today, and Julian had asked Hetty not to serve the rashers and eggs that she normally enjoyed. He was spreading her a slice of toast with marmalade. Peter was still hovering.

"Is it all right, Mum? Can I stay?" he asked.

She nodded, mutely, too choked to speak. He smiled, that slow, enchanting smile that tore at her heart. It was Nigel Bannister's smile.

It seemed a long morning to Midge, but still not long enough for John, who discovered a sitting hen had hatched out a brood of chicks, and two were dead. This small catastrophe was enough to upset the fragile balance of his mind for the rest of the day, and he had to be coaxed out of the shed in the orchard to wash and change into his best suit. It was Carrie who found him in the shed, slumped on the stool, cradling the tiny corpses in his big, roughened hands, the ever-ready tears streaming down his face. Carrie hugged his thin shoulders. She had a special place in her warm heart for this grown-up child who went all to pieces at the slightest mishap in his small world. She spoke soothingly, for he would be blaming himself for this latest mishap.

"It was not your fault, luv. These chicks must have been weaker than the rest and got smothered."

"But it's never happened before, has it, Mum? In the incubators, yes, but not under the mother hen."

"There is always a first time. You can't watch over them day and night."

"The mother hen was upset. She knew they were dead. A mother hen *does* know how many chicks have been hatched. She's not stupid. She can count. The others would laugh at that, wouldn't they? But it's true. Why shouldn't a mother hen have the same feelings for her chicks as a cat for her kittens, and a bitch for her pups?"

"I'm sure you are right, dear," Carrie agreed, her mind on the several jobs still to be done before she changed into the new dress and hat she had bought for the occasion of her daughter's wedding. New clothes were a rarity, and these would have to be put away for the christening.

"Are you going to bury them, luv?" she asked.

"Will you hold them while I dig a hole?"

She took the tiny bodies with a slight shudder of revulsion, while John picked up the spade and dug a small hole in the soft earth outside the hut. His lean, lanky body had none of Dick's strong muscle, or his father's stamina. Yet he lived a healthy outdoor life, and enjoyed his food now that his Gran was no longer there to cosset his faddiness.

He laid the dead chicks in their shallow grave, and covered them with earth. Fresh tears wet his cheeks. It was strange, his mother thought, that he felt such sorrow over two dead chicks, but felt nothing — unless it was relief — over the departure of his twin sister. Strange and rather sad, but they had never been close. From the very beginning Midge had taken the lead. She was the first to walk and talk, the first to feed herself, the first to push away her potty and sit on the lavatory. Every day had been an adventure for Midge, and a nervous, questioning agony for John, who could never catch up. Her forceful personality and lively intelligence had seemed a stumbling block to his own slow progress at the village school. Lessons were a nightmare. He cried too readily, and became the butt of the bullies. These twins were so different they could have been born into different families. Yes, it might be a good thing for John when Midge went away, Carrie was thinking, as she followed him out of the orchard.

He swung the gate wide and stood back for his mother to precede him, then closed the gate carefully. John had nice manners, she thought, as she hurried across the yard.

160

Hetty's two sisters at the Home Farm had volunteered to prepare the wedding breakfast at Russets while the two families attended the wedding. They had become very close neighbours since Hetty married Dick, and would become even closer with the arrival of the first grandchild. It would be a good substantial meal, laid out in the farm kitchen, because that was the biggest room in the house. The baker had called soon after breakfast, and delicious smells of meat pies, sausage rolls and freshly baked bread and cakes pervaded the house. Potatoes would be baked in the oven. Carrie had made trifles, decorated with blanched almonds, cherries and whipped cream, and these were arranged on the sideboard in the front parlour with the wedding cake, also from the bakery, as a centrepiece. Tom would be in charge of the elderberry wine, and Carrie in charge of the two big teapots, and brewing tea that would probably be more popular than the home-brewed wine. Everyone would want a cup of tea with their meal and again later in the evening, when they gathered round the fire to chat companionably of Midge and Mark, after they had left Russets.

Carrie had taken over the ritual of tea-making from Aunt Lucy.

"Your Gran wouldn't think much of this kind of wedding breakfast, if she was still with us," Tom remarked, as the baker unloaded his van.

"What's wrong with it, Dad?" Dick asked.

"Outside caterers. Your Gran would have stayed up half the night baking, and Midge would have made her own wedding cake, with a little help from Hetty. It might not have looked so professional, but those two girls made a pretty good job of Peter's birthday cake."

"Times change, Dad."

"You're telling *me*, son. It saves your mother a lot of worry to have everything delivered, but it's darn expensive. It's a blessing we have to foot the bill for only one daughter. Maggie isn't likely to be married."

"You could take a bet on that."

"Queer sort of life, at that Convent, but she seems happy enough. It's a mystery to me how we came to produce four children so widely different, yet all born and bred at Russets.

Wonder what your little nipper will be like?"

"Not another cuckoo in the nest for sure. No two parents could be more down to earth than Het and me."

"That's true."

They both were thinking of what might have resulted if Dick had married the gypsy girl. Gypsy blood in the family could have started a heap of trouble for future generations at Russets. But this was no time for looking back, and father and son kept their thoughts to themselves.

"Best get changed, I reckon. The women are already getting dolled up nice and early. Between you and me and the gate post, son, I shall be glad to get the day over. Don't fancy myself giving away the bride. It's a strange custom."

"And you don't want to give Midge away, do you, Dad?"

Tom shook his head sadly. "There's something rather special about a daughter. One of these days you will feel the same way."

Tom left Dick and went indoors. Julian was waiting at the gate to tip the lad from the nursery who had just arrived with Midge's bouquet and the red carnations for the men. Tom could hear the women chatting and laughing in Midge's room. He felt almost as useless and unwanted as during those endless hours of waiting for the babies to be born. Three times over, pacing up and down in a fever of anxiety that Carrie would die in childbirth. And when the twins were born, she nearly did die.

Carrie had laid out his best suit, a clean white shirt, clean socks, and a red tie — to match the red carnation. His best shoes had a special polish. Some would say it was not a woman's job to polish her husband's shoes and press his trousers, but Carrie had always done it. It was customary at Russets. Mum had done it for Dad, and Hetty was doing it for Dick. Yet the women wore the trousers and had the last word.

"Julian — *Uncle* Julian — I'm hungry. Do you think I could have a sausage roll?" Peter asked, pensively.

"I don't see why not, old chap. There seemed to be several dozen delivered, and nobody is going to count them." Julian grinned at the boy in the Eton suit, with his shining face and plastered hair that lay on his shapely head like a little cap. It was difficult to judge the right amount of water, but the hair

162

would be dry before his mother's inspection.

"Thanks awfully." Peter shot off across the yard, and was back in a matter of seconds, munching a sausage roll. How quickly the child moved!

"Oh for the wings of a dove," Julian was humming tunelessly. "You are looking very handsome today, Pete," he said.

"It's ridiculous having to wear Eton suits for best. Did you wear one for best when you were at school at The Firs?"

"I didn't go to school at The Firs."

"Why?"

"It's a long story, but I'll make it short because we haven't a lot of time. I ran away, spent the day with a family of gypsies, frightened Aunt Lucy out of her wits and caught scarlet fever. When I had recovered, I went back to the village school for another couple of years or so, when I won a scholarship to the Grammar School."

Peter sighed enviously. "You were lucky. The village school is much the best because you come home every day."

"I agree with you there. On the other hand, you would not have been auditioned for that first pantomime had you not been a pupil at The Firs."

"That's the best part. It's super."

"You really enjoy acting, don't you, Pete?"

"I'm going to be an actor when I grow up. There isn't anything else in the whole world I would rather be. Aunt Lucy said it was a mistake not to follow your star. She said it was born in me to be an actor, and Mum shouldn't try to stop me. What did she mean?"

"Perhaps your father did a bit of amateur acting before the War. Most places have an amateur dramatic society and stage a couple of plays every year. And what was only a small talent in the father, could be developed in his son with the right sort of encouragement." (Julian was rather pleased with this impromptu explanation.)

"Mum wants me to go to Lancing College, but I'm not clever enough, and I should never pass the entrance exam."

"All mothers are ambitious for their sons, old chap."

"But if *you* talked to her. She listens to you. If you told her how I feel about being an actor, how terribly important it is, she *must* listen. She *must*. It's not fair just to say I have to do as I'm told and not to get such silly ideas in my head just because I have played the lead in a local pantomime. Everyone should have the chance to prove what they can do, even if they don't succeed. The Head says it's the journey that matters, not the arrival. It's what you put into life, not what you take out of it."

"He's right, of course, and you seem to have grasped the fundamental truth."

"The Head thinks I am good, but it's rather too soon to decide on acting as a career. It's *not* too soon. I have always known, ever since I played Joseph in the nativity plays at the village school. So will you talk to Mum, *please*, will you?"

"Let's get this wedding over, and the migraine."

"OK."

They both knew there was a right and a wrong time to ask a favour.

"Must I wear one of those carnations?"

It was typical of Peter to change the subject of conversation.

"I think you should. It will please Midge. Come closer. I will fix yours, and you can fix mine. Look, they have even included a card of small safety pins. I call that good service."

"Mark gave me half-a-crown yesterday. I wonder why? I hadn't done anything to earn it."

"I expect he was feeling good because he was getting married to Midge. I believe I gave you half-a-crown when I married your mother. It's just a token of goodwill, shall we say. What are you going to buy?"

"I'm saving for the school outing to London in the Christmas holiday."

"'Peter Pan'?"

"No, that's soppy."

"What, then?"

"'The Mousetrap' by Agatha Christie."

"Gosh, that's a bit advanced for prep school entertainment."

"Not for *seniors*."

"So you're a senior, Peter. Time flies. As man to man, we will drop the Uncle. Call me Julian."

"OK, thanks, *Julian!*"

They smiled at each other, and when they smiled, they were much alike, the man and the boy. It was not the first time Wendy had been defeated by their combined forces.

It was Mark who spoke with such assurance, and Midge whose voice was scarcely audible, as they stood before the altar on that memorable day. For Mark it was the culmination of all his dreams, and his grave young face reflected his solemn thoughts. His eyes were tender with love as he clasped the small, trembling hand in a firm grip, and the vows he made would never be broken for as long as his life would last. "Faithful unto Death" would be Mark's epitaph. Not a shadow of doubt clouded his mind, and he saw the future as a calm, uncharted voyage.

Midge was not so confident. Torn apart by the strong desire to share Mark's heart and home, and the equally strong desire to remain for ever in the bosom of her family and the beloved old house in which she was born and bred, her thoughts tumbled around her troubled mind like a squirrel in a cage. Emotionally immature, she would need Mark's steadying influence.

Walking back down the aisle, she was conscious of her own family and near relations filling the front pews, for Mark's parents could not afford the expensive journey from the Congo, and he had lost touch with the grandmother who had married the Austrian professor at The Firs. Colleagues from the bank were there, teachers from the school, friends and neighbours and all those women who could not bear to miss a wedding or a funeral. The sea of smiling faces swam before them, and their own fixed smiles were stiff as they posed for photographs. Under a barrage of confetti, they ran for the car and collapsed in a giggling heap as the car moved off.

"Those devils from the bank have tied something on the back of the car," said Mark, brushing her down.

"It's supposed to be lucky." Midge was still choked with emotion. "I do love you, darling. I'm sorry I made such a hash of it," she faltered.

"But you didn't. I heard every word."

"Honestly?"

165

"Honestly."

"You do love me?"

"I love you."

"You must never forget to tell me. A woman likes to be told."

"I won't forget. Dearest Midge."

They kissed and moved a little apart, staring out of the windows at the familiar landscape. Down in the valley, the tall chimneys of Russets stood out like sentinels among the naked branches of the trees. Somebody had opened the farm gate, and they drove straight into the yard. Rusty barked a welcome, the cows fidgeted in the byre. It was nearly milking time. The old mare had her head over the stable door, and the smell of silage was strong in the heavy atmosphere of a Winter afternoon. This was home. Only Aunt Lucy was missing. But warm arms received them at the kitchen door.

"The kettles are boiling," said old Aunt Ruby, who was deputising for the twin sister in all their thoughts today. Her daughter-in-law had brought her over from Tunbridge Wells, and she had asked to be taken straight to Russets, so that she could be there to welcome Midge. In old age, they had grown alike, the two sisters, and the plump little figure, in the clean white apron, with the welcoming smile and the warm arms could have been Lucy but for the faded blue eyes.

When she had kissed Midge and Mark, she turned her attention to Wendy, who had stepped out of the following car, and was looking pale and strained. Her favourite grandchild was very dear to her. It was for Wendy's sake she had corrected the rough speech of Richmond Row, when first she went to live with her son Freddie, and his superior wife, Cynthia. To have a daughter-in-law from the upper class had been a barrier to their relationship in those early days, and her working-class principles had been questioned. The classes *could* mix, and it was a happy marriage. They all had weathered the trials and tribulations of Freddie's home-coming from the war, a physical and nervous wreck, but it was Cynthia's love and courage that saw him through the darkest days. Ruby was grateful for their hospitality in old age, for she had had a hard life. She was a good cook and careful housekeeper, and her sturdy independence was mollified. Now she looked at her grand-daughter, and recognised the symptoms. This was not something that could be cured with a nice cup of tea.

"Another migraine, love?" she asked, anxiously.

"Yes, Gran. I shall have to lie down. It's no use fighting it, for it won't go away. Will you look after Julian?"

"Of course I will. Now don't you worry. Go straight up and lie down, and I'll send Peter up with a hot water bottle."

"Bless you, Gran."

"Bless you, child." It was a very close relationship.

"Tell them I'm sorry," the hoarse voice whispered as she moved away. Weak tears wet her cheeks as she climbed the stairs. It was not fair. To miss all the fun of a family wedding was a real punishment, but she was used to being punished. Julian said it was foolish to have such thoughts, for God did not punish indiscriminately, and anyway, it was not her fault. She was not to blame for that unfortunate affair. The fact remained she had the first migraine attack on that awful day when she had heard her adored Julian was reported missing in his Spitfire. Nigel Bannister had comforted her, made her drink whisky, then seduced her. Once every month for nearly eleven years she was forced to endure this agonising pain in her head and the sickness in her stomach. There was no cure for migraine, and she had to endure it for 24 hours, with all the nerves in her body seemingly tied in a knot at the back of her head. There was a time when they offered her tea and aspirin. Now they left her alone, and Julian would sleep on the sofa in the parlour.

Lying alone in a darkened room, on Midge's wedding day, she would sink once again into the depths of despair, wishing she could die. But migraine did not kill. It only tortured its victim into a state bordering on madness. Shivering, sweating and vomiting through the long hours, then, at last, exhausted sleep. That was the pattern, and it never varied.

When Peter crept in with the hot water bottle, the room was in darkness, and the weak voice murmured "Thank you" as he handed it over.

"You feeling proper poorly, Mum?" he asked, anxiously.

"Yes."

"Julian said to give you his love."

"Thank you." She was feeling too weak to reprimand him about dropping the Uncle.

"Can I do anything else for you, Mum?" he enquired.

"Yes, go away."

Peter fled, clattering noisily down the stairs. Wendy winced and buried her throbbing head in the pillow. Nigel Bannister's son — Oh, *God*! And he wants to be an actor. Over my dead body! As if she hadn't suffered enough. That beast of a man. Why did her child have to inherit a talent for acting — they all said he was good — when he could have inherited her own musical talent? Why?

The pain clawed at her. She mustn't get upset. Try to put it out of her mind. But she was obsessed by the pain and the punishment, beating out the rhythm with little hammers on her skull. Shouts of laughter floated up from below. She was forgotten. Nobody cared.

But she was mistaken. The three people who loved her best — her husband, her father, and her grandmother — were sharing a pot of tea at the small table in the window recess. A little withdrawn from the noisy party at the big table, they were talking of Wendy and wishing they could ease the pain. Ruby was still wearing her sister's long white apron over her best dress, though she hadn't been allowed even to lift a cup and saucer from the dresser. It was habitual, and she still clung to the early training of her own working-class mother. As soon as you came home from Sunday School, you put on your pinafore and you kept it on for the rest of the day. Woe betide if you so much as damaged that Sunday best with the smallest spot or stain. There was a Winter Sunday best and a Summer Sunday best. They were worn for two years, then the hem was let down and they were worn to school (second best). They finally finished up in the hop-garden (third best).

Even after her marriage, at the age of sixteen, Ruby continued to take the greatest care of her clothes, bought from hard-earned shillings in a clothing club, and she taught her children to do the same. All through the years, her Sunday best was covered with a white apron, and her second best with a flowered apron. Ruby and her twin sister, Lucy, were seldom seen without an apron, so now, in old age, at a family wedding, her working-class upbringing was still evident, as on

168

her son's wedding day, when Freddie had married a daughter of Sir Nigel Franklin, and Ruby had confessed to being proper flummoxed.

The two men watched her anxiously, for her hands were crippled with arthritis. So were her feet, and she could no longer climb the stairs. They did not offer to pour the tea, however, for they understood only too well what it meant to be crippled. A small measure of independence must be preserved at all costs. The older man had lost a leg in the war, and the younger man would never walk again without his two sticks. The three of them had two things in common — they adored the sick girl lying alone upstairs, and they had the courage to battle on. The old woman in her Sunday best draped in the long white apron, and the two men, in the best suits they had worn for Aunt Lucy's funeral, would be sitting there, similarly attired, for the christening of Dick's infant son.

The old farmhouse echoed to the noisy singing and the loud thumping of Dick's heavy hands on the keyboard. He was proud of the fact that he couldn't read a note of music, and he often played for a hearty round of community singing in the late evening at The Three Nuns. The family always concluded any kind of party in the same way, and the elderberry wine had loosened their tongues. They sang all the old favourites, and two world wars had given them such gems as "Keep the Home Fires Burning" — an appropriate choice with a fire roaring up the chimney — "Roses of Picardy", "The White Cliffs of Dover" and "Lili Marlene". The older generation, with fond memories of the irrepressible Marie Lloyd, waxed sentimental over "If you were the only Girl in the World". Mark's deep baritone and Hetty's pleasant contralto blended so well together they were persuaded to sing a duet, and chose one from the film of "Rose Marie", followed by one from "The Student Prince". Peter had his turn to entertain the company earlier in the evening. The children of Russets had always been encouraged to entertain their elders. As soon as they were old enough to stand on a chair to recite "Little Miss Muffet" and "Three Blind Mice", they were part of the impromptu concert.

Peter had chosen the love scene from "Romeo and Juliet",

and had given such a convincing performance, Aunt Ruby and Carrie were in tears.

"An odd choice for a ten-year-old boy," Hetty's Dad commented, dryly.

"Not for Pete. He's a natural," said Hetty, fondly.

"Tell me when you are ready to leave," Tom whispered to his daughter, when the grandfather clock struck eight.

"Soon, I think, Dad."

Mark was sitting on the arm of Aunt Ruby's chair, in deep conversation. Midge caught his eye, and he smiled reassuringly. They had finished the singing with "Auld Lang Syne" which seemed to suggest the party was nearly over, and startled Carrie into prolonging it.

"Would anyone like another cup of tea?" she called.

"Yes!" came the prompt response, for their throats were dry.

"Stay a bit longer, luv," she told her daughter, as she went through to the kitchen to put on the kettle. It was Hetty who followed her to put out cups and saucers, for it would not occur to Midge to offer help in the house. Carrie had spoilt her, but she had spoilt *all* her children. It was her nature to serve rather than to be served. After today, there would be no Midge to wait on. She had never done her own washing and ironing, never boiled an egg, never made her bed or tidied her room. You would think a girl would have more pride in her pretty bedroom, for Tom had spent money and time on decorating, and Carrie had made curtains and matching bedcover and flounces for the dressing-table. But Midge was careless, and very untidy. She left everything in a mess and a muddle. Had she made a mistake in not training her daughter to be a good wife? Carrie was thinking as she filled the kettles. But her own mother had spoilt *her*, probably because she was the only girl in a family of boys. And boiling eggs for breakfast was not such a simple task, as she had discovered the morning after Aunt Lucy died. Her eggs were hard — picnic eggs John had called them. It was too late now to make amends. Mark would have to cook and tidy the house, but he had been warned what to expect, and didn't seem to mind. Dear Mark. He would carry on with the spoiling.

"They will be coming to tea every Sunday. That's settled,

170

anyway. And only two miles away," she told Hetty. Then she burst into tears.

"Don't cry, dear. It's no distance at all," Hetty comforted. But her own mother had cried when she left home on her own wedding day, and that was Home Farm, only half a mile away.

"I'm sorry," Carrie sniffed, miserably. She hadn't meant to break down before the end of the party. There was a time and a place for everything, and the time and the place for a good cry was in bed, with her head on Tom's shoulder.

So she fixed a brave smile on her face and handed round cups of tea. Only Tom knew the heartache she was hiding, because he was feeling the same way.

Then it was over, the noisy farewells, the hugs and kisses, and they all were gathered in the yard. The lanterns cast a small patch of light on the cobbles. Midge and Mark climbed into the cab of the van with Tom. Their suitcases had been dumped in the back, and Carrie had filled a tea chest with provisions, for the larder would be empty at the cottage.

"Goodbye!"

"Good luck!"

"Have a happy honeymoon!"

Their good wishes followed them out of the gate.

"You would think you were going to the South of France instead of just a couple of miles down the road," Tom muttered, irritably.

Peter had pushed open the gate and jumped on the running-board for a final kiss from the bride, who was wedged between the two men.

"Goodbye, darling."

After today, no more kissing, he promised himself. Then he shook hands with Mark, who slipped a half-crown into his hand.

"Golly, the third half-crown today! Thanks, Mark. So long."

"So long, Pete!"

They covered the short distance in silence. It was quiet and peaceful after the noisy send-off. Wedged between the two people she loved best, Midge wished the journey could last for ever. Then, suddenly, round a bend in the lane, they came

171

upon the cottage, and she gasped with surprise and pleasure. There were lights in every window, and smoke poured from the chimney.

"We came along an hour ago, your Mum and I. Thought it would be a nice welcome," Tom explained.

"Oh, Dad, you're such a darling." Her warm hug was all the thanks he needed.

"That was very thoughtful. Thank you ... Dad," said Mark, quietly. It was all part of the strangeness of this new chapter, calling Midge's parents "Mum and Dad". His own parents, thousands of miles away, had always been Mother and Father. Not a close relationship. He felt he belonged to the family at Russets.

Midge had scrambled out of the cab and was away down the garden path like a bird to its nest. He ran after her, lifted her in his arms, and carried her over the threshold. Tom followed with the cases, and went back for the box of provisions. The young couple were so engrossed in each other they hadn't noticed he was playing the porter.

"Well, I'll be getting along," said he, his voice gruff with emotion and the twinge of jealousy that all fond fathers experienced when parting from a dearly loved daughter. He pecked Midge's cheek and shook Mark's hand. "Take good care of her," he barked, and turned away.

"I will," Mark promised for the second time that day. They stood in the doorway, their arms entwined about each other's waist. They were so young, so in love, they were hardly aware of his leaving.

Back round the winding lanes to Russets. The bare hedgerows flew past in a blur of tears, an owl hooted in the barn as he pulled into the yard — and Carrie stepped out from the kitchen door to enfold him lovingly in her warm arms.

When the tail lights had disappeared round the bend in the lane, Mark closed the door, switched off the light, and took Midge in his arms. They stood there for a long moment, the firelight playing on Midge's fair curls, and Mark's shapely head. He was so desperately anxious to please her, and his grave young face was pale with the earnestness of his thoughts and the intensity of his feelings. When she reached up and wound her arms about his neck, he could count the beats of

172

her racing heart, and the trembling of her slight body matched the trembling of his own body.

"Midge," he whispered, hoarsely.

"Yes, darling?" she answered.

"I want you."

She giggled happily, and asked, "Shall we go to bed?"

This was his Midge. No shyness. No maidenly modesty. Now he could smile and relax. He had been a little bothered about the lack of facilities when he had shown her round the cottage. No bathroom and an outside loo was a bit primitive in this day and age, and they had long since enjoyed the luxury of a bathroom at Russets. Would she wait until he could afford to pay for the scullery to be converted into a bathroom?

"Of course, darling. It will be fun," she had answered, gaily.

So no need to have worried. But it was his nature to worry about those he loved. Gran had been his first consideration, now it was Midge. Of course he would spoil her. He would wait on her hand and foot, and probably be thought a fool for his pains. So he put her gently away, and went into the kitchen to boil a kettle on the gas stove.

"What are you doing?" she asked from the doorway.

"Madam would like a can of hot water for her toilet, would she not?" he teased.

"Madam would be delighted." She touched his mouth with her warm lips. Then she took his hand and pressed it to her cheek. All her gestures were warm and loving. His dearest Midge!

When the kettle boiled, he filled the brass can. "Leave the water for me," said he, and watched her climb the stairs.

"Darling, there's a fire in the bedroom," she called down.

"Your Dad is a marvel," he called back.

Midge poured the water into the rose-patterned basin on the wash stand, and dropped her clothes on the floor. Mark would pick them up! She could hear him busy downstairs, banking up the fire, pulling curtains, and the clatter of china in the kitchen. Would he be laying the breakfast?

Dad had carried up the cases, and she knew exactly where to find the clean nightie and pyjamas that Mum had washed and ironed. Mum had also run up the new curtains on her machine, and Dad had hung them. What would she do without Mum and Dad? she asked herself. She would have Mark. That was the answer. She had always been spoilt, and Mark would carry on with the spoiling. It was natural.

Sponging her firm, pointed breasts she hummed contentedly. "If I were the only girl in the world, and you were the only boy". Then she slipped the dainty garment over her head and climbed into bed.

"Hurry up, darling. I'm ready!" she called.

And he bounded up the stairs. "You've been quick," he said, and stopped, framed in the doorway, suddenly shy and uncertain. It was Midge who held out her arms, sat on the edge of the bed, and took off his clothes. She watched him splashing the water over his long, lean body. He was beautiful. She had not known that his nakedness would affect her so deeply. They would not bother with the pyjamas.

Now she snatched the nightie over her head and dropped it on the floor. "I love you," she said, as they clung together.

"I love you," he echoed.

And they came together as if their naked bodies had always known each other. They made love and slept, exhausted.

Mark was the first to wake, his limbs stiff with cramp, and a weight on his chest. Dazed with sleep, it was several seconds before he recognised the weight, and the joy was indescribable. Never in his short life had he known such happiness. The tumbled curls under his chin smelled faintly of lemons. She was curled into his body, her legs entwined in his legs. How long had they slept, locked together in this close embrace?

Moonlight flooded the room, and all the treasured belongings he had known since childhood stood out, stark and clear – the model sailing ship he had built when he was a pupil at the Grammar School had pride of place on top of the tallboy. He was proud of that ship. It had taken first prize in the exhibition of handicrafts. In this room, where Gran had slept with her schoolmaster husband after his retirement, his small treasures had been spread out, but there was still plenty of room for Midge's personal collection. The moonlight touched her silver-backed hair brush and clothes brush – a

174

present from the family when she won the scholarship to the College of Art — he would not let his thoughts dwell on that traumatic year. Her pictures had replaced the old-fashioned prints on the walls, and her teddy-bear sat comfortably in the little blue chair he had brought in from his own room, together with the handmade bookshelves. All his favourite authors were there, and the middle shelf, confiscated by Midge, held a collection of her Sunday School prizes — "Little Women" and "Good Wives", "The Swiss Family Robinson", and all the other children's classics, and a Bible with coloured illustrations, similar to his own from prep school days. There were no signs of any sporting activities other than a fishing rod. Sport had been compulsory at both schools, but his poor performance on the playing fields had been a drawback to his popularity. Good academic results could not compensate for a boy's clumsiness with a ball. He had no close friends, except at Russets. It did not matter that he had no taste for parties, or dancing, or London shows, or holidays abroad, or fast cars, or pub crawling, because nobody at Russets did any of those things either. "Life was real, life was earnest." His own seriousness had been complemented by Midge's gaiety, his shyness by her cheeky self-assurance.

The moonlight picked out the colours on Gran's patchwork quilt, draped over their naked bodies. He had no recollection of covering themselves, but he supposed the room had felt chilly after the fire had died down. He lay perfectly still, not wanting to disturb her, for his first thought was for her comfort and contentment. His dearest Midge! There was no urgency. They had a whole wonderful week to discover the mysteries and delights of their unclothed bodies, and the deepest thoughts in the secret places of the heart. Companionship they had known since childhood, but not this sweet communion of the senses, or the soul's awakening. He was both proud and humble, if that were possible. His virginal body rejoiced in the act of intercourse, and he smiled at the memory of that extraordinary initiation. "To have and to hold, from this day forward, till death us do part." What a glorious sensation!

Midge stretched and yawned, and lifted her head. "Kiss me," she said. And he kissed her.

It was a tender kiss, tender as his thoughts, but tenderness was not enough for Midge. Her warm young body pressed closer, in trembling urgency, and his own young body responded, yearning towards her.

"Again, my darling," she breathed.

And he needed no persuasion. Instinctively their lips parted to a probing tongue. Nobody had told them this was the instrument on which to play the melody of sexual desire, and it was infinitely disturbing.

"Take me! Take me quickly!" she gasped.

They came together again, each giving and receiving the utmost, holding nothing back. Mark was a gentle lover. It was not his nature to be forceful, but Midge would discover his gentleness was not weakness, and he was sensitive to her every mood, satisfying her every impulse, not with passion, but persuasion. Then they fell apart, choked with laughter and delight in each other.

"Oh, my clever darling. I never guessed you were such a wonderful lover," Midge sighed ecstatically. Mark's smile in the moonlight held a tantalising sweetness. "I could have told you" it seemed to say.

Wrapped in each other's arms, they slept again till daybreak, when Midge was the first to wake. Leaning on one elbow, she looked down on the boyish face on the pillow, and marvelled afresh at the miracle of their love, that could change overnight from the complacent relationship of familiarity to this exciting clamour of the senses. Reborn, they both had discovered that old relationships had nothing in common with this new desire to "have and to hold", and the ecstasy of fulfilment, the consummation of their marriage vows, held a promise of such profound joy and understanding that it made all other relationships of secondary importance, all other loves but a poor reflection of this one true abiding love. Self-absorbed, from henceforth they would not admit to selfishness. It was natural. It was inevitable. Father and mother, brothers and sisters had already receded into the background, and Midge was aware only of this one beloved personality. Her small world had shrunk in dimension in this one night, her wedding night. Mark was her world. Mark was her reason for living.

176

Now she had to wake him, to tell him of this marvellous discovery, just in case he had not already discovered it for himself! It could not wait. She was impatient to have it confirmed. He woke to the touch of her warm, wet lips, and was instantly aware of her.

"Darling, tell me, truthfully, do you love me best in all the world?" she demanded, breathlessly.

"Dearest Midge, what a question. You know I do." He kissed the tip of her pert little nose, and rumpled her curls. "You don't look a day over twelve. Are you sure you're a married woman?" he teased, affectionately.

"You haven't answered my question," she pouted.

"But I have."

"You haven't!" She was so intense. He had to soothe her.

"What must I say?" he asked.

"Say you love me best in all the world," she prompted.

"I love you best in all the world," he echoed, dutifully.

She smiled.

"Satisfied?" he asked.

She nodded, tremulously.

"But it's nothing new, sweetheart, I have always loved you best," he told her, and held her close.

"Why didn't you tell me?" Her breath was warm on his cheek.

"You were not ready."

She sighed, remembering Brad. She must have been mad. But even before Brad she had taken Mark's devotion for granted. So Brad was not entirely to blame.

"If Aunt Martha had not died, would you still be waiting?"

"Perhaps I was only waiting to be asked."

"No, you were not ready," he insisted.

"How did you know?"

"It was obvious. You were still wrapped in your snug little world of childhood and Russets. You had to grow up. It was a rude awakening. I was sorry you had to be hurt, but that year in London was the best thing that could have happened from my point of view. You were so naive, so trusting. I could only stand aside and wait for it to finish."

"Supposing it hadn't finished? Supposing he had asked me

to be his mistress? I would have been so terribly flattered, I would have agreed."

"I had to take that risk, sweetheart. If I had asked you to marry me when you were so infatuated with that art master, you would probably have told me not to be silly."

"Yes, it *was* infatuation. Yet when he discarded me for that other girl, I thought I would die. It seemed like the end of the world. I could understand why girls commit suicide." She shivered, and Mark held her closer, protectively. "Why am I telling you all this, my darling, when it means nothing to me now, and if I met him in the street, I would feel nothing but shame and regret. I might even hate the sight of him. I didn't mean to tell you. I have only ever told Gran."

"They say confession is good for the soul."

"I won't mention it ever again, I promise."

"That's good."

"You were jealous?"

"I was madly jealous. Aunt Lucy kept me informed."

She stroked his face – his dear, calm, familiar face. "I would never have guessed you were jealous, Mark. Where do you hide all your feelings?"

"In my heart. Isn't that the right place for them?"

"Not now we are married. You must let me see them."

"I'll try."

"I love you so much. I want you to be happy."

"But I'm the happiest man in the world."

"Honestly?"

"Honestly."

"You will tell me if you feel unhappy or upset about anything. Promise."

"I promise."

"And no secrets?"

"No secrets."

"I don't want to share you with anyone, my darling. Just you and me. You understand?"

"I understand, perfectly." There was a hint of amusement in his voice, and she lifted her head to say, accusingly, "You're teasing."

"It's a husband's privilege. Don't be cross."

"I'm not cross."

"That's good. I was going to suggest a nice cup of tea. Isn't that the duty of a new husband?"

Midge squealed excitedly. "One more kiss, please, darling."

"One more kiss." He reached for her little pointed breasts, then plunged out of bed. "Gosh, it's freezing!" He shivered, and went in search of his dressing-gown. Midge giggled and wrapped herself in the bedclothes. Then he flung open the door and ran downstairs. Cups rattled in the kitchen. The front door opened and closed. Why? She wanted to know everything. It did not occur to her that a pint of milk would be left on the doorstep. It usually came in a jug, fresh from the dairy. Now he was singing. He really was happy, wasn't he? It was strangely quiet. Apart from Mark's singing, and the rattle of the tea cups, there was no other sound — no cows mooing in the byre, no cocks crowing, no dog barking, no coughing in the stables. This was home, this was her small world from henceforth. Mark and Midge — husband and wife. Just the two of them, to live happily ever after.

Two mugs of tea and a tin of biscuits on a tin tray. The mugs were inscribed MARK and MATTHEW, and the biscuits were soft, but it seemed like a feast for the gods.

"Are you coming back to bed?" Midge asked, coyly.

"No, I don't trust myself." He smiled disarmingly, and sat on the edge of the bed, sipping his tea.

"Why, have I been naughty?" Her blue eyes danced with mischief.

"Very naughty."

"Did I shock you?"

"Profoundly!"

"You were so beautiful, my darling."

"Me, beautiful? You must be joking."

"No, honestly."

He shook his head. "And I thought you would be the one to be shocked, even disgusted. I was dreading the moment when I must take off my clothes. Supposing you had turned your face away? Your face is so expressive, I would have known immediately that you found my nakedness disgusting. Imagine the embarrassment and the mortification. Dearest Midge, and you were quite unaware that I was scared stiff, bless you."

179

"Silly darling. Why be scared? I was no stranger."

"It might have been less of an ordeal if you *had* been a stranger, my love. I *thought* I knew you, but when I stood in that doorway and saw you waiting for me in this big bed, you looked too young and vulnerable to be a married woman, ridiculously young, like a little girl in fact. It was then that I had an awful feeling that it was a mistake, and I should have waited another year, perhaps two. That you were not yet ready for marriage. But you shamed me, my love, for you had no doubts, no shyness, and you welcomed me with open arms. You had never seen me naked, yet you recognised me as the same person, and gave yourself whole-heartedly. It was so very sweet of you, love."

Midge gazed at him with wide, adoring eyes. She had asked him to share his true feelings with her, and not to hide them, but she hadn't expected that he would do so quite so quickly, for it was not his nature. She was touchingly pleased by his confession, and near to tears. She was conscious of being admitted to that secret place he had always kept hidden. Time and again she had tried to force her way into that sanctuary of the heart, but had been rebuffed by a barrier of stubborn silence. She remembered that he had closed up like a clam when she tried to probe into the relationship between himself and his parents. She hadn't realised that he was so acutely sensitive to his own unhappy relationship as compared with her own at Russets. To be separated from parents at the tender age of eight, and to be left at boarding school with a little brother depending on him for comfort and companionship, had been an unforgettable experience. When Matthew was killed, the sense of guilt and grief only added to the misery, and he shrank from all the well-meaning sympathisers, to huddle closer to the one person who seemed to understand – his dear Gran. Such reserve was unnatural, unchildlike, but he could not escape from its strangling hold on his emotions, even with Midge at Russets.

Now he looked at her with love and gratitude. In giving herself, she had received the very essence of his manhood – body, soul and spirit.

"You look very handsome in that new dressing-gown," said Midge.

180

"Yes, don't I?" Mark preened himself. He wondered whether to tell her that he felt more comfortable in the old one that Gran had bought for him when he was rushed into Tunbridge Wells hospital with appendicitis at the age of sixteen, but he decided against it because the new dressing-gown was a wedding present from her parents. They both had received new dressing-gowns and slippers. Midge's was a pretty shade of blue and quilted. It was hanging on the door, and he reached for it, draped it over her bare shoulders, and gave her a hug.

"You're so sweet. I love you so terribly," she said.

"And I love you."

The language of lovers the world over. Yet they saw themselves as unique on this first morning together as man and wife. Mark wanted only to please her, to feel her trusting dependence on him, and Midge would find pleasure in washing his shirts and socks — and probably shrinking them in boiling water!

"You stay here, sweetheart, and keep warm. I will get the fire going in the sitting-room, and cook the breakfast. I will call you when it's ready," Mark told her.

"I love being married to you, darling. I feel so cherished." Midge snuggled back among the pillows. He was going to spoil her, but she would make it up to him, she promised herself. "I will love, honour and obey him till death us do part. To have and to hold, from this day forward." What a delicious thought! Those vows were sacred. She felt very pure and good, and altogether superior in her marriage to Mark. To lie here, so warm and comfortable, and so blissfully happy, listening to Mark raking out the dead ashes, rattling buckets, and dashing around with firewood and coal, was most pleasant. Then a cloud of smoke belched from the bedroom chimney, spoiling the illusion of perfect bliss, and she scrambled out of bed, coughing and choking, and ran downstairs. She found Mark on his knees, also enveloped in a cloud of smoke.

"What's happened?" she gasped.

"It's the east wind. The chimneys always smoke in an east wind. Sorry, love. Come into the kitchen. It will be all right when the fire is well alight." And he threw open the window, letting in a blast of cold air, closed the door, and pushed her gently into the kitchen. It was cold in the kitchen, and she stood there, shivering, till he opened the oven door and lit the gas. "Sit here, with your feet on the fender. There, that's better," said he, well pleased with himself.

Suddenly she wished she was back in the kitchen at Russets. It was always warm and comfortable there. Chimneys never smoked at Russets, no matter which way the wind was blowing. Mum and Dad must have been surprised by all this smoke when they lit the fires last evening. They would be missing her today. She was always at home on Sunday. Peter would have nobody to listen to his rehearsal. Dad would have nobody to sit on the gate and watch him feeding the pigs. Mum would have nobody to finish reading "David Copperfield" while she knitted those interminable socks for her menfolk. Was she homesick for Russets? Just a teeny bit. It seemed disloyal to Mark, and he was such a darling.

Now he was unpacking the box of provisions. They were having eggs and bacon for breakfast. Mum had remembered everything, even the tomato sauce. What would she do without Mum? Watching Mark, busy as a bee, while she sat with her feet on the fender, she felt guilty, confused and unhappy in this poky little kitchen, where even the geranium on the window sill had died!

"Could you lay the cloth?" Mark was asking, as he deftly broke an egg into the frying pan.

"Yes, of course." Her voice was choked, and he turned his head to smile at her. He knew she was homesick for Russets. It was natural.

"We could have a cat or a dog, or both," he suggested, brightly, "and a few hens at the bottom of the garden. What do you say?"

"That would be super. And could we have a rocking chair?"

"Why not?" He broke a second egg into the frying pan. Plates were warming on the rack, and bread toasting under the grill.

"Thank you, darling. Shall I make fresh mustard?" Midge was asking.

It was going to be all right. Mark made fresh tea when the

182

kettle boiled, and they sat in quiet companionship on either side of the kitchen table, their eyes reflecting their happiness. A copy of the *Kent Messenger* had been delivered the previous day, and when they had finished breakfast, they scanned the advertisement pages, their feet on the fender, and the warm current of air from the open oven door fanning Midge's bare legs.

"Listen to this," Mark exclaimed, and read aloud, "'Good home wanted for retired guide dog. Preferably country. Please phone.' It's a local number. What do you think?"

"Retired? Would it be old and grey, like a retired person?"

"I shouldn't think so. It probably means retired from guiding a blind person. Hang on, I'll find out."

Midge had forgotten they were on the phone. It was nice feeling she could have a chat with Mum. She could hear Mark talking in a low voice in the sitting-room. He had a nice voice, but everything was nice about Mark, and she could depend upon him staying that way.

"The dog is only seven years old, but its working life is over," he told her. "I spoke to the mother of the blind girl who has gone to Exeter to get acquainted with another young guide dog. They have to work together for a month before they are allowed to leave. I've got the address. I said we would walk over there this afternoon. It's only a couple of miles or so, on the Lamberhurst Road. Her name is Sheba, and they don't want any money for her, only a good home." The *Kent Messenger* was spread over the floor, and Mark picked it up as naturally as he had picked up Midge's nightgown in the bedroom. Mark was a very tidy person, and if he found her untidiness irritating, he gave no sign of it. It was no surprise to discover she dropped things on the floor, so why complain? Such a philosophical outlook would save many matrimonial quarrels in the years ahead.

"I'm going to phone Mum. We haven't thanked her for all those provisions," Midge decided — and left her obliging husband to wash the dishes! To be so childishly eager for the sound of that familiar voice was inconsistent with her new status as a married woman, but Midge was a creature of impulse and instinct.

"Hullo, Mum!" she shouted, excitedly.

"Why, hullo, Midge. Is anything wrong?" Carrie sounded anxious.

"No, everything is marvellous. I just wanted to thank you for that super box of provisions. We had bacon and eggs for breakfast, and Mark will cook the chicken for dinner. Mark is a wizard cook. He says I can pick the sprouts, and that will be my contribution. Isn't he a scream? We are going to have a dog, Mum. Its name is Sheba, and it's a retired guide dog. We are going to fetch her this afternoon. We thought it would seem more like home if we had a dog and a cat. Could we have a kitten from Russets? And would you ask John if he could spare a broody hen and a clutch of eggs? Aunt Martha had hens during the war, and the chicken house and the run are still here at the bottom of the garden. It would be fun to have our own eggs for breakfast, wouldn't it?" Midge babbled on about this and that, but Carrie was not deceived by that excited monologue. Her little girl was homesick. She was missing her Mum and Dad. It was natural. But Mark was a dear boy, and Midge would settle down. She mustn't interfere.

"Here's your Dad. He would like a word with you," she said. "I'll ask John about the sitting hen, but don't bank on it. You know what John is like."

Tom took the receiver. "Hullo, Midge. How are you?" His voice was gruff with emotion.

"Hullo, Dad. I'm fine. How are you?"

"Fine."

"You missing me, Dad?"

"Sure thing."

Midge sighed. Mark was listening, so she couldn't tell Dad she was homesick, but Tom understood. They were very close, these two.

"See you next Sunday, luv?" he asked.

"You bet!"

"So long, Midge."

"So long, Dad."

The receiver clicked. Midge shivered. The fire was blazing now, and she went to kneel on the hearth. Mark finished the washing up, and came to kneel beside her, his arm round her waist. She looked at him with tear-wet eyes.

"I'm such a baby, aren't I?" she said — and cried on his shoulder.

Chapter Seven

Sheba was a Labrador, the colour of cream. She was gazing pensively out of the window when they arrived, but she came obediently to be introduced when she was called, her limpid eyes reflecting their sadness.

"She is missing Sheila. She can't understand why her normal routine has been disrupted. She is such a creature of habit, and she accompanied my daughter everywhere. Sheila is a telephonist at Clark's," Sheila's mother explained.

"Poor old girl." Mark held out a tentative hand, and Sheba licked it obligingly, then sidled up to Midge, for it was female company she was accustomed to, and it would be Midge, not Mark, she would adopt when she left her old home for the new. Simultaneously, the newly-weds were seeing a problem, however. Could they leave a dog like Sheba alone in the cottage all day?

The woman must have been reading their thoughts, for she asked, "Are you both working?"

"Yes," Mark answered.

"Then I'm afraid I must look for another home for her. Such a pity, for she seems to have taken quite a fancy to your wife, and she hasn't taken any notice of anyone since Sheila went away a week ago."

It was Mark who settled the matter with quiet authority. "There is no need for my wife to work. I should much prefer that she stayed at home. They can keep each other company," said he, smiling indulgently.

But Midge was unprepared for such a hasty conclusion, and opened her mouth to protest, when Sheba's gentle prodding seemed to suggest she agreed with Mark.

"All right, I don't much care for the job anyway," she shrugged. It was true. She was too impatient to make a good teacher. She would be letting the school down, but just at the moment other matters were more important.

"Then you will take her?" the woman asked eagerly.

"Yes."

"Thank you. My daughter will be so delighted. They have been so attached for the past seven years. Now I can assure her that Sheba will have a good home with you. Please sit down. I am sure you are ready for a cup of tea after that long walk." And she hurried away to the kitchen, leaving them to get acquainted.

"Darling, are you sure we can manage on your salary if I give up my job?" Midge asked, with Sheba's paw in her lap.

"I shall ask for a rise," said he, with the confident air of one who sees himself as indispensable to the banking authorities. Midge gazed at him with adoring eyes.

"We could all walk to the station together to see you on the train, and we could meet the train in the evening," she said.

"Thank you, sweetheart. The morning walk together would be nice, but I wouldn't want you to meet me in the evening, not even with Sheba for protection. Wait till the Spring and the lighter evenings. In the meantime, I shall take my bike and dash home full speed."

"And I shall have supper waiting. You must teach me to cook."

"OK." He smiled at her with the indulgence of a newly-wed husband, ready to believe in anything, though he must have known he would have to accept a few burnt offerings with good grace from a flushed and tearful little spouse.

"It's going to be fun, isn't it, darling?" she was saying.

"It's going to be fun, my love," he agreed. Then he leapt to his feet to take the loaded tea tray from their hostess.

"Such a nice young couple. Sheba will be happy with them," she thought, as she poured the tea.

Sheba stretched on the hearthrug while they drank tea and ate dainty sandwiches and cake.

"We don't feed her at mealtimes. She has a big meal in the early evening," Sheila's mother explained. "Regular feeding

186

and a good walk every day keeps a dog healthy. Sheila always gave her a good brush every morning before they started out. If you can manage to take her basket and all her odds and ends, she will soon settle down, won't you, girl?" she asked, kindly.

The dog glanced from one to the other, still puzzled by the presence of strangers, and still no sign of her beloved young mistress. When they had finished tea, however, and her basket was fetched, she stood up to watch it being packed with her chin on the table, as though making certain nothing was left behind – an old rug, a drinking and feeding bowl, a brush and comb, a packet of dog biscuits, and several tins of dog food. Only the white harness was left behind.

"You won't need this any more. You are going to enjoy your retirement," she was told. Did she understand? A small packet of chocolate drops was handed to Midge at the last moment.

"Just one a day. Don't spoil her," Sheila's mother admonished. And the dog received the small sweet as eagerly as a child, but, unlike a child, did not expect a second. Midge and Mark were both wondering how long they could keep up such disciplinary measures. Surely she had earned a bit of spoiling?

"We shall miss her," the woman said. "Now we have to start all over again when Sheila gets back with the young dog," she sighed, as she bid them goodbye, and watched till they were out of sight.

They were carrying the basket between them, and Sheba, with a backward glance at the woman in the doorway, loped along close to Midge, her heavy body taut with anxiety every step of the way, as they left behind the familiar sounds and smells she had known all her working life.

"All right, Sheba?" the strange girl's voice would ask from time to time, and she lifted her drooping head, for her canine instinct assured her that she could trust this stranger.

It was nearly dark when they reached home. Mark had banked up the fire, and the sitting-room was pleasantly warm. They stood watching while Sheba inspected the hearthrug, then stretched out, her head between her paws.

"Poor darling. She's homesick," said Midge, kneeling

down beside her. Sheba's tail wagged gently, and she lifted her head. Was it recognition in those limpid eyes?

"I think she likes me," Midge hugged the dog affectionately.

Slumped in Gran's armchair, Mark had mixed feelings. Could one be jealous of a dog? The firelight played on the dog's shapely head and the girl's tight curls. Did he really want to share Midge with anyone, human or animal, after waiting so long to claim her? He sighed, reflectively. If Midge had suggested it, then she must feel the need of a dog and a cat about the place. For her sake he must feel the need of them also. Sharing Midge at Russets should have prepared him for this. It was natural. His grave young face in the firelight held a calm serenity while he watched them together. Ten minutes or so later, Midge left the dog and came to sit between his outstretched legs. His whole body trembled.

"Tired, sweetheart?" he asked, gently.

She nodded.

"Hungry?"

She shook her head.

"Shall we give Sheba her supper, and settle her down for the night?"

"Yes, she's tired, too."

"She won't want to share our bed, will she?"

Midge giggled happily and hugged his knees. "There is a time and a place for everything, my darling, as Gran would say. I'll settle Sheba. You go on up and warm the bed."

"Yes, Ma'am!" he grinned. Aunt Lucy was right. She was always right, bless her — a time and a place for everything. He was whistling as he raced upstairs.

Stripping off his clothes, he could hear Midge clattering about in the kitchen, opening and closing drawers. What on earth was she doing?

Then she called up to him. "Mark! Where do you keep your tin-opener?"

"Who wants a tin-opener?"

"I do, silly! Sheba is waiting for her supper."

"Hang on a minute." Wrapping his dressing-gown round his naked body, he ran downstairs. She had turned everything upside down and looked in all the wrong places. It was there,

188

in front of her nose, and she didn't even recognise it, for the simple reason she had never opened a tin in her life. They didn't open tins at Russets. Their dogs and cats were fed on the same kind of food as themselves. There was always enough to spare. Rusty would not have recognised food out of a tin, but apparently for Sheba it had been her staple diet.

"What you never have, you never miss," said Mark, opening the tin. They were still quoting Aunt Lucy.

"After today, Sheba will eat what we are eating," Midge decided. "And she is going to like it, you'll see."

They watched her licking the bowl clean, then lapping the water from the other bowl. She was a creature of habit and strict routine, but she would soon begin to realise her familiar little world had been left behind with the white harness, and in this new environment, there was something more than kindness and affection. It was called FREEDOM, and it lasted for more than a brief ten minutes on a windswept hill. With that realisation would come the unexpected joy of discovering she was still young at heart. But her dreams were disturbed that first night in her basket on the hearthrug, in a room that smelled of dusty books and beeswax. Her basket belonged in the bedroom where her young mistress slept, and she had expected to lead the way upstairs. The clatter of the fireguard startled her tense nerves. Now they stood together, the man and the girl, and the girl was cuddling the man. They were very close, and it was strangely disturbing.

She barked politely, and they looked at her and laughed, happily. She could not share their happiness on this first night, for they were going to leave her alone. The word STAY was one of the first words of command she had learned as a puppy, and in her canine vocabulary, a word to be obeyed.

For the second time the girl told the man, "I'll settle Sheba. You go on up," and the man ran back upstairs.

"Poor darling. Come and talk to me," she coaxed, and sat down, smiling and relaxed. Sheba went to her and laid her head in her lap. It was warm and comforting, and reminded her of the girl she had left behind. Pleasantly aware of her femininity, she stood there, passively acknowledging the small caressing hands on her strong body. Acutely sensitive to touch and the voice of one particular person, she was grateful for the girl's affection. She had been puzzled and embarrassed by those fond embraces between the man and the girl, for this had never been a part of the old system. No man had yet claimed that young mistress, and Sheba was possessive in her loyal attachment. Could a dog be jealous of a man? — a man who called out, in a deep, rich voice, "Hurry up, sweetheart. I'm waiting!"

Sheba accepted a second chocolate drop, and climbed into her basket with mixed feelings.

Wrapped in each other's arms, they woke late and made love again. The sensuality of their warm young bodies was irresistible, and all their latent senses responded to the touch of caressing hands and lips. They would have slept again, all else forgotten in their new-found happiness, but a scratching on the back door reminded them they were not alone in the cottage.

"It's Sheba asking to be let out," said Midge, drowsily.

Mark muttered something unintelligible, rolled off the bed, reached for his dressing-gown, and ran downstairs. The man and the dog greeted each other with yawning tolerance, then Mark unlocked the door and Sheba stepped out into the garden.

"May as well make a cup of tea. I suppose this will be my normal routine from henceforth," Mark told himself, still a little disgruntled by the rude awakening to reality from the blissful dream. His dearest Midge was so incredibly alive to the urgency of sex in a lover so long denied. Even in her sleep her small hand would move, subconsciously, over his body, arousing all the intimacy of intercourse. Because he was feeling so sated and satisfied in his new role as a husband, he was more kindly disposed towards the dog, and called her to the door to receive one of the *petit beurre* biscuits from the new packet Midge's Mum had included in the box of provisions. Sheba was surprised to be offered such a rare titbit in the early morning, and wagged her tail in grateful appreciation. She was even more surprised to find sweet tea in her water bowl, and went back to explore the mysteries of her new territory, feeling amply repaid for the long, lonely night.

A garden was another source of pleasure to a dog whose normal routine had been restricted by the white harness to a steady pacing of hard pavements to the place of employment, a short run in the lunch hour, then back on duty till the early evening when all her senses were alerted to the dangers and obstacles to be avoided. For the last walk of the day, after supper, she ran free once they had reached the top of the hill, and the grass was soft on her paws. She always stayed within hailing distance, listening for the shrill whistle that called her back on duty.

Half expecting to be reminded of her responsibility, she kept within sight of the back door. The man had left it open and gone back upstairs. There seemed to be no sense of urgency in this new home. Perhaps it was something called a holiday. Even for a guide dog there must be a break from routine for two weeks once a year, and there were days when they stayed at home, at Easter and Christmas, and on Sunday. The word SUNDAY had a special significance. They went to church. Yesterday was Sunday, but there was no church, only a disturbing disruption of everything she had known all her working life. In the peace of this strange garden, however, Sheba found the answer to her future habitat, and when the girl ran out to join her some time later, they greeted each other like old friends. Savoury smells wafted out into the garden. Mark was cooking breakfast. They were inspecting the chicken house when he called them in, and they ran together, carefree and happy, into the warm, welcoming kitchen.

A small portion of fried bread awaited Sheba in her feeding bowl. It was indeed a day of delightful discoveries! But when she wandered into the garden after breakfast and returned a few minutes later to find the door closed, she was puzzled, and scratched on the door to be let in.

"It's too cold to leave the door open," the girl explained. "Be patient, darling, and we will take you for a nice walk."

Sheba stretched out on the kitchen floor, anxious to please. She did not want them to think she was ungrateful, for they were being so kind. It was just that she was waiting for a word of command. Her canine intelligence had not yet registered the fact that a walk without the white harness could be one of the daily pleasures in her new environment.

When they had finished washing the dishes, they set forth, Mark and Midge dressed alike in the thick jerseys Carrie had knitted, corduroy trousers and sturdy shoes. Swinging along the country lanes, hand-in-hand, with Sheba loping along beside Midge, they made an attractive trio. It was mid-morning now, and they met only the milkman and the postman returning homewards from their delivery rounds. Both stopped to admire Sheba, and to hear the story of her adoption. Country postmen and milkmen like to be informed of what is going on!

Climbing over a stile, they followed a footpath across a field, already hardened by Winter frosts. The cold, bracing air was no hardship to Midge, born and bred in the Weald, but for Mark, who had spent the first eight years of his life in the Congo, the Winters were still uncomfortably bleak. From time to time they stopped to kiss, and Sheba stopped too, more than a little puzzled by the performance. Leaning on a farm gate, their arms entwined about each other's waist, Midge's thoughts flew home to Russets. Monday morning, and Katie busy in the wash-house. She had refused the offer of a washing machine — "Them new-fangled gadgets don't do the job proper!" Generations of farmers' wives and their servants had lit the copper before breakfast, boiled the "whites", steeped the "coloureds" in a deep sink, prepared a bath of "blue" water and a bowl of starch, and spent the morning in a cloud of steam. Katie revelled in a job that most women, in this day and age, would find laborious. Red-faced and sweating, she tackled the big family wash with energy and enthusiasm. To see the sheets billowing in the orchard was Katie's contribution to the order and cleanliness of her adopted family. In the bleak mid-Winter, the sheets would freeze on the line, and resist all the impatient tugging of her strong arms. "Stiff as boards. Bugger it!" Katie would mutter, while John laughed at her struggles from the safety of his cosy little hut. They were sworn enemies, these two, and it was John who bolted himself in the lavatory when Katie was on the warpath.

Monday morning, and Mum busy in the dairy, while Hetty pottered about the house. She was nearing her time. Dick's concern for Hetty was matched by Dad's concern for Tinker Bell, expecting her first calf!

Monday morning. Julian off to Cranbrook in his little car,

192

and Wendy and Peter catching the train to Tonbridge.

Midge sighed, and Mark tightened his arm about her waist. Sheba pressed closer, both trying to compensate for the ties that bound her to Russets. But the ties were too strong to be broken. Marriage to Mark had only strengthened the ties. Russets was still there, would always be there, a solid foundation on which to build the future. No place could ever compare with Russets, so it was foolish to allow comparisons to spoil these precious hours with Mark and Sheba. The home-sickness was still there, might always be there, she now realised, and maturity was a gradual development, not something you acquired automatically with the marriage lines, or even in the marriage bed.

Mark did not have to ask, "What are you thinking?" because he knew, and he cared, profoundly. On this second day of the honeymoon, he was disturbed by her wandering thoughts and her need for the family at Russets. He had been mistaken in his assumption that marriage to Midge would finally separate her from that close family. Her roots were too deep. They all felt the same way. That was something he had to accept here and now, or it would spoil their own special relationship.

"I've been thinking, sweetheart," he began, tentatively. "We don't have to wait until Sunday to collect the kitten and the sitting hen; we could go any day this week, and your Dad would bring us back in the van."

"Oh, my darling. I do love you so terribly much."

"It's all right, I do understand."

"You don't mind?"

"No, I don't mind sharing you," he lied. He *did* mind. He was hurt, but there was no bitterness or reproach in the discovery. Midge was not to blame, and she was too fundamentally honest to hide her true feelings. The child in Midge still clung to Russets, while the woman he loved, more than life itself, gave all of herself in the marriage bed. This was the paradox he had to accept, the truth behind the façade. Perhaps he was not alone in this dilemma. Could it be that man was destined to be defeated by his own relentless pursuit of happiness? By his own masterful interpretation of love? To possess and be possessed by the beloved? The surrender of

193

self, body and soul and spirit he had envisaged, but had not sufficiently understood, or so it seemed? The sensitivity, and the depth of his thoughts as he leaned on the gate with Midge, had not reached her. Her thoughts had wandered, were still wandering.

"Shall we go back now?" she was asking.

He noticed she did not speak of going home, only of going back, to a place not yet surrounded by all the familiar associations of home. That would come later. He must be patient.

Looking down at the bright, expectant face, so trusting and childlike, in her simple deductions, and so very much like Aunt Lucy in her loving ways, Mark was still her devoted slave. Taking her hand, they ran back across the field, with Sheba loping along beside Midge, enjoying every moment of this new found freedom.

Back at the cottage, they were welcomed by the appetising smell of baked potatoes.

"What a husband! I hadn't given a thought to dinner," Midge exclaimed, happily unconcerned, as usual.

Sheba lay stretched on the kitchen floor, her tail thumping the cold linoleum in pleasurable gratitude for the unexpected scamper, her panting breath sweet with the bracing air she had inhaled as they raced for the place she would soon recognise as her natural habitat. Not yet, however. It was too soon, and she shared the loyalty and longing for familiar sounds and smells of her new young mistress. Her canine affections were still divided between the old and the new environment, and she still felt guilty about her working day in the white harness. So she watched them furtively, the man and the girl, not understanding why they had taken her away from the place she had known since she was only a year old, and the familiar routine that in seven years had become second nature. Her limpid eyes were sad as she recalled the sense of responsibility and the importance she had known in conducting her young mistress to her place of employment. The white harness was a symbol of her duty and devotion. Now it was gone, and her momentary pleasure in her new environment was lost in the sense of guilt that would continue to haunt her for some time to come.

"Cheer up, old lady. It's time for dinner!" the man told her, cheerfully, as he filled her feeding bowl with baked potato and gravy.

She made no move to sample it because it was not her proper dinner time, but her big strong body was tense with the effort to refuse the temptation.

"Come on. Eat up!" the man insisted.

And the girl coaxed, "It's all right, darling. You're retired. You don't have to keep to that silly old routine. It's going to be fun. Eat up!"

So Sheba abandoned her canine principles regarding meal times, and thoroughly enjoyed the baked potato and gravy.

Soon after dinner, they set out for Russets, in the same close formation, with Mark and Midge holding hands and Sheba prowling proudly beside Midge. They were greeted with frantic barks as Rusty flew across the yard to inspect the newcomer. Sheba stood quietly. It was not her nature to invite intimacy from strange dogs, and Rusty felt rebuked by her gentle dignity.

"So there you are!" Carrie showed no surprise when her newly married daughter rushed into her arms, and Katie merely turned from the kitchen sink to ask, "You back then, Midge?"

John climbed over the orchard gate to join them at the kitchen door. "You can have one of my sitting hens if you like," he said, with gruff good humour.

"Thanks. That's super." Midge kissed his cheek.

Hetty walked slowly from the dairy, placidly unconcerned with her enormous belly, while Dick followed with the heavy can of milk for the house.

"Well, well, look who's here! Had enough of her already, Mark?" he teased, affectionately. He was glad to see her back. It was not the same place without Midge.

Away in the distance, Tom could be seen striding across twelve acres. He waved, and Midge waved back. Then she was running to meet him, her cheeks flushed, her blue eyes swimming with tears, to be clasped once again to that smelly old jacket.

"Oh, *Dad*," she sobbed. "I'm so happy!"

"So am I, luv. So am I." Tom held her close. Once upon a

time Carrie had felt a little jealous of her daughter, who seemed to be getting more than her share of affection, and she had to remind herself that it was natural for a father to adore a daughter. Not that Tom would have used the word "adore". It was too upper-class. A farmer was too close to the soil for such pretty talk. He believed in plain speaking, and nobody but Midge had ever called him "darling".

"Do you know something, luv?" he began, confidentially, as they walked back to the house with Midge hanging on his arm. "I actually poured your mug of tea Sunday morning, and was halfway up the stairs when I remembered you were not there. Talk about force of habit!"

"Poor darling. What a shame." Midge dried her eyes on the grubby handkerchief he took from his pocket. "If only we could live here. Like Julian and Wendy, and Dick and Hetty. It would be fabulous. But there is the cottage, and it's Mark's proper home."

"And a man needs to make roots, even more than a woman," Tom reminded her gently.

"Yes," she agreed, and changed the subject, for she knew now that her own roots were here, at Russets, and always would be. "John says we can have a sitting hen. It will be fun to have our own eggs for breakfast."

Tom chuckled. "Talk about counting your chickens before they are hatched! You won't be getting your own eggs for some time, but you can always take back half a dozen from here on Sunday. It might have been a better idea to have a dozen of our pullets to start you off, but John would think he was being robbed. Don't want to upset him. Besides, you will like to see the baby chicks running around. Pretty little creatures. Mark is quite capable of getting that old chicken house ready, isn't he?"

"I think so."

"It will need to be whitewashed inside and creosoted out. Martha was a dab hand at that sort of job in her younger days. That schoolmaster husband of hers was a brainy sort of chap, but pretty hopeless as a husband in my opinion. Left everything to Martha, and she waited on him hand and foot. Silly woman. Don't you ever make yourself a doormat, luv. I wouldn't like to see you a slave to any man."

"Not much fear of that, darling. The boot is on the other foot. Mark is spoiling me."

"It's early days yet. You keep it that way, my girl."

"OK."

"That's a handsome dog. Makes old Rusty look a bit scruffy."

Sheba was coming to meet them, her sensitive senses disturbed by all the strange sounds and smells, and the patting and stroking. She liked to be admired. It was her due. Not many dogs had the intelligence to guide a blind person, or such a knowledge of pavements, kerbs, lamp-posts and manholes, but she was not accustomed to being fondled by strangers.

"Don't touch her, and don't speak to her. She has to concentrate on what she is doing," her young mistress would say, firmly. Children were the biggest offenders, and had to be reminded a dozen times a day.

She shrank from Tom's roughened hand on her head, and stepped back in dignified protest. Midge explained the reason for this unfriendly gesture, but Tom was wondering why she had chosen such a fastidious creature. Why not a friendly little mongrel?

The rest of the family had moved into the warm kitchen, and Carrie was putting on the kettle for the mid-afternoon cup of tea. Hetty had been installed in the old rocking chair. Katie had been reminded to fetch the rock cakes. Dick and John sitting at the table, waiting to be served. Nothing had changed. Why should it? Wasn't it only two days? Midge reminded herself.

Mark was standing by the window, a little remote and uneasy, a shy smile hovering on his lips. The smile hid his thoughts — the natural thoughts of a young, newly-wed husband, coming to terms with the obvious. Midge was back where she belonged.

"Sit down, Mark," said Carrie, kindly, pushing another mug of tea across the table. She was surprised by his shyness. Mark was one of the family now, wasn't he? She wondered, vaguely, about their sex life and the marriage bed, but it was a topic never discussed by the family. It was too private, too embarrassing. Certain matters were sacred at Russets. Even

Aunt Lucy, who had defied the conventions, would blush like a schoolgirl at mention of the marriage bed.

The marmalade kitten, with arched back, spitting ferociously, was facing up to Sheba with the audacity of a David facing a Goliath.

"Can I have that one, Mum?" Midge asked.

"If you don't mind getting your stockings laddered. Ginger's a holy terror," Carrie chuckled.

Sheba had backed away from her small adversary, and they all laughed.

The diversion had released Mark from his pensive mood, and he joined in the laughter and took the kitten on to his knee. It clawed at his trousers, and he winced as the sharp claws found his flesh, and swung it over his head with a reproving shake. They stared at each other, the man and the kitten, for a long moment – a moment of mutual liking. Then Ginger settled down, purring contentedly, and licked a few crumbs of rock cake from the palm of Mark's hand. Sheba also settled down beside Midge's chair, but kept a wary eye on the kitten, while Rusty kept a wary eye on Sheba from a safe distance. Flossie yawned and stretched in her comfortable basket, watching the antics of the rest of her family with a ball of wool on the hearthrug. Carrie stepped over them with cheerful unconcern, to pour the tea. This was the atmosphere of home as Midge remembered it from her earliest days. Motherless lambs would be fed with bottles. Tom would carry them home wrapped in his jacket. The kitchen had always been at the centre of everything, and each member of the family had started life in the wicker cradle on the hearthrug, and been rocked to sleep on a mother's lap in the old rocking chair. Now the cradle was ready for Hetty's babies. Dick had carried it down from the attic, and Carrie had relined it. She was looking forward to her new role as a grandmother. Her happiest years when her own children were small had passed much too quickly. This was her life. It was a hard life, but she was content. The seasons came and went. Birth and death were all part of the pattern. It was a small world, for they were almost self-sufficient, that is, until Aunt Lucy died and the village baker started to deliver bread and cakes and pies. Carrie had felt rather guilty about the extra expense, but Tom and Julian had told her not to worry, and Tom gave up smoking.

With Midge back in her accustomed place beside Tom, and Mark crumbling a rock cake for the kitten, and John ladling three spoons of sugar into his mug of tea, and Hetty rocking gently in the old rocking chair, all was well. Julian would soon be home from Cranbrook. Wendy would be collected from the station, and young Peter would join them for the weekend. Carrie sighed happily as she refilled the mugs. She loved them all.

When the cows lowed in the byre, Tom and Carrie pushed back their chairs and went out. There were no holidays for these two, but they did not seem to mind. Katie washed up the mugs, and disappeared to have forty winks in the parlour before tackling the huge pile of ironing.

Midge settled down with Sheba to chat to Hetty. Mark joined Dick in the Dutch barn, and John went back to his hut in the orchard to mix the mash for the afternoon feed. He would be busy till dusk, feeding and watering his feathered flock. Then it would be time to see them safely into the hen houses and fasten the hatches. A prowling fox would go away hungry. John was very thorough, very conscientious in his own particular small world that Aunt Lucy had decided would be most suitable when he left the village school. On his own, surrounded by scores of White Leghorns and Rhode Islands, he felt important. Nobody interfered. It was a good life, and suited to his mentality, but he could not wring a chicken's neck. It was just another chore for Dick, and he carried the corpses into the hut the evening before market day and flung them down on the bench. Weak tears would prick John's eyes. He couldn't bear to lose them.

"Don't be such a bloody baby. How do you suppose Mum could run her market stall without the poultry?" Dick demanded, irritably. "Customers had to be satisfied, didn't they? Spring chickens for roasting, old hens for boiling. Poultry was a commodity, like eggs, butter and cheese. It was stupid to get sentimental over a few dead chickens," said Dick.

"But you haven't seen them when they were little, all fluffy and yellow, and you haven't watched them grow, running

199

about the orchard on their spindly legs. You haven't fed them and watered them twice a day, and cleaned out their houses, and collected the warm eggs from the nesting boxes. They belong to me. They're mine," John had argued tearfully.

"They are *not* yours, any more than the cows or the sheep or the pigs are mine. They belong to Russets. Can't you understand?" Dick had little patience with his younger brother. Even to this day John would cry when he found a baby chick smothered in the incubator, and Aunt Lucy was no longer there to comfort him. He still missed her, probably more than any other member of the family, and would often sit and brood over imaginary injustice in his lonely isolation from the rest of the family. Did Midge realise what a sacrifice he was making in promising a sitting hen and a clutch of eggs? he wondered, as he carried round the heavy buckets of water that afternoon. What had prompted him to be so generous? He was jealous of his twin sister. She was too clever, too bossy. She made him feel stupid, and he was not stupid! He was glad Midge had married Mark and moved away, but he hadn't expected to see her back so soon. Mum said she was homesick, and Dad was making a great fuss of her. She had always been Dad's favourite. It wasn't fair! The water splashed over his gumboots, his mouth was sulky. Then he remembered that Julian had promised to play a game of Ludo after supper. Julian was nice.

Chapter Eight

Tom had filled the lanterns with paraffin. They stood in a row on the scullery shelf. The evenings were drawing in. The lanterns reminded Maggie of the parable of the virgins — the Foolish Virgins who forgot to fill their lamps, and the Wise Virgins who filled their lamps with oil. Maggie was always quoting the Bible. Maggie was good, sweet-tempered, and devoted to the Sisters and orphans at the Convent. She kept in touch with the family at Russets, but always seemed a little remote, as though her thoughts were elsewhere. She still brought an orphan to tea every Sunday, and listened to the family talking and arguing amongst themselves, but she seldom had anything to contribute. Perhaps she thought they would not be interested. Perhaps she remembered the opposition when she claimed the right to choose the Catholic faith in those early years. Carrie had thought it was just a phase, and she would grow out of it, like sleep-walking and taking the skin off her rice pudding. But Aunt Lucy had recognised a determination and dedication of lasting value, and she was right, as usual. Yet she could not break away entirely from the family at Russets. The bond was too strong, though the sense of belonging had weakened of recent years.

Loyalty and affection brought her to Russets on Sunday afternoon, Winter and Summer, in all kinds of weather. She came and went so quietly, and was so reticent, she could not talk of her own feelings, even to her mother. Only young Peter probed into her thoughts from time to time, when he and Rusty accompanied Maggie and the orphan to Marston Park after they all had enjoyed the high tea.

"Have you got a boy-friend, Maggie?" he had asked, with mild curiosity, one Sunday evening.

"No," she answered.

"Aren't you going to get married then?"

"I am married to Christ."

"Jesus Christ?"

"Yes."

Peter was puzzled by such a strange relationship. "But you can't *see* Him. How can you be married to someone you can't see?"

"It's a spiritual, not a physical marriage."

"I don't understand."

"Never mind." She smiled. She was pretty when she smiled, he thought, but not as pretty as Midge.

"I'll be getting back now," he said, because he could think of nothing more to say, and neither could Maggie.

"Goodbye, Peter, till next Sunday. God bless you." She kissed his cheek, but when she had walked away, he rubbed it off. Kissing was silly. The orphan had smiled shyly. She was very pretty. Her hair was the colour of ripe chestnuts, and her eyes as blue as the periwinkles in the wood. Her name was Rosemary.

"So long," he said, and returned the smile. If he was looking for a girl-friend, he wouldn't mind a girl like Rosemary, but he was much too busy learning to be an actor.

Walking back across the park that Summer evening, he had rehearsed his part in the school concert, and all the other parts that he knew by heart. What would Mother say when she heard he had already been chosen to play Buttons in "Cinderella" at the Theatre Royal? Surely the youngest Buttons on record? There would be two new songs, specially written for the show, that he would sing as a duet with Cinderella, because his voice was not strong enough to sing solo. He was thrilled to be chosen out of nearly a hundred applicants. Julian had congratulated him, but Mother would be displeased, and her displeasure would spoil his pride and joy in the fascinating role. Why couldn't she be pleased, for his sake?

Dick was prodded awake in the marriage bed hardly before he

had settled into the heavy sleep he felt he deserved after a hard day's work.

"What's up?" he growled, irritably.

"The pains have started." Hetty's voice was calm. She never flapped. He was the one to get worked up in an emergency, and this was an emergency, the crisis he had been dreading since he was told he could expect to be the father of twins. Now he was groping for his trousers in trembling agitation.

"Switch on the light, luv," said Hetty.

How could she remain so calm, so practical when this tremendous upheaval threatened to disrupt the harmony they had enjoyed? After today, nothing would ever be the same again, for they would be parents, and he was not yet ready for parenthood. It was Hetty who had wanted to start a family, and she had her way, as all the women of Russets had their way with their men.

Hetty was smiling complacently at his troubled face and tousled head. He looked so young and vulnerable, not a bit like the strong, manly fellow she had married. The man who had sworn "With my body I thee worship". The marriage vows were so deceptive, and Dick's rough love-making could hardly be described as "worship"! She supposed that wild gypsy girl could be blamed for Dick's initiation into the art of making love, but those rough tumbles in the hay need not have been practised on his lawful wife in the marriage bed. For all her practical commonsense, Hetty was a romantic soul, and had visualised a gentle approach to intercourse. After all, Dick was no stranger, and she had seen his gentle handling of a new-born foal on more than one occasion. It was not something you could discuss and compare with the other wives in the family, but it would be interesting to know whether they actually enjoyed the intimacy of the marriage bed. Her strong maternity would take priority from henceforth. She would be a loving, devoted mother, and Dick would take second place to her children. She would follow in the footsteps of her mother-in-law, a dutiful wife, but her children would claim the biggest share of her love and attention.

"I'll get Mum," Dick was saying, anxious to be relieved of the responsibility.

"Phone the doctor first, and he will get in touch with the hospital. They will send an ambulance to collect me. It's all arranged. Stop worrying," said Hetty, soothingly.

Dick pulled on a jersey and clattered downstairs, barefoot, to phone the doctor. With twins there could be complications, the doctor had told Hetty. They would get her into hospital as soon as the pains started. She had not told Dick it was not a straightforward birth, but Carrie understood because her own twins were born in hospital, and the boy had been such a puny little scrap of humanity he needed very careful nursing.

Now Carrie was there, cheerfully taking control of the situation.

"Men are pretty hopeless in childbirth, luv. Tom sat on the stairs, getting in the way of the midwife, and when it was all over, and Dick was born, he was sick in the scullery!" she told Hetty, with a warm hug. "Just relax. It's going to be a long wait. How about a nice cup of tea?"

"Yes, please. Are you coming with me?"

"Of course I'm coming." It was like putting back the clock. She had always been fond of Hetty, and her marriage to Dick had ended a long period of anxiety. Now Hetty was expecting twins, and Carrie was thrilled. Would it be a boy and a girl? History often repeated itself at Russets – as Aunt Lucy would say.

Yes, history did indeed repeat itself when Hetty, twelve hours later, gave birth to a boy and a girl twin, but such tiny scraps of humanity, they were put into incubators. With such strong, healthy parents, it was disconcerting for Hetty, who had visualised bonny, bouncing babies to take home to Russets within a week of their birth. They were premature, of course. Somebody had made a mistake in the dates. Now they had to be fed every two hours, and not until they weighed five pounds would they be allowed out of the maternity wing.

Dick and Carrie visited Hetty three times during the ten days she had been kept in bed. It had been a difficult birth, and there would be no more children. Physically exhausted, and mentally depressed, Hetty wept on Dick's manly shoulder, more distressed by the fact she was not going to rear a big family as she had intended than the fact of their smallness. Dick gazed at his offspring with a sense of dismay.

204

Like two little dolls, clothed only in nappies, they were sleeping and quite unconscious of the trauma surrounding their birth.

Back at the bedside, he held Hetty's hand while she continued to cry. "Cheer up, old girl, you will be OK once you get them home," said he, surprised and embarrassed by the crying. What had happened to his sensible spouse? He hardly recognised her in this clinging, emotional creature. It was not a brusque reminder to cheer up that Hetty needed, but a warm hug, and an understanding of her feelings, and she got both from her mother-in-law. Only a woman who had suffered the depressing aftermath of a difficult birth could be expected to understand, and Carrie now confessed to her tears and depression after the birth of her own twins. This seemed to comfort Hetty, and they left her, hopefully confident that the worst was over.

During their second and third visits, however, her spirits were very low. Heavy eyed and listless, she accepted the gifts they brought, from the family and the neighbours, with barely a glance, and mumbled thanks. As they climbed into the van after the last visit, Dick was looking very serious. He was obviously puzzled by Hetty's attitude.

"It's not like Het to be so quiet, and she hardly noticed the grapes and the peaches. They cost a pretty penny in that swanky shop in the Pantiles."

"It's the depression, luv. She will be all right when we get her back home."

Dick sighed heavily. He was still feeling hurt that she hadn't mentioned the grapes and the peaches. After all, he had given up smoking since he knew he would soon be a father, and fallen over backwards to please her.

"They looked so pretty in that basket, didn't they, Mum?" he said. The basket was an extra, but it was worth it. "Put in a couple of oranges and a couple of those apples, and a couple of bananas," he had instructed the haughty saleswoman, with reckless disregard of the cost. Mum had picked the last of the flowers from her garden, and Hetty had buried her face in the flowers but almost ignored the beautiful basket of fruit. Dick would sulk all the way home. Silly boy! Carrie chattered brightly as he concentrated on the traffic. He hated driving in the town. Back in the country lanes he relaxed, and Carrie introduced the subject of names.

"Names? A bit early, isn't it?" He shrugged indifferently.

"Tom and me spent a lot of time choosing names, but then they were hardly used. A pity, really. You were christened Richard, Maggie was christened Margaret, and Midge was christened Mary."

"First I've heard of it," Dick grumbled.

"Oh, *Dick*, you must have!"

He shook his head.

"I've been thinking," Carrie began, as she brewed another pot of tea on their return from the hospital. "We need another pair of hands. I can't manage the dairy and the market stall as well as the meals and helping Katie with the housework. Why don't we have Midge and Mark back here during the week? They could go home at weekends. What do you think?" She was addressing the whole family. It was a Saturday afternoon, and they were gathered round the kitchen table.

They had been listening to Dick's account of their visit, and his disappointment over Hetty's lack of interest in the luxury grapes and peaches.

"Good idea," said Tom, approvingly, but Julian was not so sure.

"I doubt whether they would want to move back, they have hardly had time to settle into the cottage. And what about the dog and the cat?"

"That's no problem," Tom asserted, his thoughts on Midge, so obviously homesick.

"I suppose I could give up my job," Wendy suggested, tentatively.

"I could stay home from school. I hate school anyway!" Peter avoided his mother's eyes.

"Don't be silly." Wendy's voice was sharp with irritation. Her head was throbbing, and her nerves were ragged. Not another migraine! She couldn't bear it. Only three weeks since the last, and she wouldn't be fit to travel on Monday. Actually, it would be quite a relief to give up the job and all the travelling it entailed, especially in the Winter.

Carrie was glancing at Julian. They both knew that Wendy was no earthly use as another pair of hands on the farm. Her

206

hands were never soiled. They were delicate, white hands with flexible fingers, admirably suited to the keyboard, or plucking the strings of a guitar.

Julian shook his head. "It wouldn't work, my darling."

"Why not?"

"You would soon get bored. It's seven days a week, remember, and now you work only five days, and have every weekend and all the school holidays to relax and please yourself." He paused and smiled, that swift, entrancing smile that still could melt her bones after all these years. "There is also the question of money, sweetheart. I doubt if we could manage on my small salary, and we must continue to contribute our fair share to the family exchequer. We are fortunate to have your parents undertaking to pay Peter's school fees, aren't we?"

"Yes, I suppose so." Wendy sounded sulky. She didn't want Midge back at Russets. Midge still behaved like a child, with all the hugs and kisses. There was no harm in it, Julian insisted. He regarded young Midge with sisterly affection. But Wendy could never control the wave of jealousy that swept over her when she saw them locked together in a warm embrace. Midge was a married woman now, but marriage hadn't changed her. To have her back at Russets would be putting back the clock. It was insufferable.

"I think I will go and lie down. Excuse me." She pushed back her chair and left the room.

Julian sighed. He knew why she was upset. He could read that tight little face like a book. It was not only the migraine. She was so intense, his beloved, still wearing a chip on her shoulder because of Peter, and because she had lied to the child about his real father. What did it matter? What did anything matter? Only peace of mind mattered. And there would be no peace of mind until she told the truth.

"So, is everyone agreed that we get Midge and Mark to come back?" Carrie was asking.

"Yes."

It was unanimous. Julian nodded, and sipped the hot tea with mixed feelings.

So Hetty came home to Russets, leaving the babies in the incubators.

"She didn't even look at them before she left," Carrie reported to Tom, as soon as they were alone together. "When Sister Maternity suggested it, Hetty burst into tears, so we came away without seeing them. Sister had already told me, on our last visit, that acute depression was not uncommon after a difficult birth, but it would pass. They would take great care of the babies, and Hetty could see them whenever she wished. In the meantime, to let her please herself. It was just a question of patience. Some things could not be hurried."

As soon as Hetty saw Dick, she started to cry again.

"It's all right, Het, old girl. Don't worry about the babies. It's you I want to see," he comforted, gruffly.

But it was not all right, and he was baffled by her tears. Hetty was a stranger, a weak, emotional stranger, and he was wishing they had never started a family. He could understand her reluctance to look at them, for he himself had felt a little shiver of distaste, and no sense of ownership or affection. In fact, it would not have mattered if he never saw them again.

So it was a sad homecoming. Hetty said she was tired and went straight to bed, and Carrie brought her a cup of tea — that infallible remedy for all ills at Russets. While she was drinking the tea, Carrie unpacked the small suitcase, chatting brightly about this and that, but Hetty was not listening, and when she had finished the tea, she lay back, closed her eyes, and pretended to sleep. In the big marriage bed, where her babies were conceived, she shrank from the remembered intimacy. She hadn't wanted to come home, and she couldn't bear to sleep with Dick, not ever again. She just wanted to be left alone; surrounded by the family she would always feel she was being watched. Weak tears wet her cheeks. Her mother-in-law had told her the babies had been christened according to her wishes — Jacqueline and Jonathan — but she had no recollection of choosing those names. Her mind was a blank.

"How are you feeling?" they questioned her. How could she answer when she had no feeling, only the overwhelming urge to weep?

"Leave me alone. Leave me alone." Was she talking to herself? And who would listen to such a plea? You were never left alone at Russets. Even at this moment, somebody was

208

climbing the stairs — heavy, laborious steps. Someone no longer young. She closed her eyes again and pretended sleep. But the dragging footsteps came nearer, in to the room, and stopped by her bed. A roughened hand pushed the lank hair from her damp forehead, and a familiar voice asked, kindly, "What's to do then, luv?"

Her eyes flew open. "Mam!"

"Aye, it's your Mam." Then she was enfolded in her mother's arms, weeping on the breast that had nourished her.

"Take me home, Mam, I want to go home," she sobbed.

"But Russets is your home now, child."

"No! No! Don't leave me here."

"You mean, for a little holiday? Is that what you want?"

"Yes, yes, a holiday at Home Farm."

"What's Dick going to say?"

"I don't know. I don't care."

"There, there, luv. Don't get yourself in such a state. You stay right here and I'll explain to him."

"You'll come back?"

"I'll wait downstairs. Those stairs murder my rheumatics. Dad brought me over in the jeep, and he will run us back if Dick agrees."

"He will! He must!"

"We'll see."

"Mam?"

"Yes, luv?"

"Tell them ... tell them ..." she flapped her hands, helplessly.

"Aye, I'll tell them." The heavy footsteps clumped away down the stairs.

She could hear them talking. Their voices floated up to her, and Dick's voice was raised in angry protest. She shivered, and slid out of bed. In the few minutes they were discussing her, she put on the clothes she had taken off only half-an-hour before, and when Dick stood in the doorway, staring at her with baleful eyes and a sulky mouth, she was sitting on the bed, wringing her hands in an agony of desperation. Could he force her to stay?

"I'm sorry," she whispered.

He made no answer, and he did not touch her again, but his

broad shoulders seemed to sag, and he stood aside as she slipped past and down the stairs.

"I'll send your things over later," Carrie spoke quietly, already resigned to a situation she could not understand. She kissed Hetty's cheek, and watched her climb into the jeep beside her father. When they had gone, she closed the kitchen door and went to look for her son. She found him sitting on the edge of the bed, his face buried in his hands, his shoulders shaking, his big, strong body wracked with his sobbing. And she, too, with a mother's love and compassion, gathered her grown child to her breast, and listened to her heart. This was her firstborn, and his suffering was her suffering. She could find no words to comfort him, but her arms were warm, and she held him close. A man's tears were drawn from the very depths of his being, strangled, and infinitely more compelling than a woman's tears. Dick had wept only once before, in his young manhood — wept for the gypsy girl who was snatched away at the altar by her gypsy lover.

When his sobs had subsided to shuddering sighs, he asked, with pathetic earnestness, "What's wrong with me, Mum? What have I done to upset her? What have I said?"

"Nothing, son. It's not your fault. It's not anybody's fault. Hetty can't help herself. She's frightened and her mind is disturbed, so she clings to her mother, like a child again."

"But I am her husband, and she is my wife. We promised to cherish one another, in sickness and in health. Doesn't that mean anything to her anymore?"

Carrie shook her head, her own eyes wet. "Not at the moment it doesn't. But she will be back."

"When? How soon?"

"Sister Maternity couldn't say how long this depression would last, but probably not more than a few weeks."

"*A few weeks*," he echoed, chokingly. "What am I supposed to do? It's unreasonable, Mum. It doesn't make sense."

"No, luv, it doesn't make sense, not to you, or to me, and probably not to Hetty. I'm sorry for her, but I'm more sorry for you, because you are my son."

"It's a kind of jinx. This is the second time I've been rejected. It's humiliating, Mum."

210

"Yes, son."

"I feel like I can't be bothered any more. I don't care what happens."

"Don't talk that way, luv. You mustn't lose heart. It's not the end of the world. Think of those dear little innocent mites in the hospital."

"I would sooner not think of them. They started all the trouble. Whoever heard of a mother who refused to look at her babies? It's not natural. The poor little blighters didn't ask to be born."

They sat there, in companionable silence, their hands clasped, then Dick spoke again. "They *are* normal, aren't they, Mum? I mean, there's nothing missing is there? Just tiny?"

"Just tiny, but perfect."

"They will need a lot of care when we get them home."

"That could be another three months or so."

"And Hetty will be back to look after them."

"I can help. We can all help. They will need a lot of care, and a lot of love — so will Hetty."

"Yes, you're right, Mum. I didn't mean what I said about not bothering any more. I want her back. She knows I love her, even if I don't tell her in so many words."

"That's where you make a big mistake, son. A woman likes to be told. Your dad never made that mistake, son, so I always knew I was loved."

"I'll remember. Thanks, Mum." He squeezed her shoulders.

"Write her a little note. I'll put it in with her clothes. Katie can take the case over to Home Farm in the morning."

"I could drink that cup of tea now, Mum, if there's any left in the pot."

"A bit stewed. I'll make fresh."

"Then I'll get back to work."

"Thank God for work, eh?"

"You're right." Dick followed his mother down the stairs.

"It's a bit much expecting us back at Russets when we have hardly settled here," Mark grumbled, as they walked back from the station with Sheba.

Midge had just explained about the phone call from Russets, but Mark was tired after a trying day at the bank, and not at all pleased at the prospect. He hadn't wanted Midge to meet the train on these dark Winter evenings, but she had Sheba for protection, and a torch to light her path, and insisted she would come to no harm. He was pushing his bike, huddled in his overcoat, feeling pretty wretched, and this news she had sprung on him was the last straw. Why couldn't she wait till he was home, comfortably installed in Gran's armchair after supper? It was absolute bliss, this hour of the day, with Midge leaning her curly head against his knees, the dog and the kitten stretched on the hearthrug, and all the worries of the day forgotten. Now he would have to cycle back alone to Russets, for it was too far for Midge to walk, and it would be a communal meal in the kitchen, followed by an evening of television, or playing cards, neither of which appealed to him in the least. Tom and Dick would be arguing as usual, over the meal. Why couldn't they settle their differences in the fields, or the barn, or leaning on a gate? The whole family would join in the discussion, and it was always a farming matter. Their world was so small, and Mark had spent his day in a much wider world.

Midge seemed surprised at his grumbling. "What could I say? I couldn't refuse, could I?"

"You could have waited to ask me if I minded."

"Darling, don't be difficult. It's not like you to be difficult."

"No, I'm an easy-going sort of chap. Mark won't mind, they would say. Just go ahead and get it organised. Mark won't mind. Well, I *do* mind, Midge, and I think it's a bit of a cheek."

"Are we quarrelling, Mark?"

"If we are, it's your fault."

"It's *not* my fault. It's Hetty's fault for taking herself off to the Home Farm, and leaving Mum with all the work and Dick without a wife. What's come over her, for heaven's sake? Why doesn't she snap out of it?"

"Acute depression is not something that can be cured with a few kind words, or a few pep pills. It's a sickness of the mind. I seem to remember a time not so long ago when another member of the family at Russets was feeling pretty sorry for herself."

"It's mean of you, Mark, to remind me."

"It's mean of you, Midge, to blame poor Hetty for something you condone in yourself."

They walked on in silence, both feeling hurt, both blaming the other for their first quarrel. The darkness of the country lanes lit only by the streak of light from the cycle lamp, did nothing to lighten their spirits, and when Mark had put his bike in the shed, and followed Midge into the kitchen, he stood there, sniffing the unmistakable odour of a burnt supper. Midge had snatched a dish of sausages and fried potatoes from the oven.

"Another burnt offering?" he sneered.

"It's not my fault if it gets dried up in the oven. Anyway, I don't pretend to be a cook. You said it didn't matter. You said you would do the cooking."

"That was before you gave up your job. Now you have all day to please yourself, and you can hardly expect me to start cooking after a long day in the office."

They faced each other in angry resentment, and Sheba blinked her limpid eyes, puzzled by their attitude, while the kitten rubbed his tiny agitated body round Mark's legs. Mark was pale and tense, but Midge saw only his stubborn mouth and hard eyes.

"Why don't you get your lunch in Tonbridge? It would save a lot of bother."

"Because it's cheaper to take sandwiches for midday, and have a meal in the evening. Only the senior clerks who earn a decent salary have lunch at the Welcome Cafe. I explained all this to you, Midge." He sighed impatiently.

"Did you? Well, I see no reason why we can't economise on something else, so that you could have your lunch at the café."

"What, for instance? We already live on a shoe-string. I warned you what it would be like, married to a junior clerk in the bank — no holidays, no car, making do. Even with that small rise in salary as a sort of bonus after our marriage, it's still a pittance, Midge. It was a mistake to get married so young. We should have waited."

"A mistake? Is that how you see it? Just because we have to go back to Russets for a week or two, and because I burnt the supper?" Midge demanded, indignantly.

213

"It's a good enough reason."

"Is it?" Midge was beginning to feel frightened. She had never seen Mark in this belligerent mood. Still holding the dish of shrivelled sausages and chippy potatoes, she faltered, "I could make some nice hot gravy?"

Mark's sudden explosion into a shout of laughter startled both animals.

"What's so funny?" Midge was near to tears.

Mark's sense of humour was not kind. "Nice hot gravy." he spluttered.

"But we mustn't waste it, must we, not with all those starving children in the world. It would be wicked."

"I'm sorry. I really am terribly sorry."

"And I may as well confess the rice pudding may be a bit overcooked. It's been in the oven all afternoon. I meant to ask you about it before you left, but I forgot. I'm a poor sort of wife. You are entitled to complain."

"Who said you were a poor sort of wife?"

"You did."

"I said nothing of the kind. Don't talk such rubbish."

"Now we are quarrelling again and I can't bear it!"

"Oh, for Pete's sake, Midge, don't cry!" Mark took the dish, dumped it on top of the stove, sat down, and, still in his overcoat, pulled Midge on to his knees. "What's the matter with us? We must be crazy," he growled. "Stop it, sweetheart. Stop crying. It's *all right*. Everything is perfect. I wouldn't change anything for all the tea in China."

"You wouldn't?" Midge asked, chokingly, and dried her tears.

What had come over him? Could marriage do this to a man? For all his denial, he was still tense, so were the animals. She slid off his knees, gave them a reassuring pat, and went into the sitting-room to poke the fire into a blaze. They followed her, and stretched out on the hearthrug, the kitten lying between Sheba's paws. She stayed with them for a few minutes, then went back to the kitchen. Mark had taken off his overcoat and hung it in the small lobby. He was such a tidy person, who never left anything lying around. She knew her untidiness was something she should try to correct, for his sake, but the habits of a lifetime cannot be conquered in a couple of weeks.

He was frying several slices of fat bacon and tomatoes, and did not turn his head. "All it needs is a bit of flavour and fat, then that supper will be quite eatable. Get the table laid, will you?" said he, authoritatively.

"Yes, darling," Midge answered, dutifully.

Nothing more was said about going back to Russets, but their love-making was not so spontaneous that night, nor so mutually satisfying. Mark fell asleep immediately, but Midge lay awake for ages, trying to recapture the blissful sensuality of previous nights, with her arm flung across Mark's lean body and her head on his chest. His deep breathing, when she lay awake, seemed further proof of their separation, and her troubled thoughts tumbled around her confused mind till her head ached and her tired eyes were wet with tears. When the alarm clock wakened her, it seemed she had slept for only a few minutes. Stiff with cramp, she rolled over, yawning and stretching, but Mark still slept soundly. Remembering their quarrel, she sighed, and slid out of bed, determined to make amends. It was barely light on this mid-Winter morning as she pulled on her dressing-gown and slippers, and crept downstairs. Ginger greeted her exuberantly, and Sheba with her usual gentleness. Midge hugged them both, and let them out in the garden. They were quickly back, waiting for the saucer of milky tea they usually received from Mark at this hour of the day. With the mugs of tea and the tin of biscuits on a tray, Midge climbed the stairs, switched on the bedroom light and stood looking down on the boyish face and rumpled head, till his eyes opened.

"What's the time?" he growled, irritably.

It was rather a shock to discover her newly-wed husband was not at his best in the early morning, and that the special effort he had been making for the benefit of his new wife was not to be considered a permanent state of affairs. Mum could have warned her that all the males at Russets, even young Peter, had to be left alone to come to terms with a new day, and the one thing they could not tolerate was bright and breezy chatter. So Mark was only being typical of his sex when he ignored Midge's peace offering and the cheery "Good morning, darling". With obvious reluctance, he sat up and took the mug of tea.

"Would you like a biscuit?" she chirped, feeling a little discouraged by his moodiness.

He shook his head and sipped the hot tea, noisily.

Midge's spirits sank to zero. So he hadn't forgotten their quarrel and he hadn't forgiven her. She thought she knew him intimately, but she was mistaken. This moody stranger was not the Mark she had known since they were children together, at Russets, tossing hay in the hayfield, swimming in the river, sitting astride the big Shire horse, bringing in the harvest, racing each other on their bikes round the winding country lanes, helping Aunt Lucy stone the raisins for the Christmas cakes and pudding – and eating the sugar in the candied peel. Mark had been just another brother, until they discovered they were in love. Now she was hurt and puzzled because he was still sulking over last night's quarrel, and she was ready to forgive and forget. It was her nature. She never bore a grudge, or harboured resentment, and she never sulked. She had to make peace between them, and she knew, instinctively, that pride was no substitute for peace.

"Mark, will you listen to me, *please*?" she ventured. He had finished the tea, handed back the mug, and was slipping out of bed. "You don't have to go back to Russets if you don't want to. Dad can collect me in the van after breakfast, and bring me back in the early evening, so I shall be here when you get home. I will take Sheba and Ginger with me, of course. Mum will give me something to bring back for our supper. There is always more than enough for the family. It means I won't be able to walk to the station in the morning or to meet the train in the evening, but it's only till Hetty is well enough to return to Russets. I . . ."

Midge got no further. Mark had turned his head to smile at her, that shy, disarming smile that twisted her heart. "Sweetheart, you're marvellous," said he, and kissed her tenderly.

"I love you so terribly much, my darling. We must never quarrel again," said Midge.

"Never!" Mark asserted, with youthful optimism – and kissed her again.

* * *

216

Three months later the babies came home to Russets in the hospital ambulance. Carrie nursed the girl and Midge nursed the boy. They would always be known as Jackie and Johnnie. They still weighed only five pounds, but seemed as bright and healthy as normal babies.

Dick was waiting to receive them, feeling the acute anxiety that was natural under the circumstances, since Hetty was still at the Home Farm. He had visited the babies regularly every Sunday with Carrie, and watched them being fed and their napkins changed, but without any sense of ownership. But now they were home, where he could see them and touch them every day, their helplessness would appeal to his own robust manhood.

It was one of those special occasions at Russets, with all the family gathered in the courtyard to welcome them home, and the big wicker cradle waiting to receive them, swaddled in shawls in the warm kitchen. A fire had been lit in the bedroom that was once Aunt Lucy's. In that big marriage bed all her children had been born and Carrie's children. Tom and Carrie would have many disturbed nights, for the babies would be fed every three hours until Hetty came home. Surely she would want to see them now? It was not natural for a mother to ignore the existence of her own children, Dick argued, but Hetty's mother would not persuade her daughter to return to Russets until she was ready, so Dick had to watch his own mother, not his wife, preparing the bottles, bathing and changing them, and tucking them into their cosy little nest. The daily routine was disorganised to accommodate the demands of this new generation at the old farmhouse, and Carrie could not have managed without Midge. Sheba stayed guard over the cradle, and the sleeping infants, while both were busy in the dairy, for Katie was too scared to be left alone with them. She made no complaint over the extra washing, however, for every day was washing day now, and the tall fireguard, brought down from the attic, was draped with airing napkins and nightgowns, seven days a week. The sweet-sour smell of babies lingered in the kitchen long after the smells of cooking had dwindled away.

The life of Russets seemed to revolve about the cradle. Peter was fascinated by their smallness and their extraordinary likeness to one another. With Christmas over, and the Boxing Day pantomime only a memory, Peter devoted all his spare time to them at the weekends, and haunted the kitchen, fetching and carrying at bath time and feeding time, with a sense of importance that amused Wendy. It was a novelty, and like all novelties, it would not last, but it helped the Winter along very nicely, and made a nice change from rehearsing in the barn with the faithful Rusty. The mystery of their birth was never explained. How did they get out of Hetty's belly and into an incubator in the hospital? It was a question that nobody was prepared to answer, and Peter was shamed by his own ignorance into asking Dick. As the father of the twins he must have had something to do with it. But Dick was not forthcoming, and Peter was reminded he was still too young for such intimate disclosures.

One warm Spring afternoon, the twins were enjoying their first airing in the big, old-fashioned pram in which all Aunt Lucy's babies and Carrie's babies had first become aware of the smells and sounds of a farm. They went no farther than the courtyard. Propped on their pillows, one at each end of the pram, they stared about them in wide-eyed wonder, and took a lively interest in their surroundings. Sheba was stretched on the cobbles, while Ginger explored the big Dutch barn. Midge was busy in the dairy, slapping pats of butter into shape for the market stall the following day. Carrie was plucking chickens in the yard, and keeping a fond eye on the babies. John was grading eggs in the hut, and Dick was busy with the Spring ploughing. Tom anxiously awaited the birth of Christabel's first calf.

From his high perch on the tractor, Dick was the first to see the familiar figure walking slowly along the cart track that divided the two farms. His heart raced, and his weathered face flushed, as the engine throbbed beneath his buttocks and beat out the rhythm of their favourite Sinatra record — "I did it My Way". There seemed to be all the time in the world for their reconciliation, so he did not panic or stop the engine, but finished the long straight furrow while Hetty leaned on the gate. She was wearing the green jumper that Carrie had knitted as a Christmas present for her absent daughter-in-law.

They all had sent her presents and cards. The sun shone on her nut-brown hair, and she had lost a lot of weight. All this he noticed as he strode back across the furrowed field, smiling a welcome.

"Hullo, Het," was all he said.

And she answered, "Hullo, Dick" in a small, uncertain voice.

He dare not kiss her for fear she took fright and went away again, but he covered her cold hands with his own warm, roughened hands, and asked kindly, "How are you feeling, luv?"

"All right, I suppose."

"I've missed you, Het. It's not the same place without you."

She sighed and looked away towards the tractor, parked under the hedge, on which Dick spent some of the pleasantest hours of his working life. He felt like a king, perched high on the saddle, surveying his kingdom. Only it wasn't his, it was Dad's. To be heir to Russets was a fine thing to anticipate, but Dad was not yet sixty, and fit as a fiddle.

"I need you, Het. I love you." It was blurted out with self-conscious embarrassment, because it was not his nature to indulge in such endearments. His casual attitude, over the years, was taken for granted, and marriage had done little or nothing towards a more loving relationship. When he proposed marriage, she knew it was more to compensate for his hurt ego than for her own homely appearance. She had no sex-appeal, and none of the wiles of that sly little gypsy girl with hair as black as a raven's wing and eyes as black as onyx. Not once had he said, "I love you." "I need you," was a poor substitute for those three magic words that every woman wants to hear repeated time and time again. It was not pride that held her back from asking why she still played second fiddle to a gypsy whose lover had claimed her, leaving Dick a jilted bridegroom at the altar. No, it was not pride, but familiarity. They had grown up together, at adjoining farms, shared the same desk at the village school in those early years of the three Rs. With three older brothers, and Dick Blunt to copy, it was not surprising that Hetty was a bit of a tom-boy, or that she expected no sympathy if she was hurt in the process. They hardly noticed her budding breasts and her blushes, only that she suddenly stopped climbing trees, fishing for tadpoles and riding on the step of Dick's bike. Adolescence was a difficult age, of tears and tantrums, and her slavish devotion to Dick was embarrassing.

But he had said it at last, those three magic words, "*I love you*" − and her pale face flushed with pleasure.

"You do?"

"I do."

"Shall we go home?"

Now he could kiss her.

Hand-in-hand, like two young sweethearts who had just discovered Paradise, they walked slowly towards the pram in the courtyard. Hetty's hand was warm now, her mouth trembling and her eyes bright with unshed tears.

Carrie's hands stopped their plucking and she drew in her breath on a long drawn sigh of relief, but she made no move to greet Hetty, and it was doubtful if they even noticed her. This was their moment, the moment her son had waited for all the interminable Winter. Sometimes she had wondered whether the separation was final.

The babies had seen them, and tiny hands were flapping excitedly. Identical faces peered out from under their distinctive head-gear. Jackie was wearing a pink knitted bonnet and Johnnie a blue woolly cap.

"They're beautiful," Hetty whispered, chokingly. And they were hers − hers and Dick's. Still holding Dick's hand, she reached out, shyly and tentatively, for one of those tiny flapping hands, and Johnnie's fingers curled round her thumb. Dick's free hand reached for Jackie's, and her fingers clung like a limpet to his thumb. There they were, parents and children, unconsciously forging a bond of loving and lasting relationship destined to occupy a permanent place in the history of Russets. Did the babies recognise their parents in that moment, or was it simply a natural reaction to hold out their arms to be picked out of the pram? Who could resist the appeal, or the baby talk that only mothers can interpret?

Holding Johnnie in a close embrace, feeling the first emotional contact of his warm little body, Hetty knew she had a number of people to thank for her babies' survival. She had carried them in her womb, given them life and birth, then rejected them. Why? It was inhuman, inconceivable, but the private hell she had endured was too demanding to be ignored, too dominating and compelling. She was a stranger to herself and her tolerant family. They had borne with her black moods, her tears and tantrums, until her mind was at peace, and a quietness had descended on her troubled spirit. It could have been the scent of the May blossoms or the song of the blackbird, or the bleating of lambs, or even the rough tongue of Gyp, her favourite collie, that Spring day, or a combination of all three, but she knew she must go back — now, today. Russets was her home because she had married Dick and borne his children. It was as simple as that. There was no more fear, or doubt or confusion.

Carrie was watching the happy reunion from her bench in the yard, and when they walked towards her, each carrying a baby, she dusted the feathers from her white apron and smiled a welcome.

"It's good to see you back, luv," she told her daughter-in-law. "Come and sit here." She finished the plucking and walked away, back to her kitchen, to put on the kettle for tea. One by one they came to join her — Midge from the dairy, as flushed and pretty as the pictorial dairymaid — John from the shed in the orchard, bringing the graded eggs for the market — Tom to announce the safe arrival of a bull calf, all slipping past the bench in the courtyard with the same thoughtful intention. They all had suffered in some small degree and worked harder and worried about Dick, but the close bond that knitted them together as a family had survived another troubled season.

Now it was over. Hetty was back where she belonged. Dick was happy, and if anything more was needed to complete the picture of contentment on that warm afternoon in the lovely month of May, it was the sweet innocence of two blue-eyed babies.

PART 3

Chapter Nine

Mark was a poor correspondent, and had to be reminded to write to his parents. The Congo was too remote to be regarded as an essential part of his adult life, and his parents but vague figures in the pattern of his early years. He was eight years old and Matthew two years younger when they were brought to England.

Looking back on those early years, Mark remembered most vividly his sense of wonder at the first glimpse of a snow-covered landscape from the frosted dormitory window, and the itching discomfort of his first woolly vest. But much of his childhood he felt guilty about Matthew's death. Now it all seemed to have happened in another era, but Mark was constantly reminded of Matthew at Gran's cottage where they had spent their school holidays during that first year in England, and known the warmth and love of her generous nature. The swing was still there on the same bough, at the bottom of the garden, the books and toys they had shared were there in the cupboard, the bed, with the patchwork quilt and the rag rug with the stain from the blackcurrant juice Matthew had spilt one morning.

Once every five years the parents came on leave for six weeks, to visit all their relatives and friends, and to lay flowers on the graves in the churchyard. It was customary. Among the headstones was a small marble angel, that in no way resembled the naughty small boy it was intended to commemorate. This was Grandma's idea, of course, but it was Gran who kept fresh flowers on the green mound, starting with snowdrops in January and finishing with

Christmas roses in December. There they lay, side by side — the vicar and the vicar's wife, the delicate daughter who had died of consumption and the child. Martha's second husband, the village schoolmaster, lay beside his mother and Martha beside her father. Several generations of Blunts were laid to rest in a quiet corner, where Aunt Lucy had joined them. As for the Franklins of Marston Park, they had a tomb all to themselves. Even in death they were divided by the barriers of class and heredity. Though it must be acknowledged that His Lordship would probably have preferred to share that humble plot with Aunt Lucy!

It was something of a shock, that September morning, for Mark to be reminded of his parents in an airmail letter from the Congo. Scanning the monthly epistle quickly for anything of importance, he exclaimed, "Good Lord! The parents are returning! Dad's being retired early for health reasons. What does that mean exactly?" He frowned.

"Where will they live?" Midge asked.

"Not in the village, let us hope. Too close for comfort. Mother would start ordering our lives. She's very bossy, like Grandma. I just don't want them around, Midge, to be quite honest. It's different for you, at Russets. Your parents are not strangers. You have grown up together. It's impossible to feel any sort of attachment to parents you see only once in every five years."

"They probably thought this cottage would be just the place for their retirement. What was their reaction when you wrote and told them Gran had left it to you in her Will?"

"Mother didn't mention it, and she would be the one to object. Dad just goes along with her apparently. Perhaps it's the only way to live at peace with a dominant partner. Gran told me it was Mother who decided to return to the Congo, where she spent her childhood with her sister, Agnes. She had the pioneering spirit, and Dad admired her tremendously. So he left the bank and went off to London to live in lodgings for a year or so while he was training for the job at the Mission. Mother had some nursing and teaching experience. She was very keen, and rather clever, so Dad had to work hard to keep up with her after they were married. It must have been a sad day for Gran when her only son went off to the Congo for five years."

226

"I remember your Mother and your Aunt Agnes, coming to visit Aunt Lucy some years ago. I was still at school. I thought they were rather uppish."

Mark grinned. "They caught that from Grandma, and Grandma caught it from her Mamma. The Vicarage girls were a pretty uppish lot by all accounts."

"What happened to your Aunt Agnes? Did she marry?"

"Not to my knowledge. She has her own flat in London. A career woman, according to Gran. We exchange cards at Christmas, and she always encloses a cheque for me. It never varies, not since I was at Grammar School. You wouldn't exactly say we were a close family, would you?"

"Poor darling. Never mind, you share mine."

"Yes." Mark was a little doubtful of that privilege. It was good to be back on their own at the cottage, and they still spent Sundays at Russets. Both were more aware of the need to give and take and that a happy marriage had to be worked for. Midge was learning to keep the problems of the day to herself till after the evening meal. The weeks at Russets had not been wasted. She could cook the sort of nourishing meals they had always enjoyed, and she had discovered she had a light hand with pastry.

"Thanks, sweetheart, I enjoyed that," Mark would say. He would never make the same mistake as Dick. "I love you" came often and effortlessly from his lips. In so many ways, Tom and Carrie agreed, he was the right husband for Midge.

Saturday morning they did the shopping together in the village, like all the other young married couples, and Peter spent the afternoon at the cottage. Julian had bought him a second-hand bike, so he was learning independence, but Wendy insisted he got home before dark. It was a good place to rehearse, and Midge had always been an interested audience. Mark would be busy in the garden. It was a happy arrangement. Peter often wished he could live there. Russets was not the same place without Midge.

A second air-letter gave the last day of October as the arrival date. It was the first time that Mark's parents had flown from the Congo. They had always enjoyed the sea journey. It seemed to indicate that his father was needing urgent medical treatment. Their baggage would come later by sea.

"Whatever plans they have in mind they will obviously need to spend a week or two with us. They must have our room, darling," said Midge, who was not nearly so apprehensive as Mark about their homecoming and this sudden invasion of their privacy.

They went to the airport to meet them, and Mark was immediately contrite for feeling so reluctant when he saw how frail his father was looking.

"How are you, Dad?" he asked, kindly, as they shook hands.

"Exhausted!" his mother answered, impatiently. She pecked their cheeks. Her manner was brusque, and her voice held the quality that would irritate her young daughter-in-law, even more than the peck on the cheek — a cultured voice, a well-bred voice, accustomed to giving orders.

Mark was so like his father, Midge felt her throat contracting as she kissed him affectionately.

"Thank you, Midge," he smiled, and the smile was Mark's. They liked each other. "You haven't changed. I would have known you, even without my son in tow," he told her, but she was only a schoolgirl when they last met at Russets. Now she was a married woman.

"Time you dropped that ridiculous name. I shall call you Mary!" snapped Mark's mother.

"What shall I call your parents?" Midge had asked, as they set out for the airport.

Mark shrugged. "Mother and father, I suppose. Why not?"

But Midge knew already she could never call this self-important "lady" mother. They were poles apart, and could only tolerate each other for Mark's sake, and his father's sake. The war had not removed the barriers of class. They were still there, would always be there while people like Mark's mother existed, with that air of upper-class superiority.

"What are we waiting for?" she demanded when the formalities had been concluded. "Do you have a car, Mark?"

"No, Mother. Can't afford to run a car on a junior bank clerk's salary. We travel by train, or Shank's pony, don't we sweetheart?" He pinched her bottom and she tried not to giggle.

"Then we will take a taxi. We are not paupers," Harriet decided. "Come along, dear." And she took Philip's arm and led the way, leaving Mark and Midge to follow with the luggage. By the time they reached the taxi rank, she had already commandeered a cab.

"My husband is a sick man. He cannot stand about in a queue," she announced, importantly. Nobody argued, so they all climbed in. Now there was no avoiding that pertinent question.

"When did your grandmother change her Will?"

Mark seemed to shrink in stature as he searched for an answer. "I was not aware she had changed her Will." He was obviously puzzled.

"You must have known the cottage would be left to the next of kin?"

"It was never mentioned."

"Don't prevaricate, Mark. You knew we would not be here to contest the Will when your grandmother died. She was an old woman, and probably senile. It would be an easy matter to persuade her to alter the Will in your favour — deceptively easy," she added, meaningly.

It was Midge who answered, in defence of her darling, angry blue eyes challenging the older woman. "Gran knew exactly what she was doing to the end of her life. She was certainly not senile. If she did alter her Will, it must have been signed by two responsible witnesses, for it was perfectly legal, and nothing was disputed. She had every right to please herself. It was Mark who kept her company in her old age, Mark who nursed her when she was poorly and sat by her bedside when she was dying. He loved her dearly. As for deceit, he doesn't know the meaning of the word. Mark is the most honest person I have ever known!"

Philip opened his eyes to say, soothingly, "She is right, my dear. Say no more. Let it rest."

Surprisingly, and very gently, she patted his hand, and acquiesced. "We mustn't upset your father, Mark. He has angina," she told her son.

What's angina? Midge wondered. Was he going to die? After witnessing that brief moment of tenderness, Midge changed her opinion of Mark's mother. Harriet loved her husband, and that brusque manner hid a genuine anxiety for his health. It also hid a natural sadness in leaving the Mission that had been their home for so many years. The pioneering spirit that had urged her to forsake family and friends and a comfortable home in England for the hazards of a strange land and a strange people, now had to be quelled, and her own robust health and energy forced to comply with the immediate demands of an ailing husband. In her anxiety she overlooked the fact that scores of people, especially men, of a certain age, suffered with angina unknowingly, because it had never been diagnosed by a doctor. Now that he was spared the stress and strain of the Mission, Philip could live to be old and enjoy the intervening years, wherever Harriet decided to settle. During this short spell of relaxation at the cottage, his clever wife would have planned the next stage of their eventful lives. Indeed, her mind was already working on it as Philip slept for the rest of the cross-country journey in the hired car, and the lovely Autumn landscape of the Weald slipped past the window. She was holding Philip's hand in a warm clasp, so that he slept like a child in the surety of her loving care.

Watching her, still a little afraid of her, Mark wished they could have enjoyed a closer relationship. But it was too late. They would go their separate ways, live their separate lives, and never know the happy familiarity that Midge had enjoyed all her short life. They, too, were holding hands, in a young, marital relationship that had still to grow in understanding, generosity and unselfishness through the years to reach that state of mature devotion that Harriet and Philip obviously enjoyed.

With her active mind working on ways and means to earn a living – the small pension would not keep them both – Harriet had no fear of the future, and she would not allow doubt to cloud her vision. "Trust in the Lord and keep your powder dry" had been her unfailing recipe for a good life, since she first knew the meaning of service to the under-privileged, and the shining example of dedicated parents. Her own mother had left behind a loving family and a comfortable home to follow her husband, a Scot with the heart and soul of a true evangelist. Her own mother had known heartache and homesickness and the anxiety of rearing young children in a tropical climate, the anguish of parting with her only son, left behind in England for his formal education. Then the final parting when her husband died. Harriet remembered the traumatic experience of that long journey home, with her sister Agnes, and her sorrowing mother, who seemed to have lost the will to live, so strong was the personality of that zealous Scot, and so trusting her dependence on him. If early environment is the main influence in the pattern of our adult lives, then it must have been responsible for young Harriet's determination to follow in the footsteps of the father she adored. But she had chosen a partner totally unsuited to the missionary field, the climate and the culture and customs of the native population. It was not her fault, but her misfortune that she had to shoulder the burden and responsibility, the discipline and duties normally taken on by a man. Harriet was her father's daughter and she walked in his shadow, automatically acquiring his strength of character and his dedication, while Philip tried desperately, but fruitlessly, to emulate such dedication. The doctor's diagnosis of a weak heart had finally released him from the unbearable position of a square peg in a round hole.

Now they were home for good, and he slept undisturbed by conscience, at peace with himself and Harriet.

Sheba and Ginger were there to greet them as soon as Mark put the key in the lock. They must have wondered what was happening, for they had never been left alone for so many hours. Mark had banked up the fire in the sitting-room and fixed the fire-guard. Midge had left food and water in the kitchen, but they had wandered about restlessly, searching for a clue to this unexplained desertion, then finally settled down in their accustomed place on the hearthrug. Sheba twitched nervously in her sleep, but Ginger did not suffer from nerves, and his independent spirit found pleasure in chasing the mice in his feline dreams.

When four people instead of two entered the cottage, both animals hesitated for a moment, but soon recognised their owners. Sheba licked Midge's hand, and Ginger rubbed himself on Mark's trouser-legs.

"Quite an affectionate demonstration," Harriet observed as she pulled off her hat and gloves. Philip was drawn like a magnet to the fire, and Mark soon had it flaming up the chimney, with the old trick of holding up a newspaper. From a pile in the shed, he carried in an armful of small logs, and the sweet smell of applewood scented the room.

"This is very pleasant, my dear, is it not?" said his father, gratefully.

"Very pleasant," Harriet agreed, peeling off his overcoat and scarf, as though he were a small boy. Mark took them from her, then helped her to remove her own coat — the same old Harris tweed he noticed. Midge was already in the kitchen, putting on the kettle for tea.

"Midge has put you in the front room, Mother. I'll take up your bags," Mark was saying, helpfully.

"Thank you." Harriet followed her son upstairs, her throat tight with tears. It was all so strange, but she mustn't cry. She never cried.

She stood looking out of the window until she had composed herself. There was a faint smell of lavender from the open drawers, reminiscent of her mother-in-law. The last time they were here she had been sleeping in this bed, and busy as a bee with her early morning chores. She had wanted to serve their breakfast in bed, but they would not allow it.

"Just a cup of tea and a biscuit, eh love?" she had pleaded.

That word "love" must be typical of the working class. It was silly to be so touchy. "The salt of the earth, Harriet," her father would have reminded her. It was true. Philip's mother was a very nice, homely little woman, with a surprising reputation, for all her homeliness. Philip had been born "out of wedlock". Martha had been teaching the Infants at the village school, and only poor substitutes had been found to replace her. Aided and abetted by the Headmaster, Martha was reinstated, to the huge delight of the Infants. All went well until the child's bullying father arrived home from India with his regiment and insisted on making an honest woman of Martha. They left the village and for several years poor Martha endured her husband's violent temper and bitter jealousy, for Philip was the innocent go-between, and his mother's darling. Nobody seemed to be quite certain how, or when, the sergeant met his death, but Martha and Philip arrived back, and two years later she married the schoolmaster. He seemed to have been a thoroughly satisfactory step-father, and Philip passed the entrance examination to the Grammar School at Tonbridge.

Now Martha was dead, and Philip had not yet mentioned her. He was becoming very introspective lately. Tonight, in this big, old-fashioned bed, he would have a little weep, and she would comfort him.

When she turned away from the window and the memories of yesteryear, her son asked, anxiously, "Are you feeling all right, Mother?"

"Perfectly all right. Thank you, Mark." Was he deceived by her brave smile? Did it matter?

Was it coincidence, or part of the pattern of their adventurous lives, that Peter should mention, on his Saturday visit to the cottage, that their matron at The Firs was leaving to be married, and emigrating to Australia.

"She's smashing. She lets us read our comics in bed till lights out," he told them.

"Oh, Pete, you're priceless!" Midge giggled, as she spread butter on another crust to eat with his afternoon cup of tea, because he had to leave for home by 4 o'clock now the evenings were drawing in. Peter was very conservative in his habits, and always looked for a buttered crust when he arrived home for the weekend because it reminded him of Aunt Lucy.

Aunt Harriet — as he had been instructed to call this rather formidable lady — put a hand on his shoulder and asked, "Who is coming to replace the Matron?"

"I don't know."

"When is she leaving?"

"Next week. We made a collection to buy her a wedding present. Every boy in the school gave sixpence, and the head boy presented it. She was thrilled."

"What did the boys buy her?"

"A set of carvers, *real* silver. It was super."

"Let us hope she will have something to carve in Australia," Harriet commented, with dry humour.

"There's always mutton, isn't there, with all those thousands of sheep?" Peter answered promptly.

"I see you have been paying attention to your Geography lessons," said Harriet, conversationally.

233

Peter frowned. "I hate Geography. I saw it on television. If I hadn't already decided to be an actor, I would be a sheep farmer in Australia."

"Sheep farming might be a better proposition. The acting profession is so precarious and so competitive. What does your mother have to say about it?"

"She doesn't like it."

"I am not surprised."

"But I have to do it. Don't you see? It's really the only thing I care about, and I'm quite good."

"He's *very* good," Midge interrupted, defensively. "Peter has been playing the lead in the Christmas pantomime at the Theatre Royal, Tunbridge Wells, for the past three years, and this year he is playing Buttons in 'Cinderella'."

"Buttons? Rather a young Buttons. What age is Cinderella?"

"Fifteen."

"I see. Obviously a juvenile cast and an amateur production."

"The rest of the cast are quite old. The ugly sisters must be forty, I should say, and Lennie, the comedian, older than the ugly sisters, only he is so funny, you don't think about his age when he is on the stage. He's the funniest man I have ever met."

"Really?" Harriet had only half her mind on this boring subject, the other half was already exploring the possibility of that vacant post for a Matron at The Firs.

"Peter has to sing two duets with Cinderella. They have been specially written for them," Midge persisted. She thought he was not being properly appreciated by her mother-in-law, and she was probably right.

Harriet remembered the boring hours she had to sit through, with her sister, Agnes, in the Village Hall, where they occupied front seats and could not escape until after the Grand Finale when everyone assembled on stage to join in the National Anthem. There was the middle-aged spinster, warbling "Where are you going to, my pretty maid?" – the elderly baritone "On the Road to Mandalay" yet again! – the music teacher's favourite star pupil struggling through "In a Monastery Garden" – and the same rendering of "Gray's

Elegy" by the same girl. It was not surprising only half her mind listened to Peter and Midge on that Saturday afternoon.

As soon as the boy had left for home, she excused herself and went upstairs to write a letter of application to the Headmaster of The Firs Preparatory School. She wrote fluently and concisely, mentioning earlier connections with the school. Her mother had held the post of matron during the War years, and her two young sons had started their education there. He would probably remember the tragic death of the younger boy when the school was evacuated. She walked down the lane to the postbox, feeling optimistic about her chances. Surely it could not be mere coincidence. It *must* be an answer to prayer. "God helps those who help themselves" was another of her trusty maxims.

When she had dropped the letter in the box, she strode purposefully back to the cottage. Midge had laid the tea in the sitting-room. There was Philip's favourite Gentleman's Relish, Carrie's strawberry jam and a fruit cake Midge had baked. Mark was on his knees, toasting bread. She stood in the doorway, her face glowing from the biting wind, and exclaimed, gratefully, "This is very nice. Thank you, Midge."

"You're welcome!" Midge answered pertly.

Another working-class expression, much abused, thought Harriet.

She had remembered to mention the telephone number of the cottage in her application, so when the phone rang, early Tuesday morning, she hurried to answer it, in eager anticipation. Mark had left for the station, escorted by Midge and Sheba, and she had given Philip his breakfast in bed to conserve his strength. She had not told him she had applied for the job, because he would start to worry. Time enough to disturb this quiet interlude − for it *was* only an interlude − when something definite had been arranged.

The pleasant, cultured voice, apologising for the early call, was music in her ears.

"I wanted to make sure of you, before you had another offer," said he. "My wife and I have already decided you would be most suitable, but of course you have to see the place before making up your mind. How soon could you come to talk it over with us, and have a look round? ...

Today? . . . That's splendid! Hang on a minute. I will look up the trains."

Harriet took a deep breath and closed her eyes. "Thank you," was all she said, but He would understand.

Then that pleasant, cultured voice was back on the line. "There's a train at ten-fifteen. You change at Tonbridge, and you shouldn't have long to wait for a connection to Tunbridge Wells. Take a cab, and charge it up to us. You should be here in time for lunch. By the way, as a matter of interest, how did you hear about the vacancy?"

"One of your pupils — Peter Franklin — was here on Saturday afternoon, and happened to mention the Matron was leaving."

"So it was young Franklin. A bright lad in some respects, but not exactly a star pupil!" He chuckled. "Franklin has a one track mind — the stage! Mind you, he's good. In fact, he's remarkably good. The talent is there, and the personality. Did he tell you he is playing Buttons in this year's pantomime at the Theatre Royal?"

"He did."

"The youngest Buttons on record, I understand. We are naturally proud of him, stealing the part from more than a hundred applicants. If I hadn't been told that his father was an Army officer, killed in the War before Peter was born, I would have sworn that boy had show-business blood in his veins. It's just a fluke, apparently. Children are quite extraordinary. You never know what they are capable of doing. We are constantly surprised, my wife and I."

Harriet liked the way he referred to his wife as a working partner, taking her share of the responsibility. It was something she had never enjoyed.

"Would the accommodation be suitable for a married couple?" she asked, tentatively.

"We can soon make it suitable. It's a big house, and there's an annexe. No worries on that score. See you later, then. Goodbye for now."

"Goodbye, and thank you."

"My pleasure."

The line went dead. It was as good as settled, and she knew it was the right job for her. But how would Philip react to another move so soon? She knew if they stayed here for more than another week, he would not want to move at all. Mark and Midge had made them feel at home, but it was an illusion. They had no home. *Somebody* had to make an effort. He was already enjoying the traditional English breakfast of bacon and eggs, toast and marmalade, but she was not yet acclimatised, and ate sparingly of the big meals that Midge provided.

Philip was reading the *Daily Telegraph*, but he put it down, removed his spectacles, and smiled disarmingly.

"Who was that you were talking to? Anyone I know?" he asked.

"Yes, the Headmaster at The Firs."

"Poor little Mattie, he never liked it there, did he?"

"There was no alternative, dear, and he did have Mark."

"He was just a baby."

"He was six. In another five years he would have been eleven, and Mark thirteen. They both would have missed all those formative years at a preparatory school." They had been over and over it so many times. "If only" brought heartache and regret.

"He would be seventeen now, wouldn't he?"

"On the fifth of November, Bonfire Night. When he was very small, he thought all the bonfires and fireworks were specially for him, to celebrate his birthday."

"So he did. Funny little fellow ... Why did he have to die?"

Harriet sighed. "It was God's will."

"So you said, my dear, but I fail to understand why He should bless us with a lovely child only to take him away, seven years later? That, to me, is one of the unanswerable questions, but then, I haven't your faith." He shook his head sadly. "I've been a great disappointment to you, haven't I?"

"NO!"

"No?" He took her hand and raised it to his lips. She loved the way he kissed her hand. Yet where had he learned such a charming gesture, such old-world courtesy? Not from that practical little working-class mother, or that brutal father, nor yet the intellectual schoolmaster with his head buried in books. Philip was one of Nature's gentlemen, her father would say. It was true.

"I have to make a journey back in time today, my dearest. There is a vacancy for a Matron at The Firs, and I have applied," she told him, gently.

"Must you?" he asked, with a sigh of resignation.

"Yes, I must. We can't stay here. It doesn't belong to us, and we haven't much money. I prayed about it, and the answer was so prompt and so obvious, it just has to be right for us."

"If you say so, my dear. I'll tag along. What do I do while you are chasing all those small boys to wash behind their ears?"

"Don't worry. We shall find a job for you."

"Would you like me to come along with you today? Moral support?"

"No thank you, Philip. I shall be all right."

"In that case, I'll get started on the crossword."

"Yes, you do that, and we will finish it this evening."

"I might take a walk with Midge and that nice dog this afternoon."

"Wrap up well. It's a cold wind."

"I should rather like a dog, Harriet. It would be company for me whan you are busy."

"Perhaps we should wait until we get there. One step at a time, don't you think?"

"I won't argue with that."

They exchanged a kiss. Philip put on his spectacles and spread out the paper.

"God bless you," she said.

"God bless you," he echoed.

It was a pleasant journey on the branch line through the lovely Weald. Travelling by train was so much more enjoyable than car travel. The past decade had seen more and more people with cars, according to the chatty little driver of the station cab, "but it weren't a patch on the train". There were still country lanes, however, that led to quiet villages where life went on in much the same way as before the war – the village school, the small shops, Sunday School treats, Women's Institute, Working Men's Club, hay-making and harvest. Two main differences had taken effect since the War. There were no "Hoppers' Specials" from London Bridge

Station, and no servants for the gentry. Big estates had been carved up into small plots of land by property dealers with big bulldozers. The gentry had retired to small bungalows in Bournemouth, Worthing and Frinton-on-Sea. Marston Park was hardly recognisable as the ancestral home of the Franklins, with its classrooms and dormitories, bare floors and uncurtained windows. The servants' hall echoed to the voices of children at morning assembly, and the servants' bedrooms, with washbasins and hot running water, were occupied by the teaching Sisters. Bicycles had replaced the horses, but washing still hung in the stable yard.

Russets still provided all the milk, eggs, butter and boiling fowls. Marston Park was their best customer. But for Harriet, on that mellow Autumn morning, it was not the past but the future that occupied her thoughts, as the unchanged vista of fields and woods slipped past the window. It was only when they drove across the Common in the hired cab that she recalled a similar Autumn day, when they had left Mark and Matthew at the school. Small boys still swarmed about the place. A junior football team kicked the ball around the playing-field with tremendous enthusiasm. Any one of them could have been Mattie. Tears pricked her eyes, but she blinked them away impatiently. This was no time for tears. It could be the start of a new chapter.

The Head's wife opened the door to her. Only her hair had faded. The boys kept her young. She smiled a welcome and they shook hands.

"Just in time for lunch," she said, and led the way to the study. The Head was balding, but the frank, boyish features were the same as his RAF crew of "Hurricane Charlie" would have recognised.

Harriet's hand was warmly clasped, while he studied her face intently. Then he shook his head. "I must confess, I don't remember you," said he.

"I do," his wife interrupted. "It's part of my job to remember the mothers," she laughed.

"My wife's fantastic memory has saved many an embarrassing situation," he told Harriet.

"Not really, when you switch on the charm!" she teased, affectionately.

"Spare my blushes, darling. Our prospective Matron will be wondering whether she likes us. Do sit down." He indicated a comfortable chair. The sadness in Harriet's eyes was reflected in her quiet voice.

"I liked you both that day, and I haven't changed my opinion."

"Thank you, my dear. That was generous of you, considering what happened later," the Head replied, and added, "We only saw you and your husband once. It's your mother I remember, of course, because she was Matron here at that time, and my wife handed the boys over to her after you had left. In a way, it was nice for the boys to have a grandmother actually on the premises, but it must have been a little confusing to be kissed goodnight, in her private apartment, and probably reprimanded for not cleaning their teeth half an hour later!"

Harriet agreed, and her mouth twitched in response to that dry humour. It had been confusing, especially for Mattie, who was Grandma's pet. "Nobody could have foreseen the tragedy, and nobody was to blame," she told them.

"We were devastated. Matthew was our youngest boarder. We normally take them at eight, but since he had an older brother, and his grandmother to keep an eye on him, we accepted the responsibility. It was absolutely shattering to discover we had failed in our duty."

The two women exchanged a sympathetic glance, but there was no time for further reminiscence. A light tap on the door announced the arrival of the lunch trolley, and a young kitchen maid, blushing importantly.

"Cook says to tell you, Ma'am, the milkman never left no cream for the apple pie!" she explained.

"Then we shall have to manage without it, shan't we, Penny, since we don't care for custard?" her mistress answered, as she helped the girl to transfer the hot dishes to the table. "It's bound to be an excellent apple pie, even without the cream, isn't it, Penny?"

The Head was pulling out chairs. Harriet realised she was hungry after the journey and only one slice of toast for breakfast.

"Cook do make the lightest pastry I ever tasted, Sir. She's going to teach me when she 'as time."

"Splendid! One of these days you will make some lucky chap a very good wife."

"There's only one young chap I fancy to marry, Sir, and that's Angus McPherson, what delivers the meat."

"And a very good choice, if I may say so." And he held open the door while she pushed out the empty trolley. "The salt of the earth," he told Harriet. "We are lucky with our staff, aren't we, darling?"

"Very lucky indeed, when you consider our friends have to make do with a daily help these days. Very superior ladies. One would hesitate to ask them to do anything more than hoovering. It's the post-War attitude to domestic service. One can't blame them; for so many it was just plain drudgery. They were earning good wages in factories during the War, and had their evenings and weekends free. Some of the younger ones joined the forces and travelled overseas. They enjoyed a way of life they had hardly envisaged, and would never go back to domestic service. We were only middle class, but my parents employed a cook, a housemaid, a washer-woman and a gardener pre-war. During and after the War, Mother did the lot, and Dad dug up the lawn and planted a vegetable garden."

"What were you doing before all this happened?" asked Harriet, with a sweeping gesture.

"In the WAAFs." She smiled at her husband.

"It was love at first sight. A most romantic affair!" he teased.

"So it was, my darling," she agreed, complacently, as she served the Irish stew. Here was a real partnership that would stand the test of time, Harriet was thinking. They shared not only responsibility, but an attitude of mind, a sense of humour, and that indefinable quality of personality.

"My wife will show you round after lunch. We have given Debbie, our young Matron, the day off to go shopping with her sister, to buy suitable clothes for Australia," the Head was saying as he held up his plate for a second helping of apple pie. "Then we will share a pot of tea and I will run you back to the station," he added.

But Harriet knew there was really no need for a tour of inspection. Their future was here, with these two charming people.

241

Only the annexe had been added since the War. The rest of the big, rambling house was comfortably shabby, with a homely atmosphere. A stout, grey-haired woman was changing beds in one of the dormitories. She held up a comic she had found under a pillow.

"This gives the game away proper, don't it?" she chuckled. "They are going to miss young Debbie. Can't see another Matron allowing them poor little blighters to read their comics in bed."

"You are letting me down, Mrs Bailey, just when I was trying to impress our prospective new Matron!" The Head's wife teased.

Mrs Bailey clamped a hand over her mouth. "Isn't that just like me to put my foot in it!"

But Harriet was smiling. "Actually, I do know about the comics being allowed till lights out, from Peter Franklin, and I certainly won't forbid it, for it seems harmless enough," she said.

"You know young Peter?"

"I have known the family for years. My sister and I hung around that old farmhouse for hours when we first arrived in England from the Congo. There was a dear woman everyone called Aunt Lucy, and we loved to sit in her warm kitchen – we were so cold and miserable. She gave us hot cocoa and home-made gingerbread for our elevenses, and she made us feel at home when she let us have all the trimmings from the pies she was making for pastry men, with currants for eyes and noses. We were also allowed to help on the farm. I remember the smell of the pig food boiling in the old copper, and the taste of the hot mash they fed to the chickens. We collected eggs and groomed the mare that pulled the milk float. I have always remembered those happy days at Russets before we were sent away to boarding school." Harriet had almost forgotten they were on a tour of inspection, she got so carried away with her early memories, but it paved the way for a good relationship with the domestic staff, for Mrs Bailey would report to cook that the new Matron was OK, and if you were OK with Mrs B, you could expect a fair deal.

"That young Peter is going on the stage, and so he should, for he's a born actor. You should have seen him climbing up that beanstalk in 'Jack and the Beanstalk'. We was all holding our breath in case he would fall." Mrs B was a good soul, but she liked a gossip, and welcomed any interruption in the monotony of changing beds. Her mistress hid her impatience, for Mrs B was one of the pre-war "treasures" who had started at the bottom of the ladder in the servants' hierarchy, in a titled family, and worked up to the coveted post of Housekeeper. She never tired of telling her tales of the "good old days" because, in her opinion, they were good.

"Everyone knew where they belonged. They knew their place. You did as you were told. You worked hard, but you fed well and had a free Sunday once a month. Who could complain about that?" Mrs B would demand of anyone who had the time to listen. It was just another version of what some would call "slavery" but for a child of thirteen, from a big family with too many mouths to feed on a father's weekly wage of twelve shillings and sixpence, it was another world, where she tasted roast beef, Christmas pudding and mince pies for the first time in her young life. Sharing a bed with the third housemaid was no hardship when they slept four in a bed at home!

If she started on one of these oft-repeated tales, however, they would never get round the house, and Harriet had to catch her train.

"Nearly time for another cup of tea, Mrs Bailey," her mistress reminded her, and they went on their way.

"I'm glad you met her, Harriet — we may call you Harriet when we are off duty?" she asked.

"Of course."

"Mrs B can be a good friend or a bad enemy. Climbing the ladder from fourth housemaid to Housekeeper was a real achievement, and she is quite justified in being proud of the fact. It was not a pension she achieved after twenty years of honest and dedicated service, but RESPECT. It meant more to her, as she will tell you in due course, than all the tea in China."

"I understand," said Harriet, quickly. It was just another lesson in diplomacy, and she had had lots of practice in the Congo!

In one of the classrooms, a murmur of voices could be

heard reciting a scene from Shakespeare, and in another room a science master was putting across some theory of his own on sound waves, and the amazing possibilities of using satellites. The two women stood for a moment listening to the eager young voice. He was certainly holding the attention of his listeners, for there was no other sound but this one voice.

"Those are the senior boys aged between eleven and thirteen. They need something interesting and stimulating to hold their attention, and we allow our young masters a lot of rope on their own particular hobby horse," the Head's wife explained, as they moved away. "Science can be quite absorbing to the modern boy, and probably some of the girls, but we have had no experience in teaching girls. We have always preferred boys, my husband and I. They seem to have a natural tendency to keep their minds on what they are doing, whether in work or play. Even the youngest boy in that playing field will have no thought in his head but scoring a goal for his side, and when the game is over, no thought in his head but the high tea, and whether it will be his favourite beans on toast or macaroni cheese! It's true, Harriet. You will soon discover it for yourself, if you haven't done so already with your own two boys, before you left them with us."

"I see what you mean, though I hadn't thought of it with such a clear perception. You must be right, of course, and girls do tend to clutter their minds, don't they? That time I was speaking of, when we first came home from the Congo, my sister and I were torn apart by our emotions, by the longing to put back the clock, and recover what we had lost, the fear of the unknown, and trivial little things, like whether to tell Grandma you had said a swear word, torn a petticoat or forgotten to say 'thank you' to Aunt Lucy. Being the wife and widow of a clergyman, she had such high standards. I was the worst offender, and so confused with it all, and so fearful of that impending boarding school. I hated it even before I set foot in the place, and went on hating it for another seven years!"

"Poor you, what a shame to make such a bogey of it when it can be so enjoyable. I loved it, and wept when I left, but I was lucky to be good at games. Nobody seemed to notice I was such a duffer at Maths if I could save the honour of the

244

school on the playing field. Silly, isn't it? I captained the hockey and netball teams for three successive years, won the trophy for swimming and archery, and ran a mile in record time. It was just a fluke, like Peter Franklin. I was their star performer! It went to my head, not surprisingly, but I soon came down to earth when I joined the WAAFs. It didn't take me long to discover there are other things in life more worth fighting for than a silver trophy."

They had reached the dining-room on their tour of the house, where the eight to ten-year-olds would be enjoying that high tea in less than an hour. Seniors had tea at five and supper at eight. The majority were healthy youngsters, with healthy appetites. The few who were finicky eaters were soon shamed by the rest.

"Children soon conform. They don't really want to be different from their fellows."

Harriet was not sure that she agreed on this point of view. Did they expect to turn out a sort of model, that could be recognised as a scholar from The Firs Preparatory School? she asked.

"Good heavens, no! Whatever gave you that idea? We do encourage team spirit, but we also encourage individual talent and ability. Several of our boys have gone on to the London School of Music, and I wouldn't be surprised to see Peter Franklin winning a scholarship to RADA. Only about fifty per cent of the boys go on to public school, the rest to grammar school, depending on the circumstances of the parents, and the preferences of the boys themselves. We demand, and get, very high standards in our teaching staff. That young science master you heard is a Cambridge BA. He also teaches Maths, French and German."

"Goodness, I'm beginning to feel quite inadequate!"

"Don't worry, my dear, for you and me it's just a matter of keeping their bodies healthy. We will leave the men to cope with their brains!"

"Now, come and have a look at your private apartment and tell me if you like it. It's in the annexe, so when you are off duty, you won't be disturbed. Don't take any notice of the muddle. Debbie is packing. Incidentally, my husband and I deal with any emergency at night, and your weekends are free

245

from mid-day Saturday. The masters take turns to escort the boys to church, Sunday morning. Only the younger boys walk in a crocodile, the rest walk as they please, but it's one of the rules that every boy attends church every Sunday during term. Catholics attend their own church with the music master, who is a Polish Catholic and an ex-fighter pilot. We are a very mixed bunch of boys and masters from a number of countries and backgrounds, including India, Africa, Egypt, Ceylon and Malta. So you see, there is no danger of turning out a recognisable type. Every boy is an individual, and treated as such."

"It's interesting. I had no idea you were so international."

"Since the war. All our coloured boys go on to public school and university. So they should be quite useful citizens back in their own country. We keep in touch."

"That must mean a lot of work, answering all the letters?"

"It does. We do have a part-time secretary from outside, but she has a crippled husband, and can't always get here."

Harriet looked thoughtful, and after she had admired the very pleasant sitting-room, bedroom, kitchenette and bathroom, she asked, eagerly, "Would there be a job for my husband? He did have a secretarial course in his younger days, and he was a bank clerk before we were married. But perhaps you would not care to suggest it to your present secretary. She may need the job and the salary?"

"Actually, I think the poor woman might be quite relieved to hand it over. She does seem rather harassed, and her husband does get a good disability pension. It's an idea, Harriet. We will work on it."

"Thank you."

"Then you *will* come?"

"I should love to come."

"It's such a relief to get it settled before Debbie leaves. A good matron is top priority in a prep school. Debbie has been having her main meal in the dining-room, and cooking her own breakfast and supper. How would that suit you and your husband?"

"Perfectly. Thank you."

"We have two other married couples. Cook's husband is the gardener. They have a couple of rooms and a bathroom in

246

the basement. Mrs Bailey and her husband have the attic flat. He is the odd-job man about the place. She married the butler on that big estate, and a most useful person he turned out to be. There is no job he won't tackle. Now we shall have you and your husband. We are really most fortunate. Look, Harriet, there is a view of the Common from this window, and the seat where your mother used to sit and talk to the Professor when she was off duty. Wasn't that a happy arrangement for two lonely people?"

"It was indeed. It was Mother's third marriage, but it seems to have worked out quite well. I hear every week. She has learned to speak German and to make apple strudel. She says she is a typical Austrian house-frau, but I find that difficult to believe, since she always had servants to do all her work in both her former marriages. What *did* surprise me, though, was that she was prepared to risk another marriage, for the second was an absolute fiasco. The man had some kind of shady business that finally went bankrupt, and he disappeared. Everything was sold to pay off the creditors, and Mother had to get a job, a living-in job, when she was no longer a young woman."

"Yes, she was a good matron, but a fundamentally sad person, which is not surprising now that I know what she had been through before she came to us. Our Professor was a dear soul. He had lost his entire family under the Nazi regime. They must have comforted each other, mustn't they? But what a small world it is, Harriet. Who would have predicted that you would turn up here, a decade or so later?"

"It was God's will. It was not pure chance. I prayed about it."

"Bless you. Such faith deserves to be rewarded, and I am going to see that you are! Come along, time for a cup of tea. We are great tea drinkers, my husband and I."

"What's the new Matron like?" Julian asked Peter, the following weekend.

"OK. She lets us read our comics in bed till lights out, but she's a bit bossy."

"By bossy I take it you have to do as you are told?"

"Well, yes."

247

"Your smashing young Matron was probably a bit too lenient."

"What's lenient?"

"Why do you suppose I gave you my old dictionary?"

Peter grinned.

"Look it up, Pete. It's the only way to learn."

"OK. Can I ask you a favour?"

"Fire away."

"Do you think I might have another shilling a week pocket-money?"

"Can't afford it. Sorry."

"I just wondered."

"When I was your age, I had to make do with sixpence, and you are already getting half-a-crown."

"That was a long time ago, wasn't it? Everything has gone up in price since you were my age."

"That's true. What was it you had in mind, I mean, to buy with the extra bob?"

"Make-up."

"Make-up?"

"To use when I go to see Midge, then she can see how I look on the stage."

"The authentic Buttons, eh?"

"Yes."

"Couldn't you borrow some from Midge?"

"She doesn't use make-up."

"Nor does she. I'd forgotten. Our Midge is just as Mother Nature made her, and who could improve on that?"

"I like Midge."

"So do I, Pete. Next to your Mother, she's my favourite girl."

"Midge never gets bored with my acting."

"Do other people get bored?"

"The family do, especially Mum. I wish I could make her understand how terribly important it is, but she won't listen."

"She won't listen to me, either. I have tried."

"Why shouldn't acting be considered a proper career? It's a profession, after all, isn't it? Look at Laurence Olivier and John Gielgud and Roy Masters."

"That's a new one on me?"

"He's super. He's playing Shylock in 'The Merchant of Venice' at the Theatre Royal this week. The Head took six of us to see it on Wednesday afternoon, this week. It was smashing."

"Is that what you are aiming for, to be a Shakespearean actor?"

"Yes."

"Well, I suppose you could call that a profession. There might come a day when your Mother might actually feel proud to see her son on the stage. She's prejudiced, Pete. She thinks show business is just a lot of hooey."

"What's prejudice? – all right, I'll look it up! Mum was in show business during the war, wasn't she?"

"She was."

"Lennie says she was a darn good trouper."

"Did he meet your Mother?"

"He was the comedian in the same touring company."

"You seem to think a lot of this Lennie?"

"He's smashing. There isn't a lot of time at rehearsals, but I'll find out more about that touring company. It wasn't ENSA, and they weren't engaged by Basil Dean. It was a very small company. Only four, including Mum, who played the piano."

"Hasn't Lennie told you the names of the other two people in the company?" (As if he didn't know!)

"Not yet. I'll ask him when there's time. I like Lennie. He's my best friend now. Don't tell Mum. She says she doesn't wish to be reminded of those days. You would think it was something to be ashamed of, wouldn't you, but Lennie says they were every bit as good as ENSA, only they didn't get the publicity, because they were off the beaten track, entertaining small units in isolated Army and RAF bases and in factory canteens. It was their own contribution to the war effort." Peter was quoting Lennie. One of these days he would be quoting Nigel Bannister – his own father! One of these days his poor darling would have to tell the boy the truth. The net was closing in, and Peter was no fool. His natural curiosity concerning the wartime concert party must eventually disclose what Wendy had been trying to hide for so long. And Bannister had every right to interfere in his son's future if that future was being jeopardised by an unimaginative mother. Any father would be proud of this boy, Julian was thinking. If only ... if only ... but why disturb their close relationship in wishful thinking? It was too late.

"I'll be getting along to the cottage now, to see Midge," Peter was saying, as he swung a leg over the saddle and tinkled the bell.

"About that extra bob. I think I could manage it," his step-father told him, quietly.

"You can? Gosh, that's super! Thanks a lot." Then he was gone.

Julian's eyes were wistful as they followed the boy on his bike. Leaning heavily on his two sticks, he remembered his own happy boyhood here, at Russets, and saw himself racing off, head bent over the handlebars, pedalling furiously right up to the time he joined the RAF.

One morning, en route to the station to catch an early train to Tonbridge for Grammar School, taking a short cut across the park, he was accosted by a beautiful girl on a beautiful horse.

"You're trespassing," she told him, haughtily.

He laughed, and flew past. What did he care about that spoilt little bitch, anyway? *Diane Maloney* — that was her name. "Too much money and no breeding". That was the general opinion in the village, of the man who had bought Marston Park and his stuck-up daughter. They had a name for such people — THE NEW RICH. They had to bring their servants down from London, a mixed bunch of refugees from Europe, who were homesick and miserable, and soon began to drift back to London. But his latent senses had been aroused, at seventeen, by that vision of beauty, like an oil painting framed in a vista of trees. He had been equally attracted to the horse — a *real* beauty, like the one his Grandfather used to ride. Grandfather had a title and Aunt Lucy always referred to him as "His Lordship". It was one of his proudest moments, as a small boy, to be swung into the saddle, and to ride with him across the park and round the estate, sitting very straight and upright, with Grandfather, on the big stallion.

But a whole decade had passed, and there had been many

changes at Marston Park. At seventeen he had only one absorbing ambition − to join the RAF. With his head in the clouds, gazing skywards, Aunt Lucy would remind him, "One of these days you are going to walk straight into that lake, my lad!" She was afraid for him, her youngest, and perhaps the most dearly loved of all her boys.

Quite suddenly, and surprisingly, he found himself thinking not of aeroplanes but a girl in a green riding habit, and the fury in her flashing eyes as he flew past. What did she expect? That he would touch his forelock, like a country yokel? That he would raise his cap? That he would apologise for trespassing? Not a hope in hell! Wasn't he the grandson of a *gentleman*? Wasn't he entitled to ride across the park, now and when he chose? If he had a horse, he could match her for horsemanship, because Grandfather Franklin had given him a spirited Welsh pony at the age of seven or thereabouts. Since he had to make do with a bike, he could show her a thing or two. But he was disturbed by her image, and by the newly awakened sensuality in his young, virile body.

Even now, as he stood there, leaning heavily on his two sticks, his back aching intolerably, his legs barely functioning after years of massage and therapy, he could feel his heart beating faster under his thick, woolly jersey, and a faint reminder of that first awareness of the opposite sex, and a challenge to his budding manhood. But it was not all on his side, the curiosity, and the remembrance of a boy's mockery and defiance. It was a novelty for Diane Maloney to meet a boy on a bike, who had the arrogance of the upper class. Was he upper class? He had come from the direction of Russets, and the Blunts were a farming family, one of several families who had inherited their farms and their land from the last of the Franklins. Her father, a self-made man of Irish-American descent, a wealthy industrialist, with the good sense to recognise the potentials of steel in a pending war, had reflected, "That guy must have been off his rocker. *Giving away land* as if it was some kind of sweepstake!" And Diane agreed.

She had recently finished an expensive education in France. Now she was bored, and looking for a new attraction. The big house came to life at weekends, when she brought her friends

251

down from London, especially her German boy-friend Carl. They drove fast cars, made love, drank cocktails and swam naked in the heated swimming pool her father had installed in the basement. Sex-appeal was an absorbing passion, and she had recognised it also in the good-looking intruder on her father's estate. So when he was invited to a late-night party at Marston Park, young Julian Franklin put on his best suit and school tie, and went like a lamb to the slaughter.

Diane was dancing cheek to cheek with a tall, blond youth in a silk shirt, open to the waist, and tight-fitting red trousers. It seemed to be a kind of uniform, for all the boys were similarly dressed in coloured trousers and silk shirts. Julian felt very foolish, and was just about to slip away, when Diane spotted him, whispered something to her frowning and frustrated partner, and darted across the room to the rescue of the new arrival.

"Come and dance!" said she, authoritatively. "And don't look so worried. Mother and Dad don't mind. They stay in London when I have a party."

Diane laughed. She always seemed to be laughing. Life was fun. Life was a game you played, using people as pawns. She thought it would be fun to see her two suitors fight over her. And what better place than in the pool? Julian remembered how her body drew him like a magnet through the warm, green water. Swimming under water, he shot up under her floating body, and she screamed with pretended fright. It was only pretence because she had seen him dive, and knew exactly what he intended. It was an old trick that Carl often practised. And she had not been mistaken. Julian Franklin's lean, virile body was a good match for Carl.

Wet and slippery, they clung together, breast to breast, stomach to stomach, legs and arms entwined. Was it only for a few brief, ecstatic moments, or an eternity that they clung together? Memory was teasing him again, and the scene had a dreamlike quality. If he closed his eyes, he could see their wet, shining bodies emerging from the depths of the pool, but he could not feel the sensuality. That was gone for ever.

It was not the first time he had tried to recapture some of the exquisite torture of that traumatic experience, and only

252

succeeded in being more aware of his aching back and crippled legs.

The fight that followed was real enough, as he dropped Diane and grappled with the furious attack of the enraged Carl. It must have been quite an interesting spectacle. It was a good fight, he remembered, but he was beaten, bashed and bruised, by flaying fists and feet. Diane watched, and winced as her latest conquest was flung out of the pool and lay sprawled on the tiles, panting and breathless. Snatching up his clothes, he disappeared up the stairs to a chorus of catcalls.

Had it really happened in such a dramatic fashion? And how did he reach home? And what did Aunt Lucy have to say about such "shocking goings on"? The climax to that extraordinary night had been lost in the mists of time! But he still had a small white scar over his left eye.

Still leaning heavily on his sticks, he wondered if Wendy was feeling better. These wretched migraine attacks had ruined so many weekends. They seemed to be getting more frequent, probably because of Peter's increasing contacts with the stage, and his fondness for Lennie, the comedian. If she had told the boy the truth about his father, she would have been spared this burden of guilt, and he himself would have been spared the anxiety. It had spoilt the relationship between mother and son that had been so loving and caring in those early years.

He sighed, but his sombre thoughts were soon dispelled by the excited squealing of the twins — Jackie and Johnnie — out for their afternoon airing. They looked adorable, in matching pram-sets. The new generation at Russets!

"You should think they knew it was Saturday afternoon, wouldn't you? All this excitement when they catch sight of me," he told Hetty.

"I believe they do know, Julian. It's quite uncanny. They don't get so excited on other afternoons when I'm dressing them up to go out. There is not much that escapes their notice now." Hetty was a proud mother who rightly supposed her babies were the nicest and brightest in the Weald! They certainly made a lively contribution to the atmosphere at Russets. For their size, it was amazing how far their shrill voices could reach from their pram in the yard. Dick, the

253

proud father, would hear their gleeful shrieks across the field, and wonder how they could ever have lived without them. The twins were healthy and happy, and at their happiest outdoors, which was understandable with both parents country born and bred. Farming was in their blood, as Carrie would say. And what better environment could they wish for than Russets?

It was Carrie who knitted the pram-sets, but Hetty paid for the wool, and walked to the haberdashery in the village where it was reserved for such a good customer. It was her only outing in the week without the twins, and she quite enjoyed meeting other young mothers in the Bakery every Wednesday morning, to chatter about their respective offspring over cups of coffee and jam doughnuts. They all had been glad to welcome her back. The grapevine had spread the news of her breakdown, and the village gossips had made it seem much more serious as they passed their embroidered version, with grave nods and much speculation about her recovery.

Now here she was, looking so bonny and buxom, and it was difficult to believe there had been a time when she shrank from her own husband and clung to her mother with a child's dependence. Several of the young mothers also bought wool at the haberdashery at the rate of four ounces weekly, because it was all they could afford on such limited incomes. Even the small luxury of coffee and doughnuts could only be managed by economising on such items as hairdressing and cosmetics. They washed their own hair, and used their Pond's lipstick and face powder sparingly. The one topic of conversation was children and husbands, in that order, for maternity had established motherhood as a woman's most important role.

Hetty had joined their ranks quite naturally. She loved Dick, but she adored her babies. Blissfully content in her new relationship with Dick, and in caring for the twins, she met her old school friends, compared their methods of bringing up their children, listened to their grievances, and decided she would not wish to change places with any one of them.

Julian was an interested spectator most of the time, but on Saturday afternoons, a willing participator of a game he had invented for the sheer pleasure of hearing their squeals of delight when they saw him waiting, leaning on his sticks,

254

smiling disarmingly. Hetty would put the brake on the pram, fetch his wheel-chair, and help him into it. His sticks would hang on the handles of the pram until he tired of the game — the twins could have played it for the rest of the day! With his legs protected by the stiff, waterproof cover, Hetty would lift the twins from the pram and place them very gently and carefully on the cover, and Julian would hold them firmly and securely, for his arms had acquired abnormal strength over the years, to compensate for his weak legs. Then Hetty would push the wheel-chair round and round the cobbled yard. Jackie would sit quietly. Johnnie would shout and wave his arms. That was the only difference between the boy and the girl, but an indicator of what to expect in the future.

Carrie watched from the kitchen doorway, smiling and waving — a proud grandmother, who would live to see them grow up and take their rightful place at Russets.

John was leaning on the orchard gate, watching the frantic flutterings of several adventurous hens from the path of the oncoming chariot.

"Serves you right!" he muttered irritably.

John kept his distance with the twins. He thought the rest of the family had gone dotty, and he was the only sane one. Talk about a bloody fuss! The smell of babies in the kitchen left no room for the lovely smell of cooking, and the tall fireguard, draped with airing napkins, shut off the warm glow of the fire. They sat in their high chairs for dinner, and were fed with lightly boiled eggs and baked custard, because Hetty was a modern mother who read a lot of rubbish in magazines about starting babies early on solid food. What a bloody waste of his lovely eggs! They only ate the yolks, and Johnnie spat out the baked custard.

"When I was their age, I ate what was put in front of me, and no nonsense!" he told Carrie.

"When you were this age, luv, you were still at the breast," she told her disgruntled son.

Everything revolved around them, and anything that was inconvenient to their welfare had been changed to suit their convenience. The Home Farm had taken over the Saturday market and Russets was responsible for the Wednesday market stall. John was still complaining that the new system disturbed the hens' routine, and he wasn't ready with graded eggs and boiling fowls for the Wednesday market.

"What difference does it make? Hens don't know if it's Wednesday or Saturday. And I still do all the plucking," Carrie had pointed out, reasonably.

Wednesday was the happiest day of the week for Hetty's Mum, when she collected the twins in their pram, and pushed them along the cart track to Home Farm. Her eldest daughter, Pam, who had lost her husband in the war, would finish her dairy work early in order to share the honours of stripping off the pram-sets. Then she would nurse Jackie, while Mum nursed Johnnie, and both babies would drain their feeding bottles of the mid-morning orange juice. Vitamin C – or was it Vitamin D? Hetty insisted on it.

Husband and sons had to make do with cold meat and pickles, and potatoes in their jackets for Wednesday dinner, but were provided with a good fry-up for high tea, after Hetty had collected the twins.

"Who says everything stops for tea? Seems to me every damn thing stops for those two young 'uns," Hetty's Dad was heard to complain one Wednesday afternoon at four o'clock, when the entire family gathered in the yard to watch their noisy departure.

"No swearing, Dad, please," said Hetty's Mum, automatically. Could "damn" be considered a swear word? It was still a debatable point after forty years of marriage. "It's good for us to be disturbed out of our regular routine one day a week, Dad. Don't look so cross," she coaxed, and slipped her arm round his thick waist.

"I'm not cross, Mother, only I do like my regular routine."

"I know you do. You're a real old stick-in-the-mud."

"If you mean I'm conservative, you're right – only I vote Labour, don't I? There's a conundrum for you."

"What's a conundrum?"

"Look it up in the dictionary. That's what dictionaries are for."

"That sounds like Julian. Talking of Julian, Dad, we thought of making a collection among the two families for one of those new-fangled wheel-chairs what run on a battery – I *think* it's a battery."

256

"Good idea. Let me know what it costs. Be glad to contribute. He's such a decent, uncomplaining chap. It must have been a bit irksome being pushed around all these years, though he has got that little car to get to work."

"It's sad. I'm sure he would have liked a family. He's so good with the twins."

"He's got Peter."

"A step-son's not quite the same as a son of his own. Hetty seems to think there is a bit of a mystery about Peter's father."

"What gave her that idea?"

"Wendy is so dead set against Peter's acting. Why should she be? You would think she would be proud of him, being chosen to play the lead in the Christmas pantomime for the past three years. Hetty says he's marvellous, but all he gets from his mother is discouragement."

"It could be a bit of snobbery. Isn't Wendy partly upper class? Her mother was a daughter of His Lordship, and her father was working class."

"Then so is Julian. I mean, Julian is a Franklin, and the Franklins were definitely out of the top drawer."

"That's true, but wasn't there a bit of a mystery about *his* father? Born on the wrong side of the blanket, as Aunt Lucy would say. She was a caution, that woman, and no mistake. Matriarch of Russets, and one time mistress of His Lordship. Remember the scandal when young Charles was born, and her husband in his grave for nigh on a couple of years? What a woman! There won't ever be another like her."

"Never," Hetty's Mum agreed, as they went indoors. Another Wednesday over all too quickly. Being a grandmother was even more satisfactory than being a mother.

The twins would not remember their first Christmas, nor the stockings that were hung on the kitchen mantelpiece on Christmas Eve – and bulged with soft toys half-an-hour later.

"Are you too big for a stocking this year, luv?" Carrie asked Peter, as he helped himself to a freshly baked mincepie.

"No, I'm not too big if I can open it at five o'clock, when there's just the three of us, you and Uncle Tom and me, before you start milking."

257

"Yes, luv." She gave him a hug. He was very good about the twins getting so much attention, but he had been the youngest of the family for such a long time, it was natural he should feel a little jealous. Whenever she could find an opportunity Carrie would think of something specially for Peter, and Christmas morning would provide just such an opportunity. Poor lamb, he was usually sick Christmas night. What with all the extra food, plus sugar mice, candied fruit, dates, nuts and chocolates, and being all worked up about the Boxing Day matinee and the first performance of the Christmas pantomime. Lennie's pep talk at the dress rehearsal was not very convincing, in his broadest Cockney – "Nah listen ter me, young-un. You're goin' to be okey-dokey. Once that curtain goes up on Boxing Day af'noon, you won't know what's 'it yer. All them fousands of kids will start clappin' an' 'ollerin' when they see you an' Cinderella sittin' by the fire. You'll forget them butterflies in the stomach an' you'll love every bloody minute. Course you will. You're one of us, a real trouper, an' don't yer forget it, me ole cock-sparrer! Shall I tell yer somethink else?"

Peter had nodded, mutely.

"I get them bloody butterflies buzzin' around me ole tum when I stand in the wings, waitin' for me call."

"You do? Honest?"

"Cross me 'eart an' 'ope ter die."

Peter smiled with relief and gratitude. It was the sort of smile that could coax a bird from a bough, Lennie was thinking. And it was Nigel Bannister's smile. Mind jew, there were quite a few bloody wrinkles under the make-up, for he wasn't born yesterday. But since he lost that little bitch, Nancy, the poor old sod was having a whale of a time with all them chorus girls!

"Yer know somethink else, young-un," he continued, as though his private thoughts had not interrupted the conversation. "After the matinee on Boxing Dye, I got a nice surprise lined up for you, kid."

"Couldn't you tell me now?"

"There's a time an' a plyce for everythink, Pete."

"That's what Aunt Lucy used to say."

"An' she was right."

"Can I have three guesses?"

"Yer wouldn't guess it, chum, in a fousand guesses!"

Peter frowned. "It must be something super."

"It's a bit of orl right. You'll see."

"I wish it was Boxing Day now, then you would be telling me this super surprise."

"An' miss all the bloody excitement, all them kids clappin' an' 'ollerin' an' jumpin' abaht on their arses! Cor blimey, it makes me 'air curl jus' ter think abaht it!" Since Lennie's very bald pate was a standing joke in his role as the show's comedian, Peter joined in the shout of laughter, and almost forgot the super surprise – almost, but not quite.

Even on Christmas Day there were moments when he remembered, and gave himself three guesses. Holding the mug of tea in both hands, rocking gently to and fro in the old rocking chair, warmly wrapped in dressing-gown and slippers, he gazed at the three bulging stockings in frowning concentration.

"You all right, luv?" Carrie asked, anxiously.

He nodded, and went on rocking, but the train of thought had gone.

"Drink up your tea, lad, and open your stocking," prompted Uncle Tom, who thought the child looked peaky. For a boy brought up on a farm, he hadn't the stamina or the healthy looks of himself and his brothers at that age, or of Dick. Carrie would say he had outgrown his strength and that could be the reason for he had shot up several inches in the past twelve months. There was a delicacy and refinement in the features that were lacking in the Blunts, but Peter was not a Blunt. In the firelight, his silky hair shone like a cap of gold on his shapely head, and his blue eyes held that faraway expression that was often there these days. Tom guessed he was not even thinking of Christmas, or the bulging stocking, or the presents piled under the Christmas tree in the parlour. And Tom's intuition was usually somewhere near the mark.

"You worried about tomorrow, lad?" he asked, kindly, with a quick glance at the clock. The cows didn't know it was Christmas Day, and they would be getting restless.

"Not worried, Uncle Tom. Just wondering about the surprise."

"What surprise?"

"Lennie says he's got a surprise lined up for me, but I have to wait till after the show is over tomorrow night. He says it's a super surprise, and I couldn't guess it even in a thousand guesses."

"He's pulling your leg."

"No, he wouldn't do that. Lennie is the funniest man I know on stage, but off stage, he can be quite serious."

"Whatever can it be?" Carrie was also glancing at the clock, and wishing the child would forget about tomorrow and show a little interest in that stocking she had taken such time and trouble to fill, and even sent away for several small articles she had seen in the catalogue that came by post in October. In the toe of the stocking was the sugar mouse and half-a-crown wrapped in silver paper. She could remember the time when her own children were wildly excited to find sixpence. It was getting to be quite a problem to know what to buy for Peter. Books, of course, about the stage and famous actors, and Shakespeare plays. She couldn't make any sense of Shakespeare, neither could Tom.

"A lot of silly twaddle," Tom reckoned.

Peter didn't mind receiving a jersey or a blazer, but it had to be similar to what other boys were wearing, for he wouldn't care to look conspicuous. He was always polite, and he had nice manners. Wendy was strict with him.

"Thanks very much. It's smashing!" he would say, and give you a hug. Last year they had given him a new fishing rod. That was Julian's idea, and he really did seem pleased with it, though he hadn't used it more than once. This year he was getting roller skates. That was also Julian's idea.

"I remember I had a lot of fun on roller skates when I was Peter's age," he had reflected, with a sad smile. But no two boys were alike, and Carrie was not so sure about skates. He would pretend to like them, for he was a sensitive child and wouldn't hurt their feelings.

"Aren't you going to open your stocking, luv?" she asked, wistfully.

"Sure!" he grinned. "Can't wait to get to that sugar mouse. Happy Christmas, Auntie Carrie! Happy Christmas, Uncle Tom!"

Boxing Day dawned bright and frosty. There would be no snow in the Weald till early January, when heavy falls would cover every inch of the green landscape. The village would lie under a blanket of white, remote and beautiful as a village in "Grimms' Fairy Tales". The village pond would be frozen hard for weeks, and the children would glide across its glassy surface on the way to school, and on the way home. Peter stayed away from the pond at weekends, because he was no longer a pupil at the village school and no longer welcome. They had their own little pond at Russets, where he used to catch tadpoles and bring them home in a jam jar, and when they grew into frogs, he put them back in the pond. Aunt Lucy hadn't cared for the tadpoles on her kitchen window-sill, but was too kind-hearted to refuse. All her boys had fished for tadpoles in the same little pond, and brought them home in jam jars, as proud as though they had caught a salmon! Peter stayed away from the pond when it was frozen because he didn't want anyone to know he was scared of falling. So perhaps the roller skates were not such a good idea after all.

Boxing Day morning he was allowed to stay in bed, because he couldn't eat any breakfast, and the hangover from Christmas Day was pretty awful. Being sick in the scullery sink was regarded with tolerant amusement by the majority of the adults, apart from Wendy, who was obviously disgusted, and John, who was also inclined to over-indulge his particular fancies on Christmas Day.

"Greedy little pig!" was his only comment, as he helped himself to another marzipan pear!

The mug of scalding hot tea at 5 o'clock tasted good. His stomach was empty, and his breath was sour.

"No breakfast, luv?" Carrie asked, kindly. "Well, it won't hurt to give your stomach a bit of a rest. Just the usual cold turkey and ham, with pickles and baked potatoes for dinner. You might feel ready to eat something by that time. No? We shall see, luv. We must have dinner prompt at twelve, then off we go to Tunbridge Wells. I really look forward to this outing. It makes my Christmas."

"I don't. I feel awful. I may not be well enough to go."

"That's what you said last year, and the year before,"

Carrie chuckled. "And you love every minute once you get on that stage. You know you do." She hugged his small shoulders. To look at him now, with his pallid face and shadowed eyes, you would think he was sickening for something if you didn't know how quickly he recovered.

She could hear the twins waking up their parents in Aunt Lucy's old room. Dick would be taking them to Home Farm for the day. He had acquired a second-hand car quite recently, so he would drive Hetty, Midge, Mark and Peter to Tunbridge Wells. Tom, Carrie, John, Katie and several members of the Home Farm family would travel in the van. Mark had been hoping to spend the first Christmas Day of their married life at the cottage, but Midge had her way, as usual, and they arrived in time for dinner, with Sheba and Ginger.

"I must be off. The cows are calling. Take it easy, luv. Get up when you are ready." Carrie took the empty mug, kissed his cheek, and went away.

When Midge came in, some time later, Peter was hugging his knees, a haunted look in his eyes.

"Midge! I can't remember a single word! I've forgotten everything!" he wailed.

"Move over, darling. Don't panic." Midge remembered last Boxing Day, and the one before that. "Now, start at the beginning."

He cuddled close to her warm young body, and sighed. "I do love you, Midge. You're super."

"I love you too, Pete. Next to Mark, you're my favourite boy-friend!" she giggled.

Cinderella had no nerves, and no apprehension. She was pert and pretty, with golden curls and cornflower blue eyes. She knew she was the star of the show, and the envy of all the other ninety-nine girls who had been auditioned. An only child, of nice ordinary working-class parents who could never understand how they had managed to produce such a beautiful creature, she was too precocious to be popular with the rest of the cast.

Prince Charming, two years her senior, had also been chosen for her good looks and long, shapely legs.

"It's so stupid, having a *girl* to play Prince Charming,"

262

Cinderella had complained when the fact was made clear to her. With her tiny waist and pointed breasts, at the age of fifteen she had naturally expected a romance — a real romance, between boy and girl, not a silly fairy-tale romance.

"It's traditional. Prince Charming has always been a girl," the producer explained, brusquely, for he was already regretting his mistake after the first rehearsal. "Silly, empty-headed little madam," he was heard to mutter, and his first impression had not changed by the final rehearsal. It was not prettiness that comprised an actress, or mere good looks an actor. It was Personality. And Personality was an indefinable quality, to be found in the most unexpected characters. It was there in Lennie, the comedian, with his ugly face, near-bald pate, and Cockney wit. (Some said he hadn't been born within the sound of Bow Bells, but in a village slum, and had once had a barrow in a street market.) Everyone loved Lennie. He was a real trouper. Nigel Bannister, one of the ugly sisters, had Personality, hidden behind the mask of ridicule. Bannister could play any part in pantomime, from the tail of a dragon to an ugly sister (some said he had once been quite a star in musical comedy, but had made the mistake to marry his leading lady). There was an old-world charm and courtesy about him, and a dedication to show business that was almost fanatical. It was his life, his mistress and his reason for living.

The third member of the cast, and the youngest — Peter Franklin — must have been born with both Personality and Talent. A rare combination, the producer had recognised in the eight-year-old boy at his first audition. It was a bit of a gamble to give such an important role as Buttons to such a youngster, but that's what show business was about — gambles, speculation and instinct.

"And I would bet my bottom dollar on that boy," he had declared, against strong opposition. For of course, there had to be opposition. That, too, was expected. It was a costly production, and somebody had to pay. They wanted to be sure they were not pouring their money down the drain. They wanted his assurance of success. A really good production could run to the end of February with a full house every night, as well as the Wednesday and Saturday matinees. But success could not be guaranteed. Success was elusive. Success and failure went hand in hand, and only one could survive that first performance. You must have faith. You must be able to distinguish the false from the real. And when you had made a mistake in casting, and it was too late to rectify that mistake, then you bloody well had to make do with the material you were landed with!

Such was the producer's philosophy, and he should know. Nine times out of ten he had discovered, with children to manipulate, one particular child would somehow contrive to cover up the defects of another, simply by being natural. Cinderella was over-acting, and jealous of anyone who could steal the limelight, even for a short scene. Peter Franklin, as Buttons, could diminish the artificiality of Cinderella in a nice way. Buttons was a nice character, and Peter was a nice child. His smile, his politeness, his gentle manner, were not forced. Peter *was* Buttons, and Buttons was Peter. It had worked at the dress rehearsal, and it would work on the Boxing Day matinee. For all their clapping and shouting, children could be critical, even cruel. They spotted insincerity quicker than adults.

With their three good troupers − Lennie, Nigel and Peter − the show was ninety-nine and three-quarters per cent *promising* − the producer assured the pessimists!

The Russets family, with their neighbours from the Home Farm, had reserved seats in the front stalls, together with the parents of Cinderella, who sat silently, awed by their surroundings, with work-roughened hands clasped in their laps, and anxious faces peering towards the footlights, waiting for the curtain to rise on their adored child. They would see nobody but Stella, hear nobody but Stella, from start to finish.

When the members of the orchestra slid into their seats to play the overture, they saw it as just one more delaying tactic. Then, at last, the curtain rose on the fireside scene, with Cinderella and Buttons.

"That's our Stella, Dad," whispered her proud Mum.

Dad nodded, too choked to reply. Their small world had revolved around Cinderella for the past three months.

"Can she see us, Dad? Does she know where to look?"

It was a loud whisper, too loud for the small boy hanging over the back of her seat.

"Shush!" he hissed.

"That's Stella, our daughter," Mum smiled proudly.

"No it's not. It's Cinderella!" the small boy contradicted.

"Please be quiet." Carrie spoke politely, but her cheeks were flushed as she strained forward. That small figure, warming his hands at an imaginary fire, was their Peter. It was all pretence. It was only a fairy story, but Carrie's heart was still young enough for fairy stories, and Cinderella was her favourite. One day, in the not too distant future, she would be reading bedtime stories to her grandchildren from the same old book with the lovely coloured pictures that Aunt Lucy's boys had treasured, because it was a Sunday School prize. Aunt Lucy's boys had wanted "Robin Hood", "Black Beauty", "The Swiss Family Robinson", and "Robinson Crusoe", all Sunday School prizes.

On Winter evenings, gathered round the fire in the kitchen, clutching mugs of cocoa, Aunt Lucy had read aloud to her boys. Peter, the youngest, listened, absorbed, to the old fairy tales, sitting on her lap as they rocked to and fro in the old rocking chair. No wonder he had played them all so realistically on stage. They were as familiar as his own family at Russets. Aunt Lucy had been the first to recognise the talent for acting a part and encouraged an individual performance on Christmas Day, when Dick, John and Katie would sneak away to watch television, and Wendy would remind her son it was nearly time for bed.

So Carrie, waiting for Buttons to reappear on stage, let her mind wander back to earlier Christmases, when Aunt Lucy was alive, before television claimed an audience and Wendy would play all the well-known and loved carols on the piano in the parlour. What did it matter that only Mark and Maggie knew the words, and the rest of the family hummed? Aunt Martha would persuade Mark to sing the first verse of "Once in Royal David's City" as a solo, because it reminded her of her son, Philip, in far away Congo, who sang like an angel in his boyhood. Mark's voice was deep, and he was too shy for the choir, but Philip had been a choir-boy, and his voice, pure as a lark's song, soared tremulously to the rafters as the choir and clergy moved slowly down the aisle on Christmas morning.

Now Buttons was back on stage — a slight, boyish figure dwarfed by the ugly sisters — and Carrie leaned forward, not wanting to miss a minute. No longer afraid that his mind was a blank, no longer pale, but flushed and starry-eyed. Farther along the row, Wendy clutched Julian's hand.

"I can't bear it," she thought, but she could not drag her eyes away from her son. It was Nigel Bannister in miniature — the shapely head, the features, the smile — yet it was Peter's voice that spoke so clearly and confidently. Julian squeezed her hand. Tonight she would be lying alone in a darkened room. The Boxing Day matinee had become an obligation and a duty. The family would not allow her to be excused.

When it was Lennie's turn to hold the stage while the scenery changed behind the curtain, she shrank back in her seat lest he recognised her as the girl at the piano, in a factory canteen in wartime.

"It's all right, sweetheart," Julian whispered, not knowing those were the exact words Lennie had used. The magic was still there. He was a clown, and everyone loves a clown. He spoke in a cracked voice, he turned cartwheels, he tap-danced, and his jokes were clean and fresh to suit his young audience.

"Shall I tell you something, kids?" he whispered, hoarsely.

"*Yes*!" they yelled.

"Prince Charming ain't a boy. She's a girl."

"*We know*!" they yelled back.

"You do?" His clown's mouth, wide and red in his dead white face, drooped with disappointment. They thought he was going to cry till a small boy in the gallery called down, affectionately, "Don't cry, Mister. We think you're smashing."

"Bless yer, me ole cock sparrer," Lennie grinned, and waved a hand. Then his face straightened, he leaned forward and once again he whispered, hoarsely, "Shall I tell you something else, kids?"

"*Yes*!" they yelled.

"Them two Ugly Sisters is MEN."

"*We know! We know!*"

Lennie looked forlorn, but his heart warmed towards them. The kids were loving every minute. Jumping up and down on their arses. The best audience in the world, the matinee kids.

They were timing him. They were ready behind the curtain. So he sang a funny song about a dragon with a belly-ache, blew a kiss, and disappeared. He would be back when they changed the scenery for the final act.

Wendy had been laughing with the rest. He was irresistible. There was nobody like Lennie. She remembered his kindness. She had been so terribly homesick. She remembered she had put herself to bed on the first painful day of her monthly period, and Nancy Bannister dragged her out.

"The show goes on! Get up!" she ordered.

Then she had fainted at the piano, and Lennie had filled in for her while Nigel Bannister carried her off stage. The audience had thought it was all part of the act. Dear Lennie. She sighed reflectively, and Julian asked, "Feeling better, my love?" as the curtain went up.

She nodded. It was true. Lennie was like a tonic. She followed the rest of the age-old story with absorbed interest. It was beautifully staged. Cinderella, in her glittering coach, with four tiny ponies, crossing the stage, had her moment of glory in the awed silence from the excited children. And Peter, *her* Peter, stole the show when he sang a sad little song about his love for Cinderella. The family hadn't been told about the solo, only about the duets.

"I didn't know Peter could sing on his own," Tom whispered to Midge.

"I did. He has been practising with us at the cottage on Saturday afternoons. Mark accompanied him on the piano. Pete said his Mum wouldn't play for him."

Tom shook his head. They were not very fond of Wendy, but they put up with her for Julian's sake.

They all had ice-cream in the interval. Dick and John, yawning with boredom, wondered if they would be back in time to see the circus on the television. Katie received her small dish of ice-cream in a state of dreamy-eyed wonder. "It's ever so real, ain't it?" she breathed. "Our Peter ain't arf enjoying hisself."

Hetty's mind wandered to the twins in the interval. Perhaps she had outgrown pantomime since last year. Of course, Peter was a fine little actor, but he wasn't *her* son, and her interest was flagging.

"How much longer, Het?" Dick whispered. They consulted the programme. "Two more bloody scenes!" he groaned.

"Then we all go back stage. We shan't get away for another hour or two," Hetty reminded him. They were whispering, and feeling a little guilty to be so bored.

This was the moment when everything fell into place, and the entire cast gathered on stage, stood smiling and waving to the enchanted children. They were standing now, clapping madly, reluctant to part with the magic. Then the rest of the cast slipped away into the wings, leaving the main characters, hand-in-hand – Cinderella, Prince Charming, the Ugly Sisters, Lennie and Buttons. The clapping rose to a final crescendo, the walls of the theatre echoing to the sound that was part of its tradition, part of the magic of show business. Cinderella stepped forward to receive bouquets of flowers and curtsied prettily. She saw herself as a brilliant star of a Drury Lane production. And her name – STELLA BAILEY – in flashing lights in Piccadilly. All the little boys in the audience loved Cinderella, and would have died for her that night. All the little girls loved Buttons, and wanted to mother him. And they all loved Lennie.

The producer received his share of applause with bows and smiles. Success was sweet. The critics could go to hell! He kissed Cinderella and the ugly sisters clamoured for a kiss. The children yelled with laughter. Three times the curtain came down and was raised again to the deafening applause. Then, finally, sadly, it was all over, and the orchestra was playing the opening bars of the National Anthem. Lennie was the first to spring to attention, the others followed and the children, quick to follow their cue, dropped their hands and straightened their faces.

Cinderella's dressing-room was already crowded when the Russets family arrived. It stank of grease-paint and sweaty bodies. The producer was handing round glasses of champagne, and Cinderella, giggling excitedly after a couple of sips, declared she was already tipsy. Her fond parents, completely out of their depth in such a strange environment, hung back, not wishing to intrude, and sipped the champagne suspiciously.

268

Peter was hugged and kissed, and seemed not to mind the kisses in this atmosphere, where he felt such a keen sense of belonging.

"'ullo, ducks. Give us a kiss." Lennie's clown's mouth touched her lips, and Wendy was caught up in a warm hug.

"Hello, Lennie. It's like old times, isn't it?" she said.

"You're tellin' me! You ain't seen nuffink yet, luv. Drink up that champagne. You're goin' ter need it."

Peter was prompting. "The surprise, Lennie. You promised a super surprise."

"It's 'ere. Cor blimey. Right on cue, Pete" — and he clutched the arm of the ugliest sister, stripped off the wig of yellow curls, the false nose and eyelashes and the double chins, and revealed a familiar face and amused eyes.

"*Nigel!*" Wendy gasped, blushing like a schoolgirl. The years rolled away. They were back in the foyer of the Regent Palace Hotel, meeting for the first time — a handsome, charming man, and a shy girl, desperately anxious to be accepted into this small select company of entertainers.

"You haven't changed, my dear," he was saying in his deep, masculine voice.

"Neither have you," she said, but it was not true, of course.

Peter was getting impatient. "The surprise, Lennie. You promised."

The babble of voices and the noisy banter went on all round them, yet they seemed to be isolated, like characters on stage — Lennie, Nigel, Wendy and Peter. Even Julian, leaning heavily on his sticks, had no part in this particular scene.

"May I?" Lennie was speaking to Wendy, and she nodded, too choked to speak.

His clown's face split in a wide grin. He was enjoying every moment. This was a scene he had played a number of times in his mind, during the past decade. Taking Peter's small hand, he placed it in the big hand waiting to receive it. The fingers glittered with cheap rings.

"Say 'ullo to yer Dad," Lennie prompted.

Peter looked puzzled. Was this the super surprise — this silly joke?

Then Wendy spoke, and her voice was clear and convincing. "Nigel is your father," was all she said, but it conveyed

269

the truth, the whole truth, that should have been told from the beginning.

Nigel Bannister waited. They looked at each other with appraising eyes. They were two of a kind. Show business was in their blood.

Then the boy smiled. "Hello, Father," he said.

"Hello, son," the man answered.

And Wendy wept on Lennie's shoulder.

A tall distinguished man was pushing his way through the crowded room. The producer hurried forward with a glass of champagne, but he waved it aside. Addressing the boy, he asked, brusquely, "Do you know who I am?"

"Yes, Sir," Peter answered, promptly. Everyone in show business knew this celebrated actor-manager of a certain suburban repertory theatre. Some called it the jumping-off perch to the West End. Be that as it may, Peter was proud to be seen talking to such a celebrity.

"I have been sitting in the audience, and I have discovered what I was looking for," said he. "How would you like to play the lead in 'The Winslow Boy'?"

Peter glanced appealingly at his Mother and Father. He was still a minor, and must have their consent. They smiled and nodded.

"I should like it very much. Thank you, Sir," Peter Franklin answered. And they solemnly shook hands.